VIOLA SHIPMAN

the Edge of Summer

GRAYDON
HOUSE

GRAYDON
HOUSE®

Recycling programs
for this product may
not exist in your area.

ISBN-13: 978-1-525-81142-5

The Edge of Summer

Graydon House
22 Adelaide St. West, 41st Floor
Toronto, Ontario M5H 4E3, Canada
www.GraydonHouseBooks.com
www.BookClubbish.com

Printed in U.S.A.

Praise for the novels of Viola Shipman

"Viola Shipman knows relationships. *The Clover Girls* will sometimes make you smile and other times cry, but like a true friendship, it is a novel you will forever savor and treasure."

—**Mary Alice Monroe,** *New York Times* **bestselling author**

"Viola Shipman has written a love song to long-lost friends, an ode to the summers that define us and the people who make us who we are. The minute I finished *The Clover Girls*, I ordered copies for all my friends. It's that good."

—**Kristy Woodson Harvey,** *New York Times* **bestselling author**

"Reading Viola Shipman's novels is like talking with your best friend and wanting never to hang up the phone. *The Clover Girls* is her most beautiful novel yet, and her most important."

—**Nancy Thayer,** *New York Times* **bestselling author**

"Oh, the joy! *The Clover Girls* may be [Shipman's] best yet, taking readers on a heartwarming trip down memory lane… Ideal for summer… A redemptive tale, celebrating the power of friendship while focusing on what matters most. Perfect for the beach!"

—*New York Journal of Books*

"Every now and then a new voice in fiction arrives to completely charm, entertain and remind us what matters. Viola Shipman is that voice and *The Summer Cottage* is that absolutely irresistible and necessary novel… [It] brings us the astounding importance of home and underscores the importance of a loving family and of having a generous heart. Grab a glass of sweet tea and enjoy!"

—**Dorothea Benton Frank,** *New York Times* **bestselling author**

"Shipman's evocative novel is a love letter to Michigan summers, past and present, and to the value of lifelong friendships. A blissful summer read sure to please the author's many fans, and fans of writers like Elin Hilderbrand or Kristin Hannah."

—*Library Journal* on *The Heirloom Garden*

"The emotional scars left by war unite two women, generations apart, in Shipman's sentimental family saga… *The Heirloom Garden* successfully captures these women's resilience and their hopeful desire for new beginnings."

—*Publishers Weekly*

Also by Viola Shipman

THE EDGE OF SUMMER
THE SECRET OF SNOW
THE CLOVER GIRLS
THE HEIRLOOM GARDEN
THE SUMMER COTTAGE

For my grandmothers,
who taught me the little things always matter most in life

the Edge of Summer

"Buttons are the fossils of the sartorial world, enduring long past the garments they were designed to hold together."

—MARTHA STEWART

Prologue

BUTTONHOLE

A small cut in the fabric that is bound with small stitching.
The hole has to be just big enough to allow
a button to pass through it and remain in place.

My mom told everyone my dad died, along with my entire family—grandparents, aunts, uncles, and all—one Christmas Day long ago.

"Fire," she'd say. "Woodstove. Took 'em all. Down to the last cousin."

"How'd you make it out with your little girl?" everyone would always ask, eyes wide, mouths open. "That's a holiday miracle!"

My mom would start to cry, a tear that grew to a flood, and, well, that would end that.

No one questioned someone who survived such a thing, especially a widowed mother like Miss Mabel, which is what everyone called her out of deference in the Ozarks. Folks down here had lived hard lives, and they buried their kin just like they did their heartache, underneath the rocky earth and red clay. It took too much effort to dig that deep.

That's why no one ever bothered to check out the story of a simple, hardworking, down-to-earth, churchgoing lady who kept to herself down here in the hollers—despite the fact me and my mom both just appeared out of thin air—in a time before social media existed.

But I did.

Want to know why?

My mom *never* cried.

She was the least emotional soul I'd ever known.

"How *did* you make it out with me?" I asked her countless times as I grew older, when it was just the two of us sitting in her sewing room in our tiny cabin tucked amongst the bluffs outside Nevermore, Missouri.

She would never answer immediately, no matter how many times I asked. Instead, she'd turn over one of her button jars or tins, and run her fingers through the buttons as if they were tarot cards that would provide a clue.

I mean, there were no photos, no memories, no footsteps that even led from our fiery escape to the middle of Nevermore. No family wondered where we were? No one cared? My mother made it out with *nothing* but me? Not a penny to her name? Just some buttons?

We were rich in buttons.

Oh, I had button necklaces in every color growing up— red, green, blue, yellow, white, pink—and I matched them to every outfit I had. We didn't have money for trendy jewelry or clothes—tennis bracelets, Gloria Vanderbilt jeans—so my mom made nearly everything I wore.

Kids made fun of me at school for that.

"Sutton, the button girl!" they'd taunt me. "Hand-me-downs!"

Wasn't funny. Ozarks kids weren't clever. Just annoyingly direct, like the skeeters that constantly buzzed my head.

I loved my necklaces, though. They were like Wonder Woman's bracelets. For some reason, I always felt protected.

I'd finger and count every button on my necklace waiting for my mom to answer the question I'd asked long ago. She'd just keep searching those buttons, turning them round and round, feeling them, whispering to them, as if they were alive and breathing. The quiet would nearly undo me. A girl should have music and friends' laughter be the soundtrack of her life, not the clink of buttons and rush of the creek. Most times, I'd spin my button necklace a few times, counting upward of sixty before my mom would answer.

"Alive!" she'd finally say, voice firm, without looking up. "That's how we made it out…alive. And you should feel darn lucky about that, young lady."

Then, as if by magic, my mom would always somehow manage to find a matching button to replace a missing one on a hand-me-down blouse of hers, or pluck the "purtiest" ones from the countless buttons in her jar—iridescent abalone or crochet over wound silk floss—to make the entire blouse seem new again.

Still, she would never smile. In fact, it was as if she had been born old. I had no idea how old she might be: *Thirty-five? Fifty? Seventy?*

But when she'd find a beautiful button, she would hold it up to study, her gold eyes sparkling in the light from the little lamp over Ol' Betsy, her Singer sewing machine.

If I watched her long enough, her face would relax just enough to let the deep creases sigh, and the edges of her mouth would curl ever so slightly, as if she had just found the secret to life in her button jar.

"Look at this beautiful button, Sutton," she'd say. "So many buttons in this jar: fabric, shell, glass, metal, ceramic. All forgotten. All with a story. All from someone and somewhere. People don't give a whit about buttons anymore, but I do. They hold value, these things that just get tossed aside. Buttons are still the one thing that not only hold a garment together but also make it truly unique."

Finally, *finally*, she'd look at me. Right in the eye.

"Lots of beauty and secrets in buttons if you just look long and hard enough."

The way she said that would make my body explode in goose pimples.

Every night of my childhood, I'd go to bed and stare at my necklace in the moonlight, or I'd play with the buttons in my mom's jar searching for an answer my mother never provided.

Even today when I design a beautiful dress with pretty, old-fashioned buttons, I think of my mom and how the littlest of things can hold us together.

Or tear us apart.

1

BUMBLEBUNCHING

*That annoying tangled loop of stitching on the
bobbin side of the fabric that is a result of
improper tension applied to the sewing machine.*

Spring 2020
The Ozarks

I spin my button necklace, the blue one, my mother's favorite color.

There are thirty buttons in varying shades of blue on this simple necklace. Same number of days as this month of April. I know every button on it. I can shut my eyes and see them, just as clearly as I can picture my mom the last time I saw her healthy, waving goodbye to me from the cabin on the water.

I shut my eyes.

Midnight blue, I think.

I open my eyes and smile.

The seventeenth button going clockwise from the clasp is midnight blue, the color of Lake Michigan at dawn.

Counting these buttons is the only way I can keep track of the days anymore. The nightmare started April 1st. I used to believe that if she could just make it to the end of the necklace, I could put on a new one and never have to count the buttons again.

Now, I know, it's just a matter of time.

I take a deep breath to steel myself and begin to open my

car door. I stop. I'm not ready yet. I scan the parking lot, ensuring no one is around, and reach into my bag and retrieve an airline-sized bottle of vodka. I pour it into my coffee.

Coffee is a generous noun. There is no Starbucks for hundreds of miles. Not even a Dunkin' Donuts. I am drinking something resembling coffee from a gas station whose name itself warns you not to purchase anything to consume.

The Guzzle-N-Go.

I put the lid back on and give the Styrofoam cup a swish.

It actually tastes better.

I'm not a big drinker. I just don't know how to get through another day here without blurring the edges just a bit.

I put on my mask, then pull it back down and take another sip.

I lock my car and walk through the parking lot to the little courtyard outside the long-term care facility. The courtyard is lined with tulips, and little fountains featuring happy cherubs burbling. It's all a lie, a make-believe world to make me believe that the nightmare happening isn't real.

I walk up to the window and check my cell.

Ten a.m. sharp.

I sip my coffee and wait, until she appears in the window. I pull down my mask.

"Hi, Mom!"

I wave.

The sun glints through the window, and in the light, my mother looks as small and fragile as the Hummel figurines she used to buy at yard sales for a quarter and line up on the shelves in her sewing room.

There is a bruise on her forehead. A scrape on her cheek. A sling still on her arm.

And yet it's the invisible that's killing her.

I try to focus on her eyes in the light. The gold.

I used to joke to my mom that there must be a pot of riches inside her head, like a pot of gold at the end of the rainbow.

"Ain't nothin' in there but memories," she'd say. "And they ain't worth much punk, save for the ones a'you."

My mother waves with her good arm. She is wearing one of the loose blouses I made for her. It's a simple top for a simple woman who loved to make clothes for anyone but herself and who rarely wore much color. But the light blue top has one ostentatious feature: a heart made of vintage moonglow glass buttons from the 1950s, all in shades of blue. My mom had a fancy dress made with these buttons that she kept in her closet and never wore.

Another mystery of my mother.

These were supposed to be my mother's "get-well" tops. She was only supposed to be here for two weeks, max. Miss Mabel tripped getting out of her sewing chair, fell right onto her sewing table and broke her shoulder. Surgery went fine. She was sent here for rehab.

Now it will be her graveyard. Covid came as quietly and furiously as that fire so long ago that took my family's lives, and now it rages through her body.

My mother is on oxygen. She doesn't want to eat.

I can still remember the call from the home's administrator. "Your sweet momma tested positive for Covid."

"How are you feeling, Mom?" I yell through the window.

She gives a weak thumbs-up.

"Keep fighting!"

She nods if you can even call it that. Her head slumps as she grows sleepy in the sun.

Why do the healthy tell the dying to keep fighting? For them, or for us? Are we more scared than they are? I actually feel selfish saying this to her any longer.

I look at my mother through the window.

Mysterious Miss Mabel.

Today, even near death, my mother looks decades younger than the other residents I've seen in the windows. Her skin is deeply creased but still taut. The skin on her arms still has elasticity; it is not the onion paper covering the skeletons like so many others. Her eyes are still bright. Her hair full.

Her appearance doesn't seem to match her age. She used to seem like such an old woman. Here, she seems like such a young one.

A few folks down here used to tell me my mom was still a baby when she arrived in Nevermore with one.

"A baby with a baby," Mrs. Dimmons, my favorite teacher, told me in grade school. I'd often sit alone at recess, ostracized by my schoolmates, and my fourth-grade teacher would join me, put her arm around me and tell me to never stop being myself.

"Being unique is all we've got in this world." She'd nod at the kids in their cliques jumping rope, playing dodgeball or telling secrets. "And we try our whole lives to fit in and be just like everyone else. But what do we have when we do that, Sutton?"

I'd look at her and shrug.

"Nothing," she'd say. "Because you'll lose what makes you *you*."

And then she'd give me a little hug, and I would melt at the affection from an adult, but it would give me the strength to finish the day.

No one thought much about that, though, down here. Babies had babies in the Ozarks. Some grandmas were in their thirties. That's why I used to snoop. Sneak into her purse while she was sewing and look at her driver's license, or try to find her birth certificate, anything. But a puzzle makes no sense when you don't have a picture to follow. I figured my mom was like an optical illusion, like the one from the game book I bought her one year for Christmas. It was filled with little riddles and fun picture puzzles, and we played them constantly. "My Wife and My Mother-in-Law" was a drawing of a woman that looked entirely different depending on how someone viewed it. When my mom would hold up the photo to me, I would always see a young woman with black hair and a long eyelash, bedecked in a white feathered cap and black shawl, looking over her right shoulder. When I held up the photo for my mom, she always saw an old woman, wrinkled and pale, looking off to the left.

This not only described how my mother and I viewed life but also how I saw my mother: a mystery of varying age I could never figure out no matter how long I stared at her.

I walk up to the window and tap on it, hard. "I love you, Mom!"

She is asleep, her head lolled to one side, the tube from the tank cutting right through the middle of her button heart, like the arrows I used to draw on Valentine's Day.

The aide nods at me and wheels my mother away.

I take a sip of my "coffee" and wait. A nurse will reappear in a moment with my mother's vitals. I keep track of them. They hold up handwritten signs in the window, like I'm in the movie *Love, Actually*, or I call and wait until someone in the home loses a game of rock, paper, scissors and is forced to talk to Mabel's "crazy daughter." I've heard them call me that when their hand isn't firmly placed over the receiver. I guess I'm a bit too much like Shirley MacLaine in *Terms of Endearment*. I would do anything to protect my mother, and I feel like I let her down.

A nurse appears and holds up a piece of paper with my mom's vitals written in Magic Marker:

BLOOD OXYGEN LEVEL = 77 PERCENT
TEMPERATURE = 100.1
BLOOD PRESSURE = 155/98

I check the notes on my cell. Every vital sign is getting worse, not better. I nod, and the nurse disappears. My instinct is to mask up, storm into the administrator's office and demand that my mother be taken to the ER. But I know it won't do any good. She has been in and out of the hospital twice. She won't be returning. There are too many other sick people now, too many others with longer lives and better chances. There are no beds remaining.

Only a coffin.

I know this. Everyone does. We all play pretend just like the cherubs are doing in the courtyard.

Her vitals signal the game is almost over.

I turn, my anguish building, and I put on my mask to cover my quivering chin. Suddenly, I lift my foot back to kick a tulip. I stop mid motion, bending to study its sunny happiness.

Remember this, Sutton, I tell myself. *Remember the beauty.*

I pluck the tulip and then sprint to my car with my coffee like an escaped prisoner. I dump out the remains of my now cold drink and place the tulip in the cup as if it were a prized vase.

"Are you Kristen Bell?"

A voice startles me. I look out the door and into the parking lot. A woman in scrubs is standing next to her car, looking at me.

"You look just like her!"

Many people have said I look like Kristen Bell, the actress. I've always considered it the highest compliment—as I've always considered myself more pedestrian than pretty—and even more so now, exhausted, hair a tangled mess, no makeup, a mask covering half my face.

"I wish," I manage to say. "You can only see my eyes, which is a good thing today."

She laughs. "People say I look just like my daddy. His nickname's 'Bulldog.' That should tell you everything you need to know."

I laugh.

"You have a good day," she says. "Or at least a better one if possible."

She heads inside the long-term care facility, which is tucked into a hill just outside downtown Nevermore. It sits on a busy road that leads to the big box store and row of fast-food restaurants that sprouted shortly after it did. Nevermore was once known as the "The Jewel Box City," due to the gorgeous, flower-filled window boxes that lined the storefronts around the historic square. My mom and I used to walk from store to store when I was a girl, admiring the geraniums, begonias and petunias. The square was the center of my universe growing up. My mom and I spent countless hours at the Ben Franklin on the corner. I couldn't wait to scan the sweet treats and eye the new toys—I got my first Slinky, Silly Putty and Rubik's Cube there—while my mom could spend just as much time in the craft aisle perusing needles, thread, yarn and, of course, buttons. Many days, we'd cozy up to the counter and have lunch—cheeseburgers, fries and a milkshake, sometimes hot dogs and cherry colas, other days onion rings and phosphates. It seemed like such a glorious luxury.

"A penny saved is a penny earned," my mom would often say, reciting Ben Franklin himself. "But, mark my words, Sutton, one day these ol' five-and-dimes will be gone, like the dinosaurs. We're already beginnin' to forget the value of simple things."

I earned my driver's license parallel parking on that busy

square, got my first bra from Doris Brazile—"Mrs. Brassiere," everyone in town called her—on that square, and learned to patch a roof and fix a sink from Mr. Sharperson, the man who owned the hardware store.

I head past the big box store. People are flocking inside.

The Ben Franklin was the first to go, and the other stores soon followed.

Now, the square is gone, the windows boarded, the window boxes rotted. This big box—which ran the little business owners out of town—remains solid, but it has no character.

Nevermore has finally lived up to its name and destiny.

About ten minutes outside of town, I turn left, and the highway becomes a two-lane road, which becomes a poorly paved road and finally a dirt one. My SUV bumps and jumps over the potholes, and when I turn down our long driveway, past the dilapidated mailbox that says *366 Hickory Crick, Mabel Douglas*, in little, reflective, peel-and-stick numbers and letters, the coffee cup turned makeshift vase tips over, and the tulip sails to the floorboard.

I park in the little turnaround area, gather the tulip and head down ten narrow, unsteady stone steps to my mom's cabin. Its ancient logs are painted white, brown trim framing old wavy windows, a bright red door and bell beside it the only pops of color. I ring the bell, and a crystal clear echo chimes through the surrounding bluffs. My mom used this to call me in for dinner when I was playing on the rocky beach or swimming in the creek. I had sixty seconds to hightail it back, or I knew I was in trouble. My mom would be there waiting, counting, "Fifty-seven, fifty-eight…dinner's on the table."

I head inside. I didn't bother to lock the door, despite the fact my mother always did. All of the doors have locks and dead bolts, the windows, too. My mom cut thick yard sticks she'd get for free from the local paint store to fit the track of every sliding patio door, and they had to be in place before we went to bed.

I always wondered, after surviving a fire, why she'd want to trap herself inside?

There's no one around here for at least a mile, as the crow flies, and there weren't even that many around when I was growing up, save for the townies who had little cabins by the water to escape the blistering Ozarks summer humidity.

I flip on the lights in the tiny kitchen. I glance into the refrigerator.

Out of wine.

Idiot. You should have stopped.

My mom was a teetotaler. That's what they called it in these parts. Sweet way to say she didn't drink. People 'round here thought it was because she was a woman of God, but I had my doubts.

"Loose lips sink ships, Sutton," she told me one night after I'd sneaked out to a hootenanny by the crick and returned home a little buzzed. Locals called them "hooch-enannies" because the music was really just an excuse to drink and dance in the dark. In my stupor, I'd ripped a button off one of my summer dresses, and when I woke up the next morning she'd sewn a mismatched button onto it.

"Just so you won't forget," she said.

I didn't.

I worked as hard as my mom did. I got straight A's. I played volleyball. I attended junior college for free on a sports scholarship and then worked two jobs to get my degree at a nearby state college. I used my story of hardship and humble upbringing to land internships, and I inched my way up over the years.

"My mom taught me to sew."

"I grew up making dresses with my mom from McCall's patterns."

"My designs are inspired by my family's history."

Now, I am the ready-to-wear fashion director for all women's apparel at Lindy's, one of the nation's oldest department stores. I have helped make the old new again, the unfashionable hip, 1940s fashion trendy.

Sutton's Buttons is the line that defined my career.

I meander into my mother's sewing room and take a seat in her sewing chair.

Every day after visiting with her, I come in here and sit in her chair. It's the only place I can truly feel her presence.

My mother loved going to church. She took it as seriously as she did everything in her life. She shook hands but never hugged. She sang the hymns quietly but never full-throated. She prayed without looking around to see if anyone was watching.

But I always believed she was closest to God here in her sewing room.

It was just the two of them the last few years. I stopped going to church. I got put off by the folks who gossiped or who used their faith as a way to justify their ungodly actions.

"You have to believe in somethin' to get you through this life," my mom used to tell me. "Life's too pretty and ugly, too happy and sad, too complicated to be happenstance. There has to be a reason for all this, don't there?"

Everything remains as she left it: button jars, spools of thread, a blouse in Ol' Betsy ready to be completed. On a shelf alongside her Hummel figurines is a framed piece of art we did together when we were young. I painted the trunk and limbs of an old oak in watercolor on a scrap of old fabric, and then my mom and I glued buttons as leaves on the branches.

It's actually quite beautiful. The buttons are small and colorful in myriad reds, browns, greens and oranges.

"You can make the world look any way you want," my mom had said when we were creating it. "Change it to fit what suits you. Even a damaged tree can put down roots and grow in ways you can't imagine."

"Who wants to play Button, Button, Who's Got the Button?"

Children scream. Some jump up and down. Some yank on my mother's skirt.

"I do!"

"Me!"

"Yeah!"

I am not used to having other people, much less other children, in my house, and I am certainly not used to seeing my mother interact with anyone besides me, except on church Sundays. A piece of me feels tremendously jealous that other kids like my mom, and another piece of me is thrilled to have the company of people my own age, especially kids who wouldn't otherwise choose to play with me.

My mom has taken up babysitting on occasion to earn a few extra dollars. Her days off aren't really off days: we need every penny.

The kids my mom is babysitting are schoolmates, but that does not mean they are in my "class." We are poor and live on the outskirts. They are decidedly middle-class with homes in town. They wear store-bought clothes and silk hair ribbons and shiny, new shoes. Once a week my mom picks them up, watches them for a few hours and a few bucks while their parents go to summer parties, BBQs at the club, or Chamber of Commerce dinners.

These are the same kids who make fun of me for wearing Christmas ribbon in my hair. Not only does my mother scrimp for buttons and attempt to remake Goodwill hand-me-downs, but she saves and irons all the ribbons from our Christmas gifts so that I can wear them in my hair. All the kids tug them, pull them from my hair, racing around the playground yelling and laughing, "Christmas ribbon! Not a hair ribbon!"

But they don't make fun of me in front of my mom. No one challenges Miss Mabel. And my mom doesn't coddle the children either. Instead, she keeps them busy. We search for arrowheads on the rocky beach. We pick wildflowers in the field. She teaches the difference between stalagmites and stalactites in the cool of the bluffs.

But her—and all the kids'—favorite game by far is "Button, Button."

My mother varies the game.

Sometimes, she takes us out to the stone steps. Since the staircase is so narrow, my mom divides us into two teams. Three kids sit on the bottom row of the steps, and my mom turns her back and pulls a button from her jar. When she turns to face us, she holds out both fists and asks, "Button, button, who's got the button?"

Each child fields a guess, and whoever guesses correctly advances one step. The first one to reach the top step and then return all the way back down to the first step wins the prize, usually an ice cream sandwich made from my mom's homemade cookies.

But they never win the button.

"Can I keep it?"

"No," my mother will say.

"But I won!"

"The game, not the button," she would say, hand out, unsmiling. "Rules are important to follow in life."

She would always shoot me a look when she said this. I didn't particularly care for rules, but I followed them.

Other times, all the kids formed a circle, hands out, palms cupped together. My mom would take a button and go around the circle, placing her hands in all the kids' hands one by one. In one child's hand she would drop the button, although all the kids continued to take her hands in theirs so that no one knew where the button was placed save for the giver and receiver. All the children in the circle begin to sing, "Button, button, who's got the button?" and then each child in the circle would guess.

"Billy's got the button!"

"Susie's got the button!"

Once the child with the button was finally guessed, that child would distribute the button and start a new round.

I always knew who had the button. I could tell. All you had to do was watch their little faces, and their expressions would give them away. I could tell just by looking at my mom, too. Even though she wouldn't smile, I could read her poker face. The corners of her eyes would lift imperceptibly, and her face would always relax just a bit when the button was gone, as if she'd just released a long-held secret.

I pretended not to know, though.

I knew my place amongst the hierarchy.

My mom knew, too. That's why she never gave me the button. Not once. Not ever.

We both knew a win by me could cause a kid to say I cheated and end up costing my mom a client and a buck.

"Button, button, who's got the button?"

I stare at the button tree.

The creek sings that childhood song back to me.

I look at Ol' Betsy.

"Tell me your secrets," I say to her.

I used to get jealous of my mom's old sewing machine. It was the one who constantly received her attention and touch. It was the one she talked to every evening in a whisper, and Ol' Betsy would reply in her magical voice, as if she were channeling God and speaking in tongues so that only my mother could understand.

But I was mostly envious of Ol' Betsy because she was a miracle worker. She could take my mother's miscellaneous scraps and turn them into something beautiful and complete. She could make sense of the pieces my mother tossed her way. I could never do that.

"Good job," my mom would say to Ol' Betsy, patting her when she had produced a quilt or blouse.

I can only remember my mom telling me once and only once she was proud of me.

Not when I graduated high school, junior college or college. Not when I landed my first job. Not when I was the youngest woman to be hired as Lindy's Department Store's ready-to-wear fashion director. It was when I least expected it. When I moved out of her house for good.

"You were never meant to live here," she said. "You got roots here, but it's not where you're meant to grow. Never was. I found my way here. You found your way out. With my buttons. Proud of ya, Sutton."

The day I moved to Chicago I stopped my truck at the end of our driveway to secure a box that had tumbled forward as I drove over the rocky road. My mom was standing in the window watching me leave.

She was weeping.

A bird lands in the tree outside the sewing room window, knocking me from this memory. I smile.

My mother hated "featherbedders." That was her term for pretentious folks who felt the need to fluff their own feathers, make themselves seem bigger than they really were.

"People who never had no hardship do that," she said. "When you have, you're just thankful to have a bed, feathers or not."

I shared this story with a friend from work once, and she told me we probably had German or Dutch in us. My heart raced. My only thought was, "Do we? I know nothing about my family history."

My life has been consumed with a question that will never be answered. I am a room filled with scraps. How many days, weeks, months, years have I spent Googling every possible word, name and date regarding my mother? How many calls have I made to people with similar last names? I grew tired of being Nancy Drew, so I stopped.

I think of Mrs. Dimmons.

That's what people do when they grow up in small towns and feel as if they are "different." They run.

I grew to believe maybe that's what my mother did, too. When you experience tragedy in a tiny town, you're defined by it. Maybe my mother was no longer Mabel Douglas, maybe she was the woman who lost her entire family in that fire. Maybe everywhere she turned—at the grocery, the farm stand, the ice cream shop—she saw someone she lost. Maybe it was better to be alone and in a new place than be the woman everyone whispered about and felt sorry for.

And so she ran, too.

The cabin is so silent, my ears ring. It could be the start of an early hangover, it could be exhaustion, or grief. But in my head, I can hear my mother sing, as she would only to me, making up her own lyrics, "Sutton, Sutton, Who's Got the Button?"

I know I will take the button tree when…

My stomach lurches.

I hear my mother's voice again.

"You found your way out."

But I didn't just run. I didn't just leave here. I didn't simply leave home. I left my mother *here*.

And then I left my mother *there*.

You left your mother, Sutton. And she will never come home again.

I stand to escape her sewing room and all the memories, but the world undulates, and I trip over the thick, colorful oval braided rug she's had here forever.

"Hides every color of thread," she used to say. "That's why we have buttons and rugs: to hide the things we don't want to see."

I nearly do a header into Ol' Betsy, just like my mother did, right into the machine where I learned to sew, my mother's hands on top of mine, teaching me the beauty of her art. I look at the old machine. It, too, is a work of art: black with a beautiful gold inlay pattern atop the original, old treadle oak cabinet, glowing with a rich patina. The top is peeling a bit, but it is a stunning antique.

"Ol' Betsy," I say to the Singer. "How'd you get your name?"

The cabinet has five drawers, one in the middle and two with knobs on each side of it.

As if compelled by a force greater than me, I take a seat and begin to sew, starting where my mother left off. My foot moves in a rhythm, as if I am dancing in my socks with my mom on New Year's Eve to songs from the Rat Pack—the only time of year she'd dance and have music—and the Singer hums as if it were trying to lull me to sleep.

I used to think it took an act of God just to thread the vintage round bobbin until I got the hang of it.

The blouse my mom was making has flouncy shoulders, a surprisingly bold choice for her. I glance at the pattern and look at the size, and I wonder if she was making it as a Christmas gift for me. The buttons she was to use sit in a cut glass bowl before her button jars.

Vintage tortoise Bakelite buttons. So beautiful. I haven't seen buttons like this in ages.

There are really two types of buttons: Utilitarian, rather plain buttons now made for clothes that are mass-produced. And buttons that are still created by artisans, beautiful, hand-crafted works of art made for one-of-a-kind designs or collectors.

My work bridges the gap: I recreate works of art in bulk.

But these are the real thing.

Am I the real thing anymore? Was my mom real?

The widow always seemed beyond reproach.

Without warning, I begin to cry. My body flails, and my hand jerks.

I stop, but it's too late.

Bumblebunching.

That's what sewers call the annoying tangled loop of stitching on the bobbin side of the fabric, the result of improper tension applied to the sewing machine.

I cry even harder.

That word sums up my life right now.

I am bumblebunched.

And I will be forever bumblebunched without you, Mom.

I turn a jar of buttons over on my mother's sewing desk. I run my hands through them, feeling each one, seeking an answer.

I hear my mom's voice call to me, or maybe it's God's, I don't know anymore, but I can hear it say very clearly: "Sometimes you have to search for God as long and hard as

you search for the right button. You know it's in there somewhere. You just need to keep believin' and lookin' until you
find it. You'll know when you do."

2

NOTIONS

When a pattern calls for notions, it's items like buttons,
zippers, hooks, lace, elastic, etc.
All the small accessories you need to finish the garment.

"Hello?"

"Sutton Douglas?"

"Yes?"

"I'm sorry to tell you that your mother passed an hour ago."
Silence.

"Hello?"

"Why didn't you call me?"

"We only discovered her…"

"She was alone?"

"We're short-staffed, ma'am. It happened overnight."

"I asked that she have a sitter since I couldn't be with her."

"We can't be with them all."

All?

"We've already notified the county coroner, but you will
need to make your own funeral arrangements," she continues.
"You can pick up your mother's things later today if you'd
like. Oh, and she left a letter for you."

A letter?

"I'll come by as soon as I can. Thank you."

I hang up and call Clara at Buck's Funeral Home. That's where everybody in town gets buried. My mom always used to say, "Now Buck's knows how to lay out a body."

The phone rings and rings. I glance at the clock and finally realize it isn't even dawn yet. I leave a message. A few minutes later, my phone rings.

"Hi, Sutton. It's Clara. I'm so sorry," she says as if we're lifelong friends. "We all just adored Miss Mabel."

"Thank you." I gather a breath to steady myself. My voice still comes out hitched. "She wants a funeral."

"Oh, honey," Clara says. "I'm so sorry, but we can't have funerals due to the Covid. State is recommending cremation."

"No, that's not what she wanted..." Tears fill my eyes.

"Ain't up to me," she says. "If it were, I'd have a big funeral and invite the whole town to celebrate that woman. She never had an easy life, and she never once complained about it. I guarantee God is welcomin' her right now with a choir and new sewin' machine!"

For a moment, I picture this, and then my grief subsides.

"We'll do a real nice newspaper article, and people can post condolences online. Maybe her church as a charity?"

"Let me think," I say.

"Well, your mama is havin' the time of her life in heaven right now. She don't have to work another day in her life bent over a machine."

"It wasn't her time," I say.

"Oh, honey," Clara says. "We never know when it's our time."

I think of our family in the fire.

"I'll swing by later today," I say, before I hang up.

How could something as random and savage as this virus find its way all the way down here to the middle of nowhere and into my mother's room and take her from me? The world no longer makes sense.

Sometimes, my mom would let me buy a bottle of Grape Nehi out of the old freezer at the candy store. It was so special, I'd save it. I'd get home and rush to the spring that fronted our rocky beach and flowed to Hickory Creek and put it in the icy water to drink when it got to be a hundred degrees.

"Watch out for the cottonmouths!" my mother would always warn.

The venomous snakes with the white mouths loved to dwell by cold, rocky streams, and they would lie, undetected, as if waiting for the right moment to strike. We knew many an unsuspecting fisherman to get bit on what seemed like a normal summer day.

Just when you think life is stable, the unknown strikes out of nowhere, and your entire world is poisoned, and you don't know if life will ever be right again.

I lie in bed, and grief rises like lava and consumes me. I roar in horror in the pitch-black. And then I am empty.

My mother protected me. I couldn't protect her.

I am alone in this world. Yes, I have friends, colleagues and coworkers, but I no longer have family. My entire family is gone.

I text Abby, my best friend from Chicago.

My mom passed this morning. Devastated.

I set my phone down, and it lights up seconds later, illuminating the dark room.

I'm sooooo sorry, Sutton. Want me to come to you?

Abby's selfless kindness overwhelms me, and I sob anew.

No. Thank you. Too risky. We can't even have a funeral. I don't know what to do, or how to start.

I grab some Kleenex off the nightstand and pull myself together as I watch the three little dots herald Abby's reply.

This is overwhelming, Sutton. And you don't have to deal with everything at once. Just know how much your mother loved you and how much you loved her. Know you will carry her with you forever. I know it all sounds so trite, and there are no words to ease your pain, but she loved you. I love you. And that's all that means anything right now in this messed up world of ours.

Thank you.

Want me to let some of your colleagues know?

Work. Even that feels like it's slipping away in the chaos of the last year.

No, thanks. I'll send everyone an email.

I'll call you later, okay? Get some rest. There may not be a funeral, but spend the day honoring your mom in your own way. Take care of yourself. XOXO!

XOXO!

I lay down my phone. Dawn is rising in the Ozarks. I can see the oak outside my bedroom window begin to take shape. I can see the sky begin to glow. The birds begin to sing.

The world continues.

My heart shatters.

My bedroom looks much the same as it did when I was a girl. A tiny log bedroom I tried to make look like the pretty ones in all those women's magazines. My volleyball trophies line shelves. Photos of me swimming in the creek dot the walls. Cute curtains I made out of mattress ticking line the old windows. My college diplomas sit in pretty frames in a place of prominence.

My mom asked me if she could keep my diplomas. It was her way of saying she was proud of me without ever having to say it. I knew they were as much for her as they were for me. I did something she'd always dreamed of doing.

It takes every ounce of strength I can muster to sit up and swing my legs out of bed.

As I do, my button necklace spins round to my front. I run my fingers from the clasp, counting the buttons as I go.

Day eighteen, I think, shutting my eyes. *Iridescent blue.*

I open my eyes and squint in the burgeoning dawn at the eighteenth button on my necklace. I can hear my mother's voice.

"Color 'a the scales of a big, fat bluegill."

My mom loved to fish for bluegill, right off the edge of the beach where a rocky finger reached into the current. The current slowed as it slinked around that rocky bend, and that's where the water got deep and dark. That's where the bluegill lived, down amongst the rocks, under the bottom of the bluff.

I hold the button up to the light.

And the scales were the exact, magical color of this button.

I slide my feet into slippers and grab my old robe off the back of the little chair in front of my childhood desk, and head to the kitchen to make a pot of coffee.

The silence is haunting.

It is nearly overwhelming to stop moving and be still. To

confront your aloneness. We all run from everything. And when we stop, we are often frightened to take stock of the person we've become.

Click-clock. Click-clock.

I turn as the coffee drips. The black-and-white kitty cat clock my mom bought when I was a girl watches me from above the stove. Its tail swishes left as its eyes glance right. Back and forth she goes, eyeing me, counting the seconds of my life, my loneliness.

Nearly forty years gone.

I look at the cat. It winks at me.

In the blink of an eye.

I grab a coffee cup from the old, painted pine cupboards slathered in countless coats of white paint. The silver hardware is now midcentury, as are the cups: milk glass mugs with gold daisies.

I fill my cup. It's tiny compared to today's giant mugs, and I know I will need many more cups to help get me through the day.

I take my coffee and head to the long, narrow deck that towers above the creek. Although it is early spring and the sun is just rising, it is already warm. The weather is one of the things I miss most about the Ozarks. Yes, summers are hot and muggy, but spring and fall are beautiful, winters tolerable. It "snows and goes" in the Ozarks, whereas in Chicago it snows and keeps snowing and snowing and snowing.

I grew up without air-conditioning and, thus, have become conditioned to being warm. My internal thermostat has never acclimated to Chicago temperatures. I always wear a coat, sweater or jacket. My hands are always cold to the touch.

From my perch, I have a bird's-eye view of the Ozarks landscape. The deck floats in the air as if it were a solitary cloud. It is pinned deep into the rocky terrain below by mile-high beams that have withstood a hundred-year flood. I remember my mom and I taking turns watching the water rise the summer I was twelve. It seemed near impossible to me that the water would reach this high, but it kept raining, and the creek kept rising, until it began to creep into the cabin. Water came from every direction—down the bluff, off the hillsides, and from the creek. We ran buckets of water outside for two days straight. We placed towels at every door. We sealed windows. We raised our appliances on concrete blocks. Our bedrooms became wading pools. When it was over, the water had come into the cabin a foot. You could tell by the color of the logs how high the water had reached. They turned lighter than the others. Then the mold came. Grew as fast as crabgrass in the heat and humidity. My mom scrubbed and cleaned, washed and dried. She saved this place.

I stamp the deck with my foot.

How could you both survive that? Why are you still standing, and she's not?

Directly below me runs that freshwater spring, cold as ice, that trickles into the creek. This is where I kept my Nehi, our minnows and fish in buckets and stringers. We had to place rocks on the buckets to keep the raccoons from finding our booty, and the fish were goners if we forgot to take them off the stringer.

A wide beach filled with rocks and stones, not sand, leads to Hickory Creek, a crystal clear ribbon that winds like a cottonmouth through the Ozarks. It is a beautiful creek, unspoiled and unchanged, and sycamore trees jut from the banks at odd angles, reaching for the sunlight, surviving against all odds. The creek is moving swiftly after spring rains, and it sounds as if it is humming a sad lullaby.

On the opposite side of the creek sits a field of wildflowers. It is actually farmland, but the family that has owned the land for generations left the acreage alongside the water natural. Sometimes, cattle will wander to the edge and drink from the creek, but most of the time the land resembles a Monet painting, soft, colorful, ethereal.

Bluffs hug the creek and the cottage, hold them inside their stony embrace just like family. In fact, just outside the back door where our outhouse used to sit, is a cave. It was my escape hatch as a girl, the place where I would go and read, or take my tablets of paper and draw sketches of dresses, or buttons I wanted to make. It was also my hiding place from my mom. Oftentimes, after a hard day at school, or a bad volleyball game, I would seek comfort from my mother, knowing it would never come.

"Better off alone," she'd tell me. "That way you won't get hurt."

"I don't need advice!" I'd complain. "I need a hug."

Off I'd go to the cave, hauling a blanket to ward off the damp chill even when the humidity was near a hundred percent, where I'd dream of what it would be like to get comfort from a family member or a friend, be connected to someone other than my mother.

I have long been a cave myself, an emotional and geographical replica of my mom and the Ozarks: impenetrable, seeking light, dulled by the cold. My emotions combined with a lack of family and need for answers formed internal stalactites that threatened to pierce my heart. I had to work hard to overcome my upbringing to make the few friends I now have, ones like Abby, who have become family to me. There is a gnawing cave inside me that still desires a family I will never have.

The only time my mom would join me in that cave was when there would be tornado warnings. My mom would grab me up and haul me inside when the wind picked up and skies turned the color of a nasty bruise, where we'd wait until the weather cleared.

"Nowhere safer you could ever be," my mom would say every time, seemingly as much to herself as to me.

The few times my mother opened up to me were during these moments of uncertainty, and even then her confessions would be coded, cloaked in stories about buttons that made no sense to me.

"Did you know that after the Renaissance in Europe, buttons became fancier, almost like little works of art? These fancy buttons required rich folk to need help dressin'. That's when buttons changed sides," she'd teach me. "Men put on their own shirts, so buttons faced right for their convenience. Rich ladies usually had maids, and their buttons were on the left to make it easier for their maids to dress them as they faced them."

"Why do you only read the Bible, or books about buttons from the library?" I'd ask.

"'Cause they tell me everything I need to know about this world," she'd reply. "They tell me exactly what matters. Don't need nothin' else but God, buttons and Sutton."

One time, a tornado swept through downtown Nevermore. It killed four people and leveled much of the new part of town. People who saw it said it was as wide as a tractor trailer coming down the highway, the kind you'd have to move your car over for, nearly into the ditch, to avoid it hitting you. We could hear it roar in the distance. My mom even hauled Ol' Betsy into the cave that time and held me tight, telling me stories to pass the time, admitting she was scared and telling me that she loved me in her own way.

"Did you know many buttons tell stories of families? Some were designed as keepsakes to hold hair clippin's from a baby, or dried flowers. These were as precious as any jewelry because they held someone's history. Maybe you could do that one day? Tell the story of our family through your buttons? I mean, all you have to do is study a button's face. It can be plain or quite purty. But every button has a history about a time, place and person. It's like a paintin'. An entire story written upon a tiny little canvas. Someone has touched it. Gazed upon it. Loved it. You just have to look and listen a bit more closely to see and hear its story."

"How do you know all this?" I'd ask her.

From what I could gather, my mother didn't even graduate from high school. There were no diplomas like the ones I earned, although they could have burned up in the fire. But one thing I did learn from my mom: her lack of an education didn't stop her from trying to make something of her life. Lazy she was not. Lazy I would never be.

"One thing I know is history, Sutton. You can't know where you're goin' if you don't know from where you came."

"Really, Mom?" I would reply. "So where did we come from then? Tell me! Tell me something. Anything. Please! I've seen my birth certificate! It says 'father unknown.' Do you have any idea what that feels like?"

"I do."

"Mother...please, what was he like?" and then my voice would trail off into tears.

How many times did I beg my mother for a simple story about my dad? *Who was he? Did I look like him?*

How many times did I ask about my grandparents? Did my grandma like to sew, too? Did my grampa love the water as much as you do? Did I have cousins? Aunts and uncles? Did we ever have a dog? A cat?

I remember doing a project in school about our family history. I made a path of buttons that led to nowhere.

My mother repeated that line about knowing history to me when I was older, and I laughed in her face.

"The irony is rich, Mother."

I sip my coffee and stare back at the bluffs. The sun rises high enough to illuminate every detail. I now see what my mother has so loved every spring of her life: the dogwoods in bloom.

Right now in the Ozarks, the hillsides are white. The Ozarks dogwoods—so much bigger, sturdier and beautiful than the ones up north—make it look as though it has just snowed.

My mother loved nothing more than spring in the Ozarks. Services leading up to Easter—culminating with Sunrise Service—were her favorites, and she always sat on the edge of her pew when the preacher told the story from the Bible about the dogwood.

"Dogwood was once akin to the great oak," the minister would say. "Because its wood was strong and sturdy, it was used to build the cross on which Jesus was crucified. Because of its role in the crucifixion, God both blessed and cursed the dogwood. He cursed the tree to be forever small, so that it could never grow large enough again for its wood to be used as a cross, and that its branches would grow narrow and crooked. But He also blessed the tree so it would produce beautiful flowers—its petals in the shape of a cross—just in time for Easter so we would never forget."

"That story is like all of us," my mom would say as she drove back home after church, the only time she wore a colorful spring dress. "All blessed and cursed, a reminder of the pain that people can cause and the beauty that can still come from it."

There is a small hillside between the bluffs—verdant yet dotted with white—where we would bury our pets growing up. We never actually went out and adopted a pet, but every few years, a stray dog or cat would wander up, badly injured and in need of help, and my mother could never turn a stray away. I loved having a friend, someone with whom to talk and share my secrets. When a beloved pet would die—Racer, Jolene, Sunny, Mr. Whiskers—we would carry it up to that hillside and bury it right under a dogwood, the creek, the beach, the wildflowers, the bluffs, the entire Ozarks expanse laid out before them.

"Now she'll have the best view for eternity."

I stand and move to the edge of the deck. I set down my coffee on the ledge, open my arms and scream.

A few seconds later, my grief echoes back.

It's like my mother never existed.

I have sneaked over to her bedroom window, hoping to see her, as if she's suddenly going to appear in front of me like an Easter version of Jacob Marley.

It is a warm, windy Ozarks day, the kind where you can nearly smell summer. I know this early warmth means a thunderstorm is in the future.

"Can't get this warm this early without a boomer," I can hear my mom tell me.

The tulips dance, and the grass moves as one in the wind.

Two women appear in the window. My instinct is to run or hide, but there is nowhere to go. An elderly woman sees me. She waves.

She has already been given my mother's room. My mother has been wiped away.

My heart rises into my throat.

The last few years have given all of us nearly more than we can handle. To deal with such anxiety and grief, and to do it in isolation, has changed us profoundly.

I have such anger at this virus and what it's doing not only to our physical and emotional health but also our elderly.

Will this just serve to separate us even further from one another, or will it draw us closer?

Will I be able to reconnect again? Or has this doomed me to be forever alone?

I think of meeting my first real friend, Tammy, in grade school. All she did to reach out to me was hand me one end of her jump rope without saying a word.

A connection.

And then her family moved away the next year, and the connection was lost.

But we all must make an effort again, right? Not only for the sake of ourselves but for the sake of each other.

I turn and look at the woman in my mother's window.

I smile, wave back and blow a kiss.

"Be strong," I whisper to her.

And myself.

Her hand flutters over her heart and then she blows me a kiss.

I turn into the wind and let its warmth envelop me, an invisible hug.

I walk to the entrance of the facility.

My mom's belongings—her purse, readers, hairbrush—are hermetically sealed in baggies, her name—MISS MABEL— scrawled on the side of the box which is just sitting on the sidewalk as if I've wandered up to a lost and found.

I feel as if I'm in one of those old-fashioned sci-fi movies where the world becomes infected by an unknown virus. I used to think those movies were so corny, but now, it's all come true.

I look in the box again.

Where are her clothes?

I begin to move toward the doors and then remember: no visitors are allowed inside.

I want the shirt I made for her.

No, I *need* the shirt I made for her.

I knock on the door. A care worker approaches.

"I'm so sorry about your mama," the woman says behind her mask. "She was salt of the earth. One of my favorite residents. Never asked for a thing."

"She had some clothes..." I start.

The woman ducks her head and then shakes it slowly. "I'm sorry," she says again.

She looks up, and I can see the dark circles under her eyes. My heart aches anew for her, this stranger coming here every day and fighting an invisible war, putting her own health at risk for the safety and protection of others.

None of us knew this was coming.

I think of Tammy and the jump rope. I put my hand on the window. She raises hers and places it over mine through the glass, bows her head and says a prayer.

When she's done, I grab my mother's box and head to my car. I put the box into the trunk and a tiny flash of color catches my eye: the button ring I had Abby make for my mom years ago sits in the corner of a Ziploc. It is a simple button fashioned in a silver setting to match the band. Not ostentatious, just like my mother. I blew my first bonus check after being hired at Lindy's to have Abby—a jewelry designer there—make it for my mother. It was my thank-you to her for not only inspiring my career but also giving me everything she possibly could to help me succeed.

It became like her wedding band. She never took it off.

"You should have been buried in this, Mom," I say. "I'm so sorry."

And that's when I see it. Her letter to me, sitting at the bottom of the box in another baggie as if it were medical evidence.

I open the baggie and pull out the envelope, which has my name on it in my mother's slanted cursive. My heart shatters. I unfold the letter.

My Dear Daughter:
Don't be scared. I can see the fear in everyone's eyes, but I'm not afraid. I have God on my side. I've always had God on my side.

No matter what happens, I want you to know how much I love you. You were and will always be my entire world. And you are my future.

I had a hard life, but God made it a good one because of you. That's all any of us can ask for in life: to love and be loved, without question, without conditions. I once had a life with nothing; and then I had everything. People won't see it that way. We didn't have a big house. We didn't go on trips. And I ain't leavin' you much, save for the cabin, my buttons and my love. But we really had everything we ever needed.

I hope you will always remember that.

Especially right now...

My heart stops, as if it has brakes built inside of it and knows instinctively a crash is coming. I take a deep breath and continue reading.

I know I've been anything but an open book about my past. I know I've not been the mother you often wanted or needed. And I know it's cruel to leave you alone in this world without the truth. I've sat here these last few weeks listening to my care workers—total strangers—share their lives without a second thought. They tell me the stories of their parents, grandparents, children and grandchildren, and I can feel the embers of

51

jealousy burn for all that I never had. I can feel my heart melt because I never shared who I was: Miss Mabel, The Widow of Nevermore.

So here goes:

Our family did not die in a fire. But our family is long gone. It has been forever.

I'm sorry to have lied to you. I felt as if I had no choice. The only thing I ever wanted to do was love and protect you. I did that. But to do so, I had to lie, and that had consequences.

Sutton, I grew up with a family, but it was void of unconditional love. The love I received only had strings and conditions. But I found true love with your father. Ted was the love of my life, my blue button. My family cast me aside for loving the wrong man, a good man but not the "right" man. Your father died from that heartbreak. I had to run away and hide to start over again. I had to run away and hide to have you. But all the pain was worth it because your father ended up giving me the greatest gift in the world: YOU!

I hope you can forgive me, Sutton. I know you may not, and I understand, but sometimes the pain in life is too much to endure, and we have to bury those memories in order to go on with our lives. There may not have been a fire, but my family burned all of my feelings of hope and love and forgiveness to the ground, and left me with nothing but a pile of ashes.

But you taught me to love again. You made me whole. You taught me to love, without conditions.

Always remember that.

Good can come from the bad.

Why do I love buttons, Sutton? And why did I pass that love of a forgotten and seemingly unimportant little trinket along to you?

Because we too often and too easily discard our own histories, heirlooms and family to seek worth in shiny, expensive objects and people that actually hold none.

Do you know what I've learned, my beautiful girl? That life is as short as one blink of God's eye, but in that blink, we forget what matters most: each other.

Don't ever do that, Sutton. Continue to make your blink count.

More than anything, I pray you will continue on with your life. Find peace. Don't go chasing my past. I fear it will only cost you precious time or end up burning you, too.

You have a family. Me. We've always been a family. And that's all that ever mattered.

My last request: promise me you'll have a funeral, open casket, so everyone can see me to say goodbye, and God can welcome me with open arms. I need that so I can look Him right in the eye and say, "Thank you for a wonderful life! I'm comin' home now!" Call Clara. Nobody lays out a body like Buck's. Oh, and bury me in the pretty blue dress, the one with pearl buttons that look like God made 'em Himself. Oh, what an entrance into heaven I'll make wearin' that.

Finally, promise me you'll be happy. I'm sorry I kept so much of myself hidden, but I don't think we need to burden our children with our own shortcomings. Your past was me. Your family was me. I know it wasn't what you dreamed, but I hope it was enough. I sure learned it was.

I love you, my beautiful daughter. You dressed my life up prettier than any button ever could. Take care of Ol' Betsy. Tell our story through our buttons.

I love you, and I will always love you, Sutton, my beautiful button!

Mom

I stand in the empty parking lot and cry my eyes out. We fear everything in this world—and that fear too often stops us in our tracks from pursuing who and what we love, or sets us running from everything we desire—but it's the invisible that eventually gets us all: loneliness, grief, sorrow, this virus.

Our past.

The invisible dwells inside us all. In me, it survives as a dull ache. I've had it since I was little. A gnawing hunger for the truth that needed to be filled. I knew this ache lived inside my mom, too. I could see it in her eyes.

My mother kept us alone, and I now know it was to keep herself from getting hurt again. She tried to keep me safe, too. And yet here I now sit, hurt *and* alone with even more questions than I once had.

I look at the letter and then my phone.

I must still have family out there somewhere. But how do I find them? Should I find them?

I've always wanted a "real" family.

Could they really have been as bad as my mother said?

I think of the men I've dated and brought home. My mom treated them as if they were vacuum salesmen who had entered against her will and tossed dirt on the floor to prove their product worked. But it was my mom who always swept them away, kept it just the two of us, kept her memory bank tidy.

I tuck my mom's letter back into the baggie.

"Hiding yet another secret," I say to it.

In the distance, a whip-poor-will calls.

I suddenly remember the legend of the whip-poor-will my mother used to always tell me: whip-poor-wills singing near a house were an omen of death.

"Don't call back at night," she would tell me. "It's an invitation."

"For what?" I would ask.

"Terrible things," she'd say. "Just don't go lookin' for trouble."

On the drive back home, my body begins to shake so hard that, despite how warm it is outside, I have to roll up the windows and turn on heat.

Lightning flashes in the distance, and I count the seconds—just like my mom taught me to do to track an approaching storm—until I hear the thunder.

Still a ways away.

From the deck, I can watch the storms roll in from the distance. It's a muggy spring evening, and I know the coming storm will wash away the humidity, and a north wind will make the world feel all clean and new again.

But will I? Right now, I feel as unsettled as the weather, my soul as thick as the air.

My entire life has been built on a lie.

Who am I?

I take a drink of cold water I pulled right from the underground spring, hoping it will chill my confusion and anger, refresh my spirit. I added some fresh watercress to it, which has sprung to life due to the warmer spring weather. College classmates used to call me a country girl, a redneck, even white trash when I talked about how I grew up.

Now they would pay five bucks for this glass of spring-fed, chemical-free, "real" water.

My mind wanders to work, and the flak I've caught from fellow designers and the media over my "country" collections.

"It's not country," I say over and over again. "It's classic. It's traditional. It's timeless."

And it's true. Quality and beauty never go out of style. People just rediscover trends—hairstyles, cars, music, design and architecture—and act as if they invented them.

Not me.

When I was young, I tried to imitate the leading designers, emulating their styles. No one was buying my designs, much less hiring me. I returned home depressed and watched my mother sew one night. She pulled the most beautiful button from her jar and turned the simplest of blouses into a stunning creation.

In fact, I took tons of her buttons—old tins, boxes and jars filled with them—and even scoured the drawers of her sewing machine stand. They inspired me.

No, Mom, you inspired my entire life.

Are all of my memories lies, too?

My heart pangs.

I saw my mother in a new light that visit. Sewing at home—even after sewing all day at work—was her creative outlet, her inspiration, her joy. Picking just the right button for just the right top was a world away from stitching the pocket onto an overall the same way or attaching the exact same fasteners every day of her life.

I hate to admit it, but my work has become drudgery, too, over the past few years, and the pandemic has just magnified my disillusion. Ready-to-wear means my once "unique" designs are made for the masses, my clothing is mass-produced in standardized sizes and sold in finished condition—rather than designed and sewn for one particular person.

The beautiful, one-of-a-kind buttons I select are now produced in bulk. Each and every button looks the same.

Every piece of clothing I design must be made as inexpensively—*no, as cheaply*—as possible, sewn out of the country, so each item can be marked up as much as humanly possible but still be at a price point affordable for most shoppers.

I have gotten no new emails from work since I left for Missouri, and I wonder if it's a way of giving me space to deal and grieve or if—like the approaching storm and my mother's letter—it's the winds of change a' comin'.

Retail has been in a downward spiral. I am just unsure as to whether it's a funnel cloud or temporary windstorm.

Lightning flashes again, and the wind gusts. The limbs on the sycamores jutting from the banks begin to sway, the dogwoods dance.

My heart leaps. I stand, so quickly the lawn chair in which I'm sitting flips over backward.

I go to my mother's closet—a place I wasn't allowed to snoop—and begin rummaging through her racks of clothes, sliding hangers this way and that. My mother's closet reflects her life: simple, unassuming, small. Lots of comfortable work clothes that she wore to the factory hang lifelessly. Hangers filled with worn slacks and jeans she wore for yard work. Sweatshirts and sweaters with button-eyed cardinals and bluebirds are stacked on makeshift shelves. Tennis shoes and work boots are scattered under the clothes.

In the far corner, tucked away, barely noticeable, hang a couple of garment bags. I wedge my body into the corner of the closet, hangers jangling, and unzip a bag.

Your blue dress.

I pull the bag free and lay it atop the chenille blanket on her bed. I remove the dress. It is ankle-length, with a tiny, shiny navy blue belt to offset the light blue of the fabric.

I sit on the bed and stare at the dress, the evening sun making the buttons shimmer. The dress is not fancy. *But the buttons are beautiful.*

They are vintage pearl buttons, varying shades of turquoise, each a little bit differently shaped and shaded.

Handmade.

I pick up the dress and hold it to my body. I walk around the room as if I were my mother, turning on her beloved lamp on her birch bark nightstand, spraying her favorite perfume, running her hairbrush through my hair, trying one last time not only to be around her but also understand her before the memories—as they become in life—are softened if not erased.

I touch the dress.

"Who were you, Mother?" I ask. And then I whisper, "Ted."

I walk to her window and stare at the creek, holding her dress out as if it were my mother's ghost, so she can see her home—which she didn't know she would never see again—one last time.

Lightning flashes, illuminating her dress.

I look at it more carefully, noticing that the dress has been altered. I hold it closer to my eyes. The dress has been hemmed, let out.

For some reason, I always thought she made this dress to wear at my high school graduation, or wedding. Her body didn't change that much over the years. She was always lithe and, save for her back, in good shape.

But now I realize that perhaps this dress not only survived the faux fire but was also reinvented and reimagined, just like my mother's life.

Lightning flashes again, and thunder booms.

I don't have much time.

I grab the dress and race out of the cabin. I grab a shovel from the outbuilding and then charge off toward the small hillside between the bluffs.

I throw the dress over my shoulder and begin to dig a grave with the shovel. The Ozarks terrain is as hard, rocky and unmovable as my mother, but so am I, and I dig—undeterred as always—through the clay and rock until fresh earth reveals itself. I dig and dig, as if I'm trying to unearth all my family's secrets at once. Finally, exhausted, I set the shovel down, lathered in sweat, and then lay my mother's blue dress in the grave.

"The funeral in the blue dress you wanted, Mom," I say. "You worked so hard your entire life for me. Rest in peace.

Watch over me. I love you. And I always will. Despite everything."

I say a prayer and then look heavenward. "God, help me. Please."

I stand and retrieve the shovel but stop. I kneel and lean into the grave. For some reason, I snap a blue button off of her dress, wanting to keep a piece of my mother alive with me.

A clue to the woman I never knew.

I fill the grave with dirt and then build a makeshift cross from dogwood branches, lashing it together with saw grass.

I turn and look out over the Ozarks landscape, the creek singing a hymn to my mother.

"Now you'll have the best view for eternity."

As if on cue, it begins to pour, and I run back to the cabin, soaking wet. I stand, dripping, in the kitchen, staring at the button. I dry off quickly with a dish towel and then walk back to my mother's bedroom, my head pounding, the thunder matching my grief. The windows are open, and I can feel the temperature drop with the approaching storm. A chill covers my body. I lie down on my mom's bed and cover myself in her chenille blanket.

It still smells like you.

The garment bag slides toward me, and I kick at it angrily, trying to release my anguish. My foot connects, and the bag goes flying toward the floor, but something slips onto the bed before it does.

I sit up and grab it.

It is an antique button card with aquamarine buttons like the ones on my mother's dress.

Behind the set of six buttons, in three vertical rows of two, is an old-fashioned illustration of a kindly grandmother, a button box below. Cute little flowers ring the edge.

The button card reads:

Grandma's Button Box
Ten Cents
For Blouses & Britches

"What is this?" I ask the room.

That's when I notice another tiny word written in an old-fashioned script in the middle of the illustration. I hold the card up to my eyes and squint. The lightning flashes just enough to illuminate it.

Dandy Button Co., Michigan.

3

ZIGZAG STITCH

A zigzag stitch is simply a stitch made with a zigzag pattern. Often used to sew along raw edges to prevent them from fraying.

The things I loved most about the city have now been stolen, the simplest of things, like walking the neighborhood, eating at a local restaurant, shopping, perusing art galleries and antiques shops, heading to ball games and concerts, gathering with friends.

I live in a city to do these things. I was alone too long. I yearned for noise, people, fashion, food and both celebrity and anonymity in a crowd.

One of the most monstrous aspects of Covid—in addition to its nightmarish invisibility, the ravaging effects on those we love, the devastating loss of so many—is that it strikes against our very own human nature. It challenges our vulnerabilities. The virus isolates us.

Humans are social beings. We yearn to gather, hug, celebrate, laugh, cry, comfort, befriend. And this monster teases us, laughs at us, challenges us, infuriates us by removing—in the biggest crisis of our lifetimes—what we yearn for most: connecting with one another.

And yet I know I am equipped to handle this isolation better than most.

I sit in the window seat of my second-floor condo in River North. I live in a drafty old condo with ornate woodwork that sits above an art gallery in the Gallery District. The condo has huge windows that front the street, and I used to love to perch in one with my coffee, water or wine and watch the constant bustle.

Now, there is little activity. Galleries and restaurants are closed. I wonder how many will open again once this nightmare ends.

I don't believe River North has, in its history, ever been this quiet.

"History," I say in the silence. "Where's mine start?"

How can I know my neighborhood's history better than my own?

During Prohibition, speakeasies popped up all over Chicago, and River North—with its many train tracks—became a bootlegging epicenter. Two of Chicago's most famous mob incidents happened right here, including Al Capone's murder of Dean O'Banion who ran a bootlegging business disguised as a flower shop on the corner of Chicago Avenue and North State with his wife. That started the five-year gang war that culminated in the infamous St. Valentine's Day Massacre in 1929.

Now, River North is a lively neighborhood that—as its name implies—lies north of the Chicago River, directly above the Loop. It is bordered by the Magnificent Mile to the east and is home to many corporate headquarters including Groupon, Yelp and ConAgra.

My company, Lindy's Department Store, is also headquartered here. Lindy's used to be known as Magnus Rhodes Finebaum, the quintessential Chicago department store where everyone went to shop and where every Chicagoan flocked for the holidays. Now they've become airplane hangars filled with ransacked rounders and bargain basements.

Sutton's Buttons is one of their few bright spots.

As long as I make them money.

In addition to the proximity to work, I was drawn to the area for many other reasons: the nice shops and eateries, vibrant nightlife, and multitude of cocktail bars and activities. But I was mostly drawn by the inspiration.

River North is home to the largest concentration of art galleries outside of Manhattan. Located between Orleans and LaSalle, many of these galleries are housed in converted warehouses and lofts.

When I used to walk the streets and into the galleries, I could actually feel the hum of creativity, as much as I could feel the throb of the El when it passed. The massive Merchandise Mart is also close by, drawing shoppers and retailers to its home and office design showrooms.

I picked up so many fashion ideas just walking around "First Fridays" when galleries were open late and filled to the gills with partying artists and the Midsummer Art Walk. I sketched late at night. I shared ideas with strangers. I ran after girls on the street whose outfits I admired.

My job, like me, has changed over the years, though. I feel as if I'm no longer creating a fashion line as much as I am—like my mother did—doing the same thing over and over and over again. My dream has become a recurring nightmare. The movie of my life has changed from a documentary on *Iris* to *Groundhog Day.*

I am a widget maker, a cookie cutter. I count dollars and cents. The buttons I select are watered down and plasticized so they can be manufactured for pennies. My new line of beautiful shirt dresses has been redesigned into poly-blend smocks. My life is...

I glance over at my mom's Singer sewing machine, sitting in the corner of my living room.

...*a zigzag stitch.*

I have been unable to sleep. I dream of my mother, at her sewing machine, trying to finish a dress for me that she wants me to wear to our family reunion.

"Everyone will be there," she says. "Everyone you've never met. Then it will all make sense."

She keeps sewing the same stitch over and over, creating the same button hole over and over. There is a man, back to me, no face, and he whispers to my mother, confusing her, making her start anew.

And then I wake with a start and try to sketch to calm myself. I sit and sew on Ol' Betsy.

Am I trying to bring my mom back to life?

Am I trying to say goodbye?

Or am I trying to stitch together a history I will never know?

I am trapped in life and in grief, in that place of inaction and immobility, where your mind runs rampant and your thoughts take over. I am in a holding place, treading water, unable to have closure over my mother's death, and unable to restart mine. I am taking stock of a life—after forty years—that I thought would continue seamlessly, no questions asked, and now all I have are questions.

My mom's belongings are scattered everywhere around my condo. Ol' Betsy, like her soul itself, casts a shadow in the corner. The button tree is propped against a wall. My childhood teddy bear, with button eyes, is propped in an armchair, staring at me. My mom's button jars sit on her sewing table, on the floor and on the mantel, shimmering in the light.

I tried over twenty times to start a new design in the middle of the night, inspired by Mom. I got as far as a zigzag stitch to prevent the edges from fraying, hoping against hope that might work for my heart, too, but it didn't. I simply stooped over Ol' Betsy and cried until my eyes were puffy and my throat raw.

I look back onto the street. My heart yearns to wander them. I miss wandering into the many cathedrals that populate this area. I want to light a candle for my mother, say a prayer for her, ask God why and how He could do this, to help me find my family, but I am trapped.

What if a runner were to bump into me without a mask, or a stranger were to approach and I became paralyzed in fear, or a biker passed too closely?

The virus found my mother in the middle of nowhere, and God did not save His most ardent believer and fearless warrior, so why would He spare me?

Or perhaps I should go and wander, take a chance, knowing the outcome would be a reunion with the only person in my life who ever loved me, the only one who could answer my questions.

I could escape this world.

I glance at the clock on the mantel. My heart jumps. I only have five minutes until the meeting with my boss.

I rush into the bathroom, toss on a cute sweater, not bothering to change out of my pajama bottoms or tube socks, run a brush through my hair, apply some mascara to my lashes, a little color to my wan cheeks and a touch of lipstick. At the last minute, I toss on my blue button necklace for security's sake and open my laptop.

Welcome to the new corporate world! Business on the top, comfort on the bottom.

I take a deep breath before joining the meeting.

"Good morning, Sutton."

My boss, Jamieson Kimsley, has a British accent that would make a sunny day sound cloudy. Everyone thinks British accents are so sexy, but Jamieson sounds like he's narrating a 1970s ad for Grey Poupon. And he doesn't want you to buy it.

"Morning, Jamieson."

"I...um...would like to start by expressing my deepest condolences on the loss of your mum."

"Thank you," I say. "I appreciate that."

"I take it you received the floral arrangement from our office?"

"I did. Thank you so much for such a thoughtful gesture."

He stares at me over the laptop. Human emotion is not a strength of Jamieson's. He's a boarding school kid raised without the benefit of a mother tucking him in every night.

My breath hitches thinking of my mom.

"The Ozarks," he suddenly says, picking up his cup of tea and looking off into his wood-paneled home office. I know there is a pool just beyond his office that overlooks the lake. I've been to his home—an estate in Lake Forest, a ritzy suburb of Chicago—when I was being interviewed. He tested me by asking if I'd like a cup of tea. He gave me many options. I knew only Earl Grey.

"With milk and sugar?" he asked.

"Yes, please," I said.

When my tea was placed before me and Jamieson was seated, he said, "Earl Grey is not a morning tea. And when you drink it, you should use lemon and sugar. Milk has a tendency to do strange things to black tea. It dulls the flavor. It's not as crisp and sharp. Lemon is always the way to go. I just want you to be informed for the future."

My mind whirs to the TV show, *Ted Lasso*. I think I've binge-watched every show ever created, especially the darkest ones, but turned to Ted for lighter fare. I remember his conversation with his new boss, Rebecca, after he arrives in England when she asks him how he takes his tea.

"Well, usually I take it right back to the counter because someone's made a horrible mistake."

The memory makes me laugh. Out loud.

"I'm so sorry," I say.

And that all sums it up: I was hired not because I was the most polished girl on the block. Nor did I have the most connections. I was unique. I was cheap. And I believe Jamieson knew he could always make me dance like a marionette on a string because my thirst for acceptance would always be unquenchable.

"Is it much like the TV show?" he asks.

"*Ted Lasso?*" I ask.

"No. *Ozark*. Is it like your Ozarks?"

"Not really," I say. "That show takes place in Lake of the Ozarks. That's further north than where I grew up. More city folk tend to have homes there. And Lake of the Ozarks is man-made, which is heresy for a true Ozarkian. I grew up on a crystal clear creek."

Jamieson looks disappointed. I don't think he understands a word of what I just said. To people like him, Chicago, New York and LA are real. The rest of the country is not.

Missouri? Arkansas? I might as well be speaking Esperanto and showing him a map of Mars.

A map floats in my mind. A map of Michigan. Shaped like a mitten.

"But the people are similar," I say, tossing him a bone.

"Oh, yes, yes," he says. His thick brows and upturned nose twitch.

Jamieson looks like a mix of Colin Firth and an English bulldog, which is not as awful as you might imagine. He looks quite innocent. But he's known to bite. You just never know—with his accent and personality—that you've actually been bitten.

Jamieson is Executive Vice President of Sales and Brand Management for all of Lindy's women's wear lines, and there are many. Over the last decade, Lindy's has purchased every dying department store and malnourished mall across the country, turning once-beloved and once-beautiful family shopping institutions into roller rinks filled with the same items. Jamieson is an Oxford grad and Harvard MBA, and he lets you know this, dropping it every chance he gets. He has no design training, and yet he has learned to stitch a profit-making division together by trimming all excess and hemming the remains into the semblance of a finished gown for the Bride of Frankenstein.

"Well, let's get down to business, shall we?" He doesn't as much acknowledge me through the screen as he does sear me with those brown eyes that are magnified through his ever-present tortoise frames. "And business, as you know, has not been good."

Jamieson begins to pull up a number of slides showing first quarter sales at Lindy's. The numbers aren't just down, they're the business equivalent of watching an avalanche occur in real time on the Discovery Channel. He then breaks out the retail numbers. It is a sea of red.

"Everyone is at home," he says. "People aren't buying jeans. They're not buying day wear. They're not buying business clothes. They're not purchasing dresses to wear to weddings, parties, restaurants or clubs. Consumers are only buying loungewear, pajamas, workout clothing."

I glance down at my bottom half and invisibly nod.

"If we worked at Lululemon, we'd all be golden," Jamieson says. "But we don't."

The world around me spins briefly.

He continues. "We cannot keep making clothes that people aren't buying. We can't keep paying employees who aren't working. Can we, Sutton?"

I hate it when people ask me to agree with something I don't agree with.

"No, sir," I say.

"Good, good. Well, then, we're on the same page."

What book are you reading? I want to ask.

"We're not terminating you, Sutton…"

"What?" I blurt.

"Hear me out, Sutton. As I was saying, we are not terminating you. But we are placing you and your team on indefinite leave. When things pick back up and the world returns to normal, so will we."

"And if they don't?"

"I don't like to live in a vague world," Jamieson says. "I prefer firm numbers. Reality."

"How am I going to survive? What if I were to come up with a loungewear design?"

"With buttons?" he asks. "No one is buttoning anything, Sutton."

My heart drops.

"We'll pay you for the next few months, and then…" Jamieson stops. "…there is unemployment."

His accent makes it sound like a dirty word.

He continues. "The government is being quite helpful in these situations. You are eligible to receive an additional three hundred dollars a week."

"My mortgage payment costs six times that much! Without utilities!"

I don't mean to say this out loud, but I do, my voice echoing in the condo I can no longer afford.

"Not to mention health insurance and food," I continue.

"You still have insurance, Sutton," he says. "I'm sure you have budgeted accordingly."

Jamieson's home in Lake Forest costs two and a half million dollars. I looked it up on Zillow.

"What about you?" I ask.

"What about me?"

"Are you being placed on leave?"

Jamieson gives me a look. I'm not playing the good girl any longer.

"That is a corporate decision," he says. "As of now, I am making the hard decisions to…"

Cut. Hem. Trim.

I glance at Ol' Betsy.

Zigzag stitch.

"I know how difficult this must be coming on the heels of such a profound personal loss," he is saying when I tune back into his voice. "I truly am sorry, Sutton."

I nod.

"There will be some paperwork coming your way," Jamieson says. "And I'd like you to complete your quarterly reports. And then…"

I nod again, he says goodbye, and I shut my laptop.

It's as easy as that, isn't it? I think.

The image of a cottonhead striking out of nowhere fills my mind.

I look over at my mother's Singer.

Everything hangs by a thread. Our lives. Our health. Our jobs. Our past. Our future.

We think we are in control, but we're not. Someone—something—else always is.

I stand and take a seat at my mom's sewing table. I can see her entire life on this machine: her footprints worn on the treadle, her fingers on the hand wheel, her arms on the desktop, her weight making the table bend forward ever so slightly.

Ghostly impressions everywhere.

My mom is gone. My job is gone. And yet I remain.

"Why, God?" I ask out loud. "Talk to me!"

I shake the sewing machine.

Silence greets me.

I stand, filled with sudden rage, and pick up the jar of buttons off the sewing table. I lift my arm and start to smash it onto the floor, but it's as if an invisible force stops me in mid motion. My arm hinges in the air, my shoulder shaking, the buttons quaking inside.

I take a seat on the floor, turn the jar upside down and dump all the buttons out.

They scatter and roll, and I do the only thing I can right now to calm myself: I slowly begin to sort them.

Just as I did as a child.

July 1991
Nevermore, Missouri

A bell clamors. Birds scatter.

I glance toward the cabin.

It's now or never.

The bell rings again. It echoes through the bluffs, a thousand bells chiming, each one, I know, calling my name.

Sutton! Sutton! Sutton!

My mom placed this bell by the door of the cabin to ring me in when I was swimming, floating, fishing or reading on the bluffs. The sound is not, like the new word I just learned in church, *tintinnabulation*, the sound of church bells on a Sunday morning.

No, this is loud, obnoxious, just as my mother wants it to be. It is a warning.

I have one minute to get home.

And then I hear my mother's voice actually yelling my name.

"Sutton?"

"Sutton?"

"Sutton!"

I toss my backpack into the front of the canoe next to milk jugs filled with water and just behind a Styrofoam cooler filled with bologna sandwiches and potato chips.

I step inside the back of the canoe and grab my paddle. I push off from the rocky beach. The current catches the canoe, and...

The canoe stops.

My mother is standing in the creek. Her hand is on the back of the canoe.

"Where in the heck do you think you're headed, young lady?"

My mother *never* cusses. Only if it's written in the Bible.

I look back at her.

"Away from you."

I take my paddle and try to push off of her body, but she grabs it with her free arm and tosses it onto the beach before single-handedly dragging the canoe onto the rocks.

"I hate you!" I yell, bursting into tears.

"Take that back."

"No, it's true! I hate you!"

My mother crosses her arms and looks across the creek.

"I don't have any friends. You don't let me do anything fun. I can't go to dances. I can't go to the square on a Friday night. I'm all alone in the middle of nowhere, and I'm going to be all alone just like you." I hesitate but continue. "I'm going to die all alone just like you."

My mom looks at me for the longest time.

"Am I really that bad?"

"Yes!"

She nods.

"Okay then. Go. Just go." She leans down and hands me the paddle. "I know you're goin' to leave me one day anyway. You're goin' to break my heart and then get yours shattered. It might be by a boy, or a boss, or a friend, or a job, but you will get your heart broken. But I want you to know I won't ever hurt you. I won't ever betray you. I won't ever lie to you. I would never kick you outta this house, no matter what you do. Do you understand me? Even if you leave me right now, forever, remember that you are welcome back here no matter what. Do you hear me?"

I am staring at her openmouthed.

"Do you hear me!" she screams.

I nod, and then she pushes me off into the creek.

My mom takes a seat on the beach and watches me, as casually as if I'm a turtle come to sun on a rock.

"Goodbye, Sutton," she says with a wave.

My canoe goes sideways. I grab my paddle, trying not to panic.

"I hope you know how to paddle all by yourself," she calls. "And that you have enough food. And did you remember to bring a pillow or a blanket? A change of clothes?"

I paddle left, then right, trying to straighten out the canoe.

"And remember to watch out for the Blue Man," she calls. "And don't get spooked by the Spooklight!"

My mind reels as I think of sleeping alone along the creek banks tonight.

Blue Man! Spooklight!

These Ozarks legends have frightened many a child and adult for decades. The Blue Man is a Sasquatch-like creature who relishes chasing and killing. He carries a wooden club in his huge hands, throwing boulders and feasting on livestock. He isn't blue, but those who have witnessed him say his jet-black fur shines blue in the sunlight, while others say he wears animal skins and feathers dyed blue from berries.

Whenever a chicken coop is ransacked, or a pet goes missing, people search the woods for the Blue Man. Hunters see him at night. Young lovers swear he tries to turn their car over at Makeout Point.

I believe I once saw him crossing the creek, blue in the midnight moon, a deer over one shoulder, a raw fish in the other hand. I screamed for my mom who had to sleep with me all night.

And my mom and I once drove to the country road in the middle of nowhere to see the Spooklight. We'd both heard about it for years but never believed it. We were the only car there. We waited for hours one summer waiting for dusk to fall, eating popcorn out of paper bags. That's when we saw it: a flickering ball of light, the size of a baseball, spinning down the center of the road at a high speed. It rose and hovered above the treetops, performing some sort of demonic dance for us. It would retreat and then reappear, this time swinging like a lantern being carried by an invisible force.

My mother began to pray, but I opened the car door.

"What are you doing?" my mother yelled.

I didn't answer. I just looked at her. I guess I was tired of being afraid of the unknown, of hiding from the world.

I had a desire to chase down the unknown as if it were my one and only calling.

I started to run toward the light.

It disappeared, as if my courage and bravery had spooked the Spooklight itself.

And that's the moment I steered my canoe back toward the beach, back toward my mom.

I knew running away would never solve a thing. It would never answer any of my questions, the reason behind my sadness. I had to chase down my own unknown.

My canoe rams the beach, a few yards from my mom.

"Tell me about yourself, Mom," I say quietly. "A story. Anything. Please. I need to understand why you are the way you are. Why we are the way we are. How we got here."

My mom stands and walks over to the canoe. She climbs inside and sits in the bottom of the canoe, facing me, our knees touching.

"You know everything you need to know," she says. "I'm your mother. And I love you more than anything. That is not a lie."

"Mom," I start, my voice raw. "I always feel like I do when I was taking off in this canoe. All alone. I just need to know more about us. I need some connection to you, the past, something. Please."

My mom shakes my knees.

"I'm givin' you everything I can, Sutton. *Everything.*"

"No, you're not, Mom. You don't give me anything. Who's my dad? You don't even say his name. What was he like? Do I look like him? Talk like him? I'm so alone, Mom."

I cry.

"You look like him," she finally says.

I start, and the canoe shakes.

"Really?"

She nods.

"And, oh, your passion for life…that's all your daddy, too." She stops, and, for once, I swear she's going to cry, too. But instead she takes a big breath. "Here's what I know, Sutton… what I can tell you: loss and heartbreak do funny things to a person's insides. It's like hard-boilin' an egg. Everything dries up, hardens, changes. It can never go back to the way it was. And yet it still looks the same on the outside."

I don't totally understand what she means, but I don't press her any further because it is *something*. I got something. I look like my father!

We sit in silence forever.

"Come home. For a night. To think about things?" my mom finally says.

I nod.

"We'll leave your canoe here, just in case you change your mind," she continues.

She begins to stand, and the canoe wobbles. I scoot over and pat the tiny seat. She takes a seat beside me, closer.

We remain there for hours, eating the food I'd brought, until dusk comes.

I know what my mom is waiting for.

Finally, the swallows come from the bluffs and dart over the water, looking for bugs. They jet this way and that, the hum of their wings and rush of the creek our Ozarks symphony.

My mother's calm.

The swallows dip into the water, leaving little circles in the twilight, purple ripples that eventually smooth.

"I don't think I'm gonna need the canoe after all," I finally say.

My mother and I drag the canoe across the beach and leave it by the spring. She looks at me and holds out her hand. We walk hand in hand up the steep stone stairs, back to the cabin.

As she cooks dinner, she watches the swallows feast while I take a jar of buttons and scatter them across the old Formica table my mom loves so much, dappled white top with an inlay of pretty flowers that look as if they have been sewn onto the table. Four aqua blue dining chairs with chrome legs sit around the table.

I arrange the buttons into piles by color. Sometimes, I do it by shape or feel, sometimes by personality, or ones I like and ones I don't. I have made it into a game, but it is really a trick, like counting sheep or taking deep breaths.

I do it to calm myself.

"Would you set the table, Sutton?" my mom finally asks.

I look at my mom and nod. I rake my forearm across the table to gather the buttons into a long line, and then use my hand as a scoop to push them back into the jar.

I head to the cupboard and cabinet and retrieve three plates, three glasses, three sets of silverware.

I set the table.

"What are you doing?" my mother asks, noticing the additional place setting.

"One for Daddy," I say.

I can't tell if she is nodding or shaking her head, but she doesn't say a word and returns her attention to the stove. I stare out the windows of the cabin as the sky turns dark as oil.

The beach and the water are now quiet. The swallows, like the buttons, are gone.

I look at the third place setting and then out the window again.

I will have dinner with my family and enjoy this moment, before the dishes are put away and these memories are gone, too, as if nothing before has been real.

I sit on the floor, my legs in front of me spread in a V. I use my hands as a scoop to gather the buttons. I begin to arrange them by color.

Blue in piles to the left of my left leg, white on the right of it. Red, black and green are placed in piles in the center of my legs, pink, yellow and purple go around my right leg. I stack the brown buttons down my legs, just as I did as a girl, challenging myself not to knock them off as I reach right and left.

Slowly, I can feel the world still. The jagged pieces become a complete picture once again. My breathing slows.

I grab a button and run my fingers over it, feeling its smoothness, its simplicity, its history, its meaning.

Blue there.

Yellow over there.

Brown here.

I move left and right, my legs twitching ever so slightly, and that's when I see it, an image as clear as day: a brown swallow on my leg. Or is it a whip-poor-will?

A sign from you, Mom? Are you here with me? Today? When I need you most?

My mother believed in such signs. It was a shocking sign of optimism for a woman who rarely smiled, like merging Walt Disney with Alfred Hitchcock.

After I left for college, my mom said a hummingbird used to visit as she sewed. Lots of hummers would buzz the feeders my mother hung around the cabin, but she said this one was different.

"Particularly nosy," she would tell me in her gravelly voice when I'd return home, the edges of her mouth traveling northward, something it rarely did unless she was watching Johnny Carson or Carol Burnett. I once caught her face move when a wealthy woman at church got a heel stuck in the gaps of the wood floor after asking parishioners to "give everything" we could and then not-so-subtly telling everyone how much she had given.

But my mom was right about that hummingbird. It would sit for long spells—often ten, fifteen minutes at a time on the native honeysuckle that trailed up the cabin—longer than any hummer I'd ever seen. It would just sit and watch my mother, angling its head this way and that, turning an eye directly toward my mother, as if the two were lifelong friends and used to the comfort in one another's silence.

I had no use for nor belief in such signs. I had no history or backstory and, thus, no understanding of why such a sign might matter.

Until now.

This is a vision so clear that I can see swallows on the water. Even when I shake my head, the buttons remain a bird, my dark blue pajama bottoms the creek.

My sudden movement causes the buttons to scatter. I scoop up a few, special brown ones in my hand and head to the Singer.

I have set it up just as my mother had it in her sewing room. The flouncy-shouldered blouse my mom was making waits quietly, staring at me, just like that hummingbird.

A ghost?

A sign?

A clue?

I arrange an assortment of brown buttons—the vintage tortoise Bakelite buttons my mom had intended to use on the blouse—into the shape of a swallow.

I begin to sew. Ol' Betsy's hum is like the rush of the creek, and I am lulled into another world. My heart races. It is frightening to be so alone and lost, and yet exhilarating to be creating for creativity's sake for the first time in a very long time.

When I look up again, it is dusk.

A streetlight clicks on and glows into my window.

I stand, stretching my back, and perch on the window seat looking out at the approaching night.

A man in a mask walks down the street carrying groceries. He is blue in the light, and his shadow stretches behind him, making him look twenty feet long.

Spooklight.

Blue Man.

There are so many things in this life that terrify us. Most are myths. Many are unseen.

But all exist, and they are real to us. They dwell in the corners of our minds, memories and pasts, where the monsters actually exist.

I stand and return to the blouse. The button swallow dips and dives in my mind.

What was my mother thinking and remembering when she watched these birds?

When she was sewing?

When she was sorting buttons?

I pick up the little antique button card with aquamarine buttons I discovered when I found my mother's blue dress.

What stories was my mom telling in the clothes she made and the buttons she so carefully selected?

What was real? What was myth?

What is now real, and what is myth?

I reach over and grab the blue button I snagged off her dress before I buried it. I hold it next to the button card.

They're exactly the same.

I squint and look closer.

Aren't they?

A flutter catches my attention. A pigeon sits in the window, cooing.

I think of my mother reading the Bible. She often said pigeons were the currency of mercy, the birds of sacrifice.

"Mom?" I call out loud.

The bird looks at me. It chirps.

"Ted!" it says to me.

I walk toward it, holding the buttons. It doesn't move.

"I sacrificed everything for you," I can hear the pigeon now say in my mother's voice.

I yelp without warning, ongoing grief plus the shock of the day suddenly overwhelming me. The bird's wings flutter madly in the window. It looks at me, yells at me, haunts me.

"Everything for you!"

And then the bird is gone.

Nothing is real anymore.

4

EMBELLISHMENT
A decorative item added to improve the look of a garment. Embellishments can include buttons, beads, jewels, ornamental stitching, etc.

I wake, and my childhood teddy bear is staring at me.

It is brown and shaggy with little ears, a golden muzzle with a black yarn nose and red mouth shaped like a gumdrop. He is wearing an old vest my mother and I made him, a sequined heart directly over his little bear heart. His button eyes are blue. Each button has two holes, which are lined up horizontally, and a deep line, which runs vertically, giving the bear a rather intense stare on an otherwise confused and bewildered—if not downright vacant—expression.

"Hi, Dandy," I whisper.

The late spring sun is streaming through my bedroom window, making the bear look aged. Its fur is matted, its paws are now just nubs, and its stuffing is exposed from a tear in the fabric.

Dandy has seen better days.

Like me. Like the world.

Time passes so quickly.

Nearly two years in the blink of an eye, since my mom's passing. The world is nearly back to normal. I still am not.

As a girl, I used to hold tea parties for Dandy. I used to read to Dandy. I used to dress Dandy up in the clothes my mother and I made for him. I took Dandy floating with me in the creek. A lot of kids used blankets—like Linus—as their safety net, many girls had favorite dolls. I had Dandy.

Dandy was actually my mother's teddy bear. She finally shared that with me when I was an adult and asked to take Dandy with me to Chicago.

"I need an old friend," I told her.

"So do I."

It was a simple yet shocking revelation from my mom, and it struck me like a lightning bolt.

My mother was a little girl who had a childhood just like me?

My mother had a past?

She saved Dandy from the fire? How? Why? Was I holding him?

Now those questions have become haunting statements.

My mother was a little girl who had a childhood.

My mother had a past.

There was no fire. So why did she save a teddy bear?

"How many eyes have you had?" I ask the bear. "What have you seen in your life?"

I used to nervously twist on Dandy's eyes when I was a girl. Anytime I felt anxious or sad, I would hold on to him and rub his eyes. Over time, they would eventually pop off. My mother would lead me to her button jar and tell me to pick his new eyes.

"This will be one of the most important decisions of your life," she would tell me. "Dandy's eyes are the windows to his soul, just like those of a person."

Dandy's eyes—and personality—changed greatly over the years. His eyes have been every color of the rainbow: purple, pink, red, gold.

But the last time I selected Dandy's eyes, I was older, and I knew they would last a lifetime, perhaps until I had a child, or forever if I did not. I remembered my mother's words and selected eyes that were not only beautiful and inquiring but also my mother's favorite color.

Now the bear seems to mock me with a name filled with as much mystery as my mother's past.

Dandy.

Dandy Button Company

"You lied to me, friend," I say to it. "Dandy, indeed."

After my mother died, my gut instinct—like that of so many friends and acquaintances—was to simply get rid of everything in one fell swoop. In my grief, I was poised to hold an estate sale, list the cabin and toss the rest into a bonfire on the beach.

Purge my past.

But then I looked at my mother's Singer, the button tree picture, the spools of yarn and thread, the baskets and tackle boxes filled with embellishments—beads, jewels, ornamental stitching—and I couldn't do it. The old coffee cups, the desert rose dishes, the quilts, my mom's Bible, even the Formica dining table and chairs.

These seemingly meaningless items told the story of my mother's life.

She purged her past. I couldn't do it. I still needed what little I had and knew of mine.

The letter she wrote me still sits on my nightstand, reminding me of this but also making me feel like my teddy bear with no eyes: I can no longer see my future because I am so haunted by the past.

I look at Dandy.

How can I know where I'm going if I don't know from where I came?

My whole life feels as if it's been a fraud. I feel as if I'm hanging by a thread.

I feel as if I need to know my mother's history to survive.

I've literally spent months in bed picking through the clues of her past.

I have Googled anything and everything thousands of times over.

I've located a few articles about the history of Dandy buttons but it was so long ago, before the internet and social media could track every second of one's life, when a forgotten industry was thriving.

What I've uncovered is that the Dandy Button Company was one of Michigan's largest pearl button manufacturers at the turn of the century and throughout the early 1900s. It was located in Douglas, a tiny resort town that holds my surname, and run by the Lyons family before it was sold.

Coincidence?

Living in Chicago, I know something of Michigan. The Mitten state is a favorite destination for Chicagoans in the summer and fall. Many own second homes near the lake, and many escape the city for the quiet and the beauty. I know that Michigan is dotted with resort towns up and down its coast, but I know nothing of Douglas and, believe me, the irony is not lost on me.

I've scrolled and scrolled and reread the history of Dandy from an old newspaper article a hundred times. I have it bookmarked on my phone.

I click again.

There is a photo of a man cutting a ribbon in front of the Kalamazoo River. Beside him, a two-story building has a painted sign hanging from the landing between the first and second floor: DANDY BUTTON COMPANY.

The Douglas Observer
MARCH 27, 1908

The Dandy Button Factory opened today in Douglas by the Kalamazoo River. Dan D. Lyons, 24, will serve as founder and president of the company which will manufacture buttons made from the freshwater clams found in the bottom of the river. Lyons says he hopes to hire as many as 100 workers for the summer, mainly Michigan families who would like to live and work together in free housing and earn a good wage. Dandy needs men to work as mussel men, clam fishermen and cutters, who will be the highest paid workers in the button factory. Lyons says that skilled cutters can always get as many button blanks out of each shell as possible.

I click on another saved article and read it out loud.

The Douglas Observer
JULY 1, 1918

Michigan Becomes the "Button Capital"
As button manufacturing has caught on across the Midwest, the button company started right here in Douglas, Michigan, by Dan D. Lyons continues to the lead the way. Within ten years the Dandy Button Co. has become the largest manufacturer of freshwater pearl buttons in the world. So far this year, Dandy has turned out nearly 10 million buttons!

And another:

The Douglas Observer
JULY 1, 1958

Dan D. Lyons, Jr., has bought out the claims of all the stockholders, including his father, in the Dandy Button Company. Despite the challenges to the

pearl button industry in America, Lyons proposes
to enlarge the plant and conduct the business on a
larger scale. At a recent meeting of the directors,
it was decided to dispose of the entire stock of the
company, and now it is announced that Mr. Lyons
was the successful bidder, replacing his father.

I have searched and searched, but I cannot find any Ted
Douglas, or Theodore Douglas, in Douglas, Michigan, or any
further clues. There are millions of Ted Douglases, none of
whom seem to match the mystery man I'm seeking. In fact,
the internet has so much information at our fingertips it's
nearly impossible to narrow. I think back to a time with ro-
tary phones, microfiche, written directions and phone books,
a time in which secrets were easier to hide.

Frustrated, I return—as I have the last few months—to
watching hair videos on TikTok or people baking bread. I flip
to reruns of the *Real Housewives* and episodes of *House Hunters*
and *Antiques Roadshow.*

My mother loved yard and estate sales, but I had difficulty
with the coldness often associated with the event: people's histories boxed up and on display in cardboard boxes for strangers. Photos of family members still lodged in picture frames
that were for sale. Toys children once played with, beloved
holiday ornaments, recipe boxes and cookbooks…

Memories.

So I loaded much of it up all by myself into a U-Haul, in the
middle of a pandemic, locked up the cabin and drove back to
Chicago. Some of it sits in a long-term storage facility off the
interstate—an additional expense I do not need—and some
made it home. Like Dandy.

But I know it is there if I need it.

There is a map in my soul—a heart, shaped like the one

on my teddy bear's vest—and it has always led me home. And I know that either makes me a very weak person or a very strong one.

I'm just not sure which yet.

Two years have passed since my mother's death. Hers was just one of over 700,000 Covid deaths in 2021 alone. Everyone seems so ready to be back. Why am I not? Depression? Guilt? A sense that nothing really matters anymore? I have always been such a fighter, tried to be such a positive person, and I feel as if the entire universe—the world, my mother—has let me down.

I received my final Covid vaccine a few weeks ago. I will receive a booster, too. I feel ready to reenter the world, but… it's taking more time than I imagined to feel "okay" again. I have only begun to sneak out of my condo—still wearing my mask—a nervous rabbit released from her cage. I have gone for a run in the park. I have strolled the streets. But I still hold my breath when I get too close to someone, I still get my groceries delivered, I still need time to process, recover, restart.

I grab Dandy and hold him tight. He still smells like my mother's cabin, a mix of pine, water and firewood.

I grab my phone and check the time.

"Pull it together, Sutton."

I slip into the kitchen, start the coffee and then take a shower. I pour a big mug of caffeine and spend the longest time I have in ages getting ready. I do my hair. I put on makeup. I actually slide into a real pair of pants. It's not easy.

At 9:59 a.m., I open my laptop and join the Zoom call.

"Good morning, Sutton."

"Good morning, Mr. Kimsley."

I've spoken only intermittently to my boss over the last few months. He provides updates. I provide direction of where I think my designs should head. But it's all "LimboLand."

"How are you, Sutton?"

"Great, thank you," I lie. "And you?"

"The past two years have been a struggle," he says. "I wouldn't ever want to do it over again."

I nod.

"I'm sorry," he says. "No one knows more than you." He takes a deep breath and continues. "Well, I'm excited to say—as you may already be aware—that Lindy's, like the rest of the world, is finally beginning to show some signs of a big bounce. Our projections for the third and fourth quarters look very strong. Shoppers are returning in huge numbers, and we only expect that to get stronger throughout the summer, fall and holiday seasons as everyone returns to work, school and social activities. People will be buying clothes at a fast clip."

"That's wonderful," I say.

"It is," Jamieson says. "With that said, we're beginning to ask key employees to return to work. That will mean back to the office, back to routine, back to normal."

Normal.

My heart skips.

"A full-time schedule again," I start. "Wow."

"So?" he asks.

Floor-to-ceiling windows surround Jamieson. He is at corporate headquarters, not far from where I live and yet a world away. I always loved the view from our offices: the tops of skyscrapers surrounded by clouds. So different from where I grew up. To me, the towering, thin skyscrapers always resembled the models we used in our runway shows and the mannequins I used to dress in my office, and the clouds were my clothes draped just so around their bodies.

"Sutton?" he asks cautiously.

I look around my condo at all of my mother's belongings. I see my mother's letter.

Words. Stories. History.

I was once as consumed by words as I became by fashion. I read voraciously. My mother had a library card, and we would head there after a day at Woolworths. The little library sat just off the main square, across from a park with a natural waterfall that oozed from the side of a bluff. The county pool was located in the back of the park, but I was not allowed to go there.

"Too many people, too many boys," my mother said.

But she would let me spend hours in the library. I would pick out Nancy Drew mysteries or Harriet the Spy books. I adored *Are You There, God? It's Me, Margaret.* Later, I became enamored with Erma Bombeck because my mother loved her so much. It was nice to see her attempt to smile. I chose books that helped me understand my circumstances, books that helped me escape from the world or laugh, but, mostly, books I believed would help me become a better detective to understand my mother. I would stack my week's worth of books in my arms and head off to find my mom. I always knew where she was: hunched over a giant monitor reading old articles on microfiche.

"Just a few more minutes," she would tell me.

Off I'd go to slump into a big, old leather chair next to the circulation desk next to Ms. McCarthy. Everyone around thought Ms. McCarthy—"*Ms.* McCarthy, *not* Miss or Mrs.!" she would admonish those who called her by the wrong honorific—was mean, but—like my mother—I just thought she spoke her mind.

"What are you reading this week, Sutton?" she would always ask, sliding her thick, black, cat-eye framed glasses onto the end of her nose to consider me before pushing them back up the mountain.

I would hold up my book, and she would nod. Eventually, she began to bring me more "challenging" books: *The Secret Garden, Little Women, Where the Red Fern Grows.*

"What does 'cautious' mean?" I remember asking Ms. McCarthy.

"Careful to avoid danger or misfortune," she said, right off the top of her head. "It's from the Latin *cautus*, meaning careful, heedful." She looked right at me, again lowering her glasses. "Like your mother. Your mother is cautious."

What was she doing poring through microfiche? You were still searching for answers, weren't you? You were still searching for closure because, deep down, you still cared about those who hurt you most. You were still searching in your own cautious way.

"Sutton?"

Jamieson is waiting for an answer.

"I appreciate the offer, but I think I'm going to have to pass," I finally say. "I can no longer be cautious with my life."

"Oh, Sutton," Jamieson says, neither his expression nor tone conveying that much sympathy. "You're making a horrible mistake. It's a tough landscape out there right now."

I don't mean to, but I laugh. I actually laugh.

"Sutton?" he asks again. "Are you okay?"

"No," I say. "I'm not. I lost my mother and never got to say goodbye to her. I never got to hug her, kiss her, whisper I love you to her again. She didn't get to have a funeral. I lost my family. I'm lost."

"Not with us. You've built a career here, Sutton."

"I hope you will forgive me for saying this, but that's not what matters anymore. When you lose everything, you finally remember what's important. It's the smallest of things: Our family. Our health."

"I empathize with all you're going through, but I don't know if you'll be saying that in a year," Jamieson says. "Listen, why don't we do this: you think about it. I'd also love it if you'd consider talking to one of the therapists we have working with us now to help employees who are grieving or anxious to return to work and life again."

"I appreciate that," I say, "but I think it's time I forge a new future. For myself. Before it's too late." I glance at the letter again. "Before my blink is over."

"Excuse me?" he asks.

"I cannot express how much I've loved working with you," I say. "It changed my life and career in countless ways, and I will be forever grateful for the opportunity. But..."

"The last years have changed us all," he says, his voice suddenly filled with emotion. He stops to clear his throat and take a sip of tea. "Go forge that new future. You'll never have a bigger cheerleader than me." He stops again. "But don't change who you are, Sutton. Don't let this change you. You're very special. And the world needs your goodness and connection to the past more than ever."

His words make the world spin before me.

"Thank you," I finally manage to say.

"I'll let everyone know." Jamieson looks at me—*really* looks at me—as if seeing me for the first time. "What *will* you do next?"

"Sutton's Buttons will continue," I say. "Remember my contract? I retain the rights to my brand should I ever leave."

He actually laughs, too, but it's a proper, controlled, British chuckle. "I wouldn't have let that slip through if I'd been the attorney here negotiating your final contract."

"No, you wouldn't have," I say. "I'm sure our paths will cross again in the future."

"I sure hope so, Sutton. Best of luck to you."

"Thank you. It's been a privilege and an honor."

He smiles and gives a brief wave goodbye.

And then I put my hand up to my laptop, just like I did

with the caregiver at my mother's facility, and Jamieson puts his hand atop mine.

We all still need human connection. We all still need closure to move on with our lives.

I close my laptop, and just like that it's all over.

"What have I done, Dandy?"

May 2022

Where to start?

I look around my condo, boxes stacked everywhere.

You're not moving, Sutton. You're just…

I stop, searching for the right words.

…moving on.

"Alexa, play Dolly Parton."

I need some Dolly right now. My mom's favorite. The woman who grew up in rural poverty and yet persevered with talent, grace and light.

"Here You Come Again" begins to play, and I laugh out loud at the irony of the lyrics while boxing up my mother's belongings.

"Just when I'm about to get myself together, Mom!" I sing.

I have sublet my condo to a couple who are moving to Chicago for a new job. I am following the lead of the rest of Chicago—and much of America's urbanites—who are fleeing the city to return somewhere, anywhere. While many are returning to work, the new work space continues to be our homes, and that means our office can be anywhere, and we want it to be somewhere there is open space, grass, room to breathe, a place where we can see natural beauty around us. Rents have plummeted in Chicago, and office buildings remain vacant, even as the majority of the US is now vaccinated.

Where am I going? I don't really know yet. Maybe my

mother's cabin to retreat for the summer and float, read books, sew, begin to design anew, mourn some more, seek closure.

But that means returning to a place that no longer feels real. It all feels fake. My mother's lies still haunt me.

Maybe I will rent a cheap place somewhere pretty where I can sit on a beach made of sand instead of rocks, and read like I did when I was a girl.

"Maybe Dollywood?" I say out loud to the music.

I am hesitant after being isolated so long, and I refuse to be as cautious as my mom. I want to rid myself of that burdensome baggage.

One of the most difficult things about being so isolated is that I—like so many—have learned to live apart from one another. Socially distanced is now the norm.

How do we regain the connection?

I now understand my mother better than I ever did when she was alive. This virus taught me to live alone, be alone, survive alone. And once you get used to that, the routine becomes a part of your being.

My mother's words echo in my head. *Loss and heartbreak is like hard-boilin' an egg. Everything dries up, hardens, changes. It can never go back to the way it was. And yet it still looks the same on the outside.*

I have grown tougher, harder, but in a good way. I believe in myself more. I realize I cannot continue on in this life trusting in the way things were. I want to be in charge of the way things are. Even if that means my path is filled with uncertainty.

It's the only way I can hope to change the future. Otherwise, I worry I will end up alone.

Just like you, Mom.

I place all the lids on my mother's button jars. A good many of them—like her sewing basket, tins and boxes—still feature wilted, peeling, yellowed strips of masking tape with my mother's faded handwriting on them:

MISS MABEL'S BUTTON JAR
MABEL'S FAVORITE BLUES
FANCY BUTTONS

I wonder why my mother went by Miss rather than Ms. like Ms. McCarthy or Mrs. I mean, my mother was married at one time, right? Or not? Yet another question. All of the widows I knew in Nevermore went by Mrs., but we all knew who their husbands were. Everyone went along with my mom's moniker out of respect, assuming she needed to exorcise the ghosts of her past. But what if she weren't married? What if that was the reason she ran?

My mother? The most pious woman in the world? An unwed mother? That couldn't be possible. Could it?

It is this, the constant mosquito-like questions buzzing my brain, that tortures me. I can't continue my life as if nothing has changed. *Everything* has changed.

I shake my head and sing like Dolly as I wrap my mother's jars in newspapers, another fading heirloom just like buttons.

I retrieve the framed button tree picture I made so long ago with my mom—one of my clearest, earliest memories—and, lost in thought, I trip over my fireplace hearth and stumble. Trying to remain balanced, I toss the art into the air. It hits the wood floor with an alarming crash.

"No!"

Glass shards are scattered everywhere, gleaming in the light. I tiptoe out of the living room, slip into some shoes, and grab the broom, dustpan and vacuum. When the floor is clean, I take a seat and pick up the photo to survey the damage.

With the glass gone, the chipped black frame is no longer a square but a rhombus. A couple of the buttons have popped off the tree, and the glue that once secured them is as dry as the Sahara.

My heart feels as shattered as the glass.

I turn on the flashlight on my phone, stand and stoop around the living room searching for the missing buttons.

"Button, button, who's got the button?" I sing over Dolly, trying to abate my rising tension. I stand straight, wanting to scream, and stretch my spine. "How far can a little button go?"

And then I see one, yellow and shiny, in the very corner of the room, as if it's trying to hide from me.

"Gotcha!" I say. "Now where's your little friend?"

I take baby steps around the entire living room. It's nowhere to be found. So I take a seat on my rear and scoot around the floor like a Roomba, scanning every square inch. The light reflects off of something on the floor. At first, I think it is a small piece of broken glass, but a shiny blue button sits wedged in a gap between the old wood planks.

"You're going home," I say to it. "Back where you belong."

I stand and retrieve some fabric glue I always have on hand. I take a seat by the button tree and glue on the tiny buttons, smiling that the limbs and leaves are once again full.

I lift up the tree to admire it and my handiwork, then turn the artwork over, laying the tree facedown on the newspaper, and reach back to grab some tape.

That's when I notice the old, dried paper on the back of the frame is torn and cracked.

"We have a lot in common," I say to it. "We're both falling apart."

I grab a piece of tape and use my fingers to tamp down the dried paper to draw it back together. I feel something underneath the paper.

At first I think it is simply the backing of the artwork, but when I move the frame, something behind the paper shifts.

I stick the tape on my knee and slowly use my fingernail as a knife to open the back. A picture of a man is staring directly at me.

What in the world?

I pull it free.

It is an ancient, rather blurry, photo of a handsome, square-jawed man, his piercing eyes peering from underneath a broad-brimmed felt hat. He has that look of the very young that announces to the world, "I have my whole life ahead of me!"

He is wearing high-waisted trousers and a long-sleeved white shirt, standing at an angle in a johnboat in the middle of what could be a river, creek or lake. Two long ropes hang from makeshift stick branches that run the length of the boat, about shoulder-high to the man. Clamshells, four-deep, hang from hooks tied to the ropes. Behind him is a lush backdrop of trees, as ethereal and blurred as the moving clouds. I turn the photo over. Faded words, like ghosts, hover, barely visible to the eye. I hold my cell's flashlight to them.

Sweet Belle—

My Secret Pearl.

Ted

My heart rises into my throat. I feel as if I might pass out.

Ted?

The Ted?!

My dad?

I stare into the picture. The jaw, the eyes, they certainly look like mine.

There is tape, now dried, on the back of the photo, as if perhaps it had been secured here in secret.

I rip all the backing off the frame. Another faded photo is taped to the back of the button tree. This one is of a girl in a summer dress standing in front of a giant dance pavilion, a semicircle arched roof rising above her. The girl is turned away from the camera, hands on her hips, watching the people on the crowded dance floor behind her.

Who is this?

My mother?

A stranger?

There is also a vintage postcard, hand-colored it appears, of sand dunes dotted with footprints leading to the water.

Lake Michigan Beach at Douglas, Mich.

The address on the other side looks as if it's been erased. In fact, there is a worn area, the paper pulped, as if someone released a lifetime of emotion on a few square inches.

Tucked in the corner of the frame are two button cards. I pull them free and study them.

Dandy Button Co., Michigan.

Just like the ones I found with my mother's dress in her garment bag.

My heart catapults.

I pick up the photo of the man again and stare into his eyes.

His eyes. So blue.

Suddenly, I jump to my feet. I rush into my bedroom and grab my teddy bear. I stare into its eyes.

I retrieve the button I had saved from my mother's dress and hold it up to the ones in the tree photo and then next to Dandy's eyes.

The exact same blue buttons.

Coincidence?

I unwrap one of my mother's button jars and turn it upside down. They scatter and roll onto the floor.

More buttons that match these.

My mind cannot keep up with my thoughts.

Am I exhausted?

Still grieving?

Hoping to find hope?

Or did I just find the biggest clue to my past, the button that will lead me to my family tree?

Dolly sings, but all I can hear are kids chanting, "Button, button, who's got the button?"

"Alexa! Off!" I yell.

The buttons I've scattered across the floor glimmer in the sunlight. A pigeon lands on my windowsill.

The world spins, my legs shake, and I must take a seat. I shut my eyes to close out the world.

But in the darkness, I can see my mother look up at me from her sewing machine and stare at me, just as intently as the man on the boat.

And in the silence I can hear my mother's voice say, very clearly, "Lots of beauty and secrets in buttons if you just look long and hard enough."

5

INVISIBLE ZIPPER

A zipper sewn with a special presser foot and seams.
When it's done right, it's hard to see the zipper
in the seam, hence the name.

The waves sigh.

Through my bedroom windows, I can hear Lake Michigan in the distance softly crash into the shore. It is a soothing sound, albeit much different than the sound of the creek from my childhood. The water in the Ozarks, much like me, always seemed in a hurry to go somewhere else. Here, the lake seems more content.

It comes and goes, but it never leaves.

Everything in my life is now upside down.

No, scratch that. Backwards.

Here, in Michigan, the sun sets over the lake, instead of rises as it did in Chicago. I am renting a knotty-pine cottage on the lakeshore while renting out my own condo in the city. I am unemployed. I am surviving on the salary I socked away, a chunk of my IRA I cashed in too early—some of which has already been eaten up by the tax man—the little bit of cash my mom had squirreled away at the community bank, and now my renters.

I am completely, utterly alone.

Eastern time is the only way I feel remotely ahead of where I once was.

I glance at a clock ensconced in the middle of a little white sailboat which sits atop a white nightstand with nautical knobs.

I am now an hour ahead.

I shut my eyes, listening to the waves.

Although Lake Michigan is a familiar friend, it seems like a new one here.

I open my eyes, lean up in my unfamiliar bed and look out my window at the burgeoning light over the lake, hidden behind a cottage and some trees, but just a few hundred feet away. I have my windows cracked, and a cool breeze makes the gauzy curtains dance.

"You've lost your mind, Sutton," I suddenly say out loud. "What on God's green earth is Sutton Douglas doing in Douglas, Michigan?"

I watch the white curtains float, and they answer for me.

Ghosts. That's what I'm doing here. Searching for ghosts.

I have uprooted my life in order to follow a trail of buttons that led me to a tiny resort town on the eastern coast of Michigan that shares my surname. I left a tiny town to move to the city only to return to a little lakeshore burg boasting only a few hundred year-round residents. My vision board is filled with an old postcard from here, a crumbling photo of a strange man named Ted who might be my father, a photo of a woman and blue buttons that all match.

"Hello, crazy," I say to myself in the quiet room. "How are you doing today?"

I answer myself.

"Not well. Not well at all."

My future now seems as threadbare as these curtains.

I used to know where I was going, just like Hickory Creek knew it would wind up in Grand Lake. We both had a goal of ending up somewhere bigger, better.

Now I wonder where I will end up.
Am I on the run, just like my mom?
I grab my cell and text my friend Abby.

I made it. I have no idea what I'm doing here. I don't know if I'm honoring my mother's spirit or disrespecting it, but here I am.

Abby texts back immediately.

None of us know what we're doing right now. All we know is that we made it through one of the worst times in history, and we're here. For a reason. Sometimes, it's okay just to be in the moment, Sutton. When was the last time you took a second for yourself? When you weren't working? Caring for your mom? Worrying about her? Worrying about your job? Maybe you have to get lost to get found again in this world. Maybe you're the strong one now, Sutton. Maybe you're doing what we all should be doing. Just listen to your heart, girl. Breathe!

I smile and shoot back a quick reply.

I love you.

Me, too. Will touch base later. P.S. It's only 4:58 in the morning here. So, yeah, thanks for that. XOXO!

I insert a string of "I'm sorry" emojis and then set my cell down to refocus on what my friend just told me to do.
Breathe, Sutton. Listen.
I listen to the waves and focus on breathing in sync with their motion.
In. Out. In. Out.

As we all return to normalcy, can we—can I—remember this: to still slow down and be thankful and strong? To remember, as my mom said, what matters most: each other.

Some days, these values now seem as antiquated as the heirlooms my mother so dearly loved. And yet each unspoken gesture of kindness carries an entire world of meaning—the history of a person—on its surface.

Just like that of an old button.

I get out of bed, and the chill of the morning makes me rush for my robe. It may be June, but it feels more like March in the Ozarks.

I pull on some thick socks and tread the few steps into the kitchen to make some coffee. It's a tiny kitchen—smaller than the one in my condo—but it reminds me of my mother's kitchen back in Missouri.

Well-used. Filled with memories. Chockful of love.

Simple open pine cabinets are covered with adorable, bright fabric dotted with blueberries. Sunlight filters in the wavy glass window overlooking a small patio and sliver of a backyard surrounded by a row of pines separating the yard from other homes. The appliances are buttercup yellow, the countertop a sparkly Formica.

Mom, you would adore this place, I think.

I find the coffee in a bag I tossed on the counter and start a pot.

The kitchen is open to the cozy living room and even cozier fireplace comprised of lake stones of all shapes, sizes and colors, almost as if a Keebler elf built his own little hideaway. I grab a coffee mug that reads *LESS WORK, MORE LAKE*, and—despite its corniness—I smile from the very bottoms of my feet. I fill my mug and take it into the living room, slumping onto the lumpy, bumpy sofa upholstered in sunny yellow. I pull an old camp blanket over my lap and sigh.

This is my first morning in my temporary new home. I arrived late, and rushed around unpacking the car before it got dark. I haven't seen the town. I haven't seen a soul. I do not know if this is the first day of the rest of my life, as Jimmy Buffett might sing, or if my life ended a long time ago.

I look at my mug's slogan again.

If I do need a reminder that perhaps things are looking up, it's this home. I was lucky to find it. Not only at the price it was offered but also this far into the rental season.

"It's a miracle," said Mick and Sarah, the owners who rented it to me. "Nothing is ever available in June around here. Especially this year in this town, with everyone—and I mean everyone—leaving the city, living in the moment, working remotely and wanting to, finally, have a summer to remember."

Mick's father died of Covid, too. This was their family's summer haven. The place they gathered to watch sunsets with glasses of wine, roast marshmallows, swim in the lake, simply be together as a family.

"I just can't go back yet," he said. "Too many memories."

I told him about my mother.

"You will be a wonderful steward for now," Mick said.

I found the cabin on Facebook. Through a friend of a friend of a friend of a friend… You know how that goes. It's amazing what you discover—and what you don't want to discover—when you slither down that dark online rabbit hole. This was one of the few bright spots.

The cottage has wide, wood plank floors, dotted with hooked rugs. A mishmash of furniture occupies the home—a bentwood rocker here, a plaid armchair there—almost like distant cousins who have gathered again, similar but different. The white shiplap walls are dotted with artwork. Some paintings are quite stunning, oils of big, puffy clouds—seemingly in motion—drifting over the lake. Others are watercolors of

111

flowers—blue hydrangeas and pink peonies—and some are framed crayon drawings children have done of sailboats and family pets.

The assortment melts my heart. It reminds me of my mother's button jars, filled with an assortment of plastic and heirloom buttons, all beautiful in their own right.

I finish my cup of coffee and get up to pour a second. I walk to the front of the low-slung cottage and stare out the wide windows that run the entire room.

The cottage, according to Mick and Sarah, has a fascinating and important history in Douglas. It was once a one-room schoolhouse.

A path—now overgrown with dune grass—leads directly from this tiny cottage to a towering, hundred-year-old white-gabled ghost sitting along the lakeshore. Mick said the historic home occupies hundreds of feet of lakeshore—a huge and expensive expanse of real estate—and a recent widow, well-known for her generosity to the community, lives there.

"I know she didn't need the money. She sold this place to my dad a while back when her husband was failing because she said she wanted a family near her," Mick had said. "She left us a bottle of champagne when we purchased the house. There was a note that read, 'To *good* family.' Since we couldn't come back during Covid, we both tried to phone her a number of times to make sure she's doing okay after all of this. We get the local paper online, and finally saw she's back to her very busy fundraising and social schedule. She's quite…*something*."

From the living room, I have a peekaboo view of the lake—a paper-thin slice of the water when the wind blows just right—between the widow's house in front and the thick trees that surround it.

But it's a view nonetheless.

I open the front slider and walk onto the deck. A small

screened porch filled with a daybed, perfect for reading and napping, sits off to the side.

The day is already beginning to warm, and the lake calls as if it's a long-lost friend that desperately wants to catch up.

"I hear you," I say.

I finish my coffee and hurriedly get dressed, trying to beat the crowds I've heard will swarm the lakeshore once the temperature hits the seventies.

I head out the patio, and then stop.

Mick said no one locks the doors of their homes or cars around here. "It's like Mayberry," he told me. "It'll get in your blood fast, and you'll never want to leave."

I hesitate, feeling emboldened, but then stop again.

"I forgot my mask," I say, retreating once more.

I no longer wear it outdoors, but I keep it with me like a lucky stone.

As I head through the house to retrieve it, I see the photo of Ted and the button tree sitting haphazardly in the house.

"Family roots," I say, my voice tinged with sarcasm.

I was raised in the Ozarks, and that makes a person as hard and unforgiving as the rocky terrain. But it also makes one utterly aware and in awe of her history, because it reminds you every day of how big and small you truly are, the stony faces of the bluffs staring at you, the craggy bodies of the beaches moaning as you cross them, the arched backs of the creeks showing their age.

I walk down the path, the dune grass on my legs, which feels both itchy and comforting. I wore an actual pair of pants on my drive here—not sweats or pajama bottoms—and those, too, felt itchy and yet very comforting because they marked a return to normal.

I approach the widow's house, which has a two-story

screened porch off the back. The house is huge, and it casts a long, wide shadow across the land.

I stop mid motion and hold my breath, listening—for what, I do not know. I feel like Nancy Drew.

But a whole lot older. And more deranged.

I look up and can imagine a family sitting on the porch, when there were no other houses around.

The path edges round the side of the house, just outside of a shoulder-high stone wall that runs alongside the driveway. Massive white shutters hug the many-paned windows on the happy yellow clapboard exterior. I stop and look at the front of the home.

It is simple, elegant, timeless. Almost like an old ship.

The front windows are framed by cheery red flower boxes overflowing with petunias, geraniums, zinnias, nasturtiums, and begonias. Ivy, euonymus and vinca cascade over the edges.

A very large porch extends off French doors on an upper level, and the home rises to a dramatic peak. I can only imagine what the views must be like from the porch and upstairs windows. I crane my neck and squint my eyes to try and read the old, wooden sign that dangles from the gable at the top.

DANDELION COTTAGE

How fitting.

Indeed, the home looks like a bright yellow dandelion growing happily along the lakeshore. The large front yard is filled with stunning gardens, insanely big rhododendrons and massive hydrangeas. Many of the yews look well eaten, stems sheared. The deer must roam the lakeshore at night and view these yards as smorgasbords.

I hear a creak and freeze.

The wind in the trees, I think.

114

But then I hear another creak, and the front door cracks open.

I take off running full sprint and do not stop until I am a half mile down Lakeshore Drive.

I finally stop, gasping for breath.

I haven't run that fast in ages, and I am not just winded, I am dizzy.

"Serves you right, nosy Nancy," I say, admonishing myself for my rather pathetic amateur sleuthing skills.

When I finally catch my breath and look up, I gasp.

So, this is Michigan!

Lake Michigan flows to the horizon, blue hugging blue.

I put my hand to my heart, thinking of my mom and her favorite color.

"Blue" is actually a disservice to the colors I'm witnessing. There seem to be hundreds of shades before me present in the water and the sky, changing second by second. I think of the blue buttons my mother collected, and how I used to sort them into rainbows based on their shade. I see the same today: a spectrum of blue.

The lake is cerulean near the shore, darkening to navy and then black-blue in the distance. The sky is akin to flipping through a Pantone chart, each shade a tad lighter the closer it gets to heaven. The horizon wears a scarf of pink clouds, a colorful shrug to ward off the morning chill, one it will soon toss aside as it warms.

The sand is golden and sparkles in the sun. The shoreline arcs north and south. In the distance to my north, I can see boats emerge from a channel. Their engines reverberate across land and sky, and boaters gun their motors as soon as they hit the open water. Sailboats seem to fade into the horizon, and I watch and wait for them to disappear. To the south, I can see a lighthouse jut into the lake.

Lakeshore Drive sits atop a steep bluff overlooking the lake.

Fragile dunes run from the road to the lake, winding, steep staircases leading to the water for homeowners lucky enough to live on the water.

I know Lake Michigan from living in Chicago. I've logged endless miles running and walking its paths. I've spent days on its city beaches. I've gone to corporate events overlooking the lake.

But this...*this* is not the Lake Michigan I know.

There are no high-rises. There is no development on the shoreline. There are no concrete paths. There are not hordes of people in the water. It is as unspoiled as the creek on which I was raised and baptized.

I turn and continue north.

As I walk, I pass home after home, each bigger than the next. Each is named something simple—Sunset Cottage, Bluff's Edge, Grannie's Getaway, Maggie Sue's Summer Cottage— and I can't help but chuckle at what these folks consider to be a "cottage."

In the south, we called them cabins. Here, they call them cottages. But they—and I—are literally a world apart. As a girl, I could race through our cabin in a few seconds flat, the front door banging shut just a second or two before the back door did. Here, I would need to take an elevator to get to my bedroom.

That is not a cottage.

I think of Jamieson Kimsley and his home. Even though he lived on Lake Michigan, he had a cottage in northern Michigan on the lake. I looked up it up on Zillow, too. It wasn't a cottage, it was a compound, with multiple buildings and a hundred feet of lake frontage. The taxes alone every month were more than I spent in six months of mortgage payments for my condo.

"Cottage my patootie," I say out loud.

It's only then I notice a woman in her yard watering her flowers. When our eyes meet, she gives me a wary wave, tightening her grip on the hose as if she might need to turn it on me.

I nod and increase my pace.

I've always been—*how can I put this?*—wary of the wealthy.

When you grow up poor—when Wonder Bread has served as sandwich bread, hot dog bun, hamburger bun, garlic toast and French toast—you become wary of those who have so much that they've forgotten the value of a hard-earned dollar and how hard it is for those who have so little.

It started early. My mother's blue-collar job at the factory, sewing overalls for minimum wage until she couldn't stand straight, and then babysitting our wealthier neighbors' children for a few extra bucks a week. Not to mention the clothes she made for Nevermore's society ladies, the ones who had homes on the hill, much like these, grand, columned Colonials with rolling green yards and croquet sets. The acid would rise in my stomach, even as a child, with every "Yes, ma'am," and "No, ma'am" my mother uttered to these women when she made them dresses for bridge club. These women believed they were talking to my mother like a friend, as she stooped before them, taking measurements, listening to their likes and dislikes. My mother would show them a sketch, and I could see her hold her breath.

"Now would you wear that to a bridge club, Miss Mabel?" a matriarch might ask. "May I make some suggestions that are more appropriate for spring?"

Their tone sounded as sweet as the tea their maids served, but their meaning was clear: *We know. You sew.*

I could see my mother's face flush. I watched her head bow in deference. Her humiliation was palpable, but she was paralyzed.

Although my mother always taught me to hold my tongue, I couldn't help myself that day, and I yelled, "May I make a suggestion? Sew it your damn self!"

My willfulness cost my mother good money and me a month of being grounded, but in the silence of the car ride home, I saw my mother look at me with such pride and then slowly, inch by inch, her spine straightened and her chin lifted, and after a while, she even began to whistle.

My mother. Whistling!

In college, I worked two jobs while going to school full-time. I had such resentment toward the sorority girls who tanned in the quad between classes and partied every weekend in a new outfit while I scurried to dish out food at the commons and waitress at a local pizza joint.

In every job, I was surrounded by Ivy League grads and trust-fund kids who "interviewed" only for show, as their families always seemed to know someone who knew someone, or someone who owed their fathers a favor.

My life was filled with an unquenchable thirst to prove that I was worthy. And that's an awful place to exist every day of your life. It's like waking up every day filling your lungs with fire instead of fresh air. It's toxic.

Now...

I stop, take a cleansing breath and look over the lake.

...I am free. For the first time in my life.

"Right, Sutton?" I ask out loud. The lake does not answer.

I know I am lying because there is still that quest inside me, a new desire to not only make a name for myself but also to make my mother's unspoken voice heard and her invisible life seen.

I've always wanted her life to have an exclamation point at the end. And now I want my life to have a final period at the end.

My mother lived in solitude. She sacrificed her whole life so that mine would be better than hers. Miss Mabel was a good woman, strong and unyielding as the Missouri oaks, and she asked for nothing in return from anyone. Her life was to wake, work hard, speak only when something needed to be said, sacrifice for family. I think of how society treated her.

My mom was overlooked, like far too many women in our world, and then, in an instant, she was gone.

She was hidden in a factory her whole life. She was hidden from society. Even at the end, she was hidden, this time behind a window, untouchable, silent.

And now I find that she hid her own history, too. I cannot live like that.

Your voice will be heard through me, Mother. I promise you, one way or another, I will find the end of our story.

A gust of wind rushes up and over the bluff and rattles an aspen tree.

Could this be my mother speaking to me?

I've grown to love aspen trees in the north, though we had none in the Ozarks. The trees talk to you in the wind, imparting their knowledge. I step toward the aspen, and the leaves crackle in the breeze. They are the perfect tree for "talking," with their leaves' long stems and flat, broad shapes. They practically quake.

"On your left!"

I leap out of my skin and release a startled yelp.

Two joggers trot past. I barely have time to reach for my mask when four bikers whiz past.

I turn and look down Lakeshore Drive. The world is awake and headed my way. The world is moving on without fear. The world is moving on without my mother in it.

I must find a way to do so as well.

"Are you okay?"

A girl walking with her family stops and looks at me.

Kids are still the most honest, empathetic beings in the universe. I think of myself as a girl quizzing my mother about her past and how calculated her responses always were. I start to nod yes to this girl, but I feel as if I owe her—and myself—the truth for once.

"I don't know," I say. "But thank you for asking."

What is it about riding a bicycle again that makes you feel like a kid again?

I giggle at the excitement—or perhaps it's my amazement—that I even remember how to ride a bike. My hands are gripped tightly on the handlebars, and the bike wiggles and shakes—as if I'm riding over gravel—due to my nerves.

What is about riding a bicycle again that makes you feel so old?

I chuckle at the quick juxtaposition of my thoughts.

I remembered this morning that Mick and Sarah said there were bikes in the little shed on the side of the cottage. I didn't expect to find the cutest bikes ever created, vintage Schwinns—one in aqua and one in pink—both with adorable little baskets and bells.

"Watch out!" I yell—while tinkling my bell—at people on the sidewalks, resorters crossing the narrow lanes with cups of coffee in hand, vacationers biking near me. "Watch out!"

People turn and stare as if the Wicked Witch from the *Wizard of Oz* has stolen Dorothy's bike.

And her little dog, too.

"Good morning!" I begin to call instead, though my voice remains panicked, the words sounding more like a warning than a greeting.

This bike is cuter than the one I had growing up, a steel trap with fat tires that could handle the endless dirt roads.

That bike was my connection to the world as a kid. It took me nowhere and everywhere.

We lived so far out in the boonies that it was too far to ride my bike into town, but I could ride my bike to places that were mine and mine alone, places where I could dream and plot my escape, places where I could ogle boys I would never date.

I loved the old swimming hole the locals called Straight Up Rock. You needed a truck to reach it, one that could go off road, across dirt roads with deep gullies that had nearly been washed away by floods, across creek beds with a foot of water in them, through overgrown fields and rocky inlets. Straight Up Rock rose straight up from the water and reached to heaven—the sun blinding you when you'd try to look at its highest point, and I nearly passed out the first time I climbed up and jumped.

There was the field of Indian paintbrush if I biked north and took the makeshift stone bridge that washed out every year. I could lie in the field forever, surrounded by orange-red blooms, bees buzzing all around me in the warmth.

If I biked down our road a few miles, the Brown Farm was like visiting another world. I would help Mr. Brown clean his stalls for two dollars a day and, on weekends, I would sell Mrs. Brown's freshly baked pies from a little stand along the road.

But the biggest reason I loved going to the Brown Farm was to watch the boys who came to bale hay. When it got hot, they would rip off their shirts, use them to dry their muscled torsos, and tuck them into the back of their jeans. I would watch them, wondering what it would be like to go on a date, even kiss one of them. A few boys asked me out, but I would always demur, usually lying that I had a boyfriend.

My mom never knew or even suspected this, or she would have grounded me for a decade without so much as a question or second glance.

"A girl your age don't need a boy," she would say. "Only leads to trouble."

But that planted a seed, deeper than any I ever planted for the Browns: boys are bad. Men are trouble. Better off alone.

Did my mom's love and loss of the "wrong man" set us both up for a life of loneliness? Is it possible to change the trajectory of your entire life?

"Good morning!"

The greeting of a young couple walking on the sidewalk knocks me from my trance. I try to wave, but I'm too terrified to remove my hand from the handlebars, worried my bike will just fly into the pond on the other side of a pretty sanctuary filled with heron and ducks.

"It is!" I yell like a crazy woman.

And it is a stunning Michigan morning, warmer than yesterday, and its beauty makes me feel brave. I am headed to check out the resort towns I've read so much about: Saugatuck-Douglas, sister cities, as it were. I am headed into town to have my first latte—the first cup of coffee I haven't made for myself—in a long time. I am headed into town to...

Be human again.

I turn from Center Street onto Blue Star Highway. There is a lovely, wide bike path, and it leads over a cute little bridge that spans the Kalamazoo River and, maps show, eventually leads to Lake Michigan. On one side farthest from town, fishing boats are set up along the banks, anglers standing at the ready, poles bent. On the other, speedboats zip by, American flags whipping in the breeze. I look up: summer flags in bright colors featuring cartoonishly smiling sunshines and happily waving waves line the bridge.

At the end of the bridge, just across the street where you turn into town, there is a sign that greets visitors and visually sums up Saugatuck: a large painter's palette.

A rainbow color of oils encircles the palette—just like one you might see an artist use while visiting Paris—and paintbrushes extend into the air. SAUGATUCK is written in vintage lettering.

If these towns are as cute as the sign, I think, *I'm going to be a very happy girl.*

The street leading to Saugatuck is lined with old trees and historic homes. Bed-and-breakfasts and vintage inns are dotted here and there, back from the road, the view of the water beyond dancing through the pines. Near the end of the street, a large arts center sits across from a park and marina.

When I reach the center of town, I slow my bike and look around in awe.

It's like a Currier & Ives painting come to life!

Art galleries line the street—oils, watercolors, sculptures, glassware, pottery—alongside shops filled with spices, women's clothing, shoes, jewelry, housewares and knickknacks. Quaint restaurants with outdoor patios have people lined up outside waiting for brunch.

Shoppers mill about the little streets, coffee in hand. Some already have ice cream cones and fudge, and the air is filled with the smell of sugar and butter.

And then I smell the distinctive scent of coffee beans roasting. I stick my nose into the air like an old beagle and trail the scent.

I stop my bike when I see the coffee shop. It is cute as a button, an old two-story cottage that has been converted into a coffeehouse. An expansive patio fronts the shop, with lots of tables and chairs, and a sign with an arrow says, *Garden patio in back!*

I walk my bike up to a rack and begin to retrieve the lock from the basket.

"No need for that," a man sipping coffee on a bench, a wagging yellow Lab beside him, says.

I look up.

"No one steals in this town," he says.

"Someone actually just told me the same thing," I say. "Said this was Mayberry."

"Then I'm Andy Griffith," he says. "I've lived here for forty years. I know everyone. And if I don't, I take a mental picture." He looks at me and blinks. "Click. I just got you. Isn't that right, Duke?"

The dog barks, and I attempt a smile, but I cannot ascertain if this man is friendly or insane.

"Go on," he urges. "I'll be here for a while. I'll make sure your bike is safe."

The word "safe" pops into my head.

"Trust me," he says.

Something shifts in me. "Okay," I say. "I will." I turn but stop. "This is a new leaf for me. I'm trying to change my life. I'm trying to be human again."

The man eyes me, and I can tell he's now trying to ascertain if I'm friendly or insane.

"We all are. Go get your coffee," he says. "Best in the US."

"That's a high compliment," I say.

"I know my coffee," he says.

I start to turn, but the man points at his head. "You're still wearing your helmet," he says.

"I forgot," I say, not bothering to finish my thought.

I forgot I'm wearing a helmet as big as a space shuttle, one seemingly made of concrete that looks as if it could protect me against a dragon attack.

I pull off my helmet and hang it over my bike handle. I turn and see the throng of people in the coffee shop, and my old friend panic overtakes me. I grab my mask from the bike's basket, walk to the door, open it but cannot step inside.

"Excuse me? Are you going in?" an older woman, unmasked, behind me, asks. She looks very much to be around my mother's age.

Time stopped for me and so many of us the last few years. And when I see a woman who reminds me of my mother, I want to retreat again, but I know running won't help any longer.

"I... I..."

She cocks her head and nods at me.

"I understand," she says. "The first time I went shopping in the grocery store without a mask, I wept in the cereal aisle. I was holding a canister of oatmeal and a box of shredded wheat, and I completely fell apart."

She reaches out to touch my arm. She smiles sweetly and continues.

"Part of it for me is survivor's guilt," she says. "My best friend died of Covid. I didn't. Why her? Why not me? Part of it was my ongoing mourning. And part of it was simply the fact that I was being normal again. I was shopping on a Tuesday morning in a store without a mask. For a few seconds, everything was the way it used to be. And then a man walked near me and reached for a box of Cream of Wheat, and I reacted exactly like you did just now. Everything came rushing back. It's not fair, and it will never be fair. But it can be okay again."

The line moves, and I step inside the coffeehouse.

"One baby step at a time," she says. "That's all you can do. That's all any of us can do. Be it dealing with life, or loss, or grief. Losing someone means our lives will never be the same, ever. But it can be okay. It *has* to be okay again."

I look at her, and my eyes well up.

This time, when she reaches out to touch my arm, I melt. It feels good to be touched, connected...

Normal.

I tuck my mask into the pocket of my shorts.

"Coffee's on me," the woman says when I reach the counter and order.

"No, thank you," I say. "I'm getting a scone, too. And maybe a blueberry streusel muffin."

She laughs.

"It's a ploy," I continue. "This is my third time in here today." And then I laugh, hard. It feels good to laugh.

"What's your name?" I finally remember to ask, once my order is ready.

"Joy," she says.

I look at her and tear up anew.

"Of course," I say.

She holds open her arms and hugs me, so tightly the world falls away, so sweetly I feel as if my mother is with me again.

"Thank you," I say. "For being so kind. It's a rare commodity these days."

"Everything comes back en vogue," Joy says with a wink. "Just like the unfortunate high-waisted jeans my granddaughters are now wearing."

I leave with my breakfast, feeling emboldened, and when I walk out of the coffeehouse, and the man still sitting next to my bike yells, "Told ya so!" I laugh again.

I head to the garden in back and take a seat at a little table. Tables are spaced a wide distance apart, and I feel like I'm sitting in a friend's backyard that is abloom with cottage flowers. Terra-cotta pots are filled with herbs, which the coffeehouse uses for its egg bakes and savory scones. Bees buzz and butterflies flit happily, and—just like one of the pansies—I turn my happy face to the sun.

My coffee—a honey lavender latte made with a bold espresso, whose beans are roasted right here—is beyond exquisite. It might be, just as the man said to me when I arrived, the best coffee in the US.

I take a bite of my blueberry muffin, and then another—the baked good bursting with Michigan blueberries and the brown sugar crumble topping melting in my mouth—inhaling it until it is gone. I follow suit with the scone.

I sit and sip and watch the boats putter down the river toward Lake Michigan.

Is this what it's like to be in flow with the world again? At one with nature? At peace?

I've felt this way only a few times the past couple of years, usually when I've been working, not on designs for Lindy's but on projects for myself. I've felt comfort when I've designed a dress for a friend and gone through my buttons to find just the right ones to fit her personality. I remembered why my mother sewed after she had spent all day sewing: it was pleasure, not a job.

My heart hiccups.

A job.

I don't have one. I will need one soon, especially after this summer—of either serendipity or stupidity—following a trail of buttons that has led me here.

Maybe I'm just here for this, I think, to be reminded of the beauty in the world. To be reminded to be normal again. Maybe this is what I needed to find.

My tiny inheritance, too-soon IRA gift to myself and small savings has kept me afloat, and it will through the early fall, but then what? I have agreed to rent my condo through Labor Day, but what happens next? My future seems as murky as my past.

The waves on the river glisten like I've embellished them with sequins.

Maybe this adventure, like the river, will lead me somewhere bigger.

I finish my coffee, stand and head to leave.

My bike remains.

"Told ya," the man says with a wink. "You can always trust Captain Lucky."

"Captain Lucky?" I ask.

"'Cause I ain't," he says. "Nickname's completely ironic." He looks at me. "But I always believe that your luck can change at any moment, don't you?"

I smile. "I do now," I say. "Thank you for the reminder."

"Have a great day," he says. "And I'm sure I'll see you around again. Everyone 'round here knows Captain Lucky."

I ride my bike around the streets of Saugatuck, admiring the sights. The streets are clogged with vacationers, everyone in a happy mood. I huff and puff riding my bike up a hill and into Saugatuck's old neighborhoods, admiring historic cottages— shingled with wide porches and well-kept gardens—that overlook the town and river. I find the new bike path that leads to Douglas and head down Center Street, its main thoroughfare.

My namesake of Douglas, I've read, is the "little, quieter sister" to Saugatuck. Its main street is home to a new—and old—library as well as art galleries and restaurants. But, as I've researched, Douglas is known for its home decorating and furnishings shops, and I pedal slowly down Center admiring the handsome stores. I slow, realizing the entire town is festooned with grand window boxes, much like Nevermore's square used to have. I slam on my brakes when I eye a shop with a sign that reads *One man's trash is another man's treasure.*

I perch my bike against the stand on the sidewalk, take off my helmet and venture inside, not hesitating, feeling emboldened.

I stop in my tracks as soon as I step through the door. It's like walking into the past.

The store has the feel of an old-time apothecary. It is clean as a whistle and yet filled to its beamed rafters with shelves of…

Stuff.

But "the stuff" is all well-considered and curated, akin to a Parisian shop rather than an antique mall.

There are linens, fabrics, tapestries, glassware, pillows, artwork, vases and furniture. I feel as if I've wandered into an upscale version of my mother's yard sales.

It smells like heaven, too. My mom used to grow stunning peonies, big white puffs with pink centers that would exhaust the stems on which they grew. She grew a row of them just off the back of the cabin—in the blaring sun, the heat from the rocky bluffs roasting them—and hung her laundry line over them.

"So your sheets will always smell like heaven," she said. "Like home."

I am overwhelmed and don't know where to start, but I begin by perusing the fabrics. I stop on a stunning floral cotton print. The background is midnight blue and populated, appropriately enough, with pink peonies and white roses. The leaves are a mix of colors—electric blue and grass green—that give it an air of whimsy.

I search for the tag on the fabric.

"That's a vintage floral cotton circa 1960."

I turn, and a man wearing a worn, purple baseball cap with a broken bill and Northwestern logo on it is standing before me.

I look at him, surprised.

"I'm John McCoy, the owner of this shop," he continues. "I

get that look a lot. A man who knows fabrics. And antiques. And, well, things men don't usually know."

I smile, and he extends his hand. I hesitate, as I did with the woman in the coffee shop.

"I'm sorry," I say. "I'm learning to be normal again."

This time, he laughs. "I could respond to that in so many ways," he says. "But I completely understand. Me, too."

I take his hand.

John looks to be in his late thirties. In his short-sleeved Penguin polo, he has the look of a former athlete, long and lithe, muscled but graceful. John has hazel eyes, not brown, not green, but golden, and the color changes—even turning blue—when he holds the fabric up next to his face.

"The maker of this fabric was founded in the fifties and went out of business about a decade ago," he says. "To me, this is American fabric at its most beautiful. The product was made here in the States, usually in smaller, rural areas, especially in the South and the East. These factories were often the area's biggest employers." John stops, and his eyes light up. "Wait a second. You have to see this."

He scoots off behind the long, wooden counter at the back of the store and returns with a photo. "Look."

It is a black-and-white picture of three women seated in rockers in front of huge, paned windows, pine trees just outside. They are holding up bolts of fabric, which drape across their laps and onto the floor.

"Isn't it amazing? Found it with the fabric," John says. "This is how quality control was done back in the good old days. The women would hold the fabric yardage up to the sunlight to look for imperfections. Nowadays modern factories use light meters, scales and various machinery to check for holes, discoloration and tensile strength. Nothing like the way they used to do it, though."

"I know," I say, telling him about my mother's days in the overalls factory as well as my career.

"Well, this certainly seems like destiny," he says.

For some reason, I open my mouth and begin to tell him about my mother's death, my job, my journey here, but the bell on the front door tinkles, interrupting me, and a woman calls out, "Hey, Tug! How are you! I missed you!"

"Hi, Betsy! It's good to see you again for the summer. What a year."

"Tell me about it! I feel like a kid again!" Betsy says.

"I'll be with you in a minute," John says, before turning back to me.

"Tug?" I ask, looking at John, lifting an eyebrow.

"My nickname," he says, shifting his body like a boy might do when he's embarrassed by something his mom just said.

"Meaning?" I ask.

John tugs on the bill of his cap. "Used to play baseball at Saugatuck High School. Played in college and the minors. I always tugged on my cap. Habit." He tugs on his bill. "See?"

I nod. "I like it. Name fits."

"I didn't ask your name," Tug says. "I'm sorry."

"Sutton."

"What a beautiful name. Rhymes with one of my favorite things." Tug points to a shelf on a far wall filled with jars of buttons.

"Are you kidding me?" I ask, turning on a dime. "You certainly have it all here."

"Look around," Tug says. "Take your time. Buy something!" I smile.

"Oh, I forgot!" Tug says, disappearing into a back room before returning with a glass of wine. "Glass of rosé?"

"Are you kidding me?" I repeat. "You certainly have it all here. Including a liquor license, it seems."

"I tried to think of everything," he says. Tug leans toward me and whispers conspiratorially. "License cost a small fortune, but it was well worth it. People buy more when they drink." He looks at me with a twinkle in those hazel eyes. "So drink!"

"I just had a coffee, and now I'm going directly into wine."

"Welcome to Saugatuck-Douglas!" Tug says with a laugh. "That's how every summer day is supposed to go. Coffee, then rosé all day! Hey, you're on vacation."

"And I came here on a bike," I finish. "Bring it on."

He laughs and hands me the glass. "Bonus: it's a really good wine," he says. "Highly recommended by *Wine Spectator* and comes from right here in Michigan."

I sip. "It *is* good," I say. "Or maybe I just got used to my delicious boxes of wine."

"Oh, a box. You are classy."

I laugh, and Tug says, "Back in a sec. Betsy's one of my biggest customers. Seriously, just wander. Enjoy. Be joyful. Hi, Betsy!"

Joyful. How long has it been?

I think of Joy, the woman I met this morning. I think of my mother. I think of how so many of us isolate ourselves from the world, by circumstance and by choice.

I watch Betsy and Tug hug like old friends, and I take another sip of wine.

Is this what it's like to connect with people again? To have conversation? To laugh?

My heart is skipping, the wine is already going to my head, and I feel downright giddy.

I peruse the fabrics a bit longer, trying to delay the inevitable, but I can no longer control myself, and I beeline to the buttons.

"Wow!" I sigh, setting down my glass of wine.

Tug has one of the largest collections of vintage pearl buttons I've ever seen. Many are stunningly sweet and simple—the ones my mother particularly adored—but a large number are a rainbow of colors, and many of the pearl buttons feature handmade Czech beads and Swarovski crystals.

I pull jars of buttons down from the shelves, turning them 'round in my hand. I take two jars filled to the brim with buttons over to the front counter and pour some out on the old wood.

I match a dozen of the most gorgeous round pearl buttons—pink with layers of white, similar in size and color to the bud on an emerging peony—and then retrieve the fabric I'd been eyeing with Tug.

Perfect!

"Perfect!"

I jump.

"Sorry," Tug says. "I didn't mean to startle you."

"It's okay. I'm not used to people." I stop. "That sounds odd, but it's true. I haven't been around people in quite a while."

"Strange how quickly we get used to being alone, isn't it? But it's not natural."

"No," I say. "It's not."

"You certainly have an impeccable sense of style," Tug says. "The fabric. The buttons. It's a little bit vintage, a little bit classic, a little bit traditional and a little bit retro, but mostly beautiful."

"Thank you," I say, my face flushing. "Sorry. The last compliment I received was from an Instacart delivery person for tipping so well."

Tug laughs.

"Do you want to keep looking?" he asks. "I have *so* many more buttons in back: black glass buttons, ornate eighteenth-century buttons, leather buttons, enamel, fabric, shell, wood, metal, celluloid…you name it. But our summer customers live for the pearl buttons."

"Why is that?" I ask.

"Michigan was the pearl button capital of the world for a period of time, did you know that?"

"I actually did know that," I say. "Or, rather, I just learned about that. I just found an old button card of my mom's that said Douglas, Michigan, on it."

"That's right! Many pearl buttons, just like these, were made right here. Fascinating history. I just love buttons. They are works of art, so different from how they're produced today."

"You're exactly right," I say.

I start to tell him more about my job, but he looks at me and asks, "Do you have plans on Friday night?"

Is he asking me out? I think. Already. *After we just met? This is beyond awkward.*

"I'm not asking you out!" he adds quickly and emphatically.

My eyes widen.

Now I don't know whether to feel relieved or rejected.

"That didn't come out right, either," he says. "It's just that on Friday nights Ox-Bow holds its Friday Night Open Studio."

"Ox-Bow?" I ask hesitantly.

"It's our historic artists' colony and school of art," Tug says. "Founded over a hundred years ago in affiliation with the School of the Art Institute of Chicago. Every other Friday, students and faculty feature studio demonstrations and guests are treated to a live auction of student, faculty and staff work. It's a way to pick up unique art by a famed artist or yet-to-be-discovered artist and help sustain the campus and provide scholarships. It's free, fun and has lots of wine."

"Wow," I say. "It does sound fun."

"You're an artist," Tug says. "I thought you might enjoy it. And it would be nice to introduce you to some of my friends.

Everyone in town goes. Everyone around here's like family. It's tradition on summer Friday nights. They had to cancel them the last couple of years. It's just nice to be back in a routine again."

I nod.

"Listen, I'll give you my cell number," Tug says. "You can text me, and we can go together. Or, you can just follow the signs…it's just beyond the entrance to Oval Beach and Mt. Baldhead."

He looks at me. "You don't understand a word I'm saying, do you?"

I shake my head.

"By that, I mean it's a climb by bike to Ox-Bow. And parking is limited, so you don't want to get stuck taking the bus." He hesitates. "What I'm trying to say is my offer to drive will make it much less of a headache for you than my explanation."

I laugh.

"So, here's my number. If you want to go, text me your address. Or not."

"Thanks," I finally say. "I'll think about it." I duck my head.

"So, do you want me to wrap up some of this fabric and these buttons, or do you want to think about that, too?"

I study the material and the buttons. I think of my mom and my need to start anew, as just Sutton again.

"I'll take it, thank you," I say. "I feel inspired."

Tug smiles. "Great! And you get the owner's twenty percent inspiration discount!"

As he cuts and wraps the fabric, I pick up my cell and, without thinking, text him.

I hear a big laugh a few seconds later. I look up, and Tug is reading my message.

"You surprised me," he says, his voice light and happy.

Back at'cha, I don't say.

"See you Friday night," Tug says. "Six thirty sharp."

I head out of the shop, the bell tinkling, and put my fabric and buttons into the basket on my bike. I turn once more to look into the shop. Tug is again helping Betsy. He is hauling armfuls of things to the counter.

It's then I catch myself in the reflection. My hair is matted down from the helmet. I have an indentation from the helmet imprinted across my forehead. I look as if I just completed a triathlon in a rain forest.

Way to make an impression your first day out in the world, Sutton.

6

PATTERN

A template on paper or cardboard from which all of the pieces of the garment are traced onto fabric. All the parts are then cut out and assembled to create the final piece.

I smile at the pattern I've created for the fabric I purchased.

It will not simply become a short summer dress, one that I can dream of wearing to a dinner or a party. No, this dress is a statement.

Of joy. Of hope. Of summer. Of a new beginning.

I am standing at the edge of a new life. I want to fill my summer with fun and possibility, and I want to fill my new life with happiness and answered questions.

I polish off my coffee and snap a photo of the pattern and fabric with my phone.

I had no idea why I was lugging Ol' Betsy here—it called to me to do so—but now it makes sense.

I *need* to create again. I *need* to be me again. And that all begins with a good plan.

For a dress. And a life.

I study the pretty pink buttons I purchased. A lake breeze drifts through the windows, carrying the scent of water, pine, grass, and I inhale. I shut my eyes against a flood of memories and see myself at the cabin with my mother, the windows wide-open. She is sewing. I am playing with her buttons. The curtains are undulating. I open my eyes.

If there's anything I've learned through all of this, it is that there are many patterns to life.

One is cut and created by our parents, who seek not only to make us in their own image but also to design a better life for us.

Another pattern is cut and created by each of us in an attempt to become our own person, unique, different from those before us.

And yet another, as I've learned, was cut and created by people we never knew, and we try to live inside of it, even though it no longer fits us.

Each pattern fits our bodies at different times in our lives.

But it's our hearts, minds and souls that are constantly growing, changing, evolving, shifting, and we rarely consider what pattern works best for them.

I inhale the scent of summer again and walk over to the windows. I lift, but the old window sticks. I steel myself, squat and push up the painted window frame—swollen from the humidity—with a big grunt. It flies northward. I lean toward the screen. Above the sounds of the lake, bees and birds, I hear car doors slamming, people talking and cell phones ringing.

I head onto the front porch and cock my head like a curious blue jay, listening.

I see people wander alongside the Dandelion Cottage, and it's then I finally notice tables lined with items.

A yard sale?

I scoot to the bathroom and run a brush through my hair, once highlighted with gold, now a dirty dishwater blond. I'm still cutting my own hair—you quickly realize once you step back into life again that "Zoom-ready" is not necessarily "world-ready"—and I flip it this way and that to try and cover my many mistakes.

When in doubt, add some mascara and lipstick.

I look at myself.

And then a little bit more.

I pull on some shorts and a pink T-shirt Abby got me to lift my spirits a while ago that reads, *CUTE AS A BUTTON!*

I slip into my sneakers and head out the front door, following the narrow path through the dune grass to the "cottage."

A few tables line the side of the house, and folks are perusing an assortment of typical yard sale items: old gardening tools, sets of dishes and flatware. A hand-propelled lawn mower that has seen better days, if not years, sits like an unearthed relic from an archaeological dig.

I head to the front of the house, and a throng of people are crammed into the front yard. Big signs read *ESTATE SALE.*

I chuckle.

Here, yard sales are estate sales, and mansions are cottages.

I look around warily, but take a deep breath and move toward the crowd. On the side of the yard I see standing clothing racks filled with beautiful dresses and gowns. Stunning scarves are draped over hangers.

"This is the *best* estate sale," a kindly woman with salt-and-pepper hair says to me when I approach. "I look forward to it every year."

Another woman approaches, and the seemingly sweet woman next to me bumps her out of the way with her hip.

"None of these are your size," she says.

The other woman walks away, her face red.

"Aren't these gorgeous?" the woman says.

"Whose place is this?" I ask. "I'm renting the little cottage behind it for the summer."

"The Widow Lyons," the woman says. Her voice is hushed,

her tone reverential, as though Queen Elizabeth will appear any moment, and she is here to pay her respects. "You should be honored to stay on these grounds."

"The Widow Lyons?" I ask, before remembering what Mick and Sarah had told me. "Sounds mysterious."

"She is," the woman says. "She's the matriarch of Saugatuck-Douglas! She's funded everything in town: the arts center, Ox-Bow, the Historical Society, the new stairs leading to Mt. Baldhead. She helped many of the local businesses survive the pandemic. She's as close to a saint as there is around here."

The woman looks at me and nods. "St. Lyons."

"She sounds like a wonderful woman," I say.

"Oh, she is," the woman says.

Then she eyes an embroidered ivory dress, orange poppies along the neckline and hem, coupled with a long orange scarf and crows, "Mine! All mine!"

I look at her.

"I'm not a saint," she says with a laugh.

"Me either," I respond with a wink.

She heads to another rack. The dresses are quite beautiful, but a bit too elegant, a tad too formal, a touch too much for my tastes.

I turn, and that's when I see it: an entire table filled with boxes and jars of buttons.

Bingo!

I rush over, but no one is looking at them.

I am in the land of buttons.

The buttons shimmer in the sunlight, hundreds and hundreds of them, covering a small table.

My eyes land on an old metal tin. It is a beautiful, burnished golden brown.

The color of Tug's eyes, I can't help but think.

The lid is still on, and I look around the crowd warily before trying to pry loose the lid, which seems as if it does not want to come free.

I use my fingernails to slowly pry it up, a millimeter at a time. Suddenly, the lid springs loose and goes flying. I release a surprised yelp. I turn to retrieve the lid, but it is now hiding underneath a table covered with vintage lamps and surrounded by a dozen people jockeying for position.

I turn quickly, acting as if nothing happened, and then whistle softly to myself as if I'm as innocent as Jiminy Cricket.

The old tin is filled to the brim with pearl buttons of all shapes, sizes and colors.

No wonder the lid was stuck, I think. *The mama was trying to protect its precious babies.*

I run my fingers through the mound of buttons and close my eyes, and my heart races and my mind pings with memories.

The feel of the buttons—smooth, cool to the touch—calms me.

"I think you dropped this."

I release another surprised yelp and open my eyes.

An elegant woman is standing before me holding the lid to the tin. She is wearing cropped pants, a crisp white blouse—collar flipped up like a bird's wings in flight—the most beautiful jacket, pale pink and fitted to her very taut body, lined with a row of the most exquisite ceramic buttons I've seen in ages, navy blue with what looks like a family crest in gold on each one. Her hair is silver—not gray—that resplendent silver that all women hope their hair will turn one day. It is cut in a long bob, one side pulled back with a vintage, filigree hair clip. She is in full makeup, as if she's about to head off to an event.

Like the Oscars, I think.

"Hello? Is anyone there?" the woman asks.

"Oh, my gosh," I finally say. "Oh, I'm so sorry. For, you know, not responding and for not picking up the lid."

She looks at me. Her eyes are as golden as the old tin. She doesn't respond.

"Thank you," I say, taking the lid from her hand.

I turn and continue studying the buttons, but the woman does not depart. She stands behind me, watching me.

I grow nervous and begin to sort the buttons by color.

"I used to do that when I was little," the woman says.

I turn toward her again.

"I've always done this," I say. "My mom loved buttons. Calms me." I stop. "I love them, too."

"Well, you are an either an old soul or a designer," the woman says. "No one *loves* buttons anymore."

"I do." I look at her and then at the old tin. "And I guess I'm both."

"'And thou shalt make fifty buttons of gold, and couple the curtains together with the buttons: and it shall be one tabernacle.'"

"Excuse me?"

"Passage from the Bible," the woman says. "It just means buttons have a special history. They are not only beautiful, but they are important. Buttons are our wearable history."

Her tone is polished, her voice featuring just the slightest hint of a Michigan accent. She sounds like a classic movie starlet, dramatic but hushed. She looks like one, too. Her face is strong, high-cheek boned, mysterious, like Ava Gardner, one of my mother's favorite actresses.

I cannot tell her age. She could be very old, or not. It's like when I see Dolly Parton, and I wonder: Has she aged at all these past forty years?

I think of my mother again. She called such women "well-preserved." And then I think of the optical illusion game I played with my mom. I cannot tell this stranger's age. She looks young when I glance at her, the opposite of how I saw my mom and how my mom viewed the world.

"That's lovely," I say. "That's how I think of buttons as well."

The woman moves around to the other side of the table. She is now facing me. She picks up a few buttons and lets them trail between her fingers and fall into the tin. They resemble raindrops in the morning light.

She watches me without an ounce of embarrassment. Nervously, I glance at the lid she returned to me. Then I lean and look at the side of the tin. I pick up a jar nearby. And then another. She continues to watch.

"This isn't a very well-organized yard sale," I say in a conspiratorial tone to the woman, tilting my body across the table toward her, trying to mask my nervousness. "There's not a price on anything." I laugh and then lean even closer. "I mean, wouldn't you think they would know how to slap a piece of masking tape on all this stuff? It's the first rule of yard sales."

I look at the woman, expecting her to agree, nod, laugh with me. But those gold eyes survey me, up and down, very slowly, before piercing my soul.

"Stuff?" she asks. "*Yard* sale?"

My heart sinks, and I immediately feel sick to my stomach. "I'm so sorry. I didn't mean to offend you, or imply anything. It's just that…"

"It's just that, what?" she asks.

"Never mind," I say. "I'll be going."

I turn from the table.

"Stop," the woman says.

I stop.

"How much are you willing to pay for these buttons?" she asks.

I look at her, my face perplexed.

"How much are you willing to pay for these buttons?" she repeats. "All of them."

"I don't know," I say. "I can venture a guess at their value, but I'm sure I can't afford all of these." I look at the buttons on the table. Some, I know, are rare. Some very valuable. Some I've never seen before. I pick one up and study it.

"Venture away," she says.

I name a price, and she smiles.

"Very accurate. That's how we do it here, by the way," the woman says. "I've always adored the marketplaces in Italy and Spain and Morocco, where you can barter for goods. Here, in America, everything is set. We don't allow ourselves to barter for our necessities. I know how much things are worth. I expect others to learn via this process as well. That's why I don't *slap* masking tape on my items. That's why I don't give away my *stuff* for a quarter. That's why I personally sell each and every item here. And this is an estate sale, not a *yard* sale."

"*Your* stuff?" I ask, before realizing my error. "I mean, *this* is your estate sale?"

She nods. A wry smile overtakes her face. It's very Grinch-like.

"You're the Widow Lyons?" I gasp.

Her laugh booms across the lakeshore, and everyone—literally, everyone—turns to stare. "Is that what they're calling me now?" she asks. "The Widow Lyons. Very sad. Very mysterious."

I shrug. "I'm so sorry. I didn't mean…" I fumble.

"I've been called worse, don't worry," she says. "Were you expecting some sort of Mary Engelbreit character? I'm anything but."

"No, I mean…" I fumble again.

"So you know of Mary Engelbreit?" she asks.

"I do. Born and raised in Missouri, like me. My mother and I adored her."

"Well, you both certainly have unique taste."

She makes *unique* sound like a curse word.

"If that's a dig," I start.

"No, no," she says, raising a perfectly manicured nail. "Just that you really are an old soul."

I eye her as warily as she is eyeing me. She extends her hand.

"I'm Bonnie. Bonnie Lyons." She leans over the table and says in a chilling whisper like Vincent Price might have done in an old horror movie, "The Widow Lyons."

I smile ever so slightly. "Sutton," I say, taking her hand. "Sutton Douglas."

I lean over and try to match her whisper. "The Single Sutton."

She laughs.

"How mysterious in your own right," she says. "Your name matches the town."

"I know," I say. "That's what brought me here." I stop, trying not to sound crazy. "Long story. *Very* long story. Actually I'm renting the cottage behind yours."

"I know," she says matter-of-factly.

"You do?"

"Yes, of course. I know everything."

She states this not as a joke but as fact.

I feel prickly all over, chilled, and in need of some water.

"The owners bought the cottage from my late husband and I. They own the cottage, but we still own the land." She looks at me. "Long story. *Very* long story. They left me a voice mail telling me you were renting. It's nice to officially meet you."

"Well, it's certainly nice to meet you, too," I say.

"You can have all of these buttons for a penny, Sutton," she says.

"What?"

"You understand the value of something valuable," she says. "That's all I expect of those who wish to possess my possessions."

"I can't," I say quickly.

"Why?" she asks. "I have thousands of buttons. Attics full. Basements full. I have more buttons than money."

I can't help but stare at her. My body is all tingly.

"I just can't," I say. "I feel like I'd owe you in the future, and my mom taught me to never put myself in that position."

"Your mother was a wise woman," Bonnie says. "Or a fool."

My eyes blaze. "I don't know whether you're being serious or whether you're joking, but I can't tolerate someone speaking ill of my mother. Not right now. Not after...well, not ever."

I turn on a dime, my walk turning into a full sprint.

When I return to the cottage, my heart is racing. I head to the kitchen for some water, and it's then I finally realize I still have one of Bonnie's buttons in my hands.

"No way!" Tug laughs. "You talked like that to Bonnie Lyons? The Button Queen?"

"The who? I thought she was the Widow Lyons. Everyone's got a nickname is this town."

"Didn't you do a Google search on her when you got home? Weren't you curious?"

"I've kept Google in business the last year," I say. "I was actually more irked than curious, to be honest. She was a bit dismissive of me and my mom. Or at least I think she was. It was hard to tell. She's got a way about her."

"That's the understatement of the century," Tug says. "She's a force of nature around here."

"Well, I just can't tolerate anyone saying anything about my mom. Not right now."

"I get it," Tug says. "Maybe she was kidding with you."

I shoot him a look.

"Or not."

Tug shakes his head and tugs at his ball cap. Standing on the front porch of the cottage, the light angled across his face, he suddenly looks like a little boy who just realized there is no Easter bunny.

"Sorry," I say.

"I guess I've just always sort of considered her a mythical character, like a unicorn. I respect what she's done for the community, but she's always been this mix of public and private. Very social in community affairs, very private about her own life. And she's actually spoken to me like that before—fundraising for her events—and I can't tell if she's being funny or dismissive."

"Why did you call her the Button Queen?" I continue. "I thought she was the Widow Lyons?"

"The Dandy Button Company? That was her and her husband's business."

"What?" I yelp.

"That's how they made their fortune. Took it over from his father. It's the one I was telling you about," Tug says. "They had the largest, and I believe the very first, button-finishing factory in the United States. It was located right here in Douglas on the shores of the Kalamazoo River."

I freeze. I feel as if my body has been cast in concrete.

"Are you okay?"

"I'm sort of freaking out," I say. "I knew about the company. I just never put two and two together." I take a breath. "I don't mean to dump so much on you so soon, but I feel as if I'm about to explode, or go insane, or something. Can I share something with you?"

Tug nods.

"I came to Douglas because before my mom died she left me a letter that told me that the story of my entire family history was a lie. I grew up believing my whole family died in a fire, and my mom survived with just me. But her letter explained that she had fallen in love with a man that her family didn't approve of, and she had run away and never looked back. I grew up with no family history. She never talked about her family and rarely talked about my father. And then, out of the blue, this."

I take another deep breath and continue.

"After that, I found a button card that said Dandy Button Company on it and Douglas. My last name is Douglas. I found a postcard of the Douglas beach. I found a picture of a man named Ted who might be my father. And I have so many pearl buttons that all look the same and now live behind the Button Queen. Not to mention I'm a designer whose collection for Lindy's was called Sutton's Buttons."

"I think that's meaningful coincidence," Tug says. "And a lot to process."

"You think?"

"Look you've got a lot on your plate and a lot on your mind. Why don't you just start asking some questions around here about your dad? People in these resort towns always know something about somebody." He looks at me for the longest time. "Or maybe you just leave it all in the past, knowing maybe your mom was trying to protect you for some reason."

I shrug.

"And, now that I think about it, I've heard of your line. I read about it in *Crain's Chicago Business*."

"Thank you," I say, pleased. "But I should have said, *was*, instead of is." I stop. "I quit my job."

"Why?" he asks.

"I don't know," I say, now shaking my head. "I think I

sort of freaked out." I look at Tug. "Long story. I keep saying that, don't I? But isn't it ironic that I make a living off of what she did?"

"No, you make a living off of what your mother did, right?"

I smile and nod.

"And I don't know if it's that ironic. I mean, is it ironic there's a baseball game on every day during the summer, and I played ball?"

"Well, isn't it ironic then that I ended up renting a place right behind her?"

"You're starting to sound a lot like Alanis Morissette," Tug says, before singing, "Isn't it ironic?"

I laugh. "You're a multitalented man."

"Maybe you two were just destined to meet," Tug says.

"Or murder each other," I add.

"What about us?" Tug asks. "I'm a button guy, too. Were we destined to meet? Or murder each other?"

"Depends on how tonight goes," I say quickly, not considering the potential innuendo in my words. "You know what I meant, right?"

He laughs. "Not at all," he says before peeking into my cottage from the front porch. "I didn't realize *this* was where you were staying."

"That sounds ominous," I say. "*Here*. Behind *her*."

"No, it's just that cottage has so much history," he says.

"Everything in my life and around here has a history, I'm learning."

"I think..."

Tug is so consumed in thought that he begins to walk around the side of my cottage.

"Where are you going?" I ask.

"Look! Back here!"

I follow Tug's voice around to the far side of the cottage to find him pointing at a plaque on the stone foundation.

"I knew it," he says. "This cottage is on the registry of historical sites."

"I heard it was a one-room schoolhouse."

"It has a lot of history."

"Thank you, Cliff Clavin," I say.

He laughs and says, "We're just filled with pop culture references, aren't we? Alanis, *Cheers*, what's next?"

"Nancy Drew," I say.

Tug nods. "Of course." He looks at the cottage again. "Mrs. Lyons held a large fundraiser for the arts center here a few years back when her husband was still alive and before she sold this cottage. She invited the entire town. For a donation, of course. I remember that tours were being given in this cottage, but I never made it back here. I was too busy being coerced by Mrs. Lyons to donate loads of free gifts to the arts center's big Summer Solstice silent auction."

"Figures," I say. "I have a thing with…"

I stop.

Tug runs his hand over the plaque and looks at me.

"With?"

"Money," I finish. "I grew up very poor. Worked my way through college. I just saw the way so many wealthy women in the town where I grew up looked at my mom. I refuse to be treated like that."

"I get it, and good for you," Tug says. "I own a small business in a town filled with wealthy resorters. Sometimes they treat me like a member of their staff. Sometimes they don't even acknowledge I'm alive." Tug rubs his hand over the plaque one more time and stands. "But sometimes, the past is the past. We either have to learn from it, or let it go."

I cock my head, considering what he's just said, and my face lifts. "Touché."

"I've had to live that lesson. Otherwise, my life would still be filled with bitterness at all the other guys I played ball with who got a big break while mine never came. I was good. I just wasn't good enough."

"Did you learn from that or let it go?" I ask.

"Both," he says. Then he looks back at the plaque and says, as if to himself, "Actually, I'm still learning from both." He turns. "We better get going, or we'll never find parking."

We walk down the little path toward the graveled parking area just on the other side of Bonnie Lyons's fence. When I look up, I stop.

"Is this your car?"

"It is," he says. "Do you like it?"

"I do," I say.

The car is a vintage Ford Thunderbird, cherry red, top down.

"My mom used to call this color 'pull-me-over-red'," I say, "because the only cars we ever saw the police pull over for speeding were this color."

Tug laughs.

I peek inside the car. It has a red leather interior, a red leather steering wheel and red leather trim. I walk around to the front. The front lights—raised like eyes—and the wide chrome grill make the car look menacingly sexy.

Like if James Dean were a car, I think.

It is in pristine shape, down to the whitewall tires, which look brand spanking new.

He bends over, using the front of his untucked short-sleeved shirt to wipe off an invisible piece of dust. I have so many questions in my life, but right now I think the biggest mystery is right before me: *What's under his ball cap?*

I try to get a closer look at his head, but his ball cap is pulled low.

You already know, Sutton. Why do men of a certain age wear a ball cap? Because they're bald as an eagle. They're trying to look young, hold on to something that's long past, like their hair.

I look at him again.

But bald can be very sexy. As long as he doesn't have a ring of hair. Or a comb-over.

Please, God. Not a comb-over.

"What's wrong?" Tug asks. "Why are you staring at me?"

I am subconsciously touching my own hair, and his question makes me jump out of my skin.

"Was this your midlife crisis car?" I ask, trying to cover. I instantly want to kick myself.

"Do I look like I'm middle-aged?" Tug asks.

"No, no, no," I stammer. "No."

"Good."

"Just trying to make a joke. A bad one obviously."

"I'm forty, by the way," he says.

I hesitate, wondering if I should reply in kind.

"I'm…" I pause but don't lie. "…forty-one."

"An older woman!" Tug grins.

"Hey."

"Just kidding," he says. "I was about to say how amazing you look."

"For my age?"

"No!" he says. "I would have guessed you to be a decade younger."

"Why, thank you."

Tug turns and places his hand over the hood of the convertible but doesn't touch it.

"This was my father's car, and he got it when he was *definitely* going through a midlife crisis." Tug smiles. "He gave it to me after my baseball career ended. Said it was a gift to celebrate all I'd accomplished and all I still had to accomplish." Tug turns toward me and continues. "When he handed me the keys, he said, 'Your summers playing ball were sacred. To you and to me. It defined our lives. I want this car to remind you that your summers should always be sacred, whether you're playing ball or not. They're special because you're a special man and a special son.' And then we popped two beers and just stood and stared at this car forever."

A tear surprises me, and I turn my head to wipe it away. Tug notices.

"Are you okay?" he asks, his voice soft.

I nod. "Just reminded me of my mom," I say. "And this car reminds me a little of her vintage Singer sewing machine she called 'Ol' Betsy.' I brought it with me here. It reminds me of her. It reminds me of summer."

"Ol' Betsy," Tug says. "I love that. How'd that name come about?"

I shake my head. "I have no idea. My mother was always a bit secretive about...well, everything."

"Well, I haven't named my car yet. What do you think? Big Red seems too obvious."

"I'll give it some thought," I say.

Tug smiles and opens my car door. I slide inside, with a little bit of effort, my knees cracking as I slink nearly to the ground, and Tug backs onto Lakeshore Drive.

"You know what I love about this car?" Tug asks. "I don't get asked to drive everyone around, which happens a lot here during the summer. People have a few drinks and expect you to serve as their Uber. 'Sorry, man,' I say. 'Only room for one.'"

It is a stunner of a June evening, warm but not humid, the landscape as green as the faux grass my mom used to put in my Easter basket. With the top down, the wind tosses my hair around, and I do feel like a girl again, seeing the world in vibrant color rather than black-and-white. Lake Michigan is calm, and the water sparkles—a blue gown bedecked in sequins—and I feel as if I could just reach right out and touch the lake. Tug turns on the radio, and I clap when "September" by Earth Wind and Fire begins to play. I lean my head back and sing, and for just a second, life is normal.

"It stays light forever in June," Tug says. He looks at the water and then at me and continues, as if reading my mind. "Michigan makes you feel like a kid again in the summer. There's just something magical about the lake, the beach, the dunes, the light...you remember who you were."

Tug points out the sights I've yet to see as we drive.

"There's the Saugatuck Chain Ferry that takes you from town across the river. It's the last existing chain ferry in America. Isn't it quaint?"

I nod.

"Only costs two bucks," he continues, pointing left and right. "Best deal in town. You can take it over and tour the history museum, walk to Oval Beach, climb the 302 steps to Mt. Baldhead, which has gorgeous views of the towns and water, or..."

The car slows to a stop.

"...walk to Ox-Bow on a Friday night."

There is a line of vehicles snaking down the winding, narrow, barely-big-enough-for-two-cars old road that sits across from downtown Saugatuck and parallels the bendy river. Boats of every type—sailboats and speedboats, pontoons and yachts—putter along the river, some returning home from a day on the lake, some just setting out for sunset.

"It's so idyllic," I say. "This truly is a summer haven."

"It's a summer *heaven*," Tug says. "This isn't just any resort area. Once this place gets ahold of you, it sinks into your soul.

It takes hold of your heart. It captures your creative spirit. There are other summer havens. There aren't any other summer heavens."

I look over at him and smile.

"You look great, by the way," Tug continues. "I meant to say so earlier."

I duck my head, unused to a compliment from a man, from anyone really. Compliments were rare from my mother—hard-earned—and ones from men have been few and far between, both personally and professionally. Jamieson was reserved and rarely gave gratuitous praise. And I've never stuck around long enough to garner many compliments from men.

Or actually believe any of the ones that were given.

Thanks, Mom.

I did try to make an effort tonight. And it felt good to try again. To do my hair, put on makeup, wear something without elastic, something other than the set of pajamas and sweats I've alternated the last two years. To look forward to something instead of sadly looking into the past. To be excited to see someone instead of scared to come in contact with anyone. To be in conversation with a real person, not just my own thoughts.

It felt good to be reminded that I can't give up on myself. I won't give up on myself.

"Thanks," I finally say.

"I was wondering if you heard me."

Tug is looking at me, and I suddenly feel claustrophobic. We aren't moving, and there is nowhere to run, no way to disguise my nervousness.

"Is it always this busy?" I ask.

Tug nods. "Summer traditions in Saugatuck are sacred."

The cars begin to move, and we go up, up, up the narrow road, snaking along a winding hill atop a dune, tottering mere feet from an overhang overlooking the river.

I grab my seat belt to make sure it's fastened, and Tug laughs.

"Is there still parking available?" Tug asks a young woman wearing a tie-dyed T-shirt that says, *FNO, BABY!*

"Sure is," she says. "Got here early! Have fun! And buy a lot to support aspiring artists!"

"FNO?" I ask as he pulls away.

"Friday Night Open," Tug says. "Baby."

Suddenly, the road curves, and we head straight downhill, into the middle of a forest. Trees canopy the road. Day turns to night. An attendant flags us into a tiny lot already crammed with cars, people spilling out of them, most dressed in either cute summer outfits or hip artsy garb.

Tug parks, gets out of the convertible and opens my door, helping me to my feet.

A gentleman.

"Thank you," I say.

He is wearing a linen shirt, brightly colored shorts and an electric-blue pair of Converse. We follow the throng, many of whom yell greetings when they see Tug.

"Hey, Tug!"

"Oh, my gosh! It's so good to see you again!"

"Missed you, man!"

"You're a popular guy," I say as we walk.

"Just a familiar face," he says.

A humble guy.

The crowd begins to split off into many directions from the main road, some following paths that lead back into the woods.

"Where is everyone going?" I ask.

"There are different art studios situated around the Tall-madge Woods," he says. "A painting and drawing studio, a ceramics studio, an open-air glassblowing facility, a paper and book studio, works on paper studio, and an open-air metal sculpture studio. In fact, I think there is a blacksmithing demonstration tonight if you want to check it out."

"Sure," I say. "Game for anything. It's my first night out since…" I stop. "I can't remember anymore, but I think *Home Alone* was in theatres."

Tug laughs, and we turn right and head up a dirt path.

A variety of structures are tucked into the woods, some historic, some with classic Michigan cottage architecture, some with a Prairie influence. Some look like old cabins, some newer-styled cottages and studios.

"You know," Tug says. "You can rent these studios, too. Like if you needed a work space to design or sew again…an inspired office in the woods."

"That would be amazing," I say.

The metals studio is a spacious open-air facility, housing equipment for welding, jewelry-making, and metal fabrication. I hear a banging as we approach. A man and woman are taking turns hammering on a piece of fiery metal, sparks flying.

I am immediately taken back in time. I am standing with my mother at Silver Dollar City, an 1880s-style theme park in Branson, Missouri, not far from where I grew up. We used to go there nearly every summer when I was a kid. I loved the rides, especially Fire in the Hole, but my mother most enjoyed watching the resident craftsmen demonstrate heritage crafts. There were candle- and candy makers, potters, glassblowers, lye soap craftsmen—all in old-timey costumes—and blacksmiths just like these, demonstrating lost American crafts.

"This is art, Sutton," my mother used to say. "Our American tradition and heritage. It is taught, learned and then passed along to a new generation so that we may never forget the beauty of who we were and who we are."

And so I became my mother's apprentice. I learned to sew.

I learned the beauty—and value—of a button. I learned an American craft.

The blacksmiths stop to catch their breaths, faces blaring as red as the metal.

"You look like you're enjoying this," Tug says.

"I am."

"I'm glad. Ready for the auction? And more importantly, a glass of wine?"

I nod, and Tug takes me on a mini-tour of the grounds as we walk, telling me about the history of Ox-Bow.

"Living in Chicago, you know the Art Institute of Chicago?"

"Of course," I say.

Tug continues. "Well, Ox-Bow was founded at the turn of the century by two artists from there who became enamored by the natural, isolated beauty of Saugatuck-Douglas. It started as a respite for artists who needed to get out of the industrialized havoc of the city. It was akin to early prep schools: fresh air and unspoiled country land would do wonders for inspiration and education, body and mind. And it did. Students from all over the world come here, mostly in the summer, and take intensive classes from renowned artists. Some students are seeking degrees, others are professional artists looking to refine their talents or explore new areas, and some are new to the arts."

Tug stops and points around. The grounds are dotted with funky shacks and adorable cabins where students and artists live. "There's over a hundred acres of unspoiled land here. It is and has remained a sacred spot for artists to commune."

"It's sort of like *Dirty Dancing* meets Woodstock," I say, looking around. "Hippy chic. Plein air Montmarte."

Tug laughs. "Yes! You understand perfectly. But you haven't seen the most beautiful part yet."

We emerge from the woods, and I stop cold in my tracks.

"Whoa!" is all I can manage to say.

An expansive lawn—with a large painting studio on one end and huge tent filled with chairs on the other—sits in front of a lagoon. The summer sun is sparkling on the water, and ghostly birch stand guard. People in bright shorts and summer dresses walk a path along the water, admiring the lagoon. Some couples are perched in tree swings, gently swaying as they hold hands, some people wander along the dock that extends into the lagoon, and some study the art for sale nestled inside the tent.

"What is that?" I ask, pointing, squinting in the sun, reaching for my sunglasses from my purse.

"Mermaids," Tug says matter-of-factly. "And mermen."

I look again.

Young men and woman wearing sequined mermaid outfits—complete with bright blue wigs—are seated on the small sandy beach in front of the lagoon flipping their tails into the water, happily splashing passersby.

"Artists," Tug says. "Youth. It's why they love this area, and why we love them. They bring a sense of wonder and joy to our towns, and we need that more than ever these days."

I nod, feeling very calm and at peace. "I think I need that glass of wine now."

We head to a long, makeshift table. Galvanized buckets filled with ice and bottles of white wine, rosé and craft beer are stacked along it. A young man in an Ox-Bow T-shirt is pouring wine.

"Red or white?" he asks.

"White, please," I say.

"Same," Tug says.

We sip our wine and head to the lagoon. I watch the mermaids and mermen pose for photos, and then Tug and I watch turtles and frogs surface near the dock, waiting to be fed. A bell rings, and it echoes across the water, and I am again transported back in time.

"The auction is starting," Tug says. "We only have a few minutes to look at the work."

We hurry back up the hill to the tent, where the chairs are already filled with people buzzing about the auction. Tug and I do a quick walk inside the tent, surveying artwork that is hung from one side like a gallery wall as well as tables filled with ceramics and glassware.

There is a range of talent, from raw to emerging—artists still finding their voice—as well as stunning works by established artists.

"How much do these sell for?" I whisper to Tug.

"Depends," Tug says. "On how much someone loves a piece. And how much everyone has had to drink."

I laugh.

"I've purchased artwork here for under fifty dollars from artists who have gone on to have their works curated in some of the world's best galleries."

I take a cursory glance at the work one more time and then stop. There's a small painting hung from a hook on the side of the tent that I hadn't noticed before where a throng of people were gathered and chatting. It's an oil of a river; a man is standing in it, the water waist-high. The man is painted in black-and-white, as if it is a vintage photo. But the landscape around him is nearly three-dimensional, thick with oils and jarringly colorful. The current of the river is a purply-black, the waves seeming to leap off the canvas along with the pink-white clouds rolling overhead. The background of trees is green, but they loom over the man and the river as if they are keeping watch.

I step closer and study it carefully.

"You like this, don't you?" Tug asks.

I nod. The painting feels so familiar and so deeply resonant that I get goose bumps. Tug leans over to read about the work.

"Oh, of course," he says. "This is from one of our local artists who teaches here. His work is revered and beloved in Michigan. He likes to capture the natural beauty of our state while telling a story from the past."

"What story do you think he is telling with this painting?" I ask.

"The history of Ox-Bow," Tug says immediately. He turns and points back toward an historic, two-story building tucked amongst the trees I hadn't noticed previously.

"What is that?" I ask, turning. "It looks like a quaint, old inn you might find on Cape Cod."

"Good eye, Sutton," he says.

"Thank you."

"That's what the locals affectionately call Ox-Bow's 'Old Inn' today," Tug continues. "It started out over a century ago as the Riverside Hotel."

"Wow," I say. "Amazing."

"The original owners built a small house in the mid-1800s on what was then an ox-bow shaped bend in the Kalamazoo River that led to Lake Michigan."

"I get it. Ox-Bow," I say slowly. "See how quick I am?"

"Impressive," Tug says with a chuckle. "They began to realize the potential for shipping trade traffic that could run through here, so they added onto their home and converted it into a twenty-room hotel. It became a hub for those who worked on the ships. At the turn of the century, the towns' major industries began to decline, and the Kalamazoo River channel was straightened to flow into Lake Michigan, cutting off the hotel from its patrons and turning this channel into a lagoon."

People begin to move toward folding chairs under the tent.

We make our way toward two near the back, and Tug continues his story.

"To make money, the owners leased the hotel to a group of artists for the entire summer just as the art and leisure industry was taking over the area. The towns reinvented themselves as a Midwestern resort community, and the hotel remained as lodging for artists," Tug says. He gestures at the young artists gathered near the podium, eager to show their works. "It still does today, housing students, although it went through a major renovation a while back to add a new kitchen and dining room. But the inn and its rooms are still as rustic and charming as they always were. Usually, when these auctions end, people gather inside to talk, drink and share stories. I've always believed I can still hear the inn's ghosts—the sea captains and fishermen—whisper."

The bell rings, and the auction starts. A young woman—festooned in a crown—takes the microphone and begins to call out the items. When a piece of art sells for a hundred dollars, music blares and the entire Ox-Bow staff dances down the aisles. They do it again at every hundred-dollar level.

When the oil painting comes up for auction, I can't help but raise my hand.

"Fifty dollars to the young woman next to Tug!" she announces.

"Young woman? Flattery will get her everywhere," I whisper to Tug.

The bidding is fierce, and I feel compelled to raise my hand—even though I don't have a job or extra cash to spend—until it reaches two hundred dollars, and the staff dances yet again.

When the bidding restarts, the auctioneer looks over at me, but I shake my head, and the piece eventually sells for two hundred and seventy-five dollars.

"You okay?" Tug asks. "I told you sometimes the bidding gets fierce."

"I am," I say, hiding my disappointment. "It just spoke to me. I don't know why." I polish off my wine and whisper, "Is there a ladies' room nearby?"

Tug nods. "In the Old Inn. I'll walk you up there."

The inn is as charming as Tug said. A screened porch lines the front, and the house is filled with tiny rooms and staircases, a dollhouse come to life. There is a bathroom, barely big enough to turn around in, hidden away in the back of the inn. When I walk out, Tug shows me around the inn. The walls are filled with eclectic artwork resident artists have done over the years. It's akin to an old gallery you might wander into in another country, every inch of wall space covered, a mishmash of frames holding the pieces in place.

There is a wall of old photos in the dining room, from the early days of the inn. Black-and-white images of men on boats, men drinking whiskey in front of the fireplace, men standing in the river.

I hear Tug yell someone's name, and I turn toward him.

"I'll be right back," he says, and heads back to the lobby.

I start toward another room when a photo catches my eye. I stop—so suddenly I have to grab the wall, nearly knocking a framed picture off of it—and stare.

A group of men—workers in overalls—are sitting atop a mountain of mussel shells.

I lean in more closely.

"I'm back," Tug says.

I jump and turn toward him. "Sorry to startle you," he continues. "It looks like you just saw a ghost. Hope this helps."

From behind his back he produces the small oil painting.

"What?" I exclaim. "How?"

"I saw how much you liked it, so I bought it off the guy

who bid on it," he says. "I know him. He owes me. And now I owe him, but it's worth it. This is your first memory of Ox-Bow, and it should be a special one. Whenever you look at this from now on, you'll remember this night. You'll remember summer in Saugatuck-Douglas."

"Tug," I say. "This is too much. You shouldn't have. I don't like to owe anyone anything."

"You don't," he says. "It's my gift to you."

"I don't what to say."

"How about 'thank you'?" he says.

"Thank you," I say.

He hands me the painting and I study it more closely.

"Oh!" I exclaim. "I didn't notice this earlier. The man's face. His eyes. They're not eyes at all. They're actually buttons. Blue buttons that reflect the world around him."

"I thought that's why you loved it so much," Tug says. "You were speaking about irony earlier. Now, this...this is incredibly ironic, isn't it?"

The room goes off-kilter for a moment, and my mind is filled with flashes of images: this man's eyes; Ted's eyes; my teddy bear's eyes; the mountain of mussels; the clamshells; the photograph of the girl at the pavilion; the button card.

"Sutton?" Tug says, taking my arm. "Are you okay?"

I look at him and then around the Old Inn.

"I think the ghosts are whispering to me, too," I say.

I stand on Lakeshore Drive gasping for air.

Five-mile run. New Sutton.

I bend over to stretch. My lungs burn.

Old Sutton.

Running has never come easily to me.

I should clarify: running as exercise has never come easily. Running from things has.

I let too few people close to me. Learned behavior.

Have I run again? From work? Friends? A future?

Am I truly seeking answers? Or am I really just running all over again? Can any of us outrun our pasts? Or am I destined to be just like my mother?

There is a stitch in my side, and that is not a bad sewing pun. I stand, stretching toward the sky and then bend slightly left and right.

In volleyball, I hated wind sprints. I didn't like our run days. Perhaps I had no one to compete against except myself, and that was a game I had played my whole life.

Perhaps I just wanted the world to know I was just as good as they were. I could beat them at their own game.

I look over Lake Michigan. The sky is heavenly blue, not even a tendril of white to tarnish its beauty, but on the horizon, dark clouds are roiling. I think of all the times my mother let me prove to her I was all grown up, and I would make my own Cream of Wheat or Malt-O-Meal on the stove. I would get distracted by a cartoon on the TV and turn to find the water roiling, the pot overflowing, the stove a mess.

My mother would make me clean the stove until it was clean as a whistle.

"Not everything is as it appears to the eye," she would say. "You always have to keep watch."

I shake my head thinking of the last few days, of the last few years, and my walk turns into a jog until I'm safely back in the cottage. I shower, dress for a morning of sewing and reading, and start some coffee. I make some oatmeal and begin chopping fresh strawberries I picked up at the local farmer's market.

I loaded up on fresh asparagus, rhubarb and strawberries and suddenly laugh, remembering Abby—a total city girl—who asked once on a fall girls' weekend to Door County why there were no fresh, local strawberries available at the market.

"They're not in season, ma'am," the kindly woman had replied.

"But I can find them at the grocery store!" Abby argued.

My mouth waters thinking of all the wonderful fruit to come this summer: blueberries, raspberries, peaches, apples.

How long will I stay?

Where will I run next?

I stop and eye the reddish-pink rhubarb. It grew like crazy in the Ozarks before the summer heat and humidity set in, and my mother made the most incredible strawberry-rhubarb pies and coffee cakes from their bounty. I plan to make one as a surprise for Tug, who asked me to go to dinner with him this week.

I can't decide if he's moving too quickly, or if any type of forward momentum right now seems fast-paced.

What is too fast?

What is too slow?

How much time do any of us have?

And how do we want to spend it?

My whole life I just wanted to run from the small town where I grew up. In college, I ran to keep pace with people from different worlds than me, who seemed to have had every advantage. In my career, I wanted to prove that I could run the world. Pressure came with success. But so did great sacrifice and even greater compromise. Somehow, thanks to all that running, I found myself distanced from the person I believed I was destined to become.

But I think somewhere between college and the pandemic, I just got tired of being on the treadmill. Being alone and losing my mom made me recalibrate and re-center as well as re-prioritize my life. Maybe my mother always understood the things that mattered most, things that a great career, or more success and money could never provide.

Perhaps I realized that I was alive but not living, and it took my mother's life to remind me of that. Perhaps success can't be defined by what people think of you, but what you think of yourself when you're finally alone with your thoughts and staring at your own reflection.

In the living room, the sun reflects on a jar of buttons. A button may be worthless in our society today, but it was priceless to so many who had so little.

Maybe buttons were what made me see the light, I think. Maybe learning my entire past was a lie made me run toward a different light source. Because when I was totally and utterly alone, I was not only haunted by why my mother would so easily run and discard our family history, but also by why I could so easily trade in everything I believed in to create clothing that no longer had any semblance of history either.

So Douglas ended up in Douglas.

I hear a burbling and look up too late to see my oatmeal boiling over and onto the stove.

"Nooo!" I wail.

I turn off the stove and move the pot to another burner.

My mother's words echo in my head.

"Is something burning?"

I yelp.

When I turn, Bonnie Lyons is standing in the kitchen doorway.

"Oh, my gosh," I say. "You startled me. How did you get in here?"

She dangles a key in the air.

"Can I help you with something?" I ask.

"I still officially own this cottage," she says, using the key to make quote marks around the word "officially."

"I don't understand. Mick and Sarah own this cottage now."

"The young couple buying this place..."

"Mick and Sarah," I repeat.

"Yes," she says in her clipped tone. "I may have sold this cottage, but I'm their bank. They refinanced through *me*, and I gave them a wonderful deal, with a wonderful rate, after the death of Mick's father. But there were conditions for my kindness. And one of them is I like to check on visitors staying on my property."

I suddenly feel more winded than I did after my run.

"Did I do something wrong?" I ask. "I'm sorry if we got off on the wrong foot the other day. I'm going through a lot of changes. I was actually just settling in here."

"Good," she says. "I'm happy to hear that."

She takes a small but rather confident step toward me.

"You know, our little towns are changing rapidly right now. So many people from the city are moving here in droves. They can live and work anywhere these days. The virus is driving them from the cities they once so loved. They're discovering what I've always known: this is the most beautiful spot in the world. The secret is out." Mrs. Lyons pauses. "I just want to ensure the wrong element hasn't moved in."

I feel as if I should be offended, but I've already overheard so many locals talk about how their beloved towns are being overrun, as if we're locusts. Same thing happened in Chicago, when rents skyrocketed and so many were forced to uproot.

"Lots of changes the last few years," I say as sweetly as I can. "But I can assure you I'm not the 'wrong element.'" I can't help but laugh. "Believe me."

"Well, I'm sorry to just pop in, but you can imagine the stories I've heard of renters tearing up a place, or having loud parties at all hours of the night." She looks at me very intently. "I may be very social in the community, but, believe me, I'm a very private person."

"I understand and respect that, Mrs. Lyons," I say. "I'm the same way."

"Well," she says, her shoulders relaxing, her entire demeanor changing.

"This cottage used to be a one-room schoolhouse," she says. "Did you know that?"

I nod.

"If you can believe it, this was still a schoolhouse when my husband and I bought this so many years ago."

"I heard about his passing," I say. "I'm so sorry. I lost my mother to Covid two years ago. It's been a nightmare for me."

Bonnie looks away. "Thank you," she says, so quietly I can barely hear her even though she's just feet away. "You know, I can still hear the sound of children's laughter in here. There was nothing like it." She turns and gestures at the space with her arm. "We let it remain the schoolhouse until the township built a big, new school. It felt like we had a large family next to us."

"Did you have children?" I ask.

She doesn't answer my question.

"This used to be all open. One big classroom. Desks lined up over there. Chalkboard on that wall. This kitchen was the lunchroom with little tables everywhere."

Her face breaks into what the most optimistic of souls might call a smile, a slight upturn of the mouth, a barely perceptible softening of the eyes.

"Speaking of which..." She takes another step, this time into the kitchen, and looks around. "We have a mess, it seems."

"My oatmeal boiled over while I was chopping fruit. I plan to clean it up."

"You always have to keep watch," she admonishes.

My heart skips a beat.

"I apologize for intruding," she says. "And please, call me Bonnie."

My heart softens.

She's just a lonely old woman trying to protect her turf. I get it. I'd be the exact same way.

"I actually came here for a reason," she says. "I came bearing gifts."

"Gifts?" I repeat.

"Lauralei?" she calls.

I hear the screened door squeak. Bonnie moves back into the living, and I follow, staying a good distance behind her.

A woman about Bonnie's age who is dressed as if she were born at the turn of the century—the last one—shuffles in carrying a box that seems to weigh as much as she does. She is wearing a maid's outfit, like one you might see in an old-time movie. She sets the box on the living room table, turns and leaves without saying a word, her shoes squeaking in the silence. She returns a moment later with another box, and then another.

"Anything else, ma'am?" she asks Bonnie, her head bowed.

I am feeling a bit creeped out by this whole situation.

"No, thank you, Lauralei. You can start lunch now."

"Yes, ma'am," she says, exiting, her feet shuffling, squeak by squeak, across the wood floor.

Bonnie turns. "As you so aptly said, I think we got off on the wrong foot the other day. I meant no ill will toward your mother. I feel very badly about that. Consider this my apology."

"Mrs. Lyons—" I start.

"Bonnie."

"Bonnie," I say. "I don't know what to say. I felt as if I offended you, too, the other day, and that certainly wasn't my intention. I've just been going through a lot."

"None taken. Now, please." She gestures at the boxes on the table.

"I'm sorry, but my mother taught me never to owe anyone anything."

Bonnie eyes me up and down, before glancing around the room. She strides—in her heels, mind you—toward a small entryway table by the door. There is a small piece of blue pottery—shaped like a narrow dish—sitting atop it where I've placed my keys and spare change from my pocket. She reaches in and grabs a penny.

"Now we're even," she says.

I smile and nod. I take a seat on the couch and open a box. It is filled with jars, tins and boxes of buttons. I open another, and another, all filled with buttons.

"From my *yard sale*," Bonnie says with a wink. "I wanted you to have them." Her eyes shift toward the Singer in the corner of the room.

"But why?" I ask, genuinely perplexed.

"I know a lot about you already. The internet is a fascinating place. No secrets there."

I stare at her. Her eyes laser on me again.

"Sutton's Buttons," she continues. "We have a lot in common, I think. United by buttons. Who would've thought the two of us would end up next to each other? It's as if it were meant to be."

Her eyes move to the Singer again.

"I can tell you appreciate the old ways," Bonnie says. "So rare these days. Especially in young people." The breeze sings through the screened door and, in the distance, there is a rumble of thunder.

"I'm having a few friends over for lunch," she says. "I just love to watch the storms roll in off the lake. It's so exciting to witness the power of nature. There are a few things over which I..." She emits a tiny chuckle. "...*we* have no control. And I find that remarkable. Well, I best be going. I need to get ready."

You already look perfect, I think.

"Speaking of which..."

She pulls an envelope from the small purse over her shoulder and hands it to me.

"I will see you soon, Sutton," she says. "Enjoy the buttons." Bonnie walks toward the door and turns at the last moment. "And the storm."

She walks out, the door banging behind her, and I stand for a few seconds, unable to move a muscle.

"What just happened?" I ask out loud.

I open the envelope. It's an invitation on very expensive, very thick card stock. There is tissue paper atop it, tied with little silk bows at the top and bottom.

TEA FOR TWO!

You Are Cordially Invited to Join Bonnie Lyons at Dandelion Cottage for Tea & Goodies on Wednesday, July 1, at Noon (Sharp!). RSVP by Saturday, June 27 Lauralei Symons at 269-214-0101

Is she being kind? Intrusive? Sweet? Nosy? Or is she just lonely?

I head to the kitchen and begin to clean the stove.

Memories of my mother, stooped over the old stove in the cabin, fill my head, and I scrub harder and harder, trying to wipe away the dried oatmeal along with my memories.

Over my cleaning, thunder booms. The storm is drawing closer.

I set down my rag and walk out to the front porch.

There are a few things over which we have no control.

A raindrop hits my head and trickles down my face. The dune grass sweeps this way and that in the wind.

I head back inside. The table is filled with buttons.

I pour a cup of coffee and take a seat on the couch. I begin to sort Bonnie's buttons until I feel like I can breathe again.

7

DRAPE
The fluid way fabric hangs in a garment.

It is a beautiful late-June morning, not a breath of wind, so still you can hear God sigh. Shafts of light are scattered around the cottage on the walls and floors. The cottage's dormers and oversized windows allow the light to be displayed in extraordinarily beautiful ways, as if I've wandered into a church.

One of my mother's favorite day trips was to the wondrous Thorncrown Chapel outside of Eureka Springs, Arkansas. Nestled in the middle of the woods, Thorncrown rose forty-eight feet into the Ozarks sky. The chapel sits atop tons of native stone and is constructed of wooden beams that crisscross like lattice toward heaven, just enough to suspend the 425 windows and six thousand square feet of glass so that you feel as if you are seated in the woods, at one with nature. The chapel is both simple and majestic.

"Like God Himself," my mother used to whisper.

I step into the light, shut my eyes and let it warm my face. I say a prayer.

"Mom, are you there? I really need you right now. I just feel so lost. Give me a sign to let me know you're okay." I chuckle, and a small, sad laugh echoes in the cottage. "Okay, okay, you got me. The woman who doesn't believe in signs needs a sign. Yes, I'm lying. I know you're okay. I need to know I'm okay. I love you. Amen."

When I open my eyes, dust motes drift in the shafts of light. "Mom?" I ask.

My mother used to say dust motes existed to show us our place in the world. I didn't really understand what she meant until I got older, but I finally figured out her parable. We are nothing really, in the big scheme of things, just little motes floating around the universe. Most of us are invisible, un-noticed, until the light shines upon us, into us, through us, and makes us bright.

Finally visible.

My mother hid her light for reasons I'm trying to under-stand. I'm trying desperately to rediscover mine.

There was nothing more magical growing up than an Ozarks summer filled with lightning bugs. Some kids used to capture them in Mason jars, but I thought that was just downright cruel. I used to lay back on the edge of the bluff, my feet dangling over the side, and watch the lightning bugs. Some, I realized, flashed only once, while some were like the stoplight on the way into town, blinking constantly.

But they had such short lives, just a few weeks in the sum-mer, so why—I always thought—shouldn't we flash our light like crazy while we had the chance?

The light shifts. If there's one thing I've already learned about Michigan, it's that the light here is magical and ever-changing. It is a soft light, a magical light, the type of light in which most women dream of being photographed.

It is a golden light that burnishes, not the harsh sun of the Ozarks that burns. Michigan light embellishes every detail: the gold of the sand, the white of the sailboat, the green of the pine, the pink of the peony, the ruby of the hummingbird's throat, the cerulean of the sky and the turquoise of the water.

The light shifts again, casting a quadrant across the living room table still filled with Bonnie's boxes.

The buttons glimmer.

I know what I must do.

Make the invisible visible.

I am adorned by a ball cap, channeling my inner Nancy Drew with a touch of Tug.

"Thank you," I say to the clerk in the adorable little T-shirt shop. I turn and look in the mirror, checking out my new cap that reads DOUGLAS in old-school lettering over my head.

"Looks good on you," she says.

"It should," I say. "It's my name."

The clerk laughs. "That's crazy," she says.

"Tell me about it," I say.

Her name is Molli, and she's all spun sugar and sunshine. She's transformed the name tag on her T-shirt from standard issue into homemade happiness. She's put masking tape over the *o* and the *i* in her name and instead drawn a happy face and turned the dot over the *i* into a heart.

She catches me staring.

"Sometimes you have to *make* it a good day, right?" she says. She looks around and whispers, "Some folks are just downright mean on vacation. I'll never understand why."

"They're not happy in life."

"Then make yourself happy!"

I smile, unsure as to whether her demeanor is purely youthful optimism or a necessary reminder.

"You're right," I say. "Hey, can I ask you a question?"

"Shoot!" Molli says, walking from behind the register to straighten T-shirts that customers have rifled through.

"I'm on sort of a hunt for my family."

"Ooh, like 23andMe?" she asks excitedly.

"Sort of," I say. I explain to her what I've found and what I know. "Any thoughts on where to start looking?"

She leans toward me and puts her hand around her mouth. "This town is filled with history and secrets. You know resort towns are like soap operas, right? Everyone knows something about someone who did something to someone else. The trouble is trying to find out what's real and what isn't."

"Where would you start if you wanted to find out some..." I stop searching for the right turn of phrase. "...soap opera secrets."

"Well, I'd either go to the town library or the town's encyclopedia."

I look at her, confused. "I'm not following."

"New library is located on Center Street as you head into Douglas," she says. "And you'll find the town's encyclopedia located either on the bench in front of Uncommon Grounds, the coffee house, with his dog, or on his boat parked in front of Coral Gables. Name's Mike McKay, but everyone in town calls him Captain Lucky."

"Oh, my gosh, I've already met him."

"Everyone has."

"Does everyone in this town have a nickname?"

She nods and laughs. "Everybody's trying to change their past, aren't they?"

"You're a wise old soul for such a young woman," I say.

"Amazing what you learn just by keeping your ears open and your mouth shut."

I bike into Saugatuck and slow as I pass Uncommon Grounds. The bench is filled with a group of teenage girls sipping iced coffee, making duck lips and taking selfies. I bike toward the big restaurant and bar on the river that resembles a giant, old three-story Dutch Colonial home with a massive front porch. The parking lot abuts a boardwalk that parallels the Kalamazoo River that runs into Lake Michigan and spans much of Saugatuck. Boats of every size are tucked into docks along the boardwalk.

I step off my bike and push it along the wooden walkway, until I see a happy Lab playfully pawing at an outstretched arm scrubbing the side of a big whaling boat. I grab my little bag from the bike's basket.

I slow and then stop in my tracks when I see the boat's name: *Knot Hers*.

"Figured I see you again."

I look up from the boardwalk.

"Permission to come aboard?" I ask.

He waves me onto his dock. I kick my stand, leave the bike and then hop on board in the back.

"Welcome aboard *Knot Hers*!" he says with a big grin.

"So I gotta ask…"

"The ex got everything but this," he says.

"You live here?"

"Until it gets cold, then I head south."

"Snowbird," I say.

"Smart bird," he says. "So what you brings you here? Guessin' you're lookin' for some information, and someone told you about me?"

"You guess right," I say.

"Everyone eventually comes to Captain Lucky. Sit!"

I take a seat on the leather bench seat in the back.

"I know you told me how you got your nickname," I say, "but is there more to the story?"

"There's always more to the story, isn't there? Let's see… Five divorces. Sold a lot of land cheap in the '80s to developers that's now worth millions. Bought an old duck boat that sprung a leak, thankfully when no one was onboard. Got struck by lightning on the golf course once. But I do have six kids and a dozen grands who love this town, the water and their old man, so I must've done something right. And I got the best darn dog in the world, too. Come say hi, Lucky."

The happy Lab trots over and sticks his face in my lap. I lean down, and he gives me a million kisses.

"Really did get lucky with this one," he says. "So, what can I do you for..."

"Sutton Douglas."

"Beautiful name."

"Thank you."

I take Captain Lucky through everything I've uncovered, pulling from my bag my mother's letter, the Douglas postcard, the picture of Ted, the picture of the woman at the pavilion, a few of the blue pearl buttons that look exactly the same.

He looks at me. "You're like the daughter of Houdini and Agatha Christie," Captain Lucky says with a laugh.

"Women can fit an elephant into any-sized purse, along with a lipstick, mascara, cell phone, keys, a credit card and pepper spray. And I would've gone with Angela Lansbury over Agatha Christie, but I'll take it."

He laughs even harder and then takes each picture and studies it for the longest time.

"One of my wives used to volunteer at the Historical Society," he says. "The Dandy Button Company used to be located..."

"I know," I say, stopping him cold.

"Okey-dokey then," he says. "This postcard is old and the real deal. Sent from here. You don't see many vintage ones like this any longer. This man here..."

"Ted," I say. "My dad. I think."

"Ted," he continues, "looks to have been a clammer."

"How do you know?"

"Just look at the photo." He hands it back to me and continues. "So many men around these parts worked as clammers from the turn of the century until the 1960s. They dragged the river bottom with hooks to get the clams to latch on. That's where the beautiful pearl buttons were born. Hard work. Long days. Little pay. A lot of these men died young."

"He did," I say, my voice suddenly quaking. "But apparently from heartbreak."

"I'm so sorry, Sutton," he says. "And I know the place in this picture like the back of my hand," he continues, flapping the photo of the woman with her back turned in it. "She's at the Big Pavilion."

"Which is what?"

"The Big Pavilion." He points just up the river where a restaurant now stands. "The Big Pavilion was one of the largest dance halls in the Midwest. Attracted bands and visitors from around the country. My parents and grandparents used to go there all the time. It opened in 1909, just when the pearl button business was booming. It was three stories high and had a 7,000-square-foot dance floor. It was painted red and was the largest wooden building in the country at the time. It even had its own power station, restaurants, movie theatre and roller rink, as well as 10,000 outdoor lights that could be seen halfway across Lake Michigan at night."

"Wow," I say.

"It held grand balls, and dance and beauty contests," Captain Lucky continues.

"What happened to it?" I say, looking up the water again.

"It burned down. Huge fire. All that history and all those memories gone in the blink of an eye."

The word *fire* blazes in my head. I think of my mother's lie. *All that history and all those memories gone in the blink of an eye.*

"Are you okay?" he asks me.

I shake my head. "Should I lie?"

"Won't do you any good." He holds the button up to the sun and then looks at the picture one last time before handing it back to me.

"So, let me think here... I don't know a Ted Douglas," he says. "And I don't know, actually, any Douglases around Douglas. But we're assuming that's your mother's married name."

This revelation hits me like a brick. "But her driver's license said Douglas," I say.

"Could've changed it. Lord knows my ex-wives have changed names enough. It was easier to get away with things like that back in the day. Who knows?" He scans the water and pets his dog. "But I do know this: the Lyons family were the kings of this town for a very long time. They ran one of the largest businesses in the US. Was one of Michigan's biggest employers. Lots of history there. Lots of money. Lots of secrets. You can head to the library to find out about it, or just search on your cell. Guessin' you've already done that, though."

I nod.

He continues. "And ol' Button Bonnie is the queen of the town to this day. Not someone you just strike up a conversation with, though. She lives in a big, yellow cottage on the lakeshore. Can't miss it."

"I'm actually renting the cottage behind hers," I say.

"Well, aren't you the lucky one?" he says. "I'd start with her then. Locals say Bonnie controls when the sun sets, so she may know a lot about what you're asking. But you may have to be at her beck and call to get her to relax. Not someone you just sit in front of a bonfire with and split a six-pack, get my drift?"

If not a six-pack, I think, *then maybe a cup of tea.*

★ ★ ★

"You bake, too?" Tug asks, looking impressed. He comes around from behind the shop counter and greets with me a big smile and even bigger hug. "You're quite the Barefoot Contessa."

"And you're quite the Little Leaguer," I say, pulling the strawberry-rhubarb pie back from his hands.

He looks at me.

"You're wearing a ball cap to dinner?" I ask. "Really? Are you eight?"

Tug looks at me, his hazel eyes surprised.

I started my walk into Douglas on this beautiful summer evening with gift in hand, feeling as high as the colorful kites that kids were flying on the beach. I felt as if I not only discovered a small lead—tea and crumpets, er, make that tea and questions with a woman I'd just happened to rent a cottage behind—but also my first date in years. I even skipped—*skipped!*—like a schoolgirl who'd just been asked to prom by the boy she liked.

But the more I walked, the more my mind began to play tricks on me.

What am I doing here?

Why am I trying to read so much into a few blue buttons?

There must've been a reason my mom wanted the past to remain in the past, why she burned her memories to the ground like the Big Pavilion.

There were hundreds of buttons in the boxes Bonnie gave me. In fact, I had ended up making piles of buttons, divided by color, all of which looked the same. My own line, Sutton's Buttons, used the exact same color and style of button—thousands and thousands of the exact same one—on blouses, sweaters and dresses. What should I read into that?

Nothing.

I began to think about Bonnie Lyons' invitation to tea, and my mind played even more tricks. How do I broach my family's past with a stranger? She's being kind. I'm now the one being intrusive and nosy. This is her town, not mine. Maybe I am a locust.

As I neared Tug's shop, I could hear my own voice, the one that sounded just like the one the bridge ladies in the Ozarks used when they discussed—*oh, they never "gossiped," they "discussed"*—a woman outside their social circle who was dating a well-established man.

"Why do you think a man like that would court such a woman?" they asked, each word cloaked with a husky "tsk-tsk."

Why? I asked myself as I walked to see Tug. *Why would a man like him be interested in a woman like me?*

I'd always been confident in my business decisions. I've been a successful entrepreneur, had successful, wonderful relationships with a few close friends and my mother, but men? Not so much.

Every time I started to get close to a man, this question reared its head: *Why would a man like this be interested in me?*

I knew it was because I'd never really put myself out there. I'd kept myself as guarded as my mother. Maybe, like her, I just didn't want to get hurt.

By the time I reached Tug's shop, I was a mental mess.

"You're right," Tug says. "You look so beautiful tonight, and I'm acting like an adolescent. My cap has always been my signature, but now I see it's probably been more of a crutch. But for you..."

He raises his arm to remove the Northwestern cap. Everything begins to move in slow motion. Even my reactions.

Oh, no! No! No! He's going to be bald. Head like an egg. Or worse! That ring of hair that makes him look like a creepy used car salesman. Or...or...a comb-over. One piece of nasty hair that looks like a shag carpet remnant that he's pulled and slicked down over his noggin.

My heart drops as his hand is now on top of his cap.

Or, worse, one endless wet noodle of spaghetti he's let grow the length of a garden hose that he's twirled and twirled atop his head like a soft-serve ice cream cone.

His cap comes off, and I brace myself, actually turning my head and wincing.

"Voila!" he says.

He not only has a full head of hair, he has a full head of the most beautiful, golden, wavy locks I've ever seen. Like Matthew McConaughey but even more sunlit.

Tug smiles, his dimples deepening.

"Not what you were expecting, was it?" he asks. "I have the hair of..." He stops and puts his hand on his chin, as if pondering the exact right words to use. "...an eight-year-old boy."

I shake my head and laugh.

"I could spend hours on my hair and it would never look like that," I say.

He smiles.

"I am so, so sorry," I say.

"For what?" he asks, as though he doesn't have a clue.

"Oh, I don't know," I say. "For being so short? For sounding like a monster? One you should run from..." I hesitate. "It's just that I've just been in a weird place for a while. The pandemic messed with my mind. My mother's death made it even worse. Now, I'm just drifting on the lake, searching for answers and a new future."

Tug nods. "It messed with a lot of folks."

"This has nothing to do with you," I continue. "I'm just... learning to live again."

"Apology accepted," he says. "I'm a nice guy. I know it

sounds like a lie when a guy says that about himself, but in this case it's true."

The bell on the front door of his store chimes, and he waves at a couple entering.

"Let me know if you need anything," he calls, before looking at me. "You know, I had a lot of bad habits ingrained in me from a young age playing baseball. Like smushing the bug, for instance."

"Smushing the what?"

"Smushing the bug," Tug says with a smile. "I was taught at an early age playing baseball to turn my back foot—or smush a bug—in order to create more bat speed and power in my swing. I was the home run king as a kid. But it was the worst habit ever. As I aged, the pitching improved drastically, and it became nearly impossible for me to hit outside pitches with the sweet spot of the bat with my back foot constantly moving. My balance was off, and my home runs turned to pop outs. I had to relearn my swing by keeping my back foot planted on the ground. I pretended it was nailed to the dirt. It took me years to perfect, but I finally did. But I think those flaws I held on to for so long held me back from being my best."

Tug continues. "Maybe you need to stop mentally smushing the bug. Stay grounded. Stop flailing."

Emotions suddenly overwhelm me, and my heart rises into my throat. I take a deep breath. "And thank you for saying that. I'm trying. It's hard."

"I know," he says. "Now, do I get that pie or not?"

I laugh and hand him the pie.

"Thank you, m'lady," he says, doffing the cap in his hand and bending at the waist as if he were in *Bridgerton.* He sets the pie on the counter and lifts the tinfoil.

"You don't know how much I just want to devour this," he says.

"Just like a little boy, huh?"

The couple in the store call, "What's the story behind this vase?" and Tug looks around. "Sorry," he says to me. "I sent Becky out on a delivery with a very chatty client. If she's not back soon, I'll just put the Closed sign in the door. Back in a sec."

"All good," I say. "You know how much I love looking around your store."

He smiles and jogs over to the couple.

"Where are you two visiting from?" he asks, his voice chipper.

I pretend to look at some vintage Fiesta dinnerware, holding up an aqua teacup as if to inspect it. But I'm actually watching Tug.

Is he a nice guy?

He sure seems like it.

Can I smush the bugs in my mind?

I sure hope so.

There are those people in this world to whom things just seem to come naturally and easily. They can talk to anyone as if they are dear friends they've known their entire lives. They can walk into parties and act as if they belong there, easily mingling amongst all the guests. They walk into a new job, day one, and have a command of their duties and respect of their coworkers. Their walk through life seems as simple as a stroll through a garden.

I am the daughter of my mother. I am her shadow. And that means living in a spotlight—something I've always desired—has never come easily. I remember taking one of those personality tests in a magazine with my mother. She was an introvert, all the way. I was an extroverted introvert. My energy came from within rather than from others, but I was an "outgoing" introvert, and that self-diagnosis seemed to unnerve my mother at the time.

"You'll only end up getting hurt being around others," she warned. "Better to stick to yourself."

My talent and internal drive pushed me to where I am now. *Or where I was.*

But it took every ounce of my being to gear up for interviews, to chat informally with people I didn't know, to lead a team. I lead by deed and example, plus loads of kindness, but not glad-handing and superfluous words.

I've met many artists and designers at parties over the years. Our work sustains and fulfills us. It gives us meaning and joy. But selling our work, getting out in front of the public, being *exposed*, was not only something that never came easily but it also exhausted us.

Tug is not like that at all.

I could say that it was because he was on a team, but I was, too. I could say that it was because he is a man, but that is not true.

My mother isolated me, and I feel as if I'm still crawling toward the light.

"I have a full set of those Fiesta dishes," Tug says.

I jump out of my skin and nearly drop the teacup.

"Jumpy much?"

"Sorry," I say. "Lost in thought. My mom used to love these dishes."

"Look at how much a full set in perfect condition costs now," Tug says. He shows me the card with the price.

"We used to buy these for a quarter," I say.

"Well, bring them to me, and we can make a fortune."

The bell jingles on the door, and a big smile breaks across Tug's face. "Becky!"

A girl who looks as if she just got her driver's permit—all dewy skin and shining eyes—comes over. "What up, boss?"

Tug walks Becky over to the couple. "Do you mind ringing up these lovely folks and helping them out with their purchases? I have dinner reservations at seven thirty."

Becky looks over at me. I can see her mouth, "A date?" and then nudge Tug in the side with her elbow.

A date, I think, the reality setting in. This *is* a date. Filled with small talk and questions about my past and maybe a first kiss and...

"Smush those bugs, Sutton," I say.

"Did you say something?" Tug asks.

"Just talking to myself," I say.

"Ready?"

I nod.

"See you tomorrow, Becky," Tug calls, opening the door for me.

"I can't wait to hear *all* about it," Becky says, her voice filled with innuendo.

It is still light, still warm. It is a perfect summer night.

"Where are we going?" I ask, as we cross the street. "Is it far?"

"We're here!" Tug says with a laugh. "Long commute."

"Long line," I say, looking at the throng of people waiting outside.

Tug winks. "I have reservations," he says. "And I know the owner. We played ball together."

I look at the pretty sign on the side of the building.

"The Bayou?" I ask.

Tug turns and opens his arms.

I follow his gaze. The sun is setting across a beautiful bayou down a hill from the restaurant. Kayakers and boats seem to be floating atop melting gold. In the distance, the marsh is abloom with hibiscus and rose mallow.

"How did I not notice this when I was biking?"

"Could've been the helmet," Tug says with a wink. "It likely occluded your vision, but it certainly protected you." He stops. "From asteroids. And falling comets."

"You'll pay for that," I say, hitting him on the shoulder.

Outdoor seating wraps around the front and side of the restaurant, and the air is filled with wonderful smells.

Tug opens the door. The restaurant is packed.

A long bar area occupies one side of the room, and a few tables sit opposite it. A doorway to the left leads to another dining room, and one in the back opens to more tables and an outdoor garden patio.

People are jammed together drinking wine and cocktails, celebrating summer and a return to life.

I need this to be the summer of Sutton, I think. *The summer I've never had.*

"You okay?" Tug asks.

I nod. "Even better after a cocktail."

"Tug!"

All at once, the entire room seems to be shouting Tug's name.

Men walk over and shake his hand. People "cheers" at the bar. Women wave.

"It's like *Cheers*," I say.

"Small town," Tug says, his face turning a touch red from the attention.

I nod, and he touches my shoulder. Tug walks toward the hostess who is perched behind a small stand, a cell in one hand, a pencil in the other, a pad of paper before her.

"Mary," Tug says fondly to the older woman with glasses

perched on the end of her nose, who is somehow managing to remain calm in a sea of chaos.

"Tug," she says, coming from behind her stand to give him a big hug.

"Great to see you! I had reservations at seven thirty. Number 123."

"As if you need them," she says. Mary returns and looks at her pad. "Your table will be ready in a few minutes. Is the old side okay?"

"Perfect," Tug says. "Thank you."

He turns to walk away, but Mary calls after him, "Where's your cap?"

"Decided not to wear it tonight."

Mary looks toward me and gives me a very big thumbs-up.

"Who wears a ball cap with hair like that?" she says, shaking her head at me.

"I know, right?" I say with a smile.

"You have a fan," he says. "I'm outnumbered already."

"We're just jealous of your hair," I say. "Women would never cover up hair like that. Do you know how long it took me to make my hair look as if I didn't just walk out of a rain forest?"

He laughs.

"What's 123 mean?" I ask. "And what's the old side? Is this code in Douglas, Michigan?"

Tug leans toward me, looking around, and whispers, "All the old-timers and locals have a secret number they give to Mary. It lets us 'bypass' some of the traffic."

"Very sneaky," I whisper. "Glad you picked a number no one else would ever think of."

He laughs. "It's the only one I can remember."

"And old side?" I ask, still in a whisper.

"Tug?" Mary calls. "Your table is ready."

People who are waiting audibly groan.

"You'll see," he says, gesturing for me to follow Mary.

We head past the bar and into another room, and I feel as if I've been swept back into another era. The room is filled with small tables draped with white tablecloths and then topped with butcher paper. One entire wall is lined with big windows that are propped open, pretty flowers from the window boxes peeking their colorful heads inside. The other wall is original art deco design and lighting, with curved shelves filled with vintage green dishware, from jade glasses to Depression-era dishes.

We are seated in a booth next to a window.

"I feel like I'm sitting at the counter of the old Woolworth sin the town where I grew up," I say, sliding in across from Tug. "My mom and I used to go there for lunch all the time after we shopped on the square. It's uncanny."

"I'm glad you like it," Tug says. "I helped them decorate it."

"Impressive," I say. "It's lovely."

"Thank you. This side of the restaurant was once an old diner, as you can tell. Jeff is the owner, and his mother used to work at this diner when she was a girl. She continued to work here after she got divorced. Her ex was terrible to her and her kids. But she never gave up. She knew she had to support her family, and her kids always came first. For decades, she served up pot-roast sandwiches to the men who worked construction or the fishermen who pulled salmon from the lake. Sunup to sundown she worked, and Jeff's dream was to buy this place and turn it into an upscale restaurant where his mother never had to work another day in her life. He attended the renowned Culinary Institute of America at Hyde Park, worked at restaurants in New York and Chicago, and eventually returned here and bought the diner and turned it into The Bayou. It's been a hit since day one. Great food, great drinks, great service, great atmosphere mean a great success."

"That is such a lovely story," I say. "What mothers sacrifice for their children…" I continue, my voice trembling. "…to have better lives. I…we…take it for granted too often. I'm sorry. I don't know what came over me."

"No need to apologize," Tug says. "And you're right. What our parents and grandparents sacrificed for us to have better lives should never be overlooked or forgotten."

"And she never had to work another day in her life," I say. "I wish I could have given that to my mother."

Tug looks at me as a young man delivers two glasses of water in front of us.

"Mary is Jeff's mother," Tug says with a straight face.

"Hostess Mary?" I ask.

Tug's stoic façade fades into a big laugh. He nods. "She still works every day. And pretty much runs the show."

"It's hard to change who we are, isn't it?" I ask. "It's pre-destined."

"I wouldn't say predestined, but it's difficult to change over-night when a lifetime of history is already ingrained inside each of us."

"How did you get to be such a wise man?" I ask.

"I thought you were going to say wiseass for a second," Tug says with a chuckle. "Actually, I was the fourth wise man. Shecky. He never got as much press."

I burst out laughing just as the waiter approaches.

"You have a way with people, Tug," the waiter says. He looks at me. "I'm Michael. I'll be taking care of you this eve-ning. And it sure looks like you'll need it."

I laugh again. "I'm Sutton. It's nice to meet you."

"A glass of wine or a cocktail to start things off?" Michael asks.

"Yes," I say too quickly.

Michael laughs. "I hear that reaction a lot when Tug brings a guest here."

"You'll pay for that," Tug says.

"Speaking of which," Michael whispers conspiratorially to me, "he sticks his guests with the check. Make him pay."

"I see a lot of people drinking Cosmos," I say.

"One of our signature drinks," Michael says.

"I'll have one then, thank you," I say.

"Starting strong right out of the gate," Tug says. "I'll have a glass of the Côtes du Rhône."

Michael presents two menus. "I'll be back in a moment with your cocktails. Take all the time you need to peruse the menu. Enjoy this beautiful evening."

I look out the window and notice we're sitting across from a baseball field.

"Really?" I ask, my eyes growing wide. "Did you plan this? Is this a way to impress me?"

Tug laughs. "No, I swear." He looks out the window at the little diamond. Kids are running around the bases, yelling in glee, as their parents watch. "Douglas fields a vintage baseball team called the Douglas Dutchers. The game is played circa 1800s with original baseball rules: we don't wear gloves, you're out if you catch a ball on one bounce, no stealing…"

"*We?*" I interrupt.

Tug smiles. "I play for the Dutchers. It's old-fashioned fun, it promotes historical education for the community, it allows us to raise funds for Beery Field to keep it going for a lot of community events. Games have been played on that field since 1860." Tug tilts his hazel eyes at me, and in the light from the window with the flowers reflected in them, they are a kaleidoscope of color, blue, green, gold. "Now I just play baseball for me. I had to make the game fun for me again. It wasn't. I felt like I'd failed when I didn't make the majors, failed not only myself but also my father. I walked over here one summer day years ago, and the stands were packed, and the guys were laughing. I watched an entire game, and it dawned on me that they were playing the game for the same reason I used to play as a kid: just to have fun. It may sound silly, but it changed me. It changed the way I looked at life. That's when I started to focus on doing things in my life that brought me joy. It's a big reason I started One Man's Trash Is Another Man's Treasure. It's a big reason why I'm able to…" He hesitates and looks out the window. "…go on after my sister. She was so filled with joy. I want to honor that."

"What? Tug! No. I'm so, so sorry."

Tug continues to look out the window of the restaurant for the longest time, as if searching the baseball diamond for a coach to shoot him a sign as to whether he should go on or stop. He finally turns his gaze on me.

"My sister, Sue, was a frontline worker, a nurse who volunteered to go to New York City at the start of the pandemic." Tug stops. "Sue died at the very beginning. She was young, the picture of health." He stops to gather himself. "I'm sorry. It's still so raw, just like your mother. Sue was fearless. She was kind. She put everyone ahead of herself. I went into a hole after she died, and it's taken me a long time to crawl back out of it. I nearly lost this business. But Sue's life taught me that sometimes it's best to just jump into something rather than think about or process it too much. Otherwise, you don't end up doing it. It's become second nature to play it safe right now. And if you're a cautious person to begin with, well…"

Is he reading my soul?

"I sort of feel like we were meant to be," he continues. "Tragedy and the pandemic forced us to reassess, and maybe that's not only a necessary thing but a wonderful one as well. We now understand how precious and limited time is, so why not do everything in our power to be happy."

Tug grows silent and turns his head.

Is he wiping away a tear?

I reach and take his hand. I can feel his pulse thump. We sit in silence and simply look at one another.

"Your drinks," Michael says, appearing at the table.

I hold my Cosmo up. "Here's to Sue," I say. "And finding joy."

"To Sue and joy," Tug says, clinking my glass. "Thank you." He takes a sip of his wine. "By the way, you should come to a game. Next game is on the Fourth of July. Best day of the year here. Fireworks, parades, baseball, barbecues, boats...it's like a series of Norman Rockwell paintings."

"I'd love to," I say. "I don't have a lot going on socially, except for..." I look around the restaurant, turning my head, eyeing each table.

"What are you doing, Nancy Drew?"

I lean over the table and whisper. "Bonnie Lyons invited me to tea tomorrow. Tea for two. Just us. I'm sort of freaked-out."

I tell Tug about her visit and her gift, as well as my talk with Captain Lucky. He listens carefully.

"Maybe she's lonely," he offers. "I mean, she did just lose her husband. Sometimes, people act tough because they've been hurt, or rejected, or lost those they've loved, and they don't know how to reach out."

"Perhaps," I say, thinking of my mother.

"Go in with an open mind," he says. "And lots of questions. What have you got to lose? And, besides Captain Lucky, if you ever need to know anything about anybody in this town, talk to Mary. She knows where the bodies are buried, and who buried them."

I laugh. "This town is starting to feel like Pine Valley in *All My Children*. I loved watching that in college."

My mind reels, and I'm about to ask about Bonnie when Michael approaches.

"Do you know what you'd like for dinner?" he asks.

I order the sesame crusted, flash seared ahi tuna, and Tug orders the Gorgonzola pork chop roasted with caramelized onion marmalade and Gorgonzola demi-glace. We share bites of each other's meals and split a handmade s'more roasted at the table for dessert. After dinner, we walk outside. It is dark, but the stars and the moon make it seem bright as day.

"Let me drive you home," Tug says.

"No, it's okay. I think I'll walk off dinner. It's just such a perfect evening."

"It's over a mile," he says. "At night."

"I want to walk," I say. "I walked everywhere growing up. It's nice to feel safe again in a small town. I missed that in Chicago."

We walk across the street until we're standing in front of his shop.

"It's been such a wonderful night," I say.

"It has. I'm so glad you enjoyed dinner."

"I'm sorry if I started our first fight tonight," I say. "My mind plays tricks on me sometimes."

"It's okay," he says. "At least you're being transparent with your emotions. That's all anyone can ask." He looks at me for the longest time. "I like you, Sutton. I don't want to rush anything, and I certainly don't want to scare you, but I want to be transparent, too."

I look into his beautiful eyes.

Tug leans in to kiss me, but at the last minute I turn my head, and his lips meet my cheek, as if I were his kindly grandmother.

"I'm sorry," I say. "Nerves." I hesitate. "Actually, I've never really been good at relationships. Or in a long-term one. I'm a relationship runner. Beware."

He smiles sweetly. "It's been a while for me, too. One day at a time, okay. I hope we can do this all again." He hesitates. "Dinner *and* the kiss."

I match his smile. "I would love that. Let me know about the Fourth, okay? I'm open to whatever you have planned. It's very nice of you to include me."

"I will."

I start to walk down Center Street when Tug calls, "Sutton? Text me to let me know you made it home okay. Please?"

"I will," I say.

I walk out of town and down the bike path that leads to the lake. The closer I get, the more I can hear the lake whisper its summer secrets to me. I turn on Lakeshore Drive. The water shimmers in the moonlight. I stop and watch the waves. I am a little girl again watching the creek at night, feeling all alone, wishing I could float away to a new world.

Here I am as an adult, watching the lake at night, still all alone, but knowing I need to just be here, be still, be in the moment, for once in my life.

I think of Tug finding joy in playing vintage baseball again.

Maybe that's what I need to do with my career, too—find the joy again.

For myself.

I turn onto the little path leading to my rental cottage. There is a light on upstairs in Dandelion Cottage, the flickering of a television. I wind my way around the stone fence, stop, and then tiptoe until I am standing underneath the open window upstairs.

Over the moans of Lake Michigan, I can hear a TV.

I hear the sounds of a little girl giggling. In the background, I hear waves.

"Button, button, who's got the button," a woman is saying in a singsong voice.

"You do, Mommy! You always do!"

I can hear something else, barely audible above the TV and the lake.

It is the sound of a woman crying.

I clamp my hand over my mouth and run back to my cottage.

Made it home safe and sound, I text Tug, knowing "sound" is not the right word to use at all.

July 2022

"Right this way, ma'am."

I follow Lauralei into the foyer. It is open and wide, painted a happy yellow like the exterior, with white trim and shiplap ceiling. I am beyond nervous, not only about being one-on-one with Button Bonnie but also about all the questions I want to ask.

And the soundtrack of last night—what sounded like an old home movie playing—keeps playing in my head, making my stomach churn.

My stomach settles a touch at the charming interior decor. I am thrilled not to have stepped directly into a mausoleum or creepy mansion of memories.

A formal living room, paneled in wood, opens to the left, a formal dining room to the right. I sigh.

The furniture isn't covered in plastic, nor is the dining room set for a surprise luncheon of twelve.

Just beyond the large staircase is a hallway that leads to a butler's pantry and then to what looks like a bright, big kitchen. I can see a man and woman scurry back and forth.

Lauralei stops in the middle of the tiled foyer. She is wearing a maid's outfit, exactly like the old-timey one she wore the other day: a long, black dress with a high collar, a crisp white apron in front. A name tag is pinned to the upper right shoulder strap of the apron. It's not a fancy name tag, more like the ones the cafeteria workers wore in my rural grade school.

"Mrs. Lyons is taking her tea upstairs on the terrace," Lauralei says. "Follow me."

She shuffles toward the stairs in her white shoes, which emit a quiet squeak akin to an Ozarks mosquito, and it is then I notice the pattern in the middle of the foyer: a big blue circle with four white tiles inside it.

My heart somersaults.

A button?

"Ma'am?"

Lauralei turns toward me.

"Yes, I'm coming," I say. "Sorry."

I feel as if I'm skating across the foyer, and the entire world has fallen away. It's just me on a button drifting in space. I lunge at the wood stair railing, thankful for the support, and follow the quiet squeak of Lauralei's shoes.

The walls are filled with artwork. Thick oil paintings of the lake, flowers, winter trees and summer clouds. Every square inch of wall space going up the two flights of stairs is covered with art.

I grip the banister and look around: not a single family photo to be found anywhere on the wall.

That's odd, isn't it?

The top of the landing is wide and covered with a beautiful old Persian rug, its colors muted. A multitude of doors encircle the second floor. One door is cracked open. I try to peek inside.

"This way, ma'am."

It's as if Lauralei secretly inserted a microchip into me when I arrived. She can detect—even above the incessant squeak of her shoes—whenever I slow down or stop moving, even for a millisecond.

"Yes, coming," I say, trying to keep my voice from sounding like that of a child who just got busted for sliding her finger across a freshly iced cake.

Lauralei opens a set of beautiful, old French doors. The wood is burnished and glows in the light. I follow her into what fancy folks in the Ozarks might call a "salon," a rather formal room where guests gather for pre-dinner drinks and conversation.

It is well-appointed with two wingback chairs upholstered in gorgeous chintz fabric that is not your standard roses on off-white, but rich, deep pink-purple foxglove with acorns scattered across a blue-gray background. An empire sofa with needlepoint pillows of birds is perched in front of another set of French doors, open wide to a tiny terrace just big enough to hold a small table and two chairs. Curtains float in the breeze.

The walls are painted an unexpected teal and lined with…

I stop and walk toward a frame on the wall.

…paint-by-number paintings?

I can tell just by looking, the shapes and colors, as if they were drawn by a child. There are paintings of the woods, the lake, a man on a boat, a dog.

"Ma'am?"

Lauralei is stopped in front of the terrace. Her back is to me. And yet she knows I'm not following.

"Coming," I say.

I turn one last time to look at the room, not stuffy at all, or what I imagined. It's as if it has been frozen in time and yet also given a recent face-lift.

"Welcome!" Bonnie Lyons calls from the terrace.

Just like the hostess herself.

Lauralei gestures with a shaky hand, and I follow it onto the terrace.

Bonnie Lyons is already standing, hand extended.

The diamond on her wedding ring is at least five carats, and I'm amazed she can even raise her arm with that on her finger. I gently shake her hand. She knows I'm staring at her ring.

"A gift from my husband," Bonnie says. "He surprised me with it on our fiftieth anniversary. A carat for every decade."

"I wasn't terribly subtle, was I? I apologize."

She laughs.

"It's hard to miss. And you like my cottage it seems?" she asks.

At first I think she means the one I'm renting, but I realize she's referring to her home, remembering everyone in Michigan calls their home—no matter its size—a cottage.

"I take it you could see me admiring all your artwork? Again, not terribly subtle."

"I'm glad you like it. I redid much of this room recently after my husband's passing," Bonnie says. "Painted it blue, my favorite color, to match the lake's many moods. My decorator found some vintage Dutch Heritage chintz fabric. You will discover that there are a lot of Dutch ancestors around here, including my husband." Bonnie looks at me. "I felt like I needed a new start." She turns and scans the room. "Sometimes it's necessary to erase the pain in order to move on with one's life."

I think of how I was unable to part with my mother's buttons and Ol' Betsy much less sell her home.

"Will you please bring the tea, Lauralei," Bonnie says with a wave of her hand.

Lauralei squeaks away.

"Those shoes of hers," Bonnie whispers. "But it's the only way I can tell if she's coming or going." She laughs. "Sit, sit, please," she says. "What a stunning day."

"It is," I say.

The lake is as smooth, flat and glorious blue as the piece

of beach glass I found on a morning walk the other day on Douglas Beach. From this vantage point, I feel as if I can see what perhaps the earliest ship's captain saw from his raised quarterdeck: the entire world spread out before him, a wondrous navy canvas, the unknown within reach.

"Penny for your thoughts?" Bonnie asks. "I still have the one you paid me the other day for the buttons."

I smile.

"I'm thinking that there is a big difference between a creek and a great lake."

"Ah, yes. The beauty of Lake Michigan is beyond words, isn't it? Like our own, private ocean. This area has been a wondrous secret," she says. "But the secret, sadly, is not so secret anymore."

I glance over at Bonnie. She is staring intensely at me. My heart flutters, but then I hear a squeak.

Saved by Lauralei's shoes.

"Tea for two," Bonnie says. "As promised."

Lauralei fills two delicate teacups with hot tea.

"I'll return with lunch in a moment, ma'am," Lauralei says.

"I have long loved a proper tea, haven't you?" Bonnie asks.

"Is sun tea considered proper tea?" I ask. "That's what I grew up having."

"I don't know what that is," Bonnie says.

"I guess it's unique to the South. The warm sun actually brews the tea."

"You grew up in the South?"

"The Missouri Ozarks."

Bonnie considers what I've said but doesn't reply.

"There is an etiquette to having tea," she says instead. "My husband and I used to travel frequently to London for business and pleasure, and I absolutely fell in love with it. It's pretty. It's polished. There are rules one should abide by for proper tea."

Bonnie continues: "We've lost all formality in society today. People disrespect one another, from family to friends. Kids on their cell phones, no one holding a door for a woman entering a building, people responding to a thank-you with 'No problem' instead of 'You're welcome.' With no rules, we have no order. With no order, we have no society. Families fail. Upside down becomes right side up."

She picks up her cup.

"Hold the teacup by the handle," she says, nodding for me to follow along. I pick mine up. "Always leave the saucer on the table. If we were having black tea, you would have the option to add milk or sugar. If so, you would stir up and down—noon to six p.m.—rather than in circles. Take small sips." Bonnie demonstrates. "Doing everything quietly is a common etiquette rule."

She waits for me to sip, and I concentrate on not slurping. I've been alone so long that I'm used to eating dinner off of my lap and drinking wine straight from the bottle.

I feel like I am not, pardon the pun, Bonnie's perfect cup of tea.

"Good, good," she says as if I'm her student.

"My former boss grew up in England," I say, trying to even the playing field. "He loved a proper tea." I think of what he taught me. "Earl Grey is not a morning tea. And when you drink it, you should use lemon and sugar. Milk has a tendency to do strange things to black tea. It dulls the flavor. It's not as crisp and sharp. Lemon is always the way to go."

"Well, aren't you full of surprises?" Bonnie says, eyebrow raised.

Lauralei appears again. She sets down an exquisite, three-tiered silver tray filled with goodies.

"It's so beautiful," I say.

"Afternoon tea comes in three courses," Bonnie explains.

"Usually all at once. We start with the savories and tea sandwiches first, which you eat with your hands. Today we have cucumber, smoked salmon and watercress–egg salad sandwiches. Scones with clotted cream and jam are eaten next, followed by the sweets."

I pick up a cucumber sandwich and pop it into my mouth.

"Tea sandwiches should be eaten in two to three bites," Bonnie says. "Never jam the entire sandwich into your mouth."

"Sorry," I mumble, lifting my napkin to my face and wiping away the crumbs and butter.

"And we dab at our mouths with our napkin rather than…" Bonnie stops and studies me as if she's at the zoo. "…exert such force."

My face reddens.

She has a knack of being both incredibly rude and insanely polite.

Bonnie looks at me again, closely.

"Thank you for dressing appropriately," she says. "That's a very pretty summer dress. And I love your application of vintage buttons. You look very nice."

Now she's making up? I feel like an emotional boomerang.

"Thank you," I say. "I designed and made it myself."

"I know. As I mentioned when we saw one another the other day, I've looked you up online. You're quite fascinating. You've certainly worked your way up in this world from what I've read. I admire that. Greatly."

"Thank you," I say. "I did work hard." I look over the lake. "Now I'm trying to find myself again after my mother's passing from Covid. I recently left my job. I feel like I'm starting over all again."

Bonnie takes a small nibble of a cucumber sandwich and follows my gaze.

"I'm going to share something with you," she says, her voice hushed. "I am not, as you may have deduced, what one might call a sharer."

Bonnie focuses her eyes on me.

"I feel as if I'm starting all over again as well," she says. "My husband also died of Covid."

"I didn't know," I say. "I'm so sorry." I scan the lake. "I think it's touched nearly everyone."

"He was my world. Our business was our life for so long, and then we just had each other."

"No family?" I ask.

Bonnie picks up her teacup and scans the liquid as if she might see her future—or an answer to my question—reflected back.

"No," she finally says. "Just the two of us."

"Me, either," I say, trying to fill the awkward silence. "Just me and my mom. The two of us."

My heart begins pounding in my chest. I've barely met this woman, and yet I feel compelled to tell her about why I came here.

Do I tell her?

Do I pump her for information?

Lauralei arrives with a plate of scones and bowl of clotted cream, giving me time to think. She sets it down and leaves without a sound.

"I had a very complicated family history," I say as if I'm verbally tiptoeing. "It seems I didn't know those I thought I loved."

I hear a clinking. Bonnie's hand is shaking, and she has spilled a touch of tea onto her saucer.

"I must be hungry," she says. "Low blood sugar."

She finishes her cucumber sandwich, and I take a scone.

"I…" she starts.

She seems as if she wants to say something, too, but only the corners of her mouth lift ever so slightly, and then it's gone, evaporated, like the bubbles in a pot of boiling water when you snap off the heat.

Lauralei appears as if on cue, now carrying a beautiful arrangement of macarons.

"Perfect timing!" Bonnie says. "What do we have here?"

"We have macarons of rose petal, framboise, pistachio, lemon and Marie Antoinette," Lauralei says.

"Marie Antoinette?" I ask.

"Estelle says it's a marriage of black teas from China and India with hints of citrus and honey," Bonnie says. "Please, have something sweet. I'll never eat all of this. Estelle is a fabulous baker. She also made lemon drizzle cake, Earl Grey panna cotta tarts, shortbread cookies, blueberry basil tartlets."

I grab a Marie Antoinette macaron and take a small nibble, as previously instructed.

"This is delicious!" I say. "So good it makes you lose your head."

I wait for a reaction, but no one laughs.

"That was a joke," I say.

"Thank you, Lauralei," Bonnie says, dismissing her with a nod.

I finish one macaron and then grab a rose petal, trying to act demure when I want to shove three of them at a time into my mouth.

"I'm glad you're enjoying them," Bonnie says in her inimitable way.

The lake sings to us, and bikers and walkers stride by on Lakeshore Drive, not seeming to notice us up amongst the trees. A hummingbird zips around us for a moment, inspecting the rainbow macarons and our tea, before settling briefly on a pine branch to watch us. And then it flits away. I lift my face to the sun and close my eyes.

I think of the bridge ladies from the Ozarks, women who had everything and treated those around them like nothing, especially my mother. They provided her work and income in exchange for undying fealty.

I wonder if Bonnie is different, if perhaps she's welcoming me into her world because we're both lonely, and she has gifts to teach me.

When I open my eyes, Bonnie is watching me carefully.

I take a deep breath and open my mouth to ask her about her family button business—I've actually compiled a list of questions I want to ask, both personally and professionally—but she cuts me off before I'm able to do so.

"I asked you here for a specific purpose," Bonnie says.

I sit up a bit straighter in my chair.

"I was hoping you might consider designing a new wardrobe for me. Something summery. Something with your signature style."

My heart skips.

Bonnie is impeccably dressed. She is wearing an expensive St. John's knit set, a marled pink tweed jacket and matching knee-length skirt. I know this outfit well. It is the uniform of choice for wealthy Chicago women of a certain age. I patterned a few of my designs after this staple, knowing how well it sells year after year, decade after decade.

"Oh, my gosh," I start.

I don't know what I was expecting from Bonnie, but it wasn't this.

"I saw what you were designing when I was in my...*your*... cottage the other day," she says. "The fabric, the buttons, the style. It was quite stunning."

"Thank you," I say.

"Did you have someone in mind when you were making that dress?" she asks.

"Me," I say. "It's going to be a short summer dress with pink buttons. I'm still working on it."

But the dress is more than that. It is my statement to the world that I'm coming back, personally and professionally. But I don't tell Bonnie that.

"I was quite taken with your choice of fabric and buttons," Bonnie says. "It was a new take on vintage materials."

"That's been the hallmark of my career."

"I know," Bonnie says into the wind. "So, might you consider designing some outfits for me to wear?"

"I'm beyond flattered, but, unfortunately, I'm not in a position—"

Bonnie puts a finger in the air and wags it, interrupting me. "But I am in a position to put you in a position."

I grab another macaron.

"It's summer season in Saugatuck-Douglas," she continues. "July and August are filled with our biggest fundraisers, galas and parties: the arts center, Ox-Bow, the Historical Society, the Garden Club, and Glow, my annual summer soiree that takes place on the beach at sunset."

"Glow?" I ask.

"That's what I've always called the time of night when the sun begins to set over the lake, and the water glows." Bonnie looks down at herself. "I've worn the same types of dresses for decades. I think it's time for me to start anew." Bonnie lifts her head and stares at the water, playing with the Liz Taylor–sized rock on her finger. "I need to re-emerge from this dark year in a new light. Do you understand?"

Her words strike a chord. "I do," I say. "I totally do."

Perhaps, despite her prickly demeanor, we are more alike than I care to imagine. Perhaps she has just lost so much that the only way she can protect herself is to be like a cactus. But perhaps deep down she is tender, wounded, a kind woman.

Perhaps she is the reason I'm here, personally and professionally. Perhaps she is the family I was meant to find.

I feel out of body up here amongst the trees, hovering above the lake, like my conscience is watching me.

Sunlight shifts through the tree and casts a light across Bonnie's face. She is old, and young, and I think of the game I played long ago with my mother.

From the earliest of ages, we are seen by society in a certain light, and it is difficult to change that perception. All of us are varying shades of light and dark, good and bad, and we often work our whole lives to have the world notice us in a new way.

My mother ran for some reason to start anew, and yet was still seen as less-than in Nevermore.

My whole life seems as if it's been a struggle between being pulled into the dark and trying to crawl into the light.

I look at Bonnie.

"I'm so glad," she finally says.

I can see her try to smile, but either she has been conditioned not to do so, or life has stolen her joy at some point. Or her plastic surgeon severed a nerve.

Stop it, Sutton. You're awful.

"I'm so glad you see it my way," she says, standing quickly, her mood suddenly sunnier. "Follow me!"

I follow Bonnie off the terrace and through the salon. She moves at warp speed for a woman of her age, spine straight, head high. Her low heels *clip-clop* across the floor and echo when we reach the landing, making it sound as if she's walking a pony.

We move through the hallway, Bonnie at a full trot. When we pass an open bedroom door, I slow, just as I'd tried to do earlier before Lauralei busted me.

The door is open a few inches, as if a ghost had just escaped. I stop, and my breath hitches.

The room is pink with frilly curtains and a four-poster bed, dolls leaning against a mountain of pillows. Ghostly silhouettes dot the pink walls, as if pictures were removed long ago and never replaced. Through the window, Lake Michigan sparkles, a beacon of blue.

Whose room is this?

She said she had no family. No children. No grandchildren. Perhaps a niece?

I look again.

And why does it appear as if only certain memories were excised from the room?

"Sutton?"

I jump.

I run, following Bonnie's voice, until I reach a door that is wide-open.

Bonnie is perched atop a round alteration fitting platform in the middle of a massive walk-in closet. She is standing tall, proud, above the world like the bronze lions outside the Art Institute of Chicago.

Her closet resembles one you might see on a tour of a movie star's home on HGTV. A large chandelier illuminates floor-to-ceiling racks for shoes and hats. Dresses and outfits hang in different areas, marked by the season. Everything is well spaced. Each outfit looks as if it's just been vacuumed. There is a vanity table, well-lighted with a huge mirror, big enough to accommodate a glam squad. A glass cabinet, lit, is filled with jewelry.

"Costume," Bonnie says, watching me carefully. "The real boys are locked away."

"This is amazing. My closet in Chicago was the size of a

postage stamp. I used to throw clothes inside and slam the door without looking."

Bonnie sighs, her breath filled with a million, silent *tsk-tsk*'s.

"You deserve better than that, Sutton. A woman of your talent. Your clothes should be one-of-a-kind, not ready-to-wear. They should be tailored for attention, not produced for the masses."

"Thank you, Bonnie."

"You made the right decision with your career."

She eyes me from her perch, like a queen on her throne. I feel the need to bow in her presence, but I know it's just my knees buckling under the weight of her gaze. I force myself to stand even straighter.

"Yes, I've done my homework," Bonnie says. "I always do my homework."

"I've been doing my homework as well," I say.

"Well…" She actually smiles. "A good businesswoman always should. Know your customers, know your base, know your product…" She pauses. "Know your competitors."

I follow the sweep of her manicured hand toward a mannequin standing in the corner of the room.

"I was so taken by the dress you were designing that I just had to seek out the fabric," Bonnie says. "Turns out you found it right here, in our little town."

"From Tug," I say.

"Yes, Mr. McCoy's shop." She looks at me. "I can never bring myself to use his nickname. It's so informal."

I walk over to the mannequin.

"You have an eye for the drape," Bonnie says. "The way the fabric hangs on the mannequin is beautiful…"

"Thank you so much," I say. "That means the world."

I touch the fabric and begin to pull, tuck and arrange it in different ways around the mannequin's body.

"...but you know just how to bring it to life. The drape is so important."

I turn. She is watching me.

"I learned in fashion design that draping is essentially fabric psychology," I say.

Bonnie's face manages to convey complete surprise. "Go on."

"Most fabrics need to be observed to see how they behave," I continue. "Just like people."

I look at the mannequin.

"Ideally, I'd start with muslin on the mannequin to see how the dress I designed might work. I'd cut, position and pin the muslin to structure the design, then remove it and start creating my sewing pattern. It's like a scientific puzzle."

"It's really illusion, isn't it?" she says. "But it's also intentional. Parallel to how we present ourselves to the world. Do we wish to drape, or do we desire dishevelment?"

Bonnie continues. "Here are my strengths, Sutton. I have wonderful shoulders, a straight back, and a surprisingly firm décolletage for a woman my age. My upper arms should be covered. I am not a fan of fads or trends. I look best in blues, grays, pinks, lavenders and shades of tree green."

"I haven't agreed to anything, Bonnie. I'm really not in any sort of a place to do this right now."

"Designing is your gift and your strength, Sutton. I would guess that, although you've been highly successful, you haven't been inspired by your work in a very long time. We've both learned life is very short. And, finally, in my long life, I've learned we should always recognize and remember our gifts and strengths, Sutton, otherwise, we'll fall prey to our foibles, wobble under our weaknesses."

"I still haven't said yes yet."

"You haven't said no either."

I can hear the lake through the window, a little girl screaming in glee on the beach.

I think of what I heard the other night.

Button, button, who's got the button?

"Sutton?"

You do, Mommy!

"Sutton?"

Bonnie knocks me from my thoughts.

"Oh, and Mr. McCoy had a few more of the same buttons
you purchased. Pink. So beautiful, aren't they? But aren't all
buttons?"

I take a deep breath to steel myself and open my mouth to
ask a question, actually a million questions, not only about
her and her husband's business, her history with buttons, Ted
and my mom, but why she is being so kind to me.

I hear a squeak.

"Ma'am?" Lauralei says in a hushed tone. "Your two-o'clock
is here. Mrs. Humphreys."

"Thank you, Lauralei. Can you show her to the salon?"

Squeak. And she is gone.

"Silent auction for the big gala," Bonnie explains. "We'll
have to finish our talk later. You'll need measurements. I'll
need to tell you more about the events I'm attending and
what's appropriate. I'll need to see sketches. We don't have
much time. This will require your full attention."

"Again," I say. "I haven't said yes. This summer was meant
for me to have a reset on my life."

Bonnie steps off her platform.

"And that's just what I'm offering you."

She walks me toward the door.

"Let me help you. Let me help you help yourself. I have
a lot of connections with the most influential women not
only around here but also in Detroit, Chicago, Milwaukee,

218

St. Louis, Cleveland. Start with me. Connect the dots. I have a lot of money. I have a lot of time." Bonnie halts and eyes me up and down once again. "I've taken an interest in you. Consider it a gift that's fallen into your lap. A million gold coins disguised as buttons."

My mouth feels full of Novocaine.

"I'll think about it. Thank you for the tea."

"It was a lovely afternoon. Now, if you'll excuse me. Lauralei will be in touch."

She escorts me to the stairway just as Lauralei walks from the salon.

"This way," Lauralei says.

I follow her down the stairs but stop midway. I turn and look up. Bonnie is leaning over the banister, watching. She disappears.

"Ma'am?" Lauralei says, knowing I've stopped moving.

"Coming," I say. "Sorry."

I start to descend once again when I notice a painting I didn't see earlier.

Amidst all the floral paintings is an oil of a young girl in a blue dress drinking tea. I lean closer.

The dress features beautiful pearl buttons in varying shades of turquoise, each a little bit differently shaped and shaded. The girl is sitting, unsmiling, under a dogwood tree in full bloom, a branch of white flowers above one shoulder casting shadows of small crosses on her dress.

"Ma'am?" Lauralei says again. This time, she is turned, her voice urgent.

But it's the eyes of the little girl that stop me in my tracks. They are gold in the sunlight, like a pot of gold at the end of the rainbow.

"Ain't nothin' in there but memories," I can hear my mom say. "And they ain't worth much punk, save for the ones a'you."

The staircase spins, and I miss a step and begin to tumble.

"Miss Douglas!" Lauralei says, alarmed.

She reaches for my arm just as I catch the banister and steady myself.

"I'm so sorry," I say. "Just a little light-headed today. My mind's playing tricks on me."

When I reach the bottom of the stairs, Lauralei grabs my hands and looks me right in the eyes.

"Ted," she whispers.

"What did you say?"

"Red," she says. "Red. Your face is so flushed. Do you need some water?"

"No, I'm okay," I say. "I'm sorry. Thank you."

Then she puts a hand tenderly on my shoulder, and opens her mouth to say something else.

"Lauralei!" Bonnie calls.

She is standing at the top of the stairs, watching us.

"Coming, ma'am."

I glance again at the portrait.

I swear I see a smile—bigger than I've ever seen—cross Bonnie's face.

And then she is gone.

8

RAW EDGE

The raw, raveling and unfinished cut edge of the fabric.

Oval Beach is packed to the gills.

I walk down the warped boardwalk, folding chair strapped to my back, beach bag slung over one shoulder, cooler in one hand, umbrella in the other.

Tug told me how beautiful Oval Beach was and of its many accolades—named one of the top beaches in the world by *Conde Nast*, *National Geographic* and MTV—but I didn't believe him until now.

I admire the expanse. The beach is golden and wide. Acres of unspoiled dunes, towering toward the sky, watch over the blue, blue water. Dune grass waves in the lake breeze. Brightly striped umbrellas dot the beach. Music and conversations drift along the shore. I hear a word, or a lyric, and then it is carried away by the breeze, gulped up by the waves.

I need this summer day.

I need it to relax, I need it to mull over Bonnie's offer, I need it to consider my career path, and I need it to organize all the questions crowding my head as well as to ask myself if what I saw and felt at Bonnie's cottage—the painting, her smile, Lauralei's look—was real or imagined.

Did she really say Ted? Or was I creating things in my own exhausted mind?

I shake my head to clear it and look out at the lake.

But mostly I need this day to contemplate how much my life—and the world—has changed and also to realize how little it has, too.

A simple day at the beach connects us all. A simple day at the beach reminds us that though the world is always changing, this simple pleasure never does. I feel the same as I did as a kid.

I walk to the end of the boardwalk. A white seagull hops spastically toward an open bag of potato chips. It looks around and then plucks a chip from the bag. And then another. A little girl turns and sees her snack being stolen and screams. The seagull flaps its wings and squawks. A father races toward the bag of chips. The seagull stares at the man and, just before the father reaches it, the bird grabs the bag in its beak and flies off.

Aviary Instacart, I think, recalling the last two years at home.

The sun warms my body, and I can't help but smile.

There's just something about a day on the beach that's more than relaxing. It's restorative. It's *necessary*. It calms your soul.

A Frisbee whizzes over my head, and a teenaged boy runs by, kicking sand.

"Sorry!" he calls. "My friend can't throw."

"I'm good," I say.

I kick off my flip-flops and step in the sand.

"Ow!" I yelp.

The sand isn't just hot, it's unexpectedly, blisteringly hot. I hop this way and that, yelping, "Hot! Oooh! Hot! Hot! Hot!"

I race to the shore like a piping plover and walk into Lake Michigan.

"Cold!" I yell. "Oooh! Cold! Cold! Cold!"

An older woman walking the shore laughs.

"First time at the Oval?" she asks. I nod. "Sand's always hotter than you think, and water's always colder." She laughs. "Welcome!" she says before continuing on her way.

I retrieve my flip-flops, the palms of my feet now numb after having been burnt and frozen, and move away from the crowd and down a narrow strip of beach that hugs a dune. There are a few walkers and some umbrellas perched in the dunes overlooking the water, but it is a relatively quiet spot. I walk about a half mile down the beach, not far from the channel that leads boats to the lake.

I dump everything off my body like a disgruntled camel. I plant my umbrella in the sand, spread out a sheet and towel and secure each corner with a flip-flop, cooler and beach chair. I toss down a book I plucked from the cottage's bookshelves, shed my shorts and T-shirt, slather my body in sunscreen, grab a fizzy water from the cooler and, finally, lie down.

I lean up on my elbows and scan the water.

I feel like I'm in another world, perhaps on the Amalfi Coast.

The color of the water, sand, sky and horizon is not simply breathtaking, it is nearly unreal.

Years ago I went with friends in Chicago to see a retrospective of Georgia O'Keeffe's work. I had difficulty believing that the color of the desert and flowers could look the way she had painted them. And then Lindy's had a retreat in New Mexico, and I saw Georgia's world anew, from her perspective. The way the sun hit the mountains at different times of day caused the landscape to age, change, shift before my very eyes. The mountains *were* dizzyingly purple just as the sky right now is as blue as the mood ring I had as a girl. The rim of the horizon is as pink as that mood ring turned when Jake Mulligan talked to me at recess.

In Chicago, the world is a bit more muted. Perhaps it's the air, perhaps it's the number of people, but here, it's as if God has used an entire bottle of Windex to make all of His magical creations even shinier, a heavenly app to make the colors more saturated.

I lay my back against the beach and let the sun warm my face. Before the pandemic, I began going to yoga with Abby. It started at six a.m.—well before work and well before I was used to making my body do anything except shuffle for a second cup of coffee—but it set an intention for the day. It made me feel anything was possible.

When we would lie still, our yoga instructor called it "grounding." It was a way to connect with the earth both physically and spiritually. She wanted us to have all of our "contact points"—head, spine, hands, feet—in contact with the earth, so we understood our connection to it. She wanted us to be both humbled by that connection and empowered by that connection.

My mother called it "hooey" when I shared this practice.

"You want to be connected to the earth, young lady?" she asked me. "Mow the yard. Weed the garden. Hang the laundry. Swim in the crick. Catch and clean a fish. I guarantee you'll be connected as well as bone tired. And I darn well guarantee you'll get your workout in for the day."

I will never forget your Ozark mom-isms, I think.

I drift off, dreaming that I am with my mom floating in inner tubes, the water cooling us on a scorching summer day, the creek moving quickly, us going nowhere. My mom would grab the branch of a sycamore jutting from the bank with one hand and hold my hand with her other, and we would be suspended in time, as if the world had stopped and would never interfere in our lives.

A boat horn toots and echoes across the water, and I sit back up on my elbows. A group of boats have anchored in the bay directly in front of where I've set up camp, protected from the wind. Four boats of varying sizes—a tri-toon, a tiny Sea Ray, a big motor yacht and an adorable vintage wood Chris-Craft—have tied together. Music comes on, and I smile.

Jimmy Buffett.

I stand and walk to the shore, and a boat horn toots again. I look over the water, and the group of boaters are waving and lifting their beers into the air to cheers me. I wave and step into the water. It is still chilly, but I'm hot from the sun, and it feels good. I edge out until I'm waist-deep. The water is crystal clear—as clear as Hickory Creek—and I can see the sand churn around my feet.

Someone on the boat tosses a float into the water—a huge, rainbow-colored unicorn—and then they leap onto it, screaming.

I take a few more steps into the lake, the water going higher, the cold causing my breath to hitch.

I stand and stare over the water, goose bumps covering my body. I push through the water until I reach the beach again, the hot sand on my feet.

"Ow," I say, edging them onto the shoreline, waves cooling them off once more.

My mother and I could both walk barefoot across our rocky beach without a wince. Every summer, the soles of our feet and nervous systems became oblivious to the sharp edges and uneven terrain. My mother took great pride in that fact.

"The human capacity to endure and withstand pain is miraculous," she once said. "But we can survive anything when our souls finally become as calloused as our feet."

I shiver and race back to my beach towel. I hear a jingling noise I at first think is coming from the boats, but then I realize the familiar tone.

My phone.

I pluck it from a pocket of my beach bag.

Texts from Abby.

I get reception out here? I think. *Now that's a miracle.*

How are you? How's the man? What's his name again, Pug?

I laugh out loud.

Tug. He's not a dog.

LOL! I've been collecting some of the mail that's not being forwarded to you. I'll get that to you. Nothing much, I don't think. A couple of letters for you. AND I did notice a credit card bill. I was NOT snooping, I promise. I was worried about when it was due.

My heart sinks. That's the one bill that's mailed. The one bill that's slipped my mind.

How much?

Abby texts me the amount. My heart sinks even further. I text back.

UGH! I hate you, Amazon!

I look out at the lake. Amazon was my BFF during this whole pandemic. I had something delivered almost every day...a sweater, a coffee mug, a book... Took the place of human companionship I think. I ordered so much when I was depressed. I started to feel weird if I didn't get a delivery every day. It was like getting excited to see a friend. It made me feel alive. I didn't actually pay attention to the fact the number was growing faster than my hair and my weight during this time. I was just worried about settling all of my mother's bills.

Abby texts.

Did you get any money from your mom? Could you sell the cabin? What about work?

I got a little, not much. Took some retirement early. I can't sell the cabin yet. Doesn't feel right. And...what work?

Do you need help? Don't be embarrassed to ask. You can be that way, you know.

I know. No. Thank you. I do have a weird story, tho...

I bring her up to date on Bonnie, her buttons, our tea and her offer.

Maybe you should do it. Just for the cash. Just for now.

Maybe. But she's odd. I can't tell if I'm her friend or her puppet.

Puppets need cash, too, honey. Even if strings are attached.

I smile, take a breath and tell Abby about the painting of the girl in the blue dress.

I feel like Nancy Drew. Or Velma from Scooby-Doo.

Or, maybe you're just in search of some closure. You never had it. Maybe this woman can give that to you.

**Maybe you can give that to yourself. Or maybe her per-
sonality reminds you a lot of your mother and that's
stirring up a lot of emotions. You are a smart woman,
Sutton. You're also kind. You're a good read of people.**

Thank you. I love you. Have a great 4th!

**You, too. And kiss Pug! TUG! Whatever his weirdo name
is. Just do it! It's time! It's summer!**

I send a GIF of a woman laughing so hard she falls down.

And then I fall back down on my towel and drift off. I
dream in fitful starts of me walking on a rocky beach. I don't
feel anything, but when I look down, my feet are cut and
bleeding. I know I should be crying, but I can't conjure the
emotion.

I reach down to pick up an arrowhead off the beach, but
when I lean over, I realize the entire beach is made of buttons.

"I'm glad you reconsidered," Bonnie says.

Bonnie is standing at the door, resplendent in a vintage
caftan that billows in the breeze. The sunlight hits her silver
hair just so, and her earrings jangle.

"Forgive my casual attire this morning," she says. "We're
taking the boat out later for a day on the lake before the tourists take over tomorrow."

She says the word *tourists* as an actress might say the word
locusts in an old movie.

Am I a locust? I think. *Invading her town? Sometimes I feel like
it, and I can see how locals might think that way, especially with so
much relocation these past two years.*

"You're a long-term renter, Sutton," Bonnie says, as if reading my mind. "Of a historic cottage. That's different.

"I thought we'd discuss your designs in the living room

this morning," she continues. "I prefer as much light as possible when I study the fabrics and the buttons."

"Design," I say. "Sketch really. And a fabric sample. I only had a few days to pull this together, remember."

"Well, then, it's a start, and I'm so thrilled you're here."

Why *am* I here? For money? Of course. To restart my career and be inspired by my work again? Yes.

Bonnie sweeps into the foyer, and I follow. My eyes drift to the button tile floor and then up the staircase to the paintings.

Where is it? Where is it?

There! The eyes!

But something bigger than money and inspiration made me agree to Bonnie's proposal. I feel as if my entire history is an early sketch—like one of my designs—and I need to complete it or I'll never be able to rest.

And something in my gut tells me this woman knows something, or at least enough to point me in the right direction.

Bonnie herds me toward the living room and takes a seat on the sofa. Bonnie pats a cushion, as if we're old friends about to sit for a chat. I hesitate. She pats the sofa again, and I take a seat.

I place my sketchbook and cell phone on a glass coffee table with bronze legs that resemble dahlias.

Squeak.

"Tea?" Lauralei asks.

Bonnie shakes her head. "I'm thinking something stronger."

"Black tea, ma'am?"

Bonnie smiles. "Stronger."

My eyes widen, and I glance at my watch.

Bonnie laughs.

"It's nearly eleven a.m. on July third in Douglas, Michigan," she says. "The entire town is either drunk or well on its way to being so. Why not join them?"

She looks at me waiting for an answer.

"I'm in," I say.

Bonnie claps. "A girl after my own heart. Lauralei, bring two glasses of that lovely Moët & Chandon Moët Imperial the sommelier sent from Champagne."

"Right away, ma'am."

Bonnie gets up and walks over to the large windows overlooking the lake. She draws back the drapes as far as they will go and then opens the wide, paned windows. Sunlight engulfs the room. It is a perfect day, the kind that actually makes your heart hurt.

I can smell the water on the wind—along with the scent of peonies, suntan lotion and boat exhaust—and I think of my day on the beach and nearly kick myself.

What have you gotten yourself into, Sutton?

When my mom was older and her back ached after a long week of work, she would stare at the beach and the creek—too tired to move even on a stunning day—and say, "I never should have wasted a beautiful summer day staying inside. You can never get these moments back."

Bonnie turns, and her caftan billows. She looks at me for the longest time. The silence is unnerving.

"That is such a lovely caftan," I say, trying to fill the void. "I love the pink and the geometric pattern. It's really wonderful."

Bonnie floats across the room like an elderly flower child, the "What they look like now" photo of a girl who was at Woodstock. The caftan is a giant fashion surprise to me, nothing like the buttoned-down knit suit she was wearing for tea. She takes a seat and smiles.

"I bought it from a designer friend in Italy. It literally just arrived. I actually purchased this in honor of you." She reaches over and pats my leg. "I wanted to inspire you. I wanted to inspire myself."

"I don't know what to say. I'm touched."

Lauralei enters the room with two glasses of champagne on a silver tray. She stoops before me, and I take a glass. Bonnie takes the other.

"Just say cheers!"

"Cheers!" I say.

"To new friends!"

I nod, unable to repeat her salutation, and take a sip. It's the best champagne I've ever had.

But what do I know?

I grew up thinking Nesquik strawberry milk *was* champagne. Pop Tarts were my croissants, fried fish my caviar, tomato sandwiches my prime rib, blackberries straight off the vine my baked Alaska. My mother didn't drink. My first drink was Boone's Farm Tickle Pink, straight from the bottle at a hoochenanny.

"The size of the bubble signifies the quality of the champagne," Bonnie explains, again as if reading my mind, as if I were her student in a course entitled "The Privileged Life" and she was presenting the syllabus. "The smaller the bubbles, the better the champagne."

Bonnie lifts her glass to the light and waits until I do the same.

"See?" she asks.

I nod, even though I wouldn't be able to discern a big champagne bubble from a small one.

Bonnie lifts the flute to her lips and takes a small sip. She closes her eyes.

"It should taste crisp, refreshing, and the mouthfeel should be creamy, soft and mellow. The bubbles should feel like crystalline pearls on the palate. Think of the bubbles as the musicians in a symphony orchestra."

I sip.

Is that an orchestra in my mouth? Or the remnants of my oatmeal?

"It's delicious," I say.

"Vintage never goes out of style, does it?" Bonnie asks. "Be it clothing or champagne, cars or homes." Bonnie lifts her glass and takes another sip. "There is a standard that comes with money, Sutton. I know I've been blessed, and I never take that for granted. But I worked hard to earn what I have. I understand that with great privilege comes great responsibility. The two go hand in hand. If someone wastes either the money or the responsibility, they are not deserving of such privilege. Don't you agree?"

I don't know exactly what she's asking, or why she's asking me, but I do understand the way in which the question is posed. I've met many wealthy people in my life, and they always speak like this. They have this innate ability to ask a question in a style and tone in which you have no option but to agree—usually when they know you have zero knowledge of the subject.

"Traveling by private jet is so much better, don't you agree?"

What is one supposed to say? *"No, taking the Greyhound is my preferred mode of travel."*

What it comes down to is that they believe in their hearts they are seeking to include you in the conversation, but they have lost complete touch with the fact that their entire lives have been built upon exclusion and privilege.

"Of course," I say.

"Speaking of vintage…"

Bonnie takes a sip of champagne and sets the flute on the table. She rubs her hands together and nods toward my sketchbook.

"So your love of buttons started with your mother?" Bonnie asks.

"It did. She was a seamstress at a local factory, but she sewed and quilted nearly every day after work. It was her joy. And she was quite talented."

"You were an apprentice of hers."

"I was," I say. "I didn't appreciate that until I was older."

"Few of us do," she says.

"She produced overalls for the masses, and then produced her own clothes for us. I thought my life would be different, but I ended up making clothes for the masses as well. But she was a laborer. I was a designer. My mother sacrificed everything for me. She stitched overalls until she couldn't stand straight."

"That's quite a legacy."

"It is, thank you for saying that."

"You know, my husband and I ran into a similar dilemma with our company. What started as a way to produce a unique, Michigan-made product began to become mass-produced as well. Everyone copied us. Buttons were no longer special. And then along came plastic, and it was so much cheaper. And then zippers became all the rage. But our 'progression' produced a lack of beauty, Sutton. We wanted cheap and fast. We wanted to do as little as possible for as much money as we could earn."

Lauralei enters the living room carrying a tray filled with cheeses, crackers, nuts, figs, baked brie and smoked salmon.

Lauralei sets the tray on the table before us, and as she passes by, Bonnie grabs her hand. Lauralei stops cold like a toy with a dead battery. Bonnie's eyes wander to her uniform. She lifts her finger to a white button on her black uniform.

"You understand the craftsmanship required to create these beauties—these perfect pearl buttons?" Bonnie asks me. "It is a far cry from the few seconds it takes to machine mold a plastic button today."

Bonnie drops her hand. "That will be all, Lauralei."

"Ma'am."

Bonnie takes a sip of champagne and continues.

"We sold our business. We could see the writing on the

wall when no one else could. We were still so young, my Dan and me. Our whole lives still ahead of us. We made a lot of money, though. And we invested it wisely, in the market and other businesses. People thought we were mad to invest in the stock market in the 1970s just as they thought we were crazy to expand our button business before that. But it was never the same. Nothing ever captured our imagination like buttons. So we stopped before anyone could make that decision for us. And it was the right one. Like the one you made. It is refreshing to see a young woman with scruples. So rare these days."

I wonder briefly if she hired a PI to investigate the woman staying in the cottage behind hers? And how would she have known? Or did she simply look online like the rest of the world?

My resignation *was* in all the business trades in Chicago. And she seems uber-savvy. All you need these days is a laptop or cell phone—and a social media history—to sniff out someone's past.

I think of my mother. Born in a time before social media.

Who were you, Miss Mabel?

"May I ask you a question?" I say.

Bonnie cocks her head and takes a sip of champagne. "By all means," she says, her voice filled with intrigue.

"I don't know how to say all of this without sounding completely crazy, but I came here to search for clues."

"Clues?" Bonnie's eyes widen.

"About my family," I say. "My family's past."

"Go on."

"My mother told me growing up that my entire family had died in a fire on Christmas."

"Oh, you poor thing. How awful."

"But it turns out it wasn't true," I continue. "My mom left me a note saying she had lied to protect me. She was in love with my father, a man named Ted. My mom said her parents cast her aside for loving the wrong man and she had to run away and hide to start over again. She said that my father died from that pain. I just have so many questions."

"I can only imagine," she says quietly.

"I found a photo amongst my mother's things from a man named Ted. He looked as if he might have been a clammer. And I found a postcard of the beach here in Douglas. Not to mention, I have hundreds of the same kind of blue pearl buttons. I just feel as if it's more than coincidence. And then when I saw the painting of the girl on your wall..." My heart is racing. "She has the same gold eyes as my mom. I know my mother's eyes. I looked into them forever...seeking answers." I look at Bonnie. "Did you know my mother? Or my father? I feel paralyzed."

Bonnie looks at me with a curious expression and then reaches out and takes my hand in hers.

"I painted that portrait of the little girl," Bonnie says. "It was a picture of the little girl I always wanted but never had." She sighs. "I have a very personal connection to that picture... a love that never came to be." Bonnie pauses. "And I'm not familiar with a Ted Douglas in town who was a clammer. I mean, our business employed thousands of men, as did pearl button factories throughout the Midwest. Have you done a genealogy search? Or gone to the library?"

"I've been doing some digging," I say. "Thank you anyway."

"Maybe I could take a look at what you found. I could ask some friends."

"That would be wonderful."

"Maybe, Sutton," Bonnie says, squeezing my hand, "you were meant to come here to find a new family. You sort of feel like the daughter I never had."

I can feel my heart rise into my throat, and I begin to tear up. Maybe she's the mother I never had. Maybe she's here to fill a void, or give me things my own mother couldn't. Maybe I can't solve the mysteries of my past, but I can solve the ones of my future.

"That means the world right now," I say.

I hear a squeak. I turn.

Has Lauralei has been standing at the doorway, listening?

She puts a hand to her eye and walks away.

"Well, I hate to move along, but is it okay if we get to the business of the day?" Bonnie asks. "I really don't have much time."

"Of course. Thank you for listening." I reach for my sketchbook.

"Remember," I caution, "this is only a sketch based on what you had broadly said you envisioned."

Bonnie nods.

"When I look at you," I say, "I see Helen Mirren."

"That's incredibly flattering," Bonnie says. "She's stunning and so polished."

"You truly are as beautiful as she is, and in just as good of shape."

"For a woman my age?"

"No, no, no," I start. "For any age."

I clear my throat. "As I was saying, Helen Mirren is the pinnacle of being both fashion-forward but also age-appropriate. She sets a standard that women of every age aspire to reach. If you want to reinvent your look and reintroduce yourself to the world, she's the trendsetter we should follow."

"Go on," Bonnie says.

"I was inspired by the fabric I purchased that you saw and loved, and I was also inspired by a powder-blue, floral embellished Valentino gown that she wore to a movie premiere," I continue. "So…"

I open my sketchbook in my lap, turning it slightly so Bonnie can see. She scoots over on the couch and then slowly leans forward over the paper until she's inches from it. Finally, she takes the book from me and lifts it to her face, turning it this way and that.

"Um," I start, unnerved. I straighten my back.

"As you can see, the dress features a rounded neckline and fitted bodice. It sweeps out at the bottom, just a touch, for a bit of formal glamour. Very simple. Very elegant. You don't want the pattern or the fabric to overpower your frame. It's the canvas. The dress is the painting. They work together."

Bonnie skews her eyes toward me.

"The elegance is found in the fabric and..." I retrieve the book and turn the page. "...the buttons."

Bonnie gasps. Audibly.

"The beautiful, round pink pearl buttons I found at Tug's... I mean Mr. McCoy's shop...are perfect for the simple, fitted sleeves. But I wanted some drama in the back. You know how at a party everyone watches everyone as they cross the room *and* as they walk away? I wanted your image to be seared in their minds. As I've said, my mother collected buttons her whole life. I found these in one of her jars: hand-embroidered pink gold buttons with central crystals. Aren't they stunning?"

Bonnie is silent.

She looks at the sketch, then at me, and then out the window.

The only sound I hear are the muted sounds of boats on the lake.

"I can always change it," I say.

"No, no, Sutton. Be confident."

I look at her and then away, waiting for a response.

Finally, Bonnie looks at me.

"It's perfection."

My whole soul exhales.

"Thank you."

"It's as though you know me. And I know you. Inside and out. We can read one another's minds. My instincts are always right. I never second-guess a decision."

Bonnie lifts her glass.

"Cheers!"

"Cheers!"

"To a wonderful collaboration." She pauses. "And friendship."

I clink her glass. We sit in silence for a few seconds.

"Zippers should be invisible, so the buttons show," Bonnie says. "You understood that without me having to verbalize it." Bonnie gazes out the window again. "I like to choose what the world sees. We all have that choice. Too few of us exercise it."

Bonnie clears her throat and turns back to me. "Your mother must have been quite the character."

I smile. "She was. She had a hard life, but she made the most of it."

"And she always loved buttons, you say? How fascinating."

"She did," I say. "They were her treasures. She told me that buttons were like beautiful mini-novels: they told a story. Of our past. Of our families. Of our histories. And we shouldn't just toss them aside. She loved to collect them. No, she *lived* to collect them. She'd even pick them up off the ground, like a penny, if she found one. 'Came from somewhere and someone,' she'd say. My mom had jars, boxes and tins filled with buttons. Just like you. I was fascinated by them from an early age, and I still am." I take a breath and smile. "Obviously."

I continue. "My mom used to say that people no longer gave a whit about buttons anymore because things of value just got tossed aside. She said that buttons are still the one thing that not only hold a garment together but also make it truly unique. 'Lots of beauty and secrets in buttons if you just look long and hard enough,' she always told me."

I look at Bonnie. Her hand is on her heart. The sun shifts through the trees and illuminates her face. I swear her eyes are misty.

"Well," she finally says, taking a gulp of air and then champagne.

"Are you feeling okay?" I ask.

"Champagne went to my head," she says. "I'm going to scurry off to the powder room for a moment. If you'd like to do the same, the closest is just out this door in the foyer, just before the staircase."

"Thank you."

"I'll be right back," Bonnie says.

Bonnie seems to steer herself with as much composure as she can into the foyer and then up the stairs. I follow behind her, locating the guest bathroom. I turn on the light and shut the door.

What a morning, I think. *I can feel the champagne, too. Or is it just adrenaline and emotion?*

I turn on the faucet and splash my face with cold water. I tamp a hand towel over my face and look at myself in the mirror.

Pull it together, Sutton.

Sometimes when I look at my reflection, I see a stranger. A woman I don't know. A woman I've never known. A shell. Is this normal for women? Or am I an emotional orphan wandering aimlessly and all alone throughout this world?

I once asked my mother if she felt the same way.

"No woman knows herself," my mother said, not bothering to look up from her sewing, "because no woman is ever allowed to know herself."

I take a deep breath and lean toward my reflection.

Who am I?

Who was I?

Who will I become?

Will I ever know?

I feel as if my mother broke the mold of her past, and I did the same as well.

But I feel as if we both never had closure. And that's a terrible place to dwell forever.

I fix my hair and make sure my supposedly waterproof mascara hasn't run and clumped and turned me into a raccoon.

I hear a squeak outside the door.

Lauralei.

Always watching like my mother. Or am I just imagining this? Is she just a kindly woman doing her job?

I wash my hands, waiting for Lauralei to squeak away. I wipe my hands on a guest towel. My heart stops.

On a wall, in an old frame, hanging just above the towel ring, is a small mosaic of the lake. The image parallels exactly what you see from the front yard of Bonnie's cottage: a pine tree in the foreground, a bluff, a ring of golden sand and the water.

Made entirely of vintage moonglow glass buttons from the 1950s, all in shades of blue.

I grasp the wall for support.

Squeak.

I open the door.

Lauralei is standing in the foyer.

"Mrs. Lyons isn't feeling well. She would like to rest before her day on the water. She will call you to continue and extends her sincere apologies."

I look at this woman, bent like my mother, but still so strong and resilient. I know she is likely working for very little probably just to put food on the table, buy medication, keep a roof over her head.

So little in the midst of such opulence. When I look at her, I see my mother.

"Thank you, Lauralei," I say. "Let me just gather my things."

I retrieve my sketchbook and phone. When I leave the living room, the front door is already open.

"Have a good day," I say.

I head out the door when I hear, "Sutton."

My name is said quietly and with great affection, like when a mother cradles her baby and whispers its name.

I turn.

"Sutton," Lauralei says again. "Are you my bluebell?"

Her hands are clasped before her heart. Tears glisten in her eyes. She is standing in the foyer, smack-dab in the middle of the blue-tiled button.

"Excuse me," I ask. "I'm not following. Are you okay?"

"Lauralei?" Bonnie calls from upstairs.

And, just like that, she turns and disappears down the hall.

"You live here?"

Tug turns and laughs at my question.

"You expected a hovel?"

He looks beyond adorable in his vintage Douglas Dutchers baseball uniform. He has eye black smeared at the top of his cheeks to reduce the sun's glare, a bat is slung over his shoulder, and the bill of his cap is broken. I have a flashback of Tom Hanks in *Big*, and I can see Tug for the first time, who he really is.

He is a kid who grew up playing a game where all the rules were established. Now, he's playing his own game with own rules, sort of like the vintage ball game I just watched.

I shake my head. "No. I expected a bachelor pad. Not this!"

Tug's home is a small white cottage with a front porch and long, little windows in front. A white picket fence fronts the property, and a cottage garden peeks over it. It's probably the cutest tiny home I've ever seen.

"It's sorta famous around these parts," Tug says, "like me."

He winks and points to a plaque on the fence.

WADE'S COTTAGE, 1851
THE OLDEST HOUSE IN DOUGLAS, MICHIGAN

I look at him, eyes wide. "Lotta history in this old town," I say.

He laughs. "You doing okay after the last Bonnie encounter?"

I shrug. I filled him in before the game about my latest conversation with Bonnie, the button artwork and Lauralei's eery utterance. "You know how you start a thousand-piece puzzle, and you work really hard on it, and you finally start getting a clear picture that matches the one on the box, and then you realize near the end that a few pieces are missing, and it will never be complete? That's how I feel. My gut says one thing, my head says another."

"Maybe just let it go today. It's the Fourth. Let it just be a holiday for your head and your heart then," Tug says. "You deserve a mental day off."

"You're right."

"Good. Now, come see my house."

Tug takes the bat off his shoulder, reaches out and takes my hand, ushering me through the gate. I can feel goosies on my skin from his touch.

"The oldest house in Douglas was built in 1851 by Jonathan Wade, whose sawmill on the riverfront in Douglas supplied the lumber for his family's small residence."

I laugh. Tug's voice sounds like a narrator from one of the old-time newsreels that used to precede the movies.

He smiles and continues in his normal tone.

"Wade had moved his family from nearby Singapore, the original site of his sawmill. Do you know about Singapore?"

"In Michigan? No."

"It's known as Michigan's Pompeii, a ghost town buried underneath the sand."

"Really?" I ask. "Wow."

"After the series of historic fires swept through Chicago, Holland and Peshtigo in 1871, Singapore was almost completely deforested supplying the towns with lumber for rebuilding. Without any protective tree cover, the winds and sands coming off Lake Michigan eroded the town into ruins and within a few years it was completely covered by sand."

"I didn't realize all the history associated with Saugatuck and Douglas."

"Our little towns love and respect their history." Tug stops and looks at me.

"And we bury our secrets even deeper than the town of Singapore."

I jump at the sound of a woman's voice. It's Mary from The Bayou.

"Sorry," she says. "I didn't mean to scare you."

I laugh at myself. "I'm a jumpy sort these days. It's good to see you."

"Tug, I brought my signature dips: my out-of-this-world corn dip and my smoked whitefish dip."

"Oh, Mary. Thank you." Tug turns to me. "These are my favorites."

"Sorry I can't stay for your party. Some of us have to work today, even though it's a holiday."

"Some of us have capable staff and know when to take a day off," Tug teases.

"Some of us don't have to herd drunken cats all day long," Mary says.

"We'll see about that," I say, wagging a finger at Tug.

"I like you," Mary laughs.

"Me, too," Tug says.

My face reddens.

"I told Sutton she should talk to you sometime," Tug says. He leans close and whispers, "About Bonnie Lyons."

"Sshhh," Mary whispers back. "She's everywhere."

Tug smiles. "I said you know everything about everyone in this town."

"And where the bodies are buried," Mary says with a wink. "Please, stop by the restaurant before it opens one night. I'll buy you a drink. Since my son owns the place."

I laugh.

"And we'll talk," Mary continues. "I'm an open book. Speaking of which, I volunteer at the new library, too, so if I don't know, I can find out."

Mary holds out the cute pink Pyrex casserole dishes heaped high with delicious dips.

I release Tug's hand and take one. He takes the other.

"See you soon, Mary," Tug says.

"Long commute," Mary says, taking off down the sidewalk that leads to the restaurant just two blocks away. "You gotta love small-town life."

"Shall we continue the tour of This Old House?"

I nod, and he opens the front door. The home is as cute as a dollhouse.

"Wade's Cottage was built in 'plank construction' style, and this little house predated the later and better-known 'balloon frame' construction method used today. My plan is to preserve the original pre–Civil War structure and add new compatible living spaces adjacent on the lot. I can go up and out. I want to respect the history and character, but I would also like a little more room." Tug looks around the cozy living room and whispers, as if to himself, "For a family."

He leads me into the kitchen, which has a beautiful view of the bayou.

"Oh, I bet the sunsets are spectacular," I say.

"They are," Tug says, opening the refrigerator. He puts his dip inside and takes the dish I am holding. "I'm going to take a quick shower. Everyone should be here in about a half hour. Do you mind if I put you to work?"

"Now I know why I was invited."

"Glasses are up here, paper plates and napkins are there, I have bags of ice in the freezer in the garage. If you don't mind filling the tubs I have set on the patio with ice for the wine and beer."

"Is there anything else?" I say with a laugh.

"Yes," he says. "You look beautiful."

"This old thing?"

I had been unable to relax after my morning with Bonnie, my mind racing from the champagne and memories. I sat down at Ol' Betsy and began to sew. I stopped only for water and to turn on lights as it grew dark. I didn't stop until I heard an owl hoot directly outside my window as I was stitching on the last button. My summer party dress.

"Love the fabric and buttons. Someone has great taste."

"We both do," I say. "I might be overdressed, though."

"It's summer in Saugatuck," he says. "Anything goes. Flip-flops to formal."

Tug winks and touches my arm, and my body again explodes in goose bumps.

"I'll be quick, I promise."

Tug leaves and shuts his bedroom door.

The windows are open, and a warm breeze blows through the cottage. For a moment, I feel like I'm back at my mother's cabin in Nevermore.

I hear a creak.

Tug's door has blown open, ever so slightly, in the cross current.

No, Sutton. Don't, I tell myself.

But my curiosity overpowers my morals, and I take a step back. And then another.

I hold my breath and stand as quietly as a cat burglar. I peer through the crack in the door.

His bedroom and bath are, literally, just off the kitchen.

Ugh.

The house may be tidy and decorated adorably, but his bedroom is not.

Tug is a bachelor at heart.

Clothes spill out of an overflowing hamper next to his bed. A beer can and a bag of pretzels sits on a nightstand. A laptop sits in the middle of his mattress. Baseball trophies line shelves. Ball caps, tennis shoes, cleats, flip-flops and dressy slip-ons are scattered across the floor, as if he just stepped out of them.

If my romantic inclinations were a balloon, I think, *well, then, it just ran into a thumbtack.*

But then I see a shadow, and Tug appears in the crack of the door. He pulls off his shirt, and it takes every ounce of strength I have not to scream.

He is ripped!

Not just in good shape, but movie star, cover of *Men's Health* ripped. As in "Why do you ever wear a shirt?" ripped.

I didn't see that coming.

Suddenly, the mess in the bedroom isn't so bad.

Just needs a woman's touch, I think. *A good clean.*

Tug turns, and I try to act invisible. He moves into the bathroom and shuts the door.

I sigh.

My guilt—and excitement—make me scurry around his house. I fill the tubs, set up for the party and even manage to put out some decorations I find in his garage—miniature American flags, red-white-and-blue bunting, a sparkly USA banner, and a red gingham tablecloth. I hurriedly pick some red roses and blue hydrangeas and place them in Mason jars filled with water.

"Wow!" Tug says, when he appears on the patio. "What a transformation."

"Just need a woman's touch sometimes."

"Is that a euphemism?" he asks.

I can feel my face blush.

Is he a good boy? Or a bad boy? Or a good boy who likes to be bad sometimes?

I'm about to ask him this when I hear, "We're here!"

Tug's friends and fellow ballplayers begin to pour in, some through the house, some through the backyard, some from neighboring parties. They bring chips, potato and macaroni salads, coleslaw, baked beans, cupcakes and strawberry shortcake.

Tug hugs everyone, introducing them to me as if we've known one another forever. He fires up the grill and barbecues hamburgers and hot dogs. I have a beer and feast on a Fourth of July spread.

I wander inside to bring out more plates and napkins. I stop at the window and watch a group of friends celebrate not only our nation's birthday but also one another. It is such a simple gesture—people coming together—but my sense of belonging has been warped by my childhood and the pandemic.

My mother had one big similarity to the virus that took

her life: they both turned human nature upside down. They both tried to thwart the basic meaning of being human—connection.

My whole life I've wanted a big family. I've wanted to be part of big celebrations like this. I even set out alone to find this, to seek a reconnection to my past and the world so I wouldn't remain that way.

Nearly all of us want to be together. We need to be together. To hug, laugh, talk, connect.

So much of my life has been spent—then and now—in isolation, fearing the company of others, thwarting my most basic human need.

I think of the last few days.

Was my mother trying to protect me, too, I wonder. Shield me from hurt? From the past? And was she trying to protect herself?

Painful memories? Or more?

"Are you okay?"

Tug is standing in the door.

I nod. "Just fine."

"My friends adore you," he says. "But the best part of the day is just beginning: the two of us together."

"How long have you had a boat?" Tug is standing at Tower Marine, untying ropes from the dock.

"My whole life. I grew up on the water, when I wasn't at the ball field."

He stops and looks around the marina. I follow his gaze. The scene resembles an old painting: yachts moored in the marina, sailboats gliding out to the lake, picnics on the grass, American flags flapping on the backs of boats.

But there's something else hidden in this picture, too, I can tell. Tug's face is etched with sadness.

"Are you okay?" I ask.

He looks at me and nods. Then he shrugs. "Don't want to be a downer on the Fourth. You don't need that today."

"Stop it," I say. "I've been a roller-coaster ride since we met."

He coils a rope on the dock—a pretty, perfect circle—and stands. "My sister loved everything about the Fourth of July. I think it was her favorite holiday. Sue relished small-town life. She always loved visiting big cities, like Chicago and New York, and I think she volunteered to work in New York to see what it might be like to live there, but she never dreamed it would no longer be the city it was. She said it was like being in a ghost town. None of us knew what we were up against in the beginning. But Saugatuck-Douglas on the Fourth, well, it made her feel like a kid again, even if for a day." Tug walks to another rope and sets to work. "We loved taking the boat out for the day. Just us. She was always my first mate. She knew how to tie the ropes, drive the boat, perfectly park it to get gas or a drink at the Red Dock..."

"I'm so sorry. She sounds amazing," I say. "I wish I would have had a chance to meet her."

"You would have loved her," Tug says, bending to tie another rope. "And vice versa."

I move from a bench on the grass toward a rope at the front of the dock. "Why don't you teach me? I'd love to learn. I'd love to be your first mate."

The weight on Tug's shoulders seems to lift, and he moves toward me.

"I grew up on the water," I continue. "It may have been a creek, and my boats may have been canoes, but I know and love the water. It's been a huge part of my life forever."

"I'd like that," Tug says. "So, here's your basic boating knots."

Tug demonstrates how to tie a boat up when it returns to

the dock and how to untie it and leave the ropes. I pick it up quickly.

"You forgot I work with tiny rope," I say. "Thread."

He laughs, and we hop onto the boat.

"Welcome aboard!"

"Now this beats a canoe any ol' day," I say. "What kind is it?"

"This is a Sea Ray 320. The number is code for a boat's length. In this case, thirty-two feet. She's an old gal, a Sundancer from the '80s."

"This boat looks like new."

"She's my baby," he says. "I take good care of her. I spend a lot of time out here on the water during the summer."

Tug walks me down a small set of stairs to the living quarters below deck.

"Wow!" I say. "It's huge."

"Not really," he says. "Small kitchen and bath, tiny bed and enough space for a few clothes. This is really where I can get away from my life. Sometimes, you have to escape the glare of small-town life in the summer. It seems so laid-back, but the spotlight can be intense and overwhelming. Work is nonstop spring through fall. I can leave everything behind on the water. Go so far out the world ceases to exist. C'mon."

We head back up, and Tug shows me the "top" of the boat.

"This is the helm, where the captain sits and steers. This is the bow and the deck in front. The deck is the 'hangout' part of the boat, where you can get sun and have a drink. The bow is the practical part of the boat: it helps the boat stay above the waves and takes it over the next one instead of breaking it in half."

"Very important," I say with a laugh. "But most importantly, what's the name of this here seafaring vessel?"

Tug laughs. "Follow me to the stern."

"I don't know where that is," I say. "We didn't have fancy language on canoes. We just said, 'Don't hit that tree in the water!' or 'Snake!'"

Tug leads me to the back of the boat, and I step out onto the dock. I peek at the name and laugh. "No!"

"Oh, yes," he says, grinning.

TUG BOAT is written in fun lettering. Sitting atop the word *TUG* at a jaunty angle is a ball cap, the bill bent.

Between nicknames and boat names, this town is slowly sneaking into my soul.

I look at Tug. He tugs on his cap before doffing it, gesturing me to move onto the boat again. Tug takes a seat in the captain's chair and turns on the motor.

"What do you need me to do?"

"Be my eyes," Tug says. "Make sure we don't hit the dock. Pull up the buoys. Tell me we're clear."

My heart begins to pound. "I feel a lot of pressure."

"No pressure," Tug says. "Just a massive boat we don't want to damage."

"As I said."

Tug preps the Sea Ray, and I stand at the stern, heart in my throat.

"Ready?" Tug yells.

"No!"

"Too late," he says, the boat easing out of the slip.

I run from one side to the other, panicked.

How can this boat even fit into this tiny slip? How can Tug drive this big of a boat without seeing the back end?

"Clear!" I call. "You're clear!"

I sprint around pulling up the buoys and scramble toward Tug out of breath.

"Your eyes are bigger than the electric donut boats all the

tourists rent," Tug says with a laugh. "You did a great job. You can relax now."

He navigates the boat into the bay that leads to the channel that flows to the lake.

"Oh, wait," he says, standing suddenly. "Steer for a second."

"What?"

He seats me in the captain's chair. "Just keep the wheel steady. It's very sensitive. We're going very slowly. Just keep a lookout and go straight."

"Where are you going?"

Tug runs down below and rushes back with his hands behind his back.

"You almost gave me a heart attack."

"Smush those bugs!" he says with a laugh. "Here," he continues. From behind his back, Tug produces a cap that reads First Mate.

"You passed your first test with flying colors. Here's your reward."

He takes off his Northwestern ball cap and replaces it with one that says Captain.

My cap and his are both white with blue bills, big yellow anchors emerging from the letters.

"I feel like I'm on *The Love Boat*."

Tug twitches his eyebrows, and his hazel eyes become chameleons. "Maybe you are," he says, sitting and steering once again. Tug looks at me for a long beat. "You earned that cap."

"I'm glad I only had one beer at the BBQ," I say. "I'd be a wreck."

"Well, now you can relax. There's nothing like seeing the town from the water, is there?"

I shake my head.

It's truly magical.

Boats navigate the channel, music blaring, flags flapping.

Boaters raise their glasses and yell "Cheers!" and "Happy Fourth!" as we pass. Shoppers clog the streets in town and line the outdoor restaurants overlooking the water. In the park, an old-time oompah band plays in the gazebo, and picnickers eat on the grass.

An air horn blares, and I jump. Tug laughs.

"That's the warning the chain ferry gives when it's about to cross the channel," Tug says, slowing the boat. "As I told you when we went to Ox-Bow, this is the last remaining chain ferry in the US. Been in use since 1838. It is hand propelled by a chain along the bottom of the channel. A lot of people take it over to the other side and then walk to Oval Beach to beat the traffic. The parking lot is usually full by noon."

The ferry resembles a well-kept Victorian home, the top of the little flat boat made of ornate gingerbread trim painted a crisp white.

"Why is it called *The Diane*?" I ask.

"A local businessman, who also owned the marina, brought the historic ferry back to life in the 1960s. He named it after his wife. He passed away not too long ago, but his love for this town and all of his memories remain intact."

"That's lovely," I say.

I watch the ferry pass, a few happy passengers taking a turn cranking the ferry, tapping someone else to take over once their shoulder tires. Parents hold their kids in their laps. Some have hauled their bicycles on board.

I think of when I would float on the creek during the summer. I used to pretend that the wildlife were the friends I never had. The cicadas would buzz, starting slowly and quietly, before building to a crescendo of deafening proportions. I imagined the cicadas were my loud friends, the ones I'd jump into a car with on Friday night to cruise the square, windows down, music blaring.

The nighthawk that soared silently over the world was my quiet friend, the one who'd come over during the week to study, cram for tests and read books for hours at a time, our legs draped over one another's in the hammock by the bluff.

At night, after the sun had set, the bullfrogs would fill the world with their low, soulful groans. My mom used to say they sounded like cows mooing—hence, their name—but I pretended they were a boy who had come to call, tossing pebbles at my window, his voice low and rumbling, calling "Sutton! Sutton!"

My mom used to go out frog hunting. She'd carry a flashlight, a homemade gigger—a harpoon on the end of a long pole—and a sack. She made me go with her a few times to hold the flashlight. When we'd come upon a bullfrog, I'd shine the light in its eyes to blind it and my mom would gig it. I cried every time, sobbing all the way home, telling my mom she'd just killed the father of the family.

"You wanna eat, or not, young lady?" my mom would ask. "People would pay a pretty penny for a frog leg dinner, and we just got one for free."

And then as we'd walk through the low-lying lands that surrounded the creek, the flashlight bobbing in front of us, she'd always say, "Survival of the fittest, Sutton. Sometimes, you have to learn to outwit everyone around you. You have to remember not to be blinded by the world. Or you'll die."

"Aren't these homes beautiful?"

Tug's question pulls me out of the past. I look along the edge of the river, where stunning private homes and cottages of every shape and size are perched on the water. Some are old cottages whose roofs and decks sway this way and that, some are log cabins that seem to disappear into the wooded landscape and some are mansions—sleek and contemporary, or all-glass midcentury, or soaring and shingled—that loom over the water seeming to scream, "Look how rich I am!"

"What do you think?" Tug asks. "You didn't answer me."

My issues with money always just simmer below the surface. "Beautiful," I say.

"Beyond those reeds is Ox-Bow," Tug says, pointing from behind the wheel. "You can see where it was cut off from the river. And dead ahead is party cove, where boats line up in a circle and party, especially on a holiday."

We motor past the cove. Boats begin to honk and wave when they see Tug's boat, people yelling his name.

"You're popular," I say.

"I know everyone," he says. "Blessing and curse of a small town."

I again think of my small town. I knew everyone, but I knew no one.

A long pier lines the river. To the left, people fish off the edge. Behind them, dunes lead to the beach, mammoth lake homes rising from the sand. Ahead, I can see Lake Michigan sparkling.

Tug slows the boat so as not to create a wake in the tight channel. Boats motor past us heading home. Behind us, boats are lined up as far as my eye can see.

"Perfect day for this!" Tug yells. "I can't remember more perfect Fourth of July weather!"

As soon as we hit the open water, Tug guns the boat and I scream in glee. I catch my cap just before it flies off my head, and I sit on it to protect it.

Tug veers the boat south. I can see where I lay out on the beach the other day, boats gathered in the protected harbor by the pier. People are packed onto Oval Beach. Bright umbrellas and beach towels dot the landscape, the dunes towering behind the sand. The sun makes everything hazy, like a mirage, the beachgoers ghosts.

"No crowds out here!" Tug jokes over the engine.

We fly down the coast. I scream and raise my arms, the wind whipping my hair around my face. It is glorious being on the water, flying over the waves, being free.

We pass the historic lakeshore cottages, Tug pointing this way and that. He slows the boat about fifty feet from the shore. The lake is crystal clear, and the water varying shades of blue-green, depending on the depth. I can see the sandy bottom and monstrous lake stones below the surface.

"That's Bonnie's house," Tug says, pointing. "See? Your cottage is right behind it. Looks completely different from this vantage point, doesn't it?"

I nod.

I spot a woman in pink tending her garden. She studies her roses carefully, and then clips them quickly with the precision of a surgeon. She turns and scans the water.

Bonnie.

Can she see me from this distance?

And what does she see when she looks at me?

My face flushes as if I just got caught spying, and I pull on my cap and tug it lower until it covers my eyes.

"Are you pretending to be me?" Tug asks.

"No," I say. "Let's go. I feel a little weird spying on her. She's been very kind to me so far. And…" I stop.

"And?" Tug asks.

"And I don't want her to think I'm any crazier than I already am."

Tug nods and veers the boat into the open water, and we fly across the lake toward the horizon until we're a half mile or so from the shore. Tug shuts off the boat and drops the anchor.

Save for the soft splish-splash of the waves against the hull, it is completely, utterly silent.

"Feels like you're in another world, doesn't it?" Tug asks.

"It does."

Water seems to go on for infinity. There is no difference between the lake, the sky, the horizon. In the distance, golden dunes rise from the water.

Tug sets up towels on the deck, retreats and reappears with a bottle of wine, and a charcuterie board.

"You're spoiling me," I say.

"You deserve to be spoiled."

He pours two glasses of rosé, and we sip it and watch the water.

"I'm reminded how big and small I am when I'm out here," Tug finally says, his voice hushed. "I'm reminded that I am part of something much bigger than me. I know all of this will remain long after I'm gone, but this also makes me want to make my own mark on this world."

"What mark do you want to make?" I ask.

"I want to inspire people to appreciate things from their past, items that we take for granted, heirlooms that are being tossed aside." He pops a grape into his mouth. "You know, everything comes back in style. Even bad taste. SPAM, for example."

I laugh. "Had a lot of that in my day. Fried."

Tug continues. "Before the pandemic, too many people took life for granted. We take photos on our cell phones and then erase them when our storage got too low. We text instead of writing letters. Nothing's permanent. The silver lining in all of this horror is that we've been reminded of what's most important in life again." Tug takes a sip of his wine. "The simplest of things mean the most. A sunrise. A sunset. Watching a ball game with your kid. Talking to a friend. Our health. Home—and everything it holds—has become our sanctuary again. At least this hell has reminded us of all that's heavenly again. If we can just remember some of that moving forward, we will all be better because of it."

I look at Tug for the longest time. I know if I try to say anything, I will cry. So I just nod and then look out over the water.

"What's your next act, Sutton?" Tug asks.

I shake my head and try to gather myself.

"To find myself again," I finally say. "Connect my past to my future, so I can finally just be in the present."

"It's okay to be just in the moment sometimes. It's okay to float every now and then." Tug laughs. "Speaking of which…"

He gets up and disappears into the cabin. I hear a whooshing noise for a few moments, and Tug finally returns carrying a giant inflatable unicorn with a gold horn and a rainbow tail, just like the one I saw when I was on the beach the other day.

I applaud.

The float is massive, big enough for two to lie out on with drink holders. Tug tosses it into the water. And then carefully tosses a bottle of wine and our two empty plastic wine glasses atop it. They bounce briefly and settle into the belly of the unicorn.

"Wow, you really are a great baseball player," I say.

"C'mon!" he yells.

He pulls off his shirt, and I stare. For far too long.

I need to burn every shirt that man owns.

And then he leaps off the boat, making a huge splash.

I stand and look over the edge. Tug is tying a rope from the unicorn to the boat. "Your turn!"

From the boat, it looks like a long way to the water.

"Just do it!" Tug yells. "Leap of faith! Water's deep out here."

I shrug out of my shorts and tank top. I look down at my body. I haven't worn a swimsuit in front of a man I know in what feels like an eternity. My body is not what it was. It shows the signs of too many quarts of ice cream.

"Hi, Ben," I say to my stomach. "Hi, Jerry," I say to my thighs.

"What?" Tug calls.

"Nothing!"

And yet, I'm still here. Healthy. Alive. And that's all that matters. I made it through to the other side somehow, to be right here, right now.

I take a deep breath and jump. I plunge through the water. I open my eyes underwater. Bubbles surround me. The water is chilly but warmer than a few days ago. It makes me feel alive. I pop up, bobbing on the waves. I swim over to the inflatable and crawl aboard with all of the dexterity of a drunk trying to tap-dance. Tug pulls me in, and I flop onto the inflatable facedown.

"How's that for a pretty entrance?" I laugh.

Tug applauds and holds out my glass. "You need a drink." He stops. "No, I think I need a drink after seeing that."

He opens the bottle of wine, pours two glasses, and we float on the unicorn on a beautiful summer day.

The unicorn softly twists this way and that on the lake's flat surface. One moment, I am facing the stunningly beautiful dunes that line the entire coastline, a ring of gold against the water. And then the next moment, I face the horizon, blue on blue, sky meeting lake.

I feel as if I'm floating on the edge of infinity. I feel as if I'm floating at the edge of life.

The edge of summer.

We float for what seems like forever, chatting and drinking, then head back to the boat as the sun begins to slowly set.

"What are we doing for the fireworks?" I ask.

"You're lookin' at it," Tug says. "No better place to be."

"How do we get home when it's dark?"

"This boat has better lights than a car," Tug assures me. "And I'm a really good captain."

Tug heads to the galley, and I follow. He has made a salad, and has two potatoes and two steaks.

"You have a grill on this, too?"

"Yep. Isn't it great?"

I sip my wine as Tug makes dinner, relishing being doted on, not having to cook for myself after so many months of opening the refrigerator and trying to figure out what to make.

For one.

And then we eat as the sun begins to disappear. It is a glorious, Dreamsicle sunset. From the boat, drifting on the horizon, I feel a part of its vibrancy and exaltation. I swear I can hear the sunset sigh, exhausted from providing such glory.

We clean the dishes and Tug has just poured me another glass of wine when I hear a boom. I look up. Fireworks are bursting across the night sky, their magnificent colors reflecting off the water.

"They shoot them off from a barge on the bay," Tug explains. "But here you can see them unobstructed."

The fireworks illuminate the dunes in flashes. Their colorful explosions look like a beautiful garden in the sky: chrysanthemums, peonies, willows, palms.

"Hold on to your hat," Tug says, grinning widely, watching the display. "The finale here is unbelievable."

And it is, going on for at least ten minutes. Like Tug, I cannot shut my mouth. I am scared to blink, worried that I might miss something. I feel like a kid again staring at the Crayola sky, echoes booming all around me.

When the last firework fizzles, I can hear boats honk their approval in the distance. I applaud wildly.

"What did you think of your first Saugatuck-Douglas

Fourth of July?" Tug asks. "Big for a small town, huh? We do our holidays right here. No one loves parades, lights, fireworks, bands and summer more than a Michigan resort town."

"Spectacular," I say. "Memorable. Awe-inspiring."

Tug laughs.

"I don't know if anything else will ever live up to this," I say.

"Well, this is probably terrible timing, but I hope this does."

Tug leans over and kisses me. It is a tender, gentle kiss. His lips are soft, the stubble on his chin rough. He leans into me, and the kiss grows in intensity.

My instinct is to stop, to slow down, to pull away, but I hear Tug's voice: *It's okay to be just in the moment sometimes. It's okay to float every now and then.*

And so I do, here on this big boat on a big lake with a sweet man I've just met in a tiny resort town I've never visited. For once, I feel present in my own life again. And that feels good.

An errant firework bursts into the sky. I look at Tug in the light. He looks at me, and I can see myself reflected in his eyes.

Hi, Sutton, I think.

I am simply a woman who is—perhaps, maybe, hopefully—finding herself, allowing herself to unbutton all those layers so her soul can finally find the light.

"You okay?" Tug asks.

I lean in and kiss him again, even more deeply.

9

SHANK BUTTONS

*Shank buttons have a hollow protrusion on the back
through which thread is sewn to attach the button.*

"Are you sure?"

Bonnie is standing atop the round alteration fitting platform in the middle of her walk-in closet. Light filters through the window and splays around her lithe body as if she were a spiritual figure in a religious painting.

She stares down at me in her inimitable way. Our last visit still buzzes in my head, and I remember her admonition to ooze confidence.

"One hundred percent," I mumble, my mouth filled with needles.

I am pinning fabric, and we have been sparring the last half hour about the length of her summer dress. Bonnie keeps pushing for floor length. I keep pushing for just above the knee.

"It's inappropriate for a woman my age," Bonnie repeats.

"Says who? Who's telling you how to dress? Society? A man? Or yourself?"

Bonnie has been taken back by my seemingly newfound confidence, but the last few days have emboldened me to find the voice I once had in my career: Tug's kiss, my design, my quest for closure.

"You have great legs. Wonderful knees. Show them off. And it's summer."

Finally, after this last push, she relented.

I finish pinning, stand and place my pins on my magnetic sewing cushion, an invention I cannot live without. The magnet grabs and holds the pins in place. My mother used a little pin tin for many years before moving to small plastic pin boxes with lids. But she knocked those off her sewing table constantly and would spend her days searching for pins, ultimately finding an errant runaway with her bare foot.

Finally, she discovered pin cushions at yard sales and became obsessed. Over the years, her pincushions became more stylish, and she switched them out every season just as she did our holiday décor: tomato and strawberry pin cushions in the summer, pumpkins in the fall, felt snowballs in the winter and birds and flowers in the spring.

I retrieve the beautiful pink embroidered buttons I've selected for the sleeves and back of the dress. I hold Bonnie's arm out and pin one just to see how it hangs.

"Ah, shank buttons," Bonnie says, her voice as wistful as the last warm autumn breeze. She holds her arm out and smiles. "They drape so beautifully from a garment. Just the right amount of space between the fabric. Today, those cheap plastic buttons are literally bolted into place. It's such a joke, isn't it? People worry that if a button comes loose, or falls off, the garment is poorly made. Well, it's already been poorly made. Our clothing should be beautiful, not indestructible. It should be tailored not mass-produced for women who are six foot four *and* five foot two."

Bonnie holds her sleeve to her eye and then moves her arm as if it's caught in a wind current—that last warm autumn breeze. She looks like a little girl you might pass on the high-way who has stuck her arm out the window and is mesmer-ized watching it fly.

"Buttons with shanks are more expensive to produce," she says in a whisper, as if in a trance. "We should have kept pro-ducing quality. The world changed. I never did."

She blinks and seems to see me again.

"Well," she says. "What next?"

"I need to take this home and work on it..." I start.

"Home," Bonnie says. "Are you?"

"I... I..." I halt, searching for the right words. "I meant that literally. It is. For right now."

A Cheshire cat grin crosses her face. "I'm thrilled you're learning to love Douglas, Sutton Douglas. I'm thrilled you're beginning to think of this as home and yourself as a local."

The word *home* trails in the air.

"One day at a time. So, I'll hopefully have something ready a week before your gala, so we have time to alter and refine."

"And what about sketches for my August Glow?"

"I'm noodling some ideas," I say.

"Noodling?" Bonnie asks. "Is that an Ozarks term?"

The platform on which Bonnie is standing seems to rotate like a disco ball.

How much does she know about me? How much do I know about her?

My mother—like many Ozarks fishermen—used to noo-dle. Noodling was "hand" fishing for catfish that lived in the muddy banks of Ozarks creeks. My mom would go out at night, as she did when she went frog gigging, and slink into the creek and feel along its banks for holes where the catfish dwelled. And then she would yank them out as easily as if she were plucking a turnip from the ground. She always tried to teach me, but I could never get over my fear of the unknown, what I couldn't see, what I felt and, worse, what I might find.

"Can't let your mind play tricks on you," my mom would say.

I look at Bonnie watching me, waiting for me to answer. *Noodling. Why would she ask that in her strange way?*

Or is my imagination continuing to play tricks on me?

"Exactly how much do you know about me?" I ask, looking directly at her.

The Cheshire grin re-emerges.

"I've told you before," Bonnie says, "I've done my research. Have you?"

My heart flip-flops. The way she asks this makes me think, *Not as much as I should have on you perhaps.*

"I'm just teasing you, Sutton," Bonnie says. "My goodness. The look on your face. It's as if you've seen a ghost."

Ghosts.

"You look as if you might need a cup of tea and a bite to eat before you go home and finish your work," Bonnie continues. "Would you join me in the garden in the front yard? There's something I'd like to speak to you about."

"Um." I hesitate. Bonnie tilts her head just so but continues to stare at me. "Sure."

"Wonderful! Lauralei!"

I follow Bonnie downstairs and out to a small patio table with two chairs tucked into one of her cottage gardens just off to the side of her cottage. The patio furniture looks vintage. It is as deeply green as the needles on her pines, wrought iron and adorned with ornate curlicues and sturdy feet that have wound themselves into the Michigan earth like tree roots.

"Have a seat."

I sit in a chair—cool to my legs, which are in shorts—just a foot or so away from Bonnie. We are tucked away from the world here, inconspicuous from the passersby on Lakeshore Drive, hidden behind her towering white phlox, red bee balm, maroon hollyhocks, lavender rose of Sharon. A natural border of boxwoods showcases rows of exquisite hydrangeas tucked just behind them, electric-blue blooms and perfectly pink panicles. An arbor with happy red roses provides even more secrecy.

"Your garden is stunning," I say.

"Thank you. It's a lot of work, to be honest. And I don't trust anyone to touch it but me. But I love gardening. There is such a perfect structure to its growth and evolution. You nurture it correctly, and it shows its undying appreciation. Ah, tea!"

Lauralei arrives with a tray and sets it on the table before us. She pours the steaming tea into two rose-covered teacups and scurries away. Bonnie picks up her tea. I follow suit. Lauralei returns almost immediately with an assortment of sandwiches and scones, much like we had the first time Bonnie and I "officially" met.

"Would you care for a sandwich, Sutton?"

Lauralei. Actually speaking to me.

I hear a tinkle of a teacup and then a crash. "Ow!"

I look up, and Bonnie has not only spilled hot tea on her leg but dropped her teacup onto the ground. She stands in a rush and begins to blot her skirt with her cloth napkin.

"Lauralei!" she yells. "We do *not* use such informality with guests! Even amongst family. What has gotten into you?"

Family?

Lauralei hurries over and begins to pick up the pieces of the teacup. "I'm so sorry, ma'am. I think the heat got to me today."

I stand and begin to help her pick up broken bits.

"Sit down, Sutton!" Bonnie orders. "Guests do not help the help."

Lauralei is stooped, but her head shoots up, and—for a second—I see a flash of fury cross her face.

"Bonnie." I look her right in the eyes. "It's no problem. And, Lauralei, you can call me Sutton."

Bonnie begins to respond, but I add, "Anytime!"

Lauralei rushes away, a rapid series of mini-squeaks, returning with a new teacup and endless apologies to Bonnie, who refuses to acknowledge her.

When she leaves, we sit in silence for a bit.

"I'm sorry, Bonnie," I say, "but I must say something: I don't like the way you talk to Lauralei. My mother was treated that way by many women of privilege, and it's not okay. Not one of us is any more important than someone else, doesn't matter if we're drinking the tea or serving it."

Bonnie's eyes widen to the size of saucers. I'm unsure if she's ever been spoken to like this.

"Lauralei and I have a very long history together. Sometimes, words are exchanged."

"That's still no excuse. I just can't abide it."

Bonnie looks at me for the longest time. "I apologize. You're right. Sometimes, I'm like a cat: I react and scratch without thinking. Maybe it's the only way I know how to survive. But it's not right."

"I appreciate you saying that," I say. "And listen, while we're 'exchanging words,' I just have to know about the artwork in your bathroom. Those moonglow buttons. I thought I was the only one who knew about them and collected them. My mother loved them. It just seems like yet another coincidence."

"Our button company specialized in moonglow buttons," Bonnie explains. "We were known for them. We had so many that I used to give them to the school for art projects. One of the children made this, and I've treasured it forever."

"Oh," I say, feeling partly relieved and partly deflated.

"And…it seems as though Lauralei seems to know me for some reason," I push on.

"She lost a child, a long time ago," Bonnie says. "Poor dear. She's never recovered from that. Work is the only thing she's had to occupy her time. I think it's a blessing we've been together so long. I might have just saved her life." Bonnie looks at me again. "So we may have words, Sutton, but believe me we have a longer history than you can ever imagine. We know each other better than you can ever know. And we have a relationship forged in…" Bonnie hesitates, seeking the right word. "…blood."

Then Bonnie tilts her head back and stares up at the sky. I sip my tea as quietly as I can, trying to be invisible, feeling guilty, as if I were responsible for initiating a fight between my parents.

"Look," Bonnie finally says.

I follow her gaze up. A canopy of sugar maples fills the sky.

"Do you see the beautiful patterns that are formed in the branches?" she asks in a quiet voice. "The sky and light you see through the tracks of empty space running through the canopy?"

It takes me a moment to visualize what she is seeing but it finally comes to me. Although the trees' upper branches have grown together, they do not touch. As a result, an intricately beautiful pattern appears in the light akin to when I used to color Easter eggs and the shell would sometimes crack over time.

"I do," I say.

"It's a phenomenon known as crown shyness, in which the crowns of fully grown trees do not touch each other, forming a canopy with small gaps. My husband and I gave a large swath of lakeshore property south of here to a nature conservancy, and a biologist explained this to us. He believed that trees in windy areas suffered physical damage as they collided with each other during winds. As a result, there is reciprocal pruning and an induced crown shyness response."

Bonnie looks at me and says in a hush, "The trees refuse to touch."

She tilts her head up again and whispers to herself, "They need personal space, too. They must maintain their distance from others."

My entire body explodes in goose bumps, and I shiver despite the temperature outside. I take a sip of tea to warm myself.

I cannot tell if Bonnie is giving me a science lesson, an insight into her own behavior, or a personal warning.

"In a surreal way, crown shyness is the arboreal version of social distancing," Bonnie continues. "Nature knew how to protect itself from harm, trees understood that even those closest to them could hurt them the most, so they learned how to survive. Maybe that's the lesson we all needed to learn these past few years."

She skews her eyes at me and continues.

"That's the beauty of isolation. The tree is really safeguarding its own health."

My heart is racing. I look up at the gaps in the trees. A breeze kicks up off the lake, and the branches sway but never touch. I stare at two trees, and their forms change. They morph into versions of me and my mother, so near and yet so distant, one so protective of herself she refuses to let the other she loves more than anything else get too close.

"I've never heard of that before," I say, trying to act interested yet unaffected. "Fascinating."

"Isn't it?" she asks in her Bonnie way.

I feel unsteady and unnerved.

"Well," I say, "I best get back to work."

"Before you do," Bonnie says, "I have something for you."

She retrieves an envelope from her pocket and hands it to me. I open it.

"A check?" I ask.

And then I see the amount. It is a healthy five figures.

"What is this for, Bonnie? I can't accept this."

"I wanted to put you on a retainer," she says.

"For what?"

"To be my designer. I think it's more than fair, don't you?"

I stare at the check, the numbers waving before me just like the branches on the trees.

"I hope it's not insulting," she continues.

"Insulting? No. Bonnie, this is a few months' salary."

"Then that's perfect right? And I hope it's just the start of our relationship." Bonnie stops. "I could even take over your rent for a few months, just to make things equitable."

"Equitable?"

I realize I'm repeating everything she's saying as a question.

"Bonnie, I'm flattered, but I can't accept this. I don't know where I'll be next month, much less what I'll be doing."

I hold out the check to her, but Bonnie fills her hands with her teacup.

"Just think about it," Bonnie says. "I promise I'll try not to be as coarse in the future. Maybe I need to learn a thing or two from you about life."

I look up at the trees and then at Bonnie.

How close should I get to her?

Am I doing this for the money? To rebuild my career? Or to have a semblance of belonging in a new place?

"Just take the check and think about it, Sutton," she says again, following my gaze up to the trees. "Opportunities like this don't come around very often."

★ ★ ★

Dan D. Lyons
Bonnie Lyons
The Lyons Trust

I pick up the check to ensure that it's real, running my fingers over the ink, touching every number.

The realist in me knows this is enough money to tide me over quite a while. It would remove the pressure of having to return to "normal" life and searching for a job I don't even want in a very competitive industry.

With Bonnie's retainer, I could stay here for the near future, spend more time with Tug, work on launching my own line just as I'd always dreamed.

This is a dream. Right?

But there is also another realist dwelling in me, and she is asking a lot of questions. In fact, her voice sounds an awful lot like my mother's.

What does Bonnie really want?

Why me?

You can't be reliant on anyone but yourself, my mom whispers.

"But I wouldn't be, Mom," I respond out loud to an empty room. "It would be my work, my life, my career."

Would it? the walls echo.

I shiver and pull a blanket around me.

It is raining outside, a cold rain that has turned July to October. The temperature is in the fifties, the rain slides down the wavy window panes in sheets. I had wanted to start a fire, but the logs outside were already wet and who knew you needed Duraflame logs in July in Michigan. Instead, I've put on my favorite hoodie and grabbed my teddy bear for comfort.

I'm a grown woman who still needs my childhood treasures to make me feel safe.

The wind blows the branches around outside, casting long

shadows along the walls, making it look as if people are dancing in the cottage.

Crown shyness.

Bonnie's story sticks with me, haunting me for some reason. I know why.

I have crown shyness.

My family tree may have been tiny—a forest of two—but we grew up alongside one another, sheltering, ever-present. But we rarely touched. My mother knew how to keep a distance, even from her own daughter. She may have never bent or broken, but she could also never embrace me in her limbs.

"Were you protecting me, Mom, and helping me reach my potential, or were you thwarting me from ever being able to connect with another living creature?"

I am talking to ghosts.

Why—even when we're cognizant of our own limitations, triggers and weaknesses—do we fall back on them, play into them?

Am I doing it again with Tug, Bonnie, my career? Not trusting my future because of my past?

Do I follow my instincts, knowing I might get hurt?

My cell blinks, illuminating the darkness. It is a text from Abby. I've told her about Bonnie's offer.

> **You're one of the smartest people I've ever known, Sutton. You got yourself into college. You got yourself a dream job. You're a good student. You know what to do.**

"Thank you," I say to my cell and my friend.

And then I open my laptop and do what I did when I was living in the Ozarks without a college counseling program or anyone to assist me with my college application process. I do what I did when I was job hunting. I became a student of the game. I became not just the girl with the interesting history, the poor girl from the Ozarks, the "button girl," but I became the most knowledgeable applicant and candidate. I learned everything about everyone.

I do what I should have done weeks ago, what I did when my mother first revealed my past was a lie: go online.

I sit and begin to research Bonnie Lyons' past as much as she's seemed to have researched mine.

I begin to Google every name and angle.

Pages of photos appear of Bonnie at fundraising galas and events. There are stories about her and her husband's charitable activities. The two owned hundreds and hundreds of acres of land around the area, in town, on the lakeshore and river, out in the country. Much of the land is now protected, but some of it was sold for development. Huge homes were built on Lake Michigan and the Kalamazoo River. Much of downtown Douglas once belonged to the Lyons. And orchards, wineries, pie pantries, and bed-and-breakfasts now dot the countryside they once owned.

How much money do they have?

Dan & Bonnie Lyons Douglas Michigan estimated net worth?

I wait as Google searches.

Fifty million dollars.

I've known people with that kind of money, but I've never *known* someone with that kind of money, and there's a big difference.

I think of my mother picking up every penny she found on the sidewalk. I think of her sewing different buttons on an old shirt to make it seem new again. I think of her fishing and gigging to put food on our table. I remember my mother once received an anonymous envelope at church one Christmas. It was stuck underneath the windshield wiper of our car when we walked into the parking lot. Someone had printed *MERRY CHRISTMAS* on the front, alternating the letters in bright red and green ink. When my mom opened it, a check for fifty dollars was enclosed along with a holiday card that read, May you have a very Merry Christmas! We looked around the parking lot, but no one looked like they had done a thing.

"Fifty dollars!" my mom screamed in the car, jumping up and down. "Fifty whole dollars! We're rich, Sutton!"

We bought a turkey and all the fixings, and my mom bought me a pair of new winter boots and lots of buttons for herself, and for one day we truly felt rich.

Without warning, tears roll down my face, and my stomach churns with sadness and anger.

Fifty whole dollars. We're rich, Sutton.

Fifty million dollars.

What does someone even do with that much money? You could never spend it all, could you? Maybe she's giving it all to her family? Or charity? Or both?

I search again: *Dan and Bonnie Lyons family children Douglas Michigan*

The first item to appear is a FIND A GRAVE memorial site. I click on it. There is a picture of a beautiful gravestone surrounded by fresh flowers.

AMBEL LYONS
BELOVED, "LOVABLE" DAUGHTER
FOREVER CUTE AS A BUTTON
BORN: 3-30-1965
DIED: TOO YOUNG

What a strange gravestone.

Too young?

And Ambel. What an unusual name? I've never heard it before.

I Google search *Ambel Lyons*. Ambel means "lovable."

Who is this? Why did it come up in my search?

I press on. The only real "news" article that appears is Dan Lyons' obituary.

Mr. Lyons was predeceased by his beloved only daughter, Ambel.

I cover my mouth with my hand.

Bonnie told me she had no children. She told me I was like the daughter she dreamed of having. That portrait on the wall. It wasn't the child she never had. It was the child she lost.

Why would she lie to me?

Is she hiding something, or are the memories and the pain too much to bear?

I certainly understand. My depression over my mother's death ate me alive for a year.

"Oh, that poor woman," I say out loud. Such loss. This explains so much about her behavior. Hurt people hurt people.

I watch it rain. Mother Nature heaving, sobbing, weeping.

I see Bonnie in a new light, as if the rain has washed away her aura, all of her confidence. How could this stranger have so much in common with my mother? Loss that has created a shell around them. The limbs wave.

Crown shyness.

I compose myself and press on with a new search: *Dan Lyons Bonnie Lyons button company Douglas Michigan*

A few articles appear about the history of buttons in Douglas, Michigan, ones I've already seen.

I scroll and scroll and scroll. Suddenly, my finger stops moving. I click.

The Douglas Observer
DECEMBER 14, 1972

One of the leading pearl button manufacturing companies in America—and once one of Michigan's largest employers—is closing its doors. The Dandy Button Company opened in 1908 and for many subsequent decades manufactured beautiful high-quality pearl buttons from Kalamazoo River mussel shells. At its peak, the company employed 240 workers and produced up to 20,000 buttons a day. Dandy buttons were sold on cardboard cards branded with the name Grandma's Button Box. For decades, Grandma's Button Box button cards were commonly found in sewing baskets throughout America.

My heart stops. How did I miss this before?

There is a photo of a button card. It is exactly like the one I found with my mother's dress.

I mean, at one time nearly every woman in America had button jars, tins and button cards, right?

I click on Images this time.

Pictures of "mussel men" and "clam fishers" populate my laptop. They are similar to the picture I found of the man hidden in the backing of my mother's button art tree.

Just like Captain Lucky had said.

Lightning flashes. Outside the window, wind blows the rain angrily. Mother Nature heaves in sorrow, her offspring the lake matching her mother's grief.

I stare at the rain crashing against the cottage. The entire world is soaking wet. I blink, and it's then I realize it's not the rain that is blurring my vision. I am crying.

I wipe my eyes with the sleeve of my soft hoodie and reach out to grab my teddy bear. I hold it against my body, so tightly, as if it's the only thing that will protect me from the storm.

"Oh, Dandy," I say. "Am I going crazy?"

My mind begins to flicker, just like the electricity now flashing in the cottage.

I look at my teddy bear, then at my laptop, then at Bonnie's check and finally out the front window.

Dandy.

Dan D.

Dan D. Lyons.

Dandelion Cottage.

"What is happening," I say to the storm. "I feel like I'm losing my mind."

My heart races, and I hold my bear to calm my rising panic.

I swear I can hear the wind howl, "Button, button, who's got the button?"

I grab my cell and text at the speed of light.

Hi, Mary. It's Sutton, Tug's friend. I think I could use that drink now.

"Pick your poison?"

I can't help but laugh at Mary's unintended double entendre as soon as she opens the door. It's four in the afternoon on a Tuesday, and although the restaurant does not open for two more hours, there is a throng of people outside acting as if Reese Witherspoon is about to exit.

As I head in, people excitedly move toward the door. Mary locks it behind her. There is an audible groan.

"People go on vacation and forget how to read," she says, pointing. "See that huge sandwich board?" It says very clearly in bold lettering, CLOSED FOR LUNCH! OPEN EVERY DAY AT 6 P.M. "Is that confusing in some way?"

Mary walks behind the long bar. She notices me eyeing the wood.

"Live edge maple," she says, running her hand along the

top of the bar. "Isn't it gorgeous? A local woodworker made this for me when my son took over this place. I used to serve him pasties to take to work for lunch every day for decades."

I look at Mary.

"Never heard of a pasty?"

I shake my head.

"Looks X-rated the way it's written, but pasty rhymes with nasty, not tasty. Got it?"

"No."

"Good," Mary says.

I laugh again.

"Pasties are Michigan's version of a portable meat pie, a sort of warm pastry sandwich, stew in a shell," Mary says. "Simple filling. Served with gravy or ketchup. Used to serve them to miners, laborers, clammers. Perfect mix of proteins and carbs. Got working men through a long day."

"Clammers?" I ask.

Mary stops. "I think that's a good place to stop. And start. Now you never answered my original question: pick your poison."

"Well, that's a loaded question," I say, "considering my life and mental state right now."

"Well, it's late afternoon, so we can go two ways: subtle or game-on."

"What's subtle?"

Mary bends down and pulls a bottle of rosé from a wine refrigerator. She holds it and then places it on the bar and gives it a high-pitched, squeaky voice, as if it's a cartoon bottle. "Hi, I'm Rosé. I'm safe. It's what all the girls have at the beach. It's what we bring to women's pamper weekend." Mary makes the bottle dance and sings in a high voice, "Wheee! Rosé all day!"

She sounds a lot like Jot, the cartoon about a glowing Christian orb that was popular in the Ozarks.

"What's game-on?" I laugh.

"Can I surprise you?"

"I have a feeling you're going to do that no matter what I choose to drink."

"Atta'girl!"

Mary begins to pull bottles from the shelves as if she's Tom Cruise in *Cocktail*. She squeezes fruit and pours alcohol into ice-filled shakers, finally siphoning out what resembles golden sunshine into a vintage-looking cocktail glass.

"Lavender gimlet," Mary says, pouring herself the same. "Nearly every ingredient, including the gin and the lavender, is locally sourced. We have one of the nation's best gin distilleries a few miles north and one of the nation's most beautiful lavender farms a few miles south. And about a hundred of the best wineries across the state. If you think we can't make a good cocktail in the Mitten, then you need to go somewhere else. Cheers!"

She lifts her glass, and I clink it. I take a sip. It's crisp and refreshing with botanical hints and subtle lavender, not at all what I expected but a perfect summer cocktail.

"What do you think?" Mary asks.

"It's one of the best drinks I've ever had," I say.

"Let's take these out to the garden, okay? It's a beautiful day. No one to stare at us through the window like we're in a zoo."

I follow Mary into the pretty back dining room. It is newer, with a beautiful fireplace and second, albeit smaller, bar. The kitchen is already packed with staff prepping for a busy summer night.

We take a seat at a small table for two perched under an umbrella. Rather than a hedge, decades-old rhododendrons and rose of Sharon form a privacy hedge. The Sharon is blooming and its flowers are multicolored, almost like little pieces of cotton candy tucked amongst the dense green. Beautiful pots of colorful flowers anchor the corners, and another, very tiny bar sits against the hedge.

"This place has changed over the years, hasn't it?" I ask.

"It has." Mary nods. "Sometimes, I don't even recognize it. Or myself. But change is inevitable. Either we fight it, we adapt to it, or we make it."

Mary takes a sip of her drink and looks at me. My mother would have called a woman like Mary "no nonsense." My mom felt the world was filled with people with the wrong intentions, seeking the wrong things. She admired people who understood the meaning of hard work.

"Too many in the world seek riches to feel powerful, but they just don't understand what it is that makes one wealthy."

Mary's readers are perched on the end of her nose. Her hair is short and tucked behind her ears. She is wearing capris and a cute dark blouse that makes her silver hair pop, as well as just a touch of lipstick so that her face doesn't just fade away.

"Now, where we should we start?" Mary asks.

No nonsense, I can hear my mother say.

"With this?" I ask, taking another sip of my cocktail and then an even bigger breath.

I tell Mary about my life, my mom, her death, the letter, the last two years of isolation, leaving my job and coming here on a whim and a prayer. I tell her about what I've discovered so far, and what I haven't as well as about Bonnie, our recent encounters and her offer. I tell her about the many coincidences in my life and ironies with Bonnie's.

"Am I crazy?"

"Listen, I'm no Nancy Drew..."

I laugh. "I'm learning her job was way harder than I imagined."

Mary smiles. "Well, as an adult, I think this all depends on if you actually want to solve the mystery or not. Sometimes, it's better not to know."

"Why?" I ask.

"That's why people bury their pasts. They don't want them to be uncovered."

"But how could I live with myself if I didn't find out?"

"Can you live with yourself if you do?"

Mary's words shake me, and I take another sip to steel myself.

"I don't know."

"Look, you don't know me from Adam, and I don't mean to sound so ominous, but I do know that life ain't always easy," Mary says, "and that family isn't perfect. The truth is hard."

I nod. "Believe me, I know. But what if I have to know?"

"At least you're being honest," Mary says. "And I don't know all the answers either. I'm not a detective, and I'm not a mathematician. I can barely put two and two together, *but* I can provide you some dirt. You're just gonna have to do all the shoveling."

"I'm good with that."

"Well, where should I begin?" Mary starts. "I was born and raised here. So was the Lyons family. Richer than God. Good Dutch folk. Knew the value of a dollar. Saved every one, too, and then built on that. Dan Sr.'s dad—so, Bonnie's grandfather-in-law—owned lakeshore land from here to South Haven and made his money transporting fruit to Chicago. Then he bought all that land from farmers after the great freeze. Dan Sr. started the button company, and Dan Jr. tried to expand it."

"Yes, I learned a lot of that online. The beauty of our world today."

Mary laughs suddenly and looks into space.

"Today versus yesterday," she says as if to herself. "What is it they say? Shirtsleeves to shirtsleeves in three generations?

The first generation creates the wealth, the second stewards it and the third consumes it."

Mary looks at me.

"In this case, the wife consumed the family."

"I don't understand."

"Bonnie was born poor. I bet you didn't you know that?" Mary asks.

My mouth drops.

"Bonnie? No."

"Dirt-poor. Her family was from the Upper Peninsula. They moved here to work for the button company. Bonnie used to help pry open the mussels."

"What? Are you sure? You're kidding me, right? I can't even imagine."

"True story. Long forgotten." Mary looks at a young woman putting out tablecloths in the nearby dining room. "They loved using little kids to do that type of work. They had small hands. And if they lost a finger, no one said a word. Sounds harsh, but that's the way it was back then. People were starving. Everybody worked if they could. Eventually, Bonnie moved up at the company, if you can call it that, and—after the buttons were tumbled in a churn with water, pumiced, washed, dried and moved onto sorting tables—she began sorting buttons according to quality, color and luster. She then moved on to hand sewing them onto cards, where they were placed in boxes for shipping."

"How do you know all this? Does anyone else know this?"

"Not anymore," Mary says. "Some of my family were employed at the button factory. Stories were passed along, until there was no one left to tell them anymore. Gone, just like all the history. And you know how people are today. They see what they want to see. And with Bonnie, they only see a rich woman who's seemingly dedicated herself to the betterment of this community. And she has. And this all happened *so* long ago. I love a success story as much as the next person, but I've never been convinced that Bonnie's entire life wasn't premeditated." Mary stops. "Lauralei was Bonnie's best friend growing up. Did you know that?"

"Her *maid*?" I throw my hands up in the air. "I'm out. I mean, I can't even with what you're telling me. It's just insane."

"Truth is always stranger than fiction, right?" Mary says. "Yep. They worked side by side at the button factory. Then, Bonnie ended up getting pregnant by Dan Jr., and they had to get married before it became public. Apparently Dan Sr. was furious. His son impregnating a button girl. Back then. Can you imagine? And Lauralei was the one who stood by Bonnie through everything."

"Okay, my head has officially exploded," I say. "Bonnie is so proper. Everything follows the rules of society. I mean, she looked at me as if I were raised in a barn because I didn't know proper tea etiquette." I look at Mary and then at the pretty flowers dotting the garden hedge. "I feel like I'm hallucinating."

"Just wait," Mary says, putting her elbows on the table and leaning closer. "Once she had the baby, Bonnie turned on her family. She was supporting them, but it's as if the birth of her baby was her key to a new kingdom. She had been supporting her parents, but then, after her daughter was born, not a penny. Not a visit. Nothing. I don't know if Dan Sr. was so embarrassed he cut them off so they would have nothing to do with the grandchild, or if it was Bonnie's decision or both, but Dan Jr. kept them employed at the button company. And when the company finally went under, her parents moved back to the UP to die. Poof! It's as if they never existed."

My heart races. "That's so sad," I say. "I can't imagine. But why is Lauralei her maid? Why would Bonnie take care of her but not her own family? It makes no sense."

"No clue. Folks say either she has something on her, or she's the one who kept Bonnie going after her daughter's death. Fealty and friendship often walk side by side."

"That's what I was going to ask you about, too," I say. "What can you tell me about Bonnie's daughter? Ambel? I just found out online that she'd died. It's so strange because Bonnie told me she never had a family. I don't understand why she would lie to me when it's public knowledge."

"I don't know that, but I do know she was devastated and refused to talk about it again. Everyone sort of just let it be."

"Do you know how Ambel died? I couldn't find it anywhere online."

"Well, it was a long, long time ago. When Ambel was a teenager, Bonnie and Dan sent her on a trip to Europe... I really didn't know her...she was homeschooled by private tutors. Never really allowed to socialize. Some folks around here assumed they were just being snooty, and others said the family was worried about a kidnapping. Seems the grandfather was consumed by the Lindbergh kidnapping after his own son was born."

Mary continues. "Ambel died in some sort of accident while traveling in Europe, and they had to have her body returned to the States. It was all so very tragic. They had a private funeral, and Bonnie sort of disappeared for a number of years, became a recluse in her own home. That's when the town really took Bonnie under its wing—and vice versa—and her past was just sort of erased along with the memory of their little girl. People began to look at Bonnie as some sort of saint, no matter what she said or did, no matter how much of her husband's fortune she spent on jewelry, travel or clothes. She loves her clothes."

Don't I know it. I think of my mother.

"Oh, my gosh," Mary says. "I forgot the most interesting part."

"Really?" I ask, my voice dripping in sarcasm.

"Bonnie wasn't even her real name growing up."

"What?" I ask. "What was it?"

"Mildred!" Mary says, unable to stifle a laugh.

"No!" I can't help but scream at the thought of Bonnie being poor, button worker Mildred.

"I'd forgotten until her husband died, and the local newspaper, of course, ran the obituary. They used her *real* name: Dan D. Lyons Jr. is survived by his wife, Bonnie Lyons, nee Mildred Bonne. I think that's how she invented her name. Bonne…get it? Bonnie? She literally became someone else right in front of everyone's eyes."

"I just Googled his obituary," I say. "I missed that! I stopped reading when I saw their daughter's name." I look at Mary. "You *are* Nancy Drew."

"No, I'm just an old local who knows way too much—and way too little—for her own good."

"So, what do you think? All coincidence?" I ask.

"No clue," Mary says, peering at me over her readers. "Your mom *was* part of another generation when most everyone sewed, collected buttons and saved pennies. My mom did that. I did, too, and still do. I mean, everyone had Dandy buttons back in the day. Maybe it's just all part of the past. Maybe she got pregnant out of wedlock, and her family couldn't deal with that. It was a different time. Who knows?"

Miss Mabel? The church widow? Unwed and pregnant?

Never.

Mary takes a sip of her drink and continues. "Tug is a great guy. I love him nearly as much as my own son. Maybe you're simply trying to find a way—after all the tragedy you've experienced and all the chaos and loss we've been through as a world—to reach for the light again."

I look up at the trees canopying part of the outdoor garden. *So close, but not touching, still reaching for the light.*

"Can I share one last thing with you?" Mary asks. "I barely know you, but I feel compelled to share it with you. Maybe it will help."

"Of course."

Mary inhales. "My dad was a mean son-of-a-gun—I mean, bad to the bone—but my mother stayed with him for the sake of her kids and society at the time," Mary says. "She should've left him because staying with him actually messed us all up worse than if she'd hightailed it outta there. I followed that cycle. My husband hurt me. I wasn't going to let him hurt my kids, and I wasn't going to stay like my mom did. I had nothing. I started as a waitress here. I socked money away. My son made all my dreams come true." Mary looks at me. "You're probably wondering why I'm telling you all this. I just feel like I have a lot in common with Miss Mabel. She worked hard. We protected our families like lionesses. Never quit. Never asked for a darn thing. Kids came first."

My heart pulses in my head.

"I guess what I'm trying to say is that family is never perfect. Sometimes, what you want from those you love isn't enough. And sometimes it exceeds your wildest expectations. But maybe sometimes it's enough to know your mother loved you as much as I love my son, and we fought and sacrificed our whole lives so you wouldn't have to endure what we did. And maybe sometimes, that's all you need to know." She looks at me. "That you were loved. So, so deeply. And no one can ever take that away."

A tear springs to my eye.

"Thank you."

"You're a very smart woman with oodles of talent," Mary says. "You're gonna figure it all out."

"And if I don't?" I ask.

"There's always another lavender gimlet waiting for you."

10

EASE

*The allowance of space in a pattern for fit, comfort and style,
over exact body measurements.*

It is one of those summer mornings that you want to bottle and open in February.

The scent, the light, the warmth, the color.

I watch a hummingbird dart around garden lilies in full splendor. The lilies are bright orange, a color so surreal in the sun that it looks fake. The hummingbird zips to a clump of pink Monarda—bubblegum in bloom—and finally to a towering coneflower the color of tomato soup before settling on the end of a mock orange branch.

The hummer sits still for so long that I begin to count to myself.

Thirty-eight, thirty-nine, forty…

I am as still as a statue, my body rigid on the bench in the corner of the little yard, coffee midair.

I think of the hummingbird that used to sit and watch my mother. I think of how long we've been isolated, but still never still.

Be still, Sutton.

My mom used to tell me this on weekends when I was alone

and antsy to do something, be like the other kids who were at the public pool, cruising the square, at the mall, doing anything but sitting idle with their mothers.

"Kids aren't supposed to be still, *Mother*," I would say.

I had a way of saying that word—*mother*—in a way, much like Bonnie speaks to me, that made it sound like a condemnation, a mistake, as if I needed to actually overemphasize the noun in order to teach her the meaning of it.

It never worked.

Fifty-two, fifty-three...

Is this my lesson? To be still—with myself, in the world—for once? To finally be at peace? Did I have the opportunity to do this, and I blew it with worry?

Fifty-eight, fifty-nine...

The hummingbird watches me.

Why are you just sitting there? I wonder. *You're a hummingbird. Do your thing.*

I shift on the bench, and the hummingbird takes off, up, up, up. I watch it soar and flit around like a drone, and that's when I notice a big branch of the sugar maple has broken off in the recent storm. I track its fall with my eyes, but there is no branch, no sticks, no debris, only a chunk in the still-damp earth—an indentation—where it landed.

A ghostly reminder.

I look up again, and there is a bigger clearing between the trees, more sunlight is filtering into the yard.

Perhaps Mary is right about how I should look at the world. Perhaps I need more light.

No, check that: perhaps I need to be the light. I need to recognize the light that is already present.

Perhaps *I* can be the change in the world and my career. Perhaps it's time I am no longer reliant upon anyone but myself. Perhaps it's time that I am not tied to the past for once.

No crown shyness.

I sip my coffee, and the hummingbird darts around the tiny garden before lighting on the end of the bench. It cocks its head at me. Its throat is ruby, its wings purple and its back the most iridescent green.

"You are wearing God's most glorious gown," I say in a hushed tone. "I should only hope to have an iota of His talent."

The bird seems to nod its approval, and it returns to the garden. I watch the colorful canvas before me, amazed at my unexpected sign of faith.

My faith has been checked royally, so much so that I began to feel as if I'd lost—along with my mother—all sense of devotion.

When I returned to Chicago after my mother's death, I couldn't get out of bed. Abby sent Instacart groceries to my condo and countless deep-dish pizzas, but for months I couldn't find a reason to go on. Every day was the same. Every month unchanged. Ironically, I felt better prepared for this isolation than the rest of the world. But I was wholly unprepared for the test of faith.

I woke in the middle of the night in the midst of my depression and sat in the window. I was shocked at the number of people who were wandering the street so late. There were many couples walking hand in hand, shoppers returning from the grocery store, runners out for some exercise.

They realized the best time to do any of this was when the world was silent, and no one was out. They realized they were the safest.

I realized the world was upside down. Night was day. Day was night. We were alone but still searching.

I was *not* alone.

"Why do people go to church?" I asked my mom once

as we were driving home on a Sunday. "A lot of them don't seem real church-y."

She had actually laughed, so hard it shocked me, so hard she had to pull the car off to the side of the road, dust flying.

"You're right, Sutton. They aren't real church-y." My mom wiped her eyes and removed her white gloves, one finger at a time. Finally, she looked at me. "Some people use their faith as a show. It's like wearing makeup or a pretty dress. But it ain't real. Ain't the same as true faith."

"What's the difference?" I remember asking.

"Well, true faith comes when you're deeply tested, when the entire world seems set against you, you're all alone, and the only one who's there for you is God. You might hear a voice, or see a sign, but mostly it will be your soul talking back to you. You'll understand one day." She put her gloves into her clutch and stopped. "But I hope not. I hope faith comes as easily as a summer day your whole life."

And then late another night, sitting in my window, I saw a man pacing the street in my Chicago neighborhood. He was holding a cardboard sign that read *FAITH*. He may have been crazy, he may have been the sanest man in the world, I will never know, but he was preaching to no one.

Or was he preaching to me?

"The world is still filled with beauty and grace!" he was yelling, thrusting his dirty sign toward heaven. "The world is still filled with God! This is all too intricate to be taken for granted. Believe! Believe now when you need Him most!"

I watched the man preach for an hour, and then he was gone.

The hummingbird flies toward the sky.

Like that branch.

I finish my coffee and shut my eyes. I hear a buzz. I open them. The hummingbird is back, resplendent in its gown.

Two rabbits jump from the garden. They leap over one another. One has white paws. She looks like she's wearing gloves.

An elderly woman runs her gloved hand along the side of Bonnie's gown, slowly, carefully and with great intention.

She resembles a vet inspecting an old horse, feeling for any lump, bump, sign of trouble.

Finally, she turns.

Three women hold their breaths awaiting her verdict.

"You've done an amazing job with the ease," she says. "This dress fits her like a glove and yet she has room to breathe, move, mingle, dance. Remember two years ago, Bonnie? You could barely make your way up those theatre stairs to give your speech. The entire room held its breath."

The women titter, relieved, and then sip their champagne.

"What do you say?"

Bonnie. Staring at me.

"Thank you," I say to Mrs. Morris.

"You're quite welcome, dear."

I haven't been called *dear* since I was a girl, certainly never since I've turned forty.

I wasn't expecting a party today. I certainly wasn't anticipating a group of Bonnie's friends to join us for her final fitting in advance of the art center's Summer Solstice this weekend.

"And thank you, dear friends, for all of the reassurance," Bonnie says. She steps off the platform and spins in her dress. The women applaud.

Bonnie's friends all have last names that I recognize from Chicago society. Their husbands and families own trucking companies, sports teams, furniture manufacturers, commercial real estate. They all live, I've learned, in an enclave of homes at the end of Douglas' lakeshore that are never sold, just passed onto the next generation. The homes are original cottages from the late 1800s, expansive, airy, throwbacks set into the dunes with stunning views of the lake. If these homes are sold, the owners must approve the buyer, and the buyer cannot hold a mortgage on the purchased home. They must pay in full—millions.

These ladies rotate "Glows," sunset parties like the one Bonnie has mentioned, all through the summer. They are not happy that—in their own, personal life's "glow"—they missed two years of tradition.

"It's so nice that you finally found your calling working for Bonnie."

One of her friends—they all look pretty much the same, like trout, eyes wide, mouths pulled too far open—says this as if it's a compliment.

"I was one of the youngest female ready-to-wear designers in America," I say. "At Lindy's."

"Lindy's," one of the women says, her face attempting but failing to show disapproval. "Remember when it was the grand dame of Chicago?"

They all nod their heads and mutter their agreements, sipping champagne.

"Well," another says. "Good. For. You!"

She says this like a mom might to a child who just earned a participation award for coming in last in the science fair.

I am so not doing this.

The woman who inspected Bonnie's gown removes her gloves, inspection over.

Always look at the hands.

This is what Abby used to say when society matrons would have her design jewelry for them. We could never tell—like with Bonnie—how old they were exactly until they removed their gloves.

"The hands never lie," Abby whispered to me.

She was right. No matter the work on their faces and bodies, their hands often resembled the crypt keeper's. And they were ice-cold when they would latch one upon your arm to garner your attention, show off a few carats or require your assistance.

I smile to myself.

She moves toward my sketchbook sitting on a side table and opens it. I am about to rush over and grab it when Bonnie asks, "What do you think, Liz?"

"I think we've all found our new designer."

The women applaud again and rush over to my sketchbook.

I look at Bonnie. She is absolutely gleaming, her shoulders back, her chest puffed.

I feel a great sense of pride in Bonnie's support showing me off to her friends. I can actually see a future on my own. My mother rarely exhibited a show of emotion toward my work. I know she was proud, but I always wanted to *hear* she was proud.

"Will you walk us through your designs for my summer appearances?" Bonnie asks.

I nod.

"This is the dress I have in mind for Ox-Bow," I say. "I thought Bonnie should actually wear a bit of its history and beauty in her dress. The floral fabric is subtle, almost nonexistent, a nod to the meadow in bloom. The color is a dusty pink, like sunset on the lagoon. And Bonnie looks so beautiful in pink."

"What's in her hair?" one of the women asks, pointing at the sketch.

"It's a headpiece," I say, casting a wary eye Bonnie's direction. "Very subtle. Gold. It will be little flowers. You've all heard of Coachella, the music festival in Palm Springs that is sort of a modern-day Woodstock? I wanted it to be an elegant play off of that."

I hold my breath. I have yet to discuss this with Bonnie, and a headpiece to her might elicit the same reaction as buying her a Kia.

"Bonnie wanted to take a bit more of a fashion risk," I add.

"Well, I love it!" Liz says, before Bonnie can respond. "It's exquisite."

She turns the page.

"And I wanted to dress Bonnie in gold for her Glow, like the color of the lake just before the sun sets, as if a pot of gold had been poured onto the water. But you'll see one shoulder is exposed, and the fabric reverses to a deep purple, another color at sunset. And Bonnie has such wonderful shoulders."

The women applaud.

"What about me?"

"What would you design for me?"

"What's your number? We must set up an appointment immediately. Do you wish to meet here or in Chicago?"

"We have the gala in Chicago coming up in October. We best get started right away!"

Bonnie looks at me, and I can tell she already views me in a different light.

I proved her right. She feels she has made me. Her confidence in me has been justified.

"Ladies, ladies," Bonnie says. "I just signed Sutton to an exclusive contract. We'll have to see how much time she has."

"I haven't signed anything yet, though, Bonnie. Remember?"

If looks could kill, I would be dead, right here in her closet.

"She's quite the negotiator, ladies. Now, everyone, scoot, scoot! There you go! Out! We have a lot of work to finish here!"

The women resist but finally finish their champagne and say their goodbyes.

Bonnie opens her arms wide.

"You're quite the rage all of a sudden," she remarks. "Let's put the finishing touches on this dress and then start on the next. I want to see the fabric. And then we can revisit that contract, okay?"

My stare has unnerved her.

It seems Bonnie and I are not that much different. We both came from nowhere. We were both poor. And today I feel more her equal than ever before.

After all I've learned, I actually feel a bit sorry for her. But confused and angry at her for lying to me.

Funny how time and image change perceptions.

"I feel compelled to ask you something, Bonnie."

She cocks her head just so. "Yes."

"I, uh, just learned about your daughter's tragic death." I take a breath. "And I'm so sorry about all you went through." I take a deeper breath. "But why did you lie to me, tell me you never had a family? You said I was like the daughter you never had. After all I've gone through, I just can't tolerate any more lies. It's cruel."

Bonnie turns from me. The room buzzes in the quiet. The lake sighs in the distance.

"I never got over Ambel's death," she says, her voice low. "Neither did my husband. It's just not something that's easy to share." She turns to face me. "No matter how much time has passed." She picks up her glass of champagne and studies the bubbles. "Your mother and I have much in common, it seems. Sometimes, it's easier to lie than face down all those memories. And then you get used to the lie."

My heart is fluttering this way and that.

"I empathize, but lying never undoes the loss or quells the

grief, it only compounds the suffering on the survivors. My mom said we can never know where we're going unless we know from where we came. She never faced her own trauma. And here I am still trying to figure out which way to go."

"I understand," Bonnie says.

"That painting of the little girl," I continue. "And that button artwork in your powder room. You painted that portrait, didn't you, Bonnie? And Ambel created the artwork, didn't she?"

Bonnie nods. "I'm so sorry for lying."

"Fool me once, shame on you. Fool me twice, shame on me."

"I hear you." She extends her hand. I stare at it.

Suddenly, I am catapulted back in time.

I picture Bonnie as a poor girl, tiny hands red and torn opening clamshells, living in tenement housing. I picture her seducing Dan Jr. as a teenager, seeing him as her way out, her secret pearl. I picture her turning on her family, on her past. I see her picking out diamond rings for each finger.

I see my mother's hands on Ol' Betsy, her knuckles swollen and red, her fingers knotted and bent like sassafras limbs. Hands that caught catfish and gigged frogs and made my clothes.

I look down at my hand stuck in mid air.

Bonnie grabs it with hers, and she sighs, believing I have given her an A-okay.

She lets go. My hand remains in front of me.

"Oh, and by the way, you are coming to the Summer Solstice."

"What?" I ask.

"I already paid for your ticket. You'll be at my table. It will be a grand time. I can't wait to show you off."

"Let me think about it," I say coolly. "I really didn't bring anything to wear. And I don't know anyone."

"You know *me*," Bonnie says. "And I know everyone."

"I'd like to bring a guest, too," I say. "Tug."

"Mr. McCoy? The shop owner?"

You know who he is. Must we play this game of surprise every single time?

"Yes."

"I'm not sure I like you running around with the help. It's not a good look."

I glare at Bonnie. If looks could kill, *she* would be dead.

"Then I'll pass," I say. "Thank you anyway."

I focus my attention on the last details of her dress and work in silence. When I'm done, I gather my things.

"I'll talk to you soon," I say. "Have a wonderful rest of your day."

I move toward the staircase and begin to exit.

"Sutton?"

I turn.

"You may invite Mr. McCoy as well."

"Thank you," I say.

I head down the stairs, shoulders back, knowing she is watching, along with the girl in the blue dress.

Ambel.

Tug settles into the back of the two-man kayak and gives the shore a mighty push with his oar.

We glide into the bayou.

It is six thirty in the morning, and the bayou—the entire town—is quiet. Our oars are the only things making a sound in the world. It is dark, the sun yawning, stretching, rising above the horizon. The water is still and flat. Slowly, the world turns amber, then purple, before settling on pink.

How many sunrises do we get? How many moments to enjoy? How many days to get it right?

Before my eyes, the world takes shape, as if I've been in a deep slumber: the trees, the water, the wispy clouds.

We paddle up river with ease, the breeze sobering me. It is a crisp morning that will warm quickly, but it is still cool without the full force of the sun, and I take a sip of coffee from the thermos Tug has brought for me.

Tug and I move our oars in sync without saying a word. I am not made uncomfortable by the silence now. I do not feel like that awkward, unworthy girl who ruled much of my life, the one who would need to fill every silence to ensure that someone liked her.

No, there is a comfort in our silence, as if we've known each other for a very long time and know each other so completely we could have an entire conversation without saying a word. That was the relationship I had with my mother. We could be in the cabin all weekend and only say a handful of words to one another, and yet it felt as though we were speaking nonstop.

To know someone that well is a rare thing. It can be a complicated thing, but it can also be an incredible blessing. But now I wonder, how well did I really know my mother?

Not well, it seems.

And does that matter? All of her secrets? Or should I focus on what Mary said: that she loved me, deeply, and I am the person I am now because of her love?

Has all of this been a lesson? A part of God's plan? To teach me that my mother—all our parents—are not perfect, and sometimes we must take them off a pedestal and look them in the eye in order to see ourselves, our past and our future more clearly.

The sun lifts above the tree line, and it's as if someone turned on all the lights in the house at once. The world gleams.

We kayak alongside a marsh that is in full bloom.

"Beautiful, isn't it?" Tug says, his first words.

So many meanings to that simple question, I think.

"Stunning. Do you know what all these flowers are in bloom?"

"The stalky, long purple flower is a loosestrife." Tug points. "Hardy hibiscus are the ones that look like pink dinner plates. See?"

"Gorgeous. They're huge."

Tug points to the other side of the marsh.

"And look at all the lily pads in bloom, too."

There is a carpet of lily pads with monstrous white flowers everywhere. White swans glide amongst them.

"It looks like a painting come to life," I say.

"I love coming out here at dawn," Tug says, "before the rest of the world is awake, before anyone has intruded on my day. I am at one with nature. In sync and at peace. Prepares me for my day and puts me in the right frame of mind. It sets my intention. And it's nice that I can just walk out my back door and be here in under a minute."

I turn in the kayak to look at Tug as I reply.

"Growing up on the water always gave me peace, too. My mom, too. She would rise at dawn to get to work. It was a hard, thankless job, sewing overalls all day long, hunched over a machine. A thirty-minute lunch break wasn't even enough time to scarf down a sandwich, go to the bathroom and try to stretch your back. Before the bus would come to get me for school—I was one of the first to get picked up and had to ride it for an hour—I would watch my mom sit on the bank of the creek. She would go down there every morning, just like you come out here, and just look into the water. I always wondered why. As I got older, I didn't know if she were remembering something, trying to forget something, or just preparing herself for the day."

"Maybe all those things," Tug suggests.

"Maybe," I say, turning forward in the kayak and placing my oar in the water again. "Maybe." I look at the river. "Even in Chicago, I felt a kindred spirit in the water. I always have. And I found myself—whenever I had a free moment—going to the lake and just staring into it like my mother did."

"What were *you* thinking of when you went there?"

"All those things I just mentioned," I say.

Two loons appear from the marsh and float alongside the kayak.

"You've heard the old tale about loons, haven't you?" Tug asks.

"No."

"People say they mate for life. They return to the same location every single year after the ice thaws. They are territorial about their home. And they speak to one another."

As if on cue, one of the loons cries a mournful wail.

Whooo-dooo-ooooh-ooooh! Whooo-dooo-ooooh-ooooh!

"What are they saying?" I ask.

"What do you think they're saying?" Tug asks.

"You're safe," I say. "You're loved."

I can feel my heart rise into my throat. The loons bob alongside the kayak for a while and then disappear into the marsh.

"What a beautiful thing to say," Tug replies.

We paddle in silence for a while longer, before I say, "The Kalamazoo River is so beautiful, too. It must get jealous of Lake Michigan sometimes, don't you think?"

"I bet it does," Tug says. "Poor thing has had a long, troubled history, though. There was a massive oil spill not too long ago that killed birds and fish. There was a massive cleanup that took way too long. A lot of damage was done to the waterway. And I'm sure Mary mentioned the harm the button industry caused a century ago."

"Not really," I say. "We were, um, focused on other things."

Tug chuckles. "I bet. The pearl button industry wreaked havoc on the environment. First, they overfished the river, cleaning out most of the mussels. In addition, pollutants were dumped into the river, along with the unused shells, and that hurt the freshwater mussels. Then ships brought in invaders to the river."

"Invaders?"

"Zebra mussels, for example. They attached themselves to the outside of the freshwater mussels' shell, which made it harder for our local species to move around and eat. They tried to solve it by having local clam and mussel hatcheries produce enough new mussels to restock the riverbeds, but the Kalamazoo was too inundated with industrial waste by then for the mussels to survive in the polluted water."

"That's awful."

I picture this river, this marsh, the way it may have been, when it was just a river that provided water and fish, unspoiled. *Can it—can we—ever return to that state after being polluted?*

"It is," Tug says. "Even the way children who worked at the button companies were treated was deplorable. We tend to think it was 'quaint' work, but it wasn't. The local Historical Society had a retrospective a long time ago that angered Bonnie and her husband to no end. They tried to get it shut it down. Kids as young as eight worked sixty-hour weeks carrying buckets of shells and acid to soften the material."

I see Bonnie as Mildred, a child laborer.

Tug continues. "Workers lost eyes and fingers stamping

buttons out of the shells, or operating lathes. One local girl was partially scalped when her ponytail got caught in a lathe."

"No," I say, smacking my oar against the water in anger.

"We never seem to learn from our past," Tug says.

"Who could do that to a child?" I hesitate. "I need to tell you about what Mary shared with me."

I tell Tug.

"I've heard the rumors," he says when I'm done. "Everyone's heard the rumors. I just thought it was small-town gossip. It's a lot to take in."

"It is," I say. "I'm processing…while working for her…and trying to figure things out. I just don't understand why she lied. And continued to lie."

"People lie to protect themselves," Tug says. "Their hearts, their feelings, their ego, their secrets. Who knows why with Bonnie? I can't imagine going on if I lost a child. Maybe that's it. At least you know a little about why your mom lied to you. She was abandoned and on her own. I don't want to excuse anyone's lies. I know I've done it."

I turn in the kayak.

"Not to you!" Tug says. "But I said I was taller and ran faster on my stat sheets to scouts. I did it to make myself look better. Maybe that's the common denominator here. Who knows?"

We head up the river and then turn at a bend, the current pushing us home in half the time.

I take a deep breath.

"I have to ask you something," I say.

"That sounds ominous."

"Bonnie invited me to be her guest at the art center's Summer Solstice gala. I told her I would only go if I could invite you."

Tug laughs. "I bet *that* went well."

"Well, she agreed," I say, turning to look back at him. "Will you go? With me?"

"Of course."

"I'm a bit nervous. I can't tell whether I'm her equal or her marionette."

"Welcome to a resort town. I feel the same way much of the time. I work with these people, but I also work *for* these people. Big difference. Tickets to that event are five hundred dollars. Not including the fact attendees are expected to buy something, too, in the live or silent auctions." Tug stops. "It's funny."

"What is?" I ask.

"Well, I donate thousands of dollars of items from my shop every year to different organizations in order to support the local community and its efforts, and I know I get to write it off at the end of the year, but I've never once been given a ticket gratis as a thank-you, or invited by a member of the committee who's asked for my donations. It's not just that it's five hundred dollars a ticket. It's that every summer gala ticket in town costs that much. I'd go broke giving away free stuff and attending each event. I've had to start rotating which fundraisers I support, and locals are not happy about that. But you're damned if you do, and damned if you don't around here sometimes: I'd be ostracized and bad-mouthed if I didn't support, and I'd go belly-up if I supported everyone year-round and attended every event."

"Well, you're sitting at a table with Bonnie."

"Thank goodness it's an open bar," he laughs.

The current carries us down the river. As we float, I think of being a girl on an inner tube, Hickory Creek heading to the lake.

As we near the bayou again, I see a woman sitting on a

bench looking at the water. She stands, picks up a stone and skips it across the water.

I did the same thing with my mom growing up. We'd find the flattest rock or piece of shale and try to skip it all the way across the creek, the goal for the rock to bounce upon the far shore.

"I did it! I did it!" I would yell—doing a jig on the rocky beach—when the rock skipped all the way across the creek. "What do I win, Mom?"

"The satisfaction that you made it," she would say.

A sudden breeze scoots across the water, ruffling the surface, making it look as if I just successfully skipped my rock from here to there.

Maybe my mom only wanted me to have a better life. Maybe she wanted me to make a splash in this world. Maybe she just wanted me to have an easier path.

I watch the water smooth again.

Maybe, just maybe, as Mary said, she wanted me to have a better life than she did, and she didn't want me to make the same mistakes she had.

Or maybe my mom just wanted me to understand the satisfaction of having made it.

From there to here.

I shut my eyes and see my mom. I see me. I see Bonnie.

Whether my mom wanted me to make it "out," or make it "somewhere," I may never know, but I do realize that making it from here to there in life is never easy. It's a long journey from one shore to the next. The current is swift. And if you don't skip or swim like heck, you might go under midstream.

"I feel like I'm entering a set for *A Midsummer Night's Dream*."

"You are," Tug says. "Although the 'dream' part is still up in the air."

I laugh. "Or the Met Gala."

"I wish this were a Mets-Tigers game."

I laugh again. "Thanks for easing my nerves."

The Summer Solstice is beyond what I'd imagined. The arts center sits in a large mid century building across from a marina, public park and a bay that forms from the Kalamazoo River before narrowing into a channel that parallels Saugatuck and leads to Lake Michigan.

A massive outdoor garden—filled with flowers and sculptures—fronts the building, and a narrow path meanders from the street through the garden to the outdoor space where the party is being held.

I turn, finally realizing Tug has been staring at me.

"You look absolutely stunning."

"Thank you." I look down at my dress. "This old thing?"

He laughs. "You made the vintage fabric you found at my shop look new again."

"Well, thank you for helping me find it."

I am wearing a Marabella dress I designed and made—in about four days, thank you very much—in bright orange, the color of a poppy. It is a very girly dress, part summer and part bohemian, but one hundred percent resort wear, which I felt was appropriate for a resort town. It is dressy but not elegant, as I did not want to outshine Bonnie, and it shows off my best features. The Marabella is a midi-length dress with a square neckline, a smocked bodice, puff sleeves and a rather daring side slit. It is slim fitting through the bodice with an easy fitting skirt. My shoes are espadrille sandals with a wedge heel, and a bright orange strap that wraps above my ankle. I am carrying a sculptural rattan tote in the shape of a crescent moon and wearing beautiful red onyx-and-orange tassel earrings I splurged on at a local gallery with some of my ill-gotten gain from Bonnie.

I look down and touch my necklace, counting.

At the last minute, I threw on my button necklace, an odd choice that not only seemed to work with the overall look but eased my nerves.

"Ready?" Tug asks.

"No," I answer.

He takes my hand, and we head down the path through the garden, admiring the flowers and the sculptures. In the middle are garden stakes of all shapes, sizes and colors. Some are ceramic, some are made with old teacups, some are glass.

I read the sign.

These garden stakes were made by migrant children from the local community who, without your support, would not have access to art classes, teachers and supplies at school and throughout the summer. Your support allows their minds, imaginations and talents to grow in ways we may never be able to measure. Your support also sends twenty underprivileged children to college every year debt-free. Your support allows the world to bloom in unimaginable ways. Thank you!

"I didn't know this," I say. "That's incredible."

"It's why I give all I can to the auctions every year," he says. "The local community has an influx of workers every year who pick the fruit and work the fields. We forget their families come with them. We forget their children are part of our community, too. The arts center has led the way in providing them with art classes in school and throughout the summer. This is the place many children spend their summers, painting, drawing, journaling, writing, nurturing their talents and also making sense of the world and their emotions. The director of the arts center is amazing and truly groundbreaking in how she approaches art, its meaning and its impact."

We turn a corner, and two tuxedoed waiters are waiting, holding trays filled with pretty glasses.

"Champagne?"

"Thank you."

We each take a glass.

"Tug!"

A woman in a black dress, funky jewelry and cool glasses opens her arms and hugs Tug tightly. She smells like roses.

"I'm so glad you could make it," she says. "I saw your name on the guest list."

"This is Sutton," Tug says. "Sutton Douglas, this is Krista Matthews, the director of the arts center."

"It's so nice to meet you," I say, extending my hand. "What you've done is just amazing. The children's art program...the garden... I'm still trying to catch my breath."

Krista beams. "Thank you. We don't shake hands around these parts, though, do we, Tug?" She opens her arms. "We're huggers. It's a resort community. Everyone knows everyone."

"Or everyone knows something about everyone," Tug adds.

"Still know how to use that fastball, don't you, Tug?" Krista opens her arms, and I give her a hug, careful not to tilt off my shoes and spill champagne down her back. It feels good to hug again. "I've heard such wonderful things about you already from Bonnie."

She takes a step back and looks at me. "Your dress is gorgeous. You made this?"

"I did. Thank you."

"And Bonnie's dress. Just breathtaking. She's the talk of the Summer Solstice in it. And we all know she likes that," Krista says in a Shakespearian whisper.

"She's already here?"

"Yes, she's helping with the auction." Krista looks over my shoulder. "We've got a line formed. Sorry to move you along, but stop and get your photo taken as a souvenir."

"It was nice to meet you," she says.

Tug puts his hand on my back, and we move toward a large backdrop covered in company logos.

"A step-and-repeat?" I ask. "This town thinks of everything."

We turn, Tug puts his arm around my back and pulls me close. I can feel the heat from his hand. The photographer aims his camera, and counts down. "One, two, three!"

"One more?" Tug asks.

The photographer lifts his camera, and, at the last second as the photographer counts, Tug points toward the step-and-repeat. I look and laugh. His finger is directed at his own logo, *One Man's Trash is Another Man's Treasure*.

"How did that happen?" I ask.

"Bonnie, I'm guessing, thanks to you," Tug says. "Krista just told me about it this afternoon. She didn't say how it happened, though. Town's good at secrets."

"Now, that's a keeper," the photographer says. He holds out his camera and scrolls the photos, the last one capturing the two of us laughing, our heads up, the sun beaming on our faces.

"It is," I say.

We move toward the party. There is a beautiful, big outdoor patio—partially covered—with a bar parked in the center, food stations at each corner, high-top tables scattered throughout and ringed by long tables filled with silent auction items. A string quartet plays from a small stage in front of the main arts center.

As soon as we enter, people begin calling Tug's name, just as they did when we entered The Bayou. He shakes hands, gives hugs, introduces me.

"I keep saying, you're like the town mayor."

"Couldn't pay me enough," Tug says. "Let's get a bite to eat and then look at some of the auction items."

We fill our plates with a slew of appetizers and share them at a table together, Tug trying to shove miniature prime rib sandwiches into his mouth between saying hello to the town.

I am laughing at him and placing a shrimp the size of the kayak we were just on—drenched in a spicy sauce—in my mouth, when I hear, "Were you ever going to say hello?"

I look up.

Bonnie.

This has long been a trend in my life. I have a mouthful of food when someone walks up to me and begins to talk. I used to try and take sip of coffee or water, or shove a bite of muffin down my throat, when I would suddenly be asked a question in a meeting, and I would choke on coconut or nearly spew liquid. Abby once set me up on a blind date with a friend of hers from high school, a sweet, smart handsome man, a doctor, no less. We went to brunch by the lake, and he ordered us Bloody Marys. He had just shared a very personal story about why he became a doctor, and asked me why I had wanted to become a clothing designer. I was poised to share an intimate story of my mom and my childhood and took a sip of my drink to wet my mouth. I didn't realize the Bloody Mary had been made by the devil himself, with enough Tabasco and hellfire to ignite an instant inferno. I began to choke, so much so that the kindly doctor rushed over and began to perform the Heimlich.

The brunch ended abruptly, Abby told me the doctor thought I was "special"—a euphemism if there ever was one— and he never contacted me again.

This time, I take my time to chew and swallow before answering. I chew and chew, Bonnie looking at me, her face growing in bewilderment.

"I'm sorry," I finally say, sipping my champagne. "Krista said you were busy with the auction."

Bonnie's shoulders ease. She turns. "How do I look?"

"Beyond stunning," Tug says, cutting me off. "You look like a work of art."

"Thank you, Mr. McCoy. And it is a work of art!" Bonnie says. "Everyone is going gaga, Sutton!"

"This is your night," I say.

"It is, isn't it?" Bonnie says, beaming. "Don't fill up on all this. Beautiful dinner coming. You're at our table inside, remember?" She looks at Tug. "You, too, Mr. McCoy. See you in a bit."

"Can't wait for dinner," Tug says, voice low, rolling his eyes. He flags down a bartender and snags two more glasses of champagne. "They probably put the bottles of bubbly right by Bonnie to chill them."

The bartender laughs, stops and looks around guiltily before departing.

We finish our appetizers and peruse the auction tables before a dinner bell chimes, and Krista appears on the tiny outdoor stage with a microphone.

"This is your ten-minute warning! Please begin to move inside for dinner and more cocktails—yes, more cocktails! I know that will get you moving!" Krista laughs. "And then we'll move on to the live auction!"

Tug gives me a quick tour of the arts center, walking me through the five-hundred seat, state-of-the-art theatre that features summer productions of hit musicals with Broadway and local talent as well as performances by singers, dancers, entertainers and authors.

There is a large gallery featuring the latest exhibit—a local, internationally known artist whose oil series on clouds is so vibrant, powerful and real I feel as though I am sitting on the beach underneath the Michigan sky being reminded of not only how—like tonight—I fit into the human race but also how I fit into the world.

Tug escorts me inside the performing arts studio.

"This is where the arts center hosts smaller, live concerts," he says.

It is a large room with a small stage at the front of the room. A wall of windows faces the back of the arts center, and pines provide a step-and-repeat of deep green.

I see an arm waving. It is Bonnie. Our table is at the very front.

"Finally!" Bonnie says dramatically. She stands and, to my surprise, gives me a big hug. "My special guest." Bonnie stops, then smiles that Cheshire cat smile. She looks at Tug. "Guests."

She continues. "You met my friends the other day, and they all want to steal you away from me. But we won't let that happen, will we?"

Her friends are all dressed to the nines in custom dresses—nearly gowns—that are a bit too formal for this type of summer soiree.

Tug pulls out my chair and whispers, "This is going well."

I try to stifle my laugh but can't, and Bonnie shoots me the exact same look my mother used to give me when I'd chuckle in church.

After I'm seated, Tug—ever the gentleman—approaches each woman at the table and introduces himself, although they all know who he is.

"So did your husband abandon you for the Cubs again, Cindy?"

The woman laughs and nods. "He's in St. Louis for the big rivalry series."

"What about you, Liz? Where's Chuck?"

"Annual boys' golf outing at Bob's place in Egg Harbor."

Bonnie leans toward me. "Mr. McCoy has impeccable manners," she says.

I can't hide the surprise on my face at Bonnie's sudden U-turn on him.

"Or he's a good showman," she adds, looking me in the eyes. "Gets the gullible to believe what they're seeing."

I blink.

"Like a shell game," she says.

My face flushes and heart races. "Maybe he's just a nice man," I say. "Such a rare trait these days, isn't it? Kindness?"

Bonnie doesn't blink. She looks at me, her expression seeming to say, *touché*.

Tug returns to his seat, as one waiter approaches with salads and another with wine.

"Red or white?"

As we eat, I notice the placard on our table: #1.

For some reason, this literal sign hits me like a ton of bricks.

I glance at Bonnie. She is looking around the room, queen of the ball, creator of the universe. People nervously wait for Bonnie to acknowledge them. She surveys her minions. I can see her consciously decide who is worthy and who is not.

When she does, she gives a small wave, and people light up as if they've just been granted special dispensation, and the rules no longer apply to them.

What must it be like for her?

What must it feel like to have been so poor and then so rich? To have a family and then none? Does her past still exist in her heart, echo somewhere deep in her soul? Or is all of that buried under a pile of emotional scar tissue and money?

Do I ask because I am jealous? Jealous that I've always had to play by the rules, that my mother had to play by rules that never worked for a woman like her?

I've done well, excelled in a difficult career where few

succeed, and made more money than my mother could have dreamed while stitching together a life on minimum wage and extra jobs babysitting and making clothes.

And yet I still feel poor. When I look at myself, the woman who looks back is still the girl in the wavy mirror at the cabin. *Unworthy.*

Do I want more because I've worked hard and deserve more, or do I want more to bury my past under a pile of money, too? Will the woman looking back ever feel worthy?

Bonnie busts me watching her. I casually laugh at something someone has said as if I don't notice.

Krista approaches our table and whispers something to Bonnie. Krista turns to me and says, "It's so great to have you in our community, Sutton. What a welcome addition."

"Thank you," I say.

"And such a coincidence, too," she adds. "Douglas came to Douglas? Such a small world."

Her joke unnerves me and sends my stomach—and mind—into somersaults.

So many coincidences.

Too many coincidences.

I eat my dessert quickly, hoping it will settle my tummy.

After dessert and enough wine, the dynamic changes: the women at the table begin to approach me, crouching beside my chair, backs to Bonnie.

"We need to talk about you designing a dress or two for me. Here's my number."

"Whatever she's paying you, I'll double."

"Your designs are so current and yet so respectful of our past. I need you to start on my fall and winter gowns. Please. I'll put you up at the Drake in Chicago. Give you an expense account for travel and food. My husband can write it all off."

I watch Bonnie carefully after each friend approaches.

She is acting as I just did, as if she doesn't notice, but her shoulders become more pinched, her back more rigid. Bonnie's demeanor gives me the feeling her pride in showing me off to her friends the other day has quickly morphed into jealousy.

"Excuse me, will you?" Bonnie announces to the table. "I want to go freshen up before my speech."

Tug stands, and Bonnie exits, all eyes in the room on her and my dress.

I sigh and take a sip of wine.

"I think she's miffed her friends are seeking my help," I whisper to Tug.

"Don't worry," he says. "She knows how to take care of herself."

The lights dim, and Krista hops onto the stage with all of the energy of a Vegas performer. She thanks the donors and volunteers, before introducing the director of the Lake Street Warehouse, who puts on all of the summer musicals. He brings out the lead cast members currently starring in *In the Heights*, and they perform two numbers.

"But the real star of tonight's Summer Solstice," Krista says, when she takes the stage again, "is Bonnie Lyons, our lifetime Platinum member whose vision and support helped make the arts center what it is today. Bonnie, will you join us to kick off the live auction?"

A spotlight appears on Bonnie standing just off to the side of the stage, and she acts as if it is all a big surprise. She places her hand over her heart and takes the stage. Bonnie looks luminous in her dress, and I feel a swell of pride.

"Thank you, thank you, thank you," Bonnie says, bowing toward Krista and then the crowd's applause. "Art changes lives. It has changed mine profoundly. Whether it is a musical performance like we just witnessed, an art exhibit, a dance troupe, an author reading, art makes us consider the world in new ways, it forces us to see things from the perspectives of others whose lives may be so different from ours, and it makes us better people."

She continues. "But, more than anything, art takes root in a child's soul and grows in ways we can never imagine." Bonnie stops and lowers her head. When she lifts it again, a tear is trailing down her cheek. "I rarely speak of my late daughter."

I gasp. People turn. Tug grabs my hand. I give him a look that reads, *"Now she's an open book?"*

"My late daughter loved art. As many of you know, Dan and I owned a button company here for a very long time, and those buttons helped kick-start my daughter's love of art. She used those buttons as one might paint. She rendered pictures of the lake, the sunset, flowers out of buttons. I still have her art hung prominently in my home, and it speaks to me to this day. What we're doing tonight will have an impact on a child's life that we may never be able to see or measure. But I assure you that impact will be felt by someone." Bonnie stops. "Forever."

The crowd stands as one and begins to cheer. I stay seated, literally, unmoved. I'm not buying this. It all just seems so planned and rehearsed following our recent talk.

"So, let's give all we can tonight for the sake of art and our future. I know there are some deep pockets here, and if you don't dig deep, I'll be watching."

Bonnie turns to Krista but then stops.

"Oh, my goodness," she says in the mic. "How ironic. Speaking of buttons."

Bonnie lifts an embroidered button into the air and shows it to the crowd as if it's a snake. She then lifts the sleeve of her dress. A button is missing.

One of my buttons.

"Sutton?" Bonnie asks. "Where are you?"

The crowd turns.

"I think we need to talk." Bonnie laughs. "Krista, let's do this."

Bonnie's friends turn to look at me as she returns to the table. They look aghast and begin murmuring to one another.

Bonnie takes a seat and places the button squarely in front of me on the table. She does not bother to look at me.

"There is no way that could have come off your dress," I insist, my words coming out in a rush. My voice is high and flustered. "I quadruple-checked every button."

Bonnie doesn't answer. She looks ahead with that smile plastered across her face.

"There is no way!" I repeat, grabbing the button and slamming my hand down on the table.

The people at our table and the ones around us turn to stare.

"Mistakes happen, Sutton," Bonnie says.

"Not with me they don't."

"Sutton, we're trying to raise money for a good cause here tonight. Let's not make this about you, shall we?"

I stand and storm out of the room.

"Sutton!" Tug calls. He follows me outside. "Stop! Please!"

I turn.

"She did that on purpose! I know it. She did it to make a spectacle of me. She did it to turn her friends away. She did all of that—the speech about her daughter, the show of the button—for a reason. To put me in my place for standing up to her. I know it! There is no way that button came off her dress. It was fine before she went to the bathroom and then it just fell off into her hand? She didn't even come to get me to fix it before she went onstage? She carried it up there? C'mon!"

I am holding in my tears, like an angry child. My breaths are coming out as short gasps. I teeter unsteadily on my shoes.

Tug opens his arms and hugs me.

"I'm so sorry," he says.

In my head, I can hear children sing, "Button, button, who's got the button?"

Why didn't I ignore Bonnie like I did the kids I knew had the button growing up?

Tug drives me home and walks me to my door.

"Are you sure you're okay?" he asks.

I nod. "I know how to take care of myself."

Repeating the words Tug said earlier is harsher than I anticipated, but they are true. I've always taken care of myself.

"I had a good time," Tug says. "For a while."

I try to smile.

"See you tomorrow, okay? I'll call you."

He hugs me, tightly, and I watch him drive away. I stand in the driveway, button still in hand, but I cannot go inside. I pull my cell out of my pocket and shine the light on the button, surveying it, studying it, as if I've dug up a diamond in the Arkansas dirt and cannot believe my eyes.

That's when I see it: a few threads are still attached to the shank on the back of the button. I shine the flashlight on the button even closer.

The threads are not frayed.

They're all even, straight, the same length.

As if they've been cut.

I don't know whether to scream or to feel vindicated.

I take a photo of it in my hand, capturing the thread around the shank.

For some reason, the word *shank* rattles in my head, and I think of its meaning.

"I just got shanked," I say to myself. "Wounded deeply. By a button."

Instead of going inside, I head to Dandelion Cottage.

Dandy.

Dan D. Lyons.

Lions.

Liars.

I stand on the doorstop. The entryway is lit, the big, tiled button illuminated under a spotlight.

The world around me disappears, and I am eleven years old and standing in a spotlight on our church stage. Our final rehearsal has just ended, and in a few moments, the church will be filled for our Christmas concert. I have been selected to sing the solo, "Mary, Did You Know?" much to the chagrin of the kids in our choir.

"Her?" they asked the choir director. "The button girl doing the solo?"

My nerves are frayed, and I cannot stop shaking. My mother beams from the pew.

"You have a voice from God," she says. "Angelic."

On my way backstage, one of the girls grabs me by the sleeve of my dress and says, "Don't mess up, got it?"

When she releases me, a moonglow button drops onto the floor, rolls away and disappears into a gap in the old wood floor. My sleeve pops open. My dress—and performance— are ruined.

I wail.

My mother appears moments later, led by the choir director. She takes me into the bathroom and, without as much as a word, pops a matching button off her own dress, pulls an always-present needle and thread from her purse and makes my dress new again.

"I got you," she said. "Always will."

I received a standing ovation after my performance.

Standing here, some three decades later, I finally realize that my mother didn't give a whit what anyone thought about us. I was her only concern. I was her world. I was her future. She was *my* past.

And even though I always hated to admit it to myself, my mom and I were made of exactly the same cloth.

She would give me anything, even a button off her own dress, to make me whole.

I leave the button on Bonnie's doorstep.

11

WRONG SIDE

The inside or back of the fabric.
The side that isn't on display.

I stop in the middle of Tug's shop and stretch my neck as far out as I can.

Am I hearing this right?

"Are you okay?" Tug asks.

I give him a look.

"I know, I know, I've asked you that question a lot lately." He walks over to me. "But you look like a confused crane. Did you hurt your back?"

I give him another look.

"We're already like an old couple, aren't we?" I ask.

"That's a goal of mine, you know. To be an old couple."

The sincerity in his voice melts the ice around my heart, and I soften just a little.

Bonnie hurt me. On purpose. Does Tug like me? Love me? Will he hurt me, too? My mother loved me more than anything in the world, and she still hurt me.

The song that just came on in Tug's store has catapulted me back in time.

"Buttons and Bows" by Doris Day.

I know every word by heart:

Let's move down to some big town where they love a gal by the cut of her clothes

And I'll stand out in buttons and bows

There was a radio station in southern Missouri that my mom listened to every evening when she got home from work: *Z100, Ozarks Oldies.*

She listened to it as she made dinner, cleaned the kitchen and then retreated to her sewing room. The reception at our cabin—down in the hollers, bookended between bluffs—was spotty at best, and the transistor radio crackled and squawked. My mom and I would fuss with that radio, turning it this way and that, moving the knob millimeters left and right, to try and improve the reception. I would hold the radio up in the air, stand on a chair, put tinfoil on my finger and turn myself into a human antenna.

I fell in love with that song. I learned every word. I dreamed of being that girl who would leave the small town and move to the city and dress in fancy clothes. In my mind, I could picture myself being rich, living in a mansion, having a chef, driver and dressmaker.

Sometimes, when this song would come on, I would dance around the house, singing, pretending I was Doris Day and every move I made in my life would be drenched in sunshine.

"Don't be that girl who forgets where she came from," my mom warned.

And then she'd look up from searching her button jar, and that momentary glance wouldn't just stop me in my tracks, it would replace the sunshine in my soul with frost.

Sometimes, late at night, especially when I got older and I would hear my mother snore, I would cry the tears she never released.

How must she view the world after escaping with me but not having a family?

Did she feel blessed or cursed?

Or both?

Did her soul feel scorched forever?

"God, my momma may have gotten the buttons but she deserves a few bows, too," I would pray. "Give her some joy."

"Did you hear me?" Tug says. His arm is on my back. I am mouthing the lyrics to the song.

"Old couple," I finally manage to say. "Old song. Old soul."

"Are you…" He stops himself before finishing.

I smile. "I am."

Tug's shop is bustling this morning. It is packed with customers whose carts are filled with heirlooms and vintage goodies. And it's not just older women in Tug's shop. Girls in their twenties and thirties are shopping who know exactly what is on trend again.

Old *is* new.

"As you said, everything eventually comes back into style," I say.

"It does," Tug says. "Good taste never goes out of style."

I look at a couple eyeing a series of vintage paint-by-numbers of the lake, deer frolicking, pine trees in winter. I glance at Tug.

Old things.

Tug is an old soul. I am an old soul.

Could we be an old couple?

Doris Day finishes, and a new, old song begins to play.

Is Bonnie lonely, too? As lonely as my mother? Unable to see the future because of her past? Is that why she did what she did? Hurt me so I would stay? Never leave her? Be her and hers alone? Manipulate me?

"Hey, can I talk to you for a second?" Tug asks, knocking me from my thoughts.

He takes my hand and leads me into a storage room.

"What's going on?" I ask. "I feel like a girl in one of those romantic high school movies."

"Go into business with me?"

It takes me a second to process what Tug has just asked.

"Sorry, what?"

"Go into business with me," he says again, very slowly, deliberately, as if he's been thinking about this for a very long time. "No strings attached."

I stare at him.

"Really, I mean it."

"Tug," I say. "That's very sweet, but I'm not ready for this, for any sort of finite decision right now. I came here on a whim, remember? Part vacation to escape the present and part investigation to uncover the past. And right now I feel as if my life has been put into a blender on high speed."

"I know," he says. "But I think—and this is a terrible analogy—the ingredients have blended really well."

I groan. "That *is* a terrible analogy."

Tug continues. "Let me just say this and then you can cogitate on it for a while."

"Cogitate?" I ask. "That's a word my mom always used."

"My grandma, too," he says. "It's a good word, isn't it? Vintage. Heirloom."

I nod.

"Which is why I think you should consider joining me here," Tug says. "You have an appreciation for heirloom style, and you have an innate talent to make it hip again. That's what I do, but I do it with my selection of products. You do it with your style. You actually remake what I find. Can you imagine what we could do together?"

"Thank you," I say. "But..."

"Look," he says, cutting me off with his enthusiasm. "When I opened this shop, I did it for me. Not for anyone else, but for me. I was a local baseball star whose career stalled in the minors. I returned home and wanted to start an antiques store. Believe me, no one expected that. It would be like Tom Brady becoming an opera singer."

I laugh.

"I did a lot of things in my life to please others. I loved baseball, but I didn't love it *enough*. I stuck with it to please everyone else, but it wasn't enough. I think you did the same thing. I mean, even the way that old song just stopped you in your tracks. You fought hard to work for a big company, and you've been very successful. That is so incredible. But did you do it for *you*, or someone else?"

I take a sharp breath.

"I know how that feels," Tug continues. "My entire life, people told me I would never make it. They told me that in baseball, and they told me that when I opened this store. A local business owner actually told me they couldn't wait for me to fail. But they didn't know me very well. I used all my savings to start this store. I barely had enough money to go a year. But I realized there is no straight line to success. There is no guaranteed future. What it takes is a leap of faith and jumping with a parachute you may not even know how to unfurl."

"Tug," I start.

"No, please. Just hear me out, and then I'll shut up."

"Okay."

"Mostly, I had to unlearn all the fear that had been driven into me from an early age. Fear that I was not good enough, worthy enough, smart enough...*enough*. Some of that was my parents—who wanted me to take the safe route after baseball because they knew it would be the least painful for me—but most of it was internal. I always felt inferior to other players. I always wanted to be like them. I learned that fear is a beast we cannot see that eats slowly at our souls. And that is, sadly, how too many of us live. Too often in our world, we let fear consume us: it drives our daily lives typically more so than passion. We worry about money, time, health, aging, our children, our future, but how often do we nurture our now, which helps nurture a healthy future?"

Tug looks away and then back at me. His voice is filled with such passion. "But when we start to do something we love, guilt and societal expectations haunt us. 'I should be making dinner.' 'I should be doing the laundry.' 'There are better things I should be doing with my time.' 'I will never make a penny doing this?' 'I should just give up.' And so it ends before it begins. My sister used to say, working on the front lines, that so many of those she was caring for who were dying were filled with fear and regret. Regret they didn't follow their passion. Fear that their lives had been wasted. 'Don't live with regret,' she told me. 'Don't end your life thinking of what you should have done, or who you should have been.' We've been reminded of just how short our blink may be these past two years."

My heart hiccups. I think of my mom and the letter she left me. Why would Tug reference this? The room spins. I feel as if I was destined be here, right now.

Tug continues. "We've confronted fear headfirst. What makes you happy, Sutton? What will you regret if you don't give it a shot? What do you want to achieve in this short blink? Sometimes, life is more than an IRA and benefits package. I know that's easy for me to say now, but it wasn't so easy a few years ago. But, after all we've gone through, I see life as a glorious opportunity. God makes each of us unique souls with beautiful voices that need to be heard in this world. But we too often silence them to fit in with the world, to not stand out, to take the path of least resistance. We deny the world our special gifts when we do this."

I take a deep breath.

"These past couple of years have been filled with unspeakable loss," Tug says. "But one, small silver lining has been that we've learned what matters again. And what matters is the simplest of things, as my sister taught me: Our health. Our family. Our friends. Our home. A sunrise. A sunset. A dog sighing in the middle of the night. Each other."

My head spins. My mom wrote this to me in her final letter.

Tug stops and takes my hand. "What matters is *you.*"

My heart rises.

"*You* matter to me, Sutton. And I think all of this—you coming here, me meeting you—was destined to happen. And if we blink, we'll miss that."

I look at him and wipe my eyes.

"Tug."

I can only say his name, before I burst into tears.

He opens his arms and holds me.

Another oldie comes on, and we rock back and forth to the song in the storage room.

I feel caught between the past and the future, but the longer he holds me, the more I realize that perhaps I'm just here, right now—like we all are—firmly in the present, half in the dark and half in the light.

I am surrounded by my past.

I can see my future.

I am in the present.

Which direction should I head?

I returned from Tug's shop with ghosts in my head. Doris was singing about the past, Tug was offering me a future, and my mom and Bonnie were standing over me like trees, shadowing my judgment.

I went for a run on the beach, hoping to clear my head. Typically, despite my dislike of running, a run will actually clear my head: the more physically exhausted I get, the more mentally alert I become. But today, the sand clogged my shoes and made every step, every thought, uneven and unsteady. Finally, I collapsed under a lone aspen perched awkwardly on a dune.

This is how I was taught to love and live, I thought, looking at the aspen growing at a thirty-five-degree angle from the sand. Just like this aspen. Just like the sycamores that survived on Hickory Creek, the water exposing their roots. And yet they hung on for dear life, as if survival was instinctual. They grew toward the light, searching for and needing it, even if it twisted and turned their bodies into strange beings.

They still needed warmth, love, a new day.

The shadow of the aspen had bent over the sand, and in it I could see my mother's silhouette, arched back, hunched over a sewing machine.

I was her sole source of light.

I started to cry, feeling guilty for being unable to give more to her, but how fair was it for a mother to need so much from her daughter? How much light could I provide before mine dimmed?

So I returned to the cottage even more confused. I opened all the windows to let in the sunshine and warm breeze, and then I began to pull out all the mementoes I'd brought here as comfort—button jars, Dandy, the button tree—and the mementoes of my mother's I'd brought here as clues—the sewing card, the blue button from her dress, the photos of the man and the girl, the postcard of Douglas.

Everything—and nothing—makes sense now.

I keep trying to win a chess game using only buttons as pieces.

I pick up the blue button from my mother's dress.

I see Bonnie's oil painting of the little girl in the dress.

Buttons and bows.

I have these placed around Ol' Betsy, as if I'm conducting a séance, summoning all the ghosts and demons to have a seat and chat.

Perhaps I am, I think. *A committee meeting to decide my fate.*

I yelp at the knock on the door. I see Tug's face.

"I'm so sorry," I say, opening the door, realizing why he's here. "Going out on the boat this afternoon totally slipped my mind."

"I can tell," he says, walking inside and surveying the cottage.

And I can tell he is about to make a joke to lighten the mood, but he stops, walks over and touches my teddy bear, the sewing machine, the jars of buttons.

"You're thinking of leaving," he says instead.

His honesty catches me by surprise. I can't lie.

No, I don't want to lie to this man.

"Let's just say I'm thinking. About a lot of things. And that's the truth."

He ducks his head.

"Please don't run," Tug says, looking up and talking to Dandy instead of me.

"I'm not. I'm just in motion."

Tug finally turns. He holds the bear in such a sweet, tender way. My heart breaks.

"Take all the time you need," he says. "I understand. It's like you've forged a new life—and a new history—in just a few weeks."

I nod. "Let me go take a quick shower. I have some wine and cheese in the fridge."

"Already taken care of," Tug says. "Go get ready. It looks like a beautiful day on the water. I've already told the staff that my 'appointment'"—Tug lifts his arms to make air quotes—"may take a while, and it's potentially very lucrative."

"Is it?" I ask.

"That's up to the customer," he says with a wink. "But today's just about being in the moment."

I change, and we head to the *Tug Boat*.

And Tug is right: it is a perfect weekday afternoon on the water.

It is low eighties with a light breeze. The channel is quiet, the resorters are still in the city earning a buck, and the weekend tourists have yet to arrive.

"We have the town and water to ourselves," Tug says.

As if on instinct, we have both pulled on our matching First Mate and Captain hats. Tug honks and waves at the couples sailing by on the channel or perched on the front of their boats enjoying a cold drink.

Old couples, I think. I look at Tug. He smiles when he catches my eye. *Old couple.*

We head past the historic cottages dotting the riverbanks, and the new ones being constructed on the dunes just before the channel. I look out at the lake, but at the last moment, Tug veers the boat into the party cove, which sits empty.

I look at him.

"Change of plan," he yells to me. "I'm in motion today, too."

Tug parks the boat and drops the anchor.

"All ashore!" he calls.

"What are you doing?" I ask.

He takes my hand, helps me down the ladder on the back

of the boat. I hop into the water, which is about chest-deep, and we wade to the sandy beach.

"Remember at the Fourth of July barbecue when I told you about the lost town of Singapore?" he asks.

"And all its buried secrets?"

"Well, I wanted you to see it firsthand."

He holds out his hand, and I take it. He leads me onto a path that cuts through the dune grass. As we walk, we drip-dry in the sun. Finally, we reach a high point—a small dune—that has a full 360-degree view of the sand, beach, bluff and Lake Michigan spread before us. The entire world sparkles.

"Michigan's Pompeii," Tug says, his voice drifting on the breeze.

"The tiny town of Singapore once stood right there," Tug continues, pointing where the river bends before ending its journey into Lake Michigan. "Picture this as a thriving little city. A few lumber mills, dozens of houses and ship docks, a school, saloons and a hotel. Three hundred people living right here where the river meets the lake. A humming lumber and shipbuilding hub with white pines everywhere. Perfect, right?" Tug takes a few steps until he's at the very edge of a dune. "The founders of Singapore had big dreams. They envisioned their town as the next Midwestern city, one that would rival the growing metropolises in Illinois and Wisconsin. But they got greedy. They depleted the landscape of its natural resources, and nothing could stop the blowing sand. It just kept coming and coming. Finally, fires destroyed much of the remaining houses. An entire history is buried underneath where we're standing."

I can feel the heat rising from the sand.

It is just the two of us out here, and yet I feel as if I'm surrounded.

By ghosts.

By kindred spirits.

By family.

The sand lifts in the breeze and sings as it moves around me. I can hear it talk, speak to me, whisper its secrets.

The past is buried here. Destroyed by human ego and consumption.

"You know," Tug says, looking toward the water, "the past continues to repeat itself. Our towns are coping with historically high lake levels that have caused incredible erosion on the lakeshore and surrounding dunes. This is a reminder of the power of nature and how humans can accelerate those forces. Just like we did on the river." Tug turns. "The dunes reclaimed the land. They reclaimed what was rightfully theirs. They engulfed their own history."

My knees suddenly feel weak, and I take a seat on the sand. Tug sits beside me.

"It's so strange—almost unnerving—to hear this and to see all of this in a completely different light," I say. "It's as though the past never existed. And yet it still remains, unseen, right before our very eyes."

"I believe Singapore buried itself under its own avarice," he says in a quiet voice, the blowing sand seeming to agree with his declaration. "The town wasn't satisfied being its own unique little place. It wanted to be bigger. It wanted to be like everyone else. It tried to be a lot of things to a lot of people, but it forgot about its own foundation. The trees that protected it were its family, its history, its line of self-defense. Its demise was self-inflicted because it wanted to be more. Sometimes, being what and who you are is enough. Sometimes, understanding your past will save you because you finally remember those roots are there for a reason: they keep us grounded."

The lake wind whistles through the trees, and the leaves seem to sing in agreement with Tug.

I watch boats drift in and out of the channel. A yacht exits the channel and moves before us, seeming to engulf all of Lake Michigan in its size and grandeur. As it sails further and further into the distance, onto the horizon, the yacht gets smaller and smaller, until it looks...

...*no bigger than the inner tube or the canoe on which I used to float.*

No different than how I used to get from here to there.

We are all in motion. Same water. Same world. Same people.

"Have they ever found anything buried in the dunes?" I finally ask.

"Someone found a sign, old and worn, but still intact," Tug says. "It read, SINGAPORE LOCATED HERE. And it still is. Even though we can't see it, it's here. And it's good to know that, remember that, embrace that, lest history repeats itself again."

He reaches out and takes my hand.

I shut my eyes.

When I open them, I can see the town of Singapore as it once was, thriving, booming, humming.

I shut my eyes and open them again.

It is still there, despite everything that happened to it.

And so am I.

Bonnie and I have barely spoken to one another since I arrived a half hour ago. We have not spoken since the Summer Solstice.

But I kept my appointment to complete her gown.

I have a job to do. And I will finish it.

Tug's offer to join him along with our visit to Singapore has occupied my mind the last day.

I *am* in motion.

To where, I'm just not quite sure.

And I'm unsure if I'm here to say goodbye, or if I'm waiting for her to say I'm sorry yet again for lying.

My past—all our pasts—are buried as deeply as Singapore's past. Too much history burned to the ground. I won't be burned again.

Bonnie shifts on the dressing stand.

Is she my lost Pompeii?

Or a mirage of my memories?

I think of what Tug said: sometimes, being what and who you are is enough. Sometimes, understanding your past will save you because you remember there are roots there that keep us grounded. Even though we can't see Singapore, it's here. And it's good to know that, remember that, embrace that, lest history repeats itself again.

I focus on Bonnie's dress for the Glow. Her dress is as golden as the lake at sunset, one shoulder exposed, the fabric reversed to a deep purple, like the sky before the sun finally goes down.

I hear a squeak in the silence and know Lauralei is approaching. She sets tea down on a side table and looks at Bonnie.

"Beautiful, ma'am."

Bonnie doesn't say a word. She lifts her hand into the air and gives a teensy, dismissive wave.

To her onetime friend.

Lauralei exits.

Squeak. Squeak.

"She refuses to wear any other shoe," Bonnie finally says. Her voice is higher than normal, almost as if she's inhaled helium. The tension in the room is palpable. I do not look at her. "She thinks they save her feet, but the rubber sole makes that hideous noise."

There is another long silence before Bonnie continues.

"Do you remember that old country song? 'The Streak'? It was on every radio station in the 1970s?"

I nod. Although the song was popular before my time, a DJ would play it on the radio every so often. My mom would act mortified by the lyrics, but I could see her face lift, her infamous unsmiling smile.

"My friends used to sing that about Lauralei," Bonnie says. "Oh, yes, they call it the squeak…"

Bonnie so completely surprises me by singing, telling a joke and sharing an old secret that I look at her as if for the first time.

"You can't leave me alone," she says out of the blue. "I have no one. Please."

Her words are barely audible, but they are tinged with pain and heartache. Her tone is wobbly. I cover my surprise by taking a seat on the floor.

I look up at Bonnie towering above me. I hear Lauralei's shoes squeak.

Servant? Friend?

"That's not an apology," I say. "I know what you did at the Summer Solstice. You not only sabotaged me, you humiliated me in front of your friends and the entire town. For no reason. Why did you do that?" I hesitate. "No, how could you do that? It's unforgivably cruel."

"I have a tendency to cut off those who don't need me," she says, even more quietly. "My friends wanted to take you from me."

"I'm not your property. I'm a designer, not a full-time employee of yours. I learned a long time ago not to sign a noncompete and not to sign over my name or my brand. Now I have to start over again."

"I will tell them what I did, I promise," Bonnie says.

"That doesn't undo what you've done, though."

Bonnie steps off the platform, holding the hem of her dress, and skitters over to a dresser. She opens her purse and pulls out an envelope.

"Here," she says, when she returns.

I open it. It's another large check with numerous zeroes.

"Stay for my Glow," Bonnie says. "Please."

I look at this woman, who seems to be both a complete stranger and so very familiar, a ghost and so very real, a woman buried underneath the sand who is trying to claw free before it's too late.

A mirror across the room reflects another woman, who seems to be both a complete stranger and so very familiar, a ghost and so very real, a woman buried underneath the sand who is trying to claw her way free, too, before it's too late.

I can see myself, my mother and Bonnie in the reflection. I can see women I know and have never known.

I see my reflection look again at the check.

In the mirror and in my mind, I can see that I have the same chain reaction of emotions my mother had when she received extra cash from townsfolk for sewing or babysitting. Her face—nearly imperceptibly, like mine when I knew who had the button when we played the game—would register initial disgust. I could see her pride had been pinged. The disgust would then morph into uneasy acceptance, before finally and publicly appearing as faux gratitude.

Such is the conflict I've always had about those with money.

I need it. I want it. But it always come with strings.

Work for a large company. Lend us your talent and your name. Be indebted.

My mother used to take any uneasy windfall and hide it in a McCoy cookie jar in the shape of a happy, wide-eyed puppy bowed before its owner, head down, tail up.

The irony was lost on me until I became an adult.

I'm so grateful! Thank you, thank you, thank you!

My mother never used that money on anything frivolous. It was squirreled away until an emergency arose: a hole in the roof, a fridge on the fritz, a fall and trip to the emergency room, a new pair of shoes for a growing girl.

To me, that made the money seem even more ominous. It was tainted and should only be used for such ends.

Tug may say that life is more than an IRA and benefits package, and he may be right in the long run, but right now I know that my Cobra insurance coverage that guarantees the same benefits as Lindy's health plan will run out in a few months, my renters will leave, I have condo association fees and taxes, I have a big credit card bill, and I have no steady income.

My cookie jar will be empty.

"I'll think about it," I finally say—to Bonnie, to myself, to my mother—folding and tucking the check into my pocket.

"I'm so glad," Bonnie says. "Now, let's finish this masterpiece."

Later that afternoon, I sip a glass of wine and work on the "wrong side" of Bonnie's dress.

I have always been fascinated by sewing terms.

For instance, the side of the fabric that is meant to be seen is known as the "right side" of the fabric. The other side, the wrong side, is hidden.

Sometimes, it's easy to tell what's the right and what's the wrong side. The right side will have an obvious pattern, or it will be velvet. The right side of the fabric is and will always be the side with the smooth edge on the holes; the wrong side has the edges relieved and pushed out.

But the two sides work in concert. You cannot have a garment with only one side. The unseen side—the wrong one—is doing just as much work. It has just as much pride.

I've always tried to make it as beautiful as the right side. I never wanted it to be a "throwaway" part of the garment. I wanted it to tell its own beautiful story, too.

For years, I've surprised the wearer, sometimes with a polka-dot pattern in a tailored blouse, or a monogram inside the sleeve, a message that might speak to her. I even managed to do this in my ready-to-wear designs for Lindy's: a hidden, looping, cursive SB for Sutton's Buttons inside the back of every blouse or jacket.

The doorbell rings.

I glance out the open screen door. A man in a brown shirt is holding a small box.

"Sutton Douglas?" he asks.

"Yes."

"Package for you. Can you sign here?"

I stand and sign. "Have a great day," he says, jogging down the path and back to his truck.

I grab a pair of scissors and open the box. It's from Abby. I set it on the living room table and take a seat on the floor. It's filled with mail that never made it to me. Most is trash— magazines, junk mail, AARP notices for my mother and her church bulletins—but there is "the bill" Abby mentioned, and although I already know the total, I still stare at all the numbers for a few minutes wondering how I could have been such an idiot, thinking shopping could fill my void. I set it in a "keeper pile" and then the rest in a "toss pile."

"Keep, toss, toss, toss," I say to myself, shuffling through the box of papers.

And then something catches my eye. A letter addressed to me with a return address of Kansas City, Missouri, and a stamp from Joplin, Missouri.

I open it, thinking it's perhaps a condolence note from an

old coworker of my mother's. It's a handwritten letter in neat cursive. I open it.

Dear Sutton,

First, please know how deeply sorry I am on the loss of your mother. I just learned about it. I just lost my mama, too. I grew up in Joplin, as you know the "big town" in the southern Missouri Ozarks. I now live in Kansas City. I never knew you or your mother, but it seems as if my parents did.

In fact, it seems as if we are connected. By a secret.

Before my mama passed, I was down helping to clear out the house so I could move her into an assisted living facility. As you can imagine, after fifty years in the same house, it was filled with stuff. Spent days cleaning until I finally made it to the attic. Even more stuff...boxes stacked all the way to the rafters. Most were filled with the usual—books, holiday decorations, dishes—and I was hauling it to the trash or putting it aside to take to the antiques store on Main. I dumped a box filled with old papers into the trash, and when I glanced down, I saw what looked like a birth certificate sitting on top of the papers. As you can see, it's a copy of yours.

My heart is pounding. I open the folded piece of paper.

The birth certificate looks just like the one I've seen before when I had to use it to get my driver's license and passport: My name. My mother's name. Father unknown. Mother born in Michigan.

I stop. Wait. My copy lists Missouri as my mother's birthplace, not Michigan. I'm certain it does.

I continue reading in a mad blur.

I found other things in the trash, too: pictures. Of a girl with a baby. Of a cabin. As soon as I showed my mom, she burst into tears. She held the photos in her shaking hand and said,

"My beautiful girls." She was so emotional, and she was so old, I had to take my time to piece her stories together.

My mama used to be a nurse at the county hospital near Nevermore. A young girl showed up in the ER one night decades ago ready to have a baby. No family. No friends. All alone. She ended up having a little girl. "Baby having a baby," my mother kept saying.

My mama told me that the girl's family was so furious that they sent her away to have the baby. But the girl found out that the father of the baby, a boy himself, had killed himself out of grief, thinking he would never see her or his child ever again, so she ran away from that home in Chicago. Hitchhiked until she found a place so remote she thought no one would ever find her again: Nevermore.

She had a healthy baby girl she named Sutton. "Rhymes with button, my favorite thing in the world," she told my mama.

After a few days, my mama finally got the girl to talk a little bit more, to tell her where she was from, and my mama contacted the family to tell her she was safe and had had a baby girl. She called. She wrote letters. "Do you want her to come home?" Her family never responded.

"Know what's worse than never being found?" your mama told mine. "Not wanting to be."

My mama and daddy let her live in their carriage house for a while. This was long before I was born. Daddy was the county judge, and he was so upset by all she'd endured that he helped your mom restart her life as Mabel Douglas.

Seems it was a lot easier to change social security information and a birth certificate back then, especially when a judge is advocating for you, telling officials and locals alike that a little girl lost her entire family in a fire and escaped with nothing but her baby. He gave her the last name of Douglas, because that's where she was from and that's what was on her original birth certificate. Did you know your mom was born in a little hospital in Douglas, Michigan? And then reborn in Missouri? Daddy gave her just a little bit of history to carry forward and changed just enough of it so no one would ever find her. They even came up with that fire story after Miss Mabel told him about being a girl and watching some big dance hall burn in her hometown, everything gone—all that history—in a matter of moments. My daddy taught her to drive, got her a driver's license and everything she needed to start over. I think my parents just understood. They grew up poor, too. They were always helping those who needed a hand up in this world.

My mama said they wanted to adopt her, offered a hundred times, but she always refused. They told her how much they loved her, but my mama said Miss Mabel couldn't get close to anyone again, said she'd lost everything and wouldn't survive losing it all again. My parents did help her get a job at a local factory because she knew how to sew, and they set her up in the old cabin they bought on Hickory Creek they used as a summer retreat to fish and swim.

They checked in on you on occasion, as much as your mama would allow, but that was it. Over time, they let her be. They were happy she was happy. And they said she was with you.

I found your Chicago address from the local funeral home. I told them I needed to contact you. I wanted you to know all this if you didn't already. I also wanted you to have these photos. You as a baby with your mama. It's your history. You need to know to be complete. I know I would want to know.

My mama adored Miss Mabel. Said she was the best mother in the world. She nearly died for you. And would die to protect you. I understand that as a parent. That's what any good mother would do.

I hope this brings you some closure. And if you ever need anything or want to talk, here's my number. My door's always open for you. I feel like you're the sister I never had. And as a mother myself, I thank God every day for the one I had.
Best,
Sammie Jo Tucker

I am weeping so hard that I fall to my knees. And when I am done crying, I say a prayer thanking God for the best mother I ever could have had.

As if in a trance, I stand and move toward the jars of buttons I have from my mom and Bonnie. I eye each one carefully. I make my choices.

I know now what I must do.

I tip over a jar filled with vintage moonglow glass buttons from the 1950s, all in shades of blue. These are the buttons that she had on her dress. The buttons that are Dandy's eyes. The buttons of Bonnie's artwork in her bathroom.

I pull some gold buttons from another jar.

I turn the wrong side of the fabric at the bottom of her dress toward me.

I make an image of a sun setting over blue waves.

In buttons.

Bonnie will notice it when she steps into the dress. Her guests will notice it when she moves just so, and the image appears.

But—I know, and I believe that she will know—that there is a hidden message in this symbol. I am speaking to her in buttons, in our secret code.

How she is willing to tell me—and how I react—is still to be determined, though.

The room suddenly turns dim.

I walk to the window. In my peekaboo view, I can see the

glow on the horizon of the lake, a brushstroke of orange over moonglow blue.

The sun is setting.

A new day is coming.

12

PATCHWORK

*A form of needlework that involves sewing together
small pieces of fabric to create a patchwork–like effect.
This is very popular for quilting.
It can be done by hand or machine.*

When I wake up, my head is as cool as the pumpkins my mom and I would pull from farmers' fields in the Ozarks in October. The curtains wave in the breeze.

I fell asleep, exhausted after the letter and having worked late into the night on Bonnie's dress like a woman possessed. In my trance, I must have left the bedroom windows wide-open. I sit up. It is very chilly in the cottage.

In fact, I must have left every window open.

I pull the quilt at the end of the mattress over my body.

Patchwork.

I went through a phase growing up where I wanted to wear, much to my mother's chagrin, anything and everything patchwork. My mother and I made patchwork shorts, shirts, jeans and jean jackets.

My mother loved to make quilts, especially when the weather turned cold. She could make all of the patterns: log cabin, flying geese, star, bear paw and traditional Celtic square. But her favorite to make was the old-school patchwork quilt.

My mother would start by pulling together the scraps she

wanted to use in the quilt. I used to believe that she went by color or pattern—my mother sorted scraps by color and size, much as she did her buttons—but, over time, I realized she sorted the fabric by history.

The dresses I wore as a little girl. The old coats we wore when we'd make snowmen on the creek banks. Even my old volleyball jerseys.

I loved the warmth the quilts provided as a girl. I could not only feel the winter wind squeeze its way through the chinks in the old logs of our cabin, I could actually hear it squeal in delight.

But, at the time, I didn't love the stories those quilts wanted to tell me.

My mother saved everything. Every button, every scrap of fabric, every found penny. She funneled water into nearly empty ketchup bottles and swished it around, acting as if the tomato liquid was a new purchase from the grocery store. She saved eggshells and scattered them in her garden to rid them of snails, slugs and deer. Used tinfoil was smoothed, folded and stacked in the cabinets. Drawers were filled with contraband condiments, sugar and jelly packets she stuffed into her pocketbook the once a month we would eat at Woolworths.

"Thou shalt not steal," she would say, "but these are fair game!"

I was reminded every day of my life of exactly how little we had. I was reminded that if we didn't save scraps, hoard buttons, extend ketchup, we would not make it to next month, much less next year.

That puts the fear of God into you.

That's why I loved making patchwork outfits instead of quilts. If I had to use scraps, then I wanted to make them look hip and cool.

It's why I do what I do.

I touch the quilt in front of me, feeling each patch.

Who made this? What is its story? How was its life pieced together?

The wind whistles through the cottage. It speaks to me, as it did when I was a girl.

I hear its question loud and clear:

Are you the woman you are today because of your mother? Or are you the woman you are today in spite of your mother?

I pull the quilt toward my face and study the pretty pieces of scraps that comprise a beautiful soft star.

Without saying a word, was my mother trying to tell me everything?

About her life? About mine? About what is most important in life?

A chill covers me from head to toe, and I sit straight up, remembering something I haven't in a very long time.

I once attended a theme party in Chicago, and the hosts had invited a psychic to do readings for the guests. I thought it was a complete and utter joke until the woman, who I had never met and who had probably already done fifty readings that night, took my hand and said, "I see buttons! Everywhere. Like ghosts."

The woman was quiet, her eyes shut, for what seemed like an eternity before she continued.

"I see buttons in your dreams and visions, flashes of your imagination. I see buttons like a path in your waking life, leading you in a certain direction. But then there will be a fork in that road, buttons leading one way, the other path free of them. I see loose buttons as the backdrop of your entire life, in paintings and pictures."

She continued. "Did you know buttons are symbolic for a phase or present concern where you may be at a crossroads with making decisions? I feel as if they've been ever-present your whole life, both holding you back and pushing you forward, but always obstructing your ability to make a big decision. Wait, wait!"

It was then she had opened her eyes.

"Two women just moved onto each fork of the path," she said. "I cannot tell if they are blocking your way forward, or inviting you to take a new path." She shook my hand, hard. "Do not be indecisive when this occurs in your life. Make a choice and move on."

"How will I know what choice to make?" I asked, my heart racing.

"The buttons will tell you."

When we left, I was so shaken I hurried to find Abby.

"Did you tell her about me?" I asked her.

"No!" she said. "I don't know her. I thought she was a kook."

I get out of bed, wrapping the quilt around my body, and walk into the living room.

The letter is open. The picture of me and my mom stares up at me. The wrong side of Bonnie's dress is facing me.

Another dress—the one I made for myself—sits beside it as closely as a mother and daughter in church.

I shut one window in the living room, but just as I am about to close the other, I leave it open, as if I need options.

I can hear the psychic's voice—raspy and low—as clear as the breeze rushing inside this summer morning.

Do not be indecisive when this occurs in your life. Make a choice and move on.

I run an iron over the seams of my dress for Bonnie's Glow party.

As I sew, I always press the stitch lines and seams along the way in order to get that lovely, crisp finish.

You must do it at the end as well, otherwise people will only notice the wrinkles.

It's a small, but important and often overlooked, step.

I pull on my dress and smile.

It's time for me to press and finish.

I head out the door, walk along the path, letting the dune grass tickle my bare legs, and take a funicular down to Bonnie's beach.

As the funicular descends and my eyes take in the lakeshore, I suddenly understand Bonnie's vision of "beach party."

"Thank you," I say to the attendant helping me off the funicular and then again to a waiter in a black tux with a gold tie handing me a glass of champagne. The stem of the glass is wrapped in burlap the color of the sand, and a button of gold is centered just below the flute.

I shouldn't have been surprised by any of this. This isn't your typical summer beach bonfire. No one is running around barefoot in wet swimsuits, roasting hot dogs and marshmallows, like my mom and I did most summer nights on the creek. Bonnie isn't going to hand her guests a stick and some bug spray and yell, "Have a good time!"

No.

Instead, Bonnie has installed a makeshift wooden runway across the sand that leads to a huge tent with a dance floor, band, bar and food stations. The tent's fabric is a glorious gold, and it is strung with lights in different shades of amber. The band is playing Rat Pack music, and a few people are already dancing.

I take a sip of my champagne and take in the sheer opulence of this spectacle.

Men are dressed in tailored suits, and the woman are dressed as if they are attending the Golden Globes: dressy, elegant but a bit more festive. Lanterns are strung in the air from driftwood posts, the lights artfully zigzagging this way and that, and tables are occupied by floral centerpieces in vases filled with beach glass and candles set in sand.

It's then I realize people are also coming down to the beach on a second funicular. The funiculars are so well designed, so hidden into the dunes, painted the exact color of the bluff, that it's no wonder I didn't notice them from a distance on Tug's boat.

But the dueling trams serve to bookend the amount and grandeur of Bonnie's property. She owns five hundred feet of lakeshore, which doesn't sound like a lot until you actually see it in person. It's the equivalent of the total frontage that five historic lakeshore cottages own here in Douglas.

I've heard Tug discuss how high the taxes are in town—and how they skyrocket on the lakeshore—and I wonder how much she pays every year.

Probably a pittance considering her net worth of fifty million dollars.

"No need to add water to your ketchup, is there, Bonnie?" I mutter to the dune.

"Did you say something?"

I jump, and slosh a bit of champagne onto the sand.

"I was just saying to myself how beautiful this is and what a wonderful job you've done."

Bonnie beams.

Way to save yourself, Sutton.

"And you look stunning," I say.

I reach out and touch her dress. For a moment, my ego balloons with pride: Bonnie's dress *is* stunning, a true work of art.

And I made it!

Perhaps I am worth every penny I earn.

"Thank you," Bonnie says, doing a small bow as if she's

meeting the queen. "Everyone is going gaga over it. I'm telling everyone what a genius you are."

I nod but don't smile. *I'm not buying your schtick any longer, Bonnie.*

"And I want you beside me when I make my speech at sunset, do you hear me? Just a tiny way for me to say I'm sorry to you and let everyone know what a talent you are. The two of us. Forever!"

My body is still. Bonnie shifts in her shoes.

"All the buttons are firmly in place," she says, doing a twirl, trying to make a joke.

"As they always are," I say.

Bonnie looks like a screen goddess standing before me bathed in the glorious glow of the sun over the lake and reflection off the sand. She is gold on gold, the deepening purple of the lake matching the reversed fabric on her shoulder perfectly. The sun sparkles off the waves, and it looks as if a million flashbulbs are popping at the same time, paparazzi fighting to take Bonnie's photograph.

How old are you? I wonder. *How old were you when you embraced who you are now, when you left "poor" Mildred Bonne buried in the sand to become Bonnie Lyons?*

When you buried your own daughter?

Bonnie finally notices my dress, and the emotions on her face change in slow motion.

I am wearing a blue dress with blue buttons.

Similar to the one my mother loved, never wore and wanted to be buried in.

Similar to the one of the little girl in the painting going up her staircase.

Bonnie's eyes finally meet mine. In them I can see a range of emotions, a thunderstorm raging in her pupils. And yet, like the actress she is, Bonnie manages a smile and says, "You look lovely in blue."

A group of women approach.

"Excuse me," Bonnie says to me. "Marybeth! Yvonne! I'm so glad you could make it! Happy Glow!"

I watch these women hug, and I miss my mom so much my soul aches. I miss her most in the summer. I can still see her at the creek watching the water, the sun set, the swallows dip. I can hear the burble of the creek, the song of her Singer, the way she'd hum to herself when she was making dinner.

Life is not fair. Life can be cruel. But it can also be as glorious as a summer night on the beach if we are simply surrounded by those we love.

Even if it's just their memories.

"Sutton? Sutton?"

Bonnie is shaking my arm.

"Look for me just a touch after nine o'clock, okay? Right over there under that tent. Sun will be setting around then. I always make my speech and toast the end of a day and the beginning of a new one. You, my dear, are a new day."

I blink, once, twice.

"Okay."

She turns to leave with her friends, but pivots at the last second and looks at me, as if a ghost has appeared right here on the beach before her very eyes.

A waiter approaches, and I grab another glass of champagne.

I chug it and grab another.

He looks at me. "Do you need some food?"

I shake my head and meander around the Glow, watching the wealthy doing wealthy things: sip Veuve as if it's tap water, gorge on caviar and lobster as if they are saltines and spray cheese, carry thousand-dollar handbags as if they are purses they picked up at Goodwill.

Are they doing anything wrong, Sutton? Or has life just smiled upon them like the sun is doing right now, and rained gold onto their lives like the light on the lake?

I think of the seven deadly sins I learned in church: pride, greed, lust, envy, gluttony, wrath and sloth.

How many am I exhibiting right now versus them?

It's a close score, isn't it?

"Don't be a glutton, Sutton," my mom always said when I'd reach for a third helping of mac and cheese instead of saving it for tomorrow's dinner or allowing my mother to take it to a coworker who always brought tomato sandwiches for lunch.

It's almost as if she named me Sutton on purpose, as a way to inflict perpetual guilt.

"One more," I say to the waiter. "Liquid courage." I look at him. "You working your way through college? I worked my way through college, too."

He nods.

That's when I notice the button on his jacket is frayed, hanging by a thread.

The irony is too much to take.

I think of Bonnie and her dress, of my mom and hers, of me in mine. I think of my life—all our lives—hanging by a thread.

I glance over at Bonnie.

I think of what she did, what my mother did, and what I must do.

It's why I am here right now. It's why I came here in the first place.

I take my champagne and sneak back toward the funicular.

"Are you leaving?" the man operating it asks.

"I need to find a little girls' room."

"Mrs. Lyons has exquisite facilities set up on the beach." The man points.

Of course she does.

"I forgot my purse," I lie.

He eyes the purse on my arm.

"I forgot my phone," I try.

He notes the cell gripped in the hand not holding the champagne.

"I made Bonnie's dress," I say. "There's an issue with a button. I'm renting the cottage behind hers, and I need to get some needle and thread to fix it. I would hate for her to wait or get upset."

The man hits the button and up we go.

A lie that's not a lie.

"Back in a jiffy," I tell him, scooting across Lakeshore Drive in the same high espadrille sandals I wore to the Summer Solstice.

When I reach Bonnie's yard, I turn. The funicular man is taking another group down the bluff.

I scan the yard, road and bluff. The coast—literally—is clear.

I race up the path, still holding my champagne, and when I reach the front door, I chug the remains in the flute and set the glass down by the entrance. I open the door, an inch at a time. I peek inside. I can see the kitchen and waitstaff scurrying about, going in and out of the side door. My heart is beating so quickly I feel as if I might pass out.

Champagne has given me courage.

I step inside and ease the front door shut.

No, champagne has made you stupid, Sutton.

My urge is to sprint across the tile, but I'm worried about the sound my shoes will make, so I tiptoe across, slowly, drunkenly. I hear the unmistakable squeak of Lauralei's shoes, and I stop. In the middle of the button.

Squeak. Squeak.

The noise slowly diminishes, and I scoot across the tile and up the stairs.

I head to the secret bedroom, open it quickly and slip inside. I close the door, my heart beating in my temples.

The room is just as I remember: pink with frilly curtains and a four-poster bed, dolls leaning against a mountain of pillows. Through the window, Lake Michigan sparkles, a beacon of blue.

I look at the ghostly silhouettes dotting the pink walls, as if pictures were removed long ago and never replaced.

When will it end, Sutton?

I turn in a circle. I begin—as quietly as possible—to open drawers in the tiny dressers.

All empty.

I look under the bed.

Nothing.

The room spins from the champagne, trepidation and fear of what I might find. I take a seat on the bed. The four posters shake as if there's been an earthquake, and the dolls tilt toward me as if they need a hug. I pick one up and hold it, just as I do with Dandy. I squeeze it so tightly that its little arms shoot straight out from its sides. One of the arms points toward the closet. I set the doll down and head toward it, opening the door.

The closet is largely empty, save for some sheets stacked on a shelf. But then I see, in the back of the big, walk-in closet, a wooden chest. I pull on its lid. It's locked.

My heart sinks, and then I remember the hope chest my mother kept for me as a girl. The key was always hidden underneath.

I lift the chest with a grunt, and a key is taped to the bottom. I pull it free and unlock the chest. A baby blanket sits inside, a tiny pair of baby booties on top of it. My heart suddenly aches for my mother.

I pick up the blanket and booties, and hidden beneath them is a cardboard box, two words written on top:

AMBEL'S THINGS

I open the lid of the box, carefully unfolding the panels that have been interlocked. It is filled with button jars. I pick one up. A peeling piece of masking tape with faded ink reads:

AMBEL'S FAVORITE BLUES

The jar is stuffed with beautiful blue buttons, similar to the ones I'm wearing on my dress, similar to the ones I've hidden inside Bonnie's dress, similar to the ones my mother dearly loved.

I set it down and pick up another button jar.

My heart stops.

MABEL'S BUTTONS!

I look again, thinking my tipsy eyes are playing tricks on me. They are not.

The writing on the label is that of a little girl, as if she's just learning to spell and has unintentionally juxtaposed the first two letters of her name.

I place one hand over my eye to stop the words from spinning. I do it with the other. I look away. This time, when I glance at the label, it reads BLAME.

Blues.

Buttons.

Ambel.

Mabel.

Blame.

History.

Twisted, juxtaposed and reversed.

I look toward the rag dolls on the bed to help me, their arms outstretched, their button eyes searching mine.

"She was just a child," I say to them. "She did nothing wrong."

"What are you doing in here?"

I scream.

Bonnie is standing in the doorway, arms crossed, face red.

I hold up the button jar.

"You're my grandmother, aren't you?"

"You're drunk, Sutton. Sober up and get yourself down to the beach before I throw you out of my house and this town."

"Stop it!" I plead. "Stop lying! For once in your life!"

"I'm not lying, Sutton. You are. To yourself. You're a very unhappy woman, and I'm trying to help you."

"Tell me what happened. Please!"

"My daughter died," Bonnie says, her voice cold as ice. "And you don't even have the courtesy to respect my feelings or my home after I've invited you into my life."

My eyes blur with tears.

"I know everything," I say. "Everything. I know you sent my mother away. How could you do that? How?"

"You didn't even recognize your own granddaughter in the beginning. I knew immediately."

Lauralei is standing behind Bonnie.

"Watch your mouth!" Bonnie shouts at her.

"She has Ambel's eyes," Lauralei says, her eyes shining with tears. "She has Ted's jaw and hair." She looks at me, her expression softening. "I knew it was you from the first time I saw you. I knew. I knew you'd find your way back one day. My grandbaby's come home."

"What?"

My legs shake.

"Tell her," Lauralei says. "Or I will."

"Don't you dare," Bonnie threatens.

Lauralei looks at me.

"My husband and son were clammers," Lauralei says, her voice barely audible. "They worked for the Lyons."

"Lauralei..." Bonnie says, approaching us.

Lauralei doesn't even acknowledge her words or presence. She continues, her voice getting stronger.

"So did we," Lauralei says, finally looking at Bonnie. "Didn't we, Mildred?"

"I'm warning you!"

"Or what?" Lauralei spits her words at Bonnie in disgust. "How could you possibly hurt me anymore? You took my only son, you took my only grandchild. I have nothing!"

"You have a job," Bonnie says, voice ice-cold.

"Had," Lauralei corrects her.

Lauralei walks me over to the bed, and we sit.

"Bonnie and I were best friends," she says. "We were so young, just girls. Our families were poor, and we came here to work for Mr. Lyons hoping and praying for a better life. Wilbur, who's now my husband, went out on a johnboat every day and dragged sets of hooks along the river bottom. The wire hooks would touch the clam's tender lips, and the precious little fool would grab ahold of it, close its shell upon it and hold on for dear life."

Lauralei looks at Bonnie. "Sound familiar?"

Bonnie takes a step back until she is leaning against the pink wall. She holds it for support.

"Wilbur would bring in his catch, and the clams were tossed into big pots of boiling water to kill them. Mildred and I would pry open the loosened shells and clean out the white meat before the shells were taken to the factory to be made into buttons." Lauralei looks away and continues. "Mildred and I bunked next to one another. She fell in love with Dan, Jr. and said she was going to marry him. We went to school in the cottage behind this one for years in the morning. It used to be a one-room schoolhouse for the poor factory workers' children. Then, we'd work in the factory all afternoon and night. No one ever saw it as a problem, using children for hard labor. When we got older, Mildred started sneaking out and going to the old Pavilion in Saugatuck. Oh, she could make any ol' leftover scraps into the prettiest dress. She'd stay up and sew by candlelight, using the blue buttons she'd steal from the factory. What was it you called that sewing machine of yours one of the women gave you? Ol' Betsy! That was it."

I blink a tear.

"Mildred ended up dancing with Dan Jr. one night. He didn't recognize her all gussied up and out of the factory. Lied to him, didn't you, Mildred? Said you were just up for the summer from Chicago with your family, right? Made him fall in love? Get you pregnant?"

Bonnie is gripping the wall, her face even redder, her golden dress like a sunset against the pink sky.

"Then it was too late," Lauralei continues. "Old man Lyons was furious, but he made his son marry Mildred. Cut him off. But no one should ever underestimate Mildred. She got him to change his trust back to his son and her when—let's just say—the elder Lyons no longer had his wits. She took the business from him, too."

The pieces begin to click together from the letters, Captain Lucky, Mary, Tug. My head is whirling.

"Fast-forward a few years: Wilbur taught my son, Ted, how to be the best clammer in the world. Mildred's daughter, Ambel, used to accompany her to the factory. Ted and Ambel hit it off immediately. Ted was so handsome, and Ambel was a beauty. Such a lonely, little girl being homeschooled all alone. Had no friends. Mildred tried to keep her and Ted apart. She couldn't stomach the fact that history was repeating itself. But it didn't work: the two were so deeply in love. And then Ambel got pregnant when she had yet to turn sixteen." Lauralei turns to Bonnie. "You tell the rest of the story, Mildred. You know it so well."

"Lauralei, please—"

"Tell her!"

I jump at Lauralei's shout.

"Ambel had her whole life ahead of her," Bonnie begins weakly. "I thought it would be best if we sent her away to a home in Chicago to have the baby in secret and give it up for adoption. Where it could have a good life."

"She!" Lauralei says. "It was a girl! Our *granddaughter*! And she would have had a good life. Right here, with her mother! Her whole family! You had all the money in the world. Every advantage."

"Ambel ran," Bonnie says. "She disappeared."

"She ran from *you*!" I say. "I know everything, Bonnie. I got a letter from the daughter of the woman who helped my mother when she was all alone. They reached out to you. You never replied. Your own daughter needed you, and you turned your back on her."

Bonnie looks away, out the window.

"I was the one who went to Chicago, to tell Ambel that Ted had taken his life," Lauralei says. "She needed to know. I tried to get her to come home and live with me, but she was inconsolable. She said she could never have a life in Douglas, in her mother's shadow. She said she just wanted to have the baby and move on with her life. I had no idea she would run away. I looked for the two of you for years. I started anew when everything went online. But nothing. Ambel knew how to hide. I tried. Believe me, I tried. I did everything I could to try and locate you. But, oh, your mother was smart. And tough. Tougher than Mildred. She made a decision to have a life in which her mother could never interfere. My beautiful Ted died of heartbreak. He loved his Belle so much." Lauralei looks at me. "Short for bluebell because she loved the color so much. Ted, ever the clammer, called her his secret pearl."

I take Lauralei's hand in mine. "I'm so sorry," I say through my tears. I turn to Bonnie. "Did *you*? Did you ever try to find us?"

Bonnie cannot look at me.

"Or were you relieved?" I ask. "That your family shame had conveniently disappeared?"

"Can you imagine being reminded every day of what I left behind?" Bonnie asks. "What I worked so hard to leave behind?"

"You're a monster," I say.

"I am, too, Sutton," Lauralei says. "Mildred hired me here to work for her after all that happened, offered me more money than I could ever dream after living day-to-day for so long. But, in return, I had to keep my mouth shut. And I did. I did." Lauralei shakes her head. "I was filled with so much shame. I still had a family to take care of. I've been trapped in my own hell forever." Lauralei turns to me. "Can you ever forgive me? Because I can't ever forgive myself."

I open my arms and hold her.

"I'm just learning to forgive myself," I whisper.

I look at Bonnie. I release Lauralei and stand to face her.

"Let me tell you about the woman and child you sacrificed for your own ego," I say. "They had a hard life. A lot like the one you left behind. A life filled with scraps, leftovers and backbreaking work. I grew up believing my entire family died in a fire on Christmas. Can you imagine a little girl living with that her whole life? All I wanted was a family. And you just left yours behind, not once, but twice. My mother sacrificed her entire life for me to have a better one, and now I can see that it was a life filled with incredible gifts despite all the hardship. I was safe and loved, and that's all a child needs."

I narrow my eyes and continue.

"You should know that you nearly killed my mother—and you did kill her dreams of loving anyone but me again—but despite all the scar tissue, she loved me with everything she had. Sometimes, all she could give me was the equivalent of the last few summer beans in a dying garden, but it was *everything* she had. She taught me to survive. She never left me. She never turned her back on me. She fought for me to have a better life. Isn't that what every parent wants for her child? If you did one thing right, it was that you made my mother stronger, more resilient and more powerful than she ever knew she could be. You made us cling to one another. You made us mother and daughter—one soul—and that is something you will *never* know."

My breath hitches, and I will myself not to cry in front of this woman, my grandmother. "You've finally made me realize that my mother was never poor, and I was never alone. We had everything. We had each other. In fact, I can now see that my mother was the richest woman I've ever known because she *got* it. She understood what mattered most, the simple things. You're still not even close. Money doesn't matter. Status doesn't matter. Image doesn't matter. What matters is our family, our friends, our health, a sunrise and a sunset, a bird singing at dawn, a dogwood in bloom, a beautiful button." I take a deep breath. "Each other."

I hold out my hand to Lauralei.

"You're choosing *her*?" Bonnie says.

"No. I'm choosing my family."

"I will ruin you in this town," Bonnie cries.

"Go ahead and try," I snap. "You don't get it. I don't need

you. I never have. And if you try to hurt me, or Lauralei, then every secret you've tried to hide will come to light. Or, you can keep your mouth shut. Like you've always done. Perhaps pretend that you died on a trip."

I take Lauralei's hand, and we walk out of the bedroom, past my mother's portrait and out of Dandelion Cottage.

I stop at the end of Bonnie's yard. The sun is setting over the lake directly in front of my eyes. I walk to the edge of the bluff and stare into the sunset.

Bonnie rushes by us, as if we do not exist, as if we are strangers, and takes the funicular back down to the beach. I can hear her voice greet her guests. It sounds so happy.

The sun looks like a gold button on the horizon, and a zig-zag stitch of ripples extends from it to the shoreline, as if my mom has skipped a piece of shale all the way across the lake and into infinity.

I now know what she was pondering when she looked across the creek.

She was grateful for another day.

She was grateful for being a survivor.

She was grateful for being stronger than she could ever imagine.

She was grateful for being a mother.

I stare into the sunset disappearing into the ripples.

"I did it! I did it!" I remember yelling when my rock would skip all the way across the creek and make it to the other side. "What do I win, Mom?"

"The satisfaction that you made it," I can hear her say.

Lauralei's cabin looks much like the one I grew up in, down to the logs and chinking. It sits on a tiny lake a few miles inland from Saugatuck-Douglas.

Lauralei throws open the front door and races down the path toward me, arms open.

She rocks me back and forth. When I look up, Wilbur is standing at the door.

"It's so nice to meet you," I call.

"My grandbaby," he says, bursting into tears. "Alive."

"This is Tug," I say. "My boyfriend."

"Know your store well," Lauralei says. "It's nice to meet you. Come in. Come in."

Her home is modest but filled with heirlooms and love. She offers us some lemonade, and we take a seat in her living room. Lined up on the coffee table are scrapbooks filled with photos of Ted and Ambel.

There is a picture of Ted on the johnboat, nearly exactly like the one my mother had hidden.

"I don't know how she kept up a lie for so many years," Wilbur comments.

"She knew what was best for her child," Lauralei says. She takes my hand. "Oh, how I wish you could have met your father. He was such a good man. He loved Ambel more than anything in the world. All he wanted was a family."

Lauralei's face is wet. "Excuse me," she says.

There is a moment of awkward silence, but she returns with a button jar.

"I saved all of these buttons," she says. Lauralei moves the scrapbook and turns over the jar, blue buttons scattering everywhere. She snakes them out across the table like a blue river. "Oh, Ambel loved the color blue."

"She did," I say.

"The blue of the water, the blue of the sky in summer, the icy blue of the snow in winter. So did Ted. He had aquamarine eyes."

I pick up a button and study it.

"I want you to have these buttons," Lauralei says. "I can't give you much except all my love and these heirlooms." She looks at me and then at Tug. "Maybe one day, these will be for your baby."

I shift uncomfortably on the couch. "I'm getting a bit old for a family," I say. "My mom may have been a baby when she had me, but I'm no spring chicken."

"Bock-bock," Tug clucks, laughing. He turns serious and looks at Lauralei. "I would love nothing more than to have a family."

There is another awkward silence.

"Well, I can't wait for you to meet the rest of our family soon." Wilbur says, clapping his hands to snap us out of it. "Let me go start the grill. Steaks will be ready in a bit. Why don't you two take a walk, and we'll get dinner going."

We nod, and let Lauralei shoo us out the back door toward the lake.

"How are you doing?" Tug asks. "This is overwhelming, I know."

"I feel..." I stop as we walk. "Remarkably at peace for the first time in a long time."

We walk out onto Wilbur and Lauralei's dock, kick off our shoes, take a seat and dangle our feet in the water.

I think of my mom telling me the story of the River Jordan, in which Jesus was baptized. I think of the creek in which she baptized me. I think of Lake Michigan and starting over anew with Tug. I look into the water and see the reflection of a woman I'm just beginning to understand. I kick my feet, hoping this little lake can wash away years of sorrow and grief.

Tug takes my hand. I look into his hazel eyes. In them, I can see more blue than I remember.

I suddenly stand. I look at the blue button still in my hand. I give the button a kiss and skip it across the lake.

The button jumps and skitters as if propelled by an invisible motor, before taking one last giant hop into the air and diving into the lake.

"Sutton!" my grandmother calls, ringing a bell. "Time for dinner!"

Epilogue

Button
A Memory
Five Years Later

"Button, button, who's got the button?"

I hold both of my hands, fists tight, in front of Tug and Melba. They are seated on the steps that lead to the upstairs addition of Wade's Cottage.

Melba points at my left hand.

I open it. It's empty.

"Ha!" Tug yells, teasing our daughter and pointing at my right hand. "Winner, winner, chicken dinner!"

I open my right hand. It's empty.

"What?" Melba asks, eyes wide. "You don't play fair, Mommy! Where's the button?"

I pull a button jar from the deep pocket of my jacket.

"Right here," I say. "All for you."

I hold out the jar to my daughter. It is filled with pink buttons of every shade. Melba is all girl, all pink, all the time.

"Where'd you get these?" she asks. "What are you going to make for me?"

I laugh. "I got these with Daddy," I say. "And what would you like me to make for you?"

"A coat! No, a dress! Wait! Wait! A princess costume for Halloween!"

She is absolutely breathless with her requests.

"First things first," Tug says. "We need to get you ready for your swim lessons. Now, scoot. And don't forget the sunscreen."

Melba races up the stairs with an excited squeal.

It is a beautiful July morning—still, so still—where summer seems as if it's holding its breath in anticipation for all that's to come this wondrous day.

I glance up at the clock. There are things to be done—so many things. I have a half-dozen clients who need fittings for summer gala dresses. My fall collection—Sutton's Buttons—is going into a series of boutiques in Chicago. And Tug's shop is busier than ever now.

We are united now, in every way.

The second hand on the clock clicks.

I think of my life, of how many times I've tried to speed up time, how many times I've tried to evade it, how many times I've run from it and tried to make sense of it.

Now I just want to stop it.

I shut my eyes, and I can hear the rush of the waves from Wade's Bayou. It sounds like the rush of Hickory Creek, the whir of Ol' Betsy, the Rolodex of memories.

Is this how my mom felt when it was just the two of us, together in our cabin, her sewing, me playing with buttons? That, just for a moment—for one tiny moment in a too-short life that is too often packed with pain, horror, shame, death, guilt and resentment—everything was perfect. Everyone was safe. Everyone was loved.

Money didn't matter. Family did.

Melba rushes down in her adorable swimsuit, and I grab a cover-up I made, decorated in pink felt applique mermaids with button eyes.

"C'mon, Daddy! Let's go!"

She rushes out the door, and the screen bangs shut.

The home buzzes with quiet. Sunlight shifts and slants across my face.

I can see my mother clearly when she was older, sitting on the beach, too tired to move, staring at the creek, back aching and arched after a long week of work, the sun setting on another stunning summer day.

"I never should have wasted a beautiful summer day staying inside when I had the chance. You can never get these moments back."

I grab my purse and keys.

"I want to take Melba to swim lessons this morning, okay? And then maybe the beach and ice cream?"

Tug looks at me.

"I think that's a grand idea," he says.

He hugs me, and the world falls away.

There is a moment in your life where the past meets the future, and you realize how hard it was to get right here, right now, and you feel as if you can see into infinity, as if you are staring at the horizon becoming one with Lake Michigan.

And time finally stands still.

★ ★ ★ ★ ★

Author Note

Dear Reader,

I grew up with my grandmas. I spent weekends and holidays in their tiny, too-hot kitchens watching them bake beloved desserts from recipe cards they pulled from their recipe boxes. I spent Saturdays at the beauty parlor watching them get their hair "did." But I probably spent the most time in their sewing rooms watching them make my school clothes or turn scraps into beautiful quilts.

My grandma Shipman (Viola, my pen name) stitched overalls at a local factory until she couldn't stand straight. And my grandma Rouse was also an accomplished seamstress. But even after sewing all day for work, nothing brought them more joy than finding the perfect pattern or creating their own designs and taking a seat at their Singers. It represented one of the first times in my life I was able to witness in real time what happens when talent meets inspiration: incredible joy. Work is no longer work. That changed my life.

My grandmothers both owned Singer sewing machines, and

I thought they were the most beautiful things in the world: black with a beautiful gold inlay pattern atop the original, old treadle oak cabinet, glowing with a rich patina.

My grandmothers were like ballerinas at their Singers, their bodies in motion and in tune with the machine. It was a gorgeous dance to watch. They were also the first artists I ever knew, though they were never called that and their cheeks would turn red today at the mere utterance of such a fancy word. But they taught me to create. To take pride in what I created. To continue perfecting my talent.

The Edge of Summer is inspired by these memories. It's also inspired by the thoughts that spun in my head as I watched them sew, especially as I grew older—what were my grandmas like before they were my grandmas? Did I know everything about them? Where did this love of—and great skill for—sewing come from? And, although I knew of their sacrifices, I wondered how much they truly had to sacrifice, and maybe even hide, in order to get here, right now, happy and sewing in a home with their grandchild watching them work.

The novel is also inspired by the loss of my father-in-law, George, to Covid in 2019. We've lost so many to an invisible virus—too, too many—and I never want their names or stories to be lost. George achieved so much in his life, rising from hardship and working his way through college, day and night, finally earning his PhD to become a school superintendent and pass along the importance of education.

Like Miss Mabel in *The Edge of Summer*, my grandmothers and father-in-law overcame so much in their childhoods. But I know it didn't come easy. It never does. In today's age, we have so much information at our fingertips. We seek out our ancestry, searching to find who we are and where we came from. We want to know how our families came to be. My grandma used to say, "We can't know where we're going if we don't know from where we came." We seek that more than ever these days.

I wrote this novel to remind readers that families are not perfect. They never will be. But if we were blessed to be loved by our family, as flawed as it may have been—and even if our parents were not who we wished they had been or the love they gave was not as much or as demonstrative as we would have liked—we were still blessed to be loved. At its heart, this novel seeks to ask if we should be thankful for those sacrifices and if maybe, just maybe, that love is enough for us to stitch together a beautiful life and future.

I truly hope you love *The Edge of Summer*. And I'm so excited my next holiday/winter novel will publish this fall! All my best for a beautiful, blessed summer!

XOXO

Wade

Acknowledgments

When I was writing my first Viola Shipman novel, I never dreamed what would transpire, and that *The Edge of Summer* would be my EIGHTH novel! I also never dreamed that writing fiction inspired by my grandma's heirlooms and memory—novels that are meant as a tribute to family and our elders, to inspire hope and remind readers of what matters most in the world—would resonate so deeply with so many. I am forever grateful and humbled.

Writing a book is a solitary task, but publishing is not. There are many, as always, to thank:

Wendy Sherman: my literary agent, since day and book one. The best. Period. (And thank you, Callie Dietrich, for all your behind-the-scenes assistance and expertise.)

Susan Swinwood: there is no more special working relationship an author has than with his or her editor. I feel as if I were always meant to be paired with Susan, my editor AND the editorial director at my publisher. We are kindred spirits and artistic souls. Her edits are always keenly insightful and pinpoint exactly how to make my work better while also granting me the creative leeway to determine that direction. Every reader needs to know she makes each and every book I write infinitely better, and I'm beyond grateful I have the opportunity to work with her on four new books.

The Graydon House Team: I am continuously grateful to work with one of the best teams in publishing. Each member does his or her job not only with great talent but also great grace. Huge, heartfelt thanks to Randy Chan, Pam Osti, Lindsey Reeder, Heather Connor, Leah Morse, Linette Kim and countless others.

To my invisible, secret weapons: Kathleen Carter of Kathleen Carter Communications, I cannot express enough gratitude for all you do on behalf of my books. When you see me on TV, or my books mentioned on TV or social media, thank Kathleen. Danielle Noe is a huge reason my books continue to reach more and more readers. You may never see her, but you will see her work—and importance—everywhere you look. Meg Walker, thank you for your marketing expertise, your author and Bookstagrammer outreach and influence, and your friendship.

Jenny Meyer: thank you for all you've done over the past fifteen years to help me reach readers all across the world—twenty-one languages and counting.

Gary Edwards: I would not be who, or where, I am without you. I simply would not be.

My readers: I write these novels because they call to me. They mean the world to me. But, above all else, I write these novels for you, and only for you. That will never change. I can never express how much you mean to me. I am not simply an author. You are not simply readers. You are my friends. We are a family. And each and every day you remind me—as my grandma did—of what's most important in life.

Each other.

THE
EDGE
OF
SUMMER

VIOLA SHIPMAN

Reader's Guide

GRAYDON
HOUSE

1. A major theme of *The Edge of Summer* is family history. Do you know your family's history? Are there any mysteries in your family you've always wondered about? Any secrets that have been revealed? Have you done any genealogy research? What did you discover that you never knew?

2. Another major theme in the novel is family itself. How do you define your family? What does it mean to you?

3. Have you ever been deeply wounded or betrayed by a family member? Why? How did that change your life?

4. Sutton's relationship with her mother is central to the novel. Did you ever wish your mother was different, or more demonstrative with her affection? Did your relationship change as you aged? And did you view your mother differently as you each grew older? How?

5. Sewing is, pardon the pun, threaded throughout the novel. My grandmothers sewed, and I spent my childhood watching them make my clothes and our quilts. Do you

sew? What do you make? Did anyone in your family sew? What does it mean to you?

6. Did the women in your family collect buttons in button jars or tins? Do you still have them? Do you collect buttons? (I do. And I still have all of my mom's and grandmas' buttons.)

7. My grandmothers were working poor, and the value—and history—of a button meant the world to them. Do you think we're losing touch with the value of a dollar? Do you think we're losing touch with our heirlooms and traditions?

8. I lost my father-in-law and dear friends to Covid, and it has changed my life profoundly. Sutton and Tug have both lost family members to Covid. Did the pandemic cause you to rethink or change your life in any way?

9. I live in the Michigan resort town about which I write. Where is your favorite place to vacation? Does it hold special significance to you?

10. I often write about characters who desperately want to be loved but often feel "unworthy" of love, a way I felt for much of my life. Have you ever felt that way? What caused that?

11. Faith is foundational in my novels. What does your faith mean to you? How does it help guide you through difficult times?

12. Every novel I write is meant as a tribute to our elders. Did your elders impact your life? How so?